About the Author

Mike Dramytinos is a man of relentless ambition and ceaseless adventure, a true embodiment of daring spirit. Whether it's conquering the business world, the thrill of love, a fierce game of tennis, the rush of swimming, or the exhilaration of hiking, Mike seizes every moment with unwavering enthusiasm. He lives by his father's wisdom: 'Be a refuse collector, but be THE Number One, the best,' and that ethos has guided his extraordinary life.

In his diverse and vast business pursuits, he's consistently achieved the top spot. But Mike's appreciation extends beyond the boardroom; he holds a deep respect and admiration for women of all shapes, sizes, and ages, recognising the profound beauty in diversity. A true gentleman and bon viveur, he understands that life without the company of these extraordinary individuals is mundane. In *Areus,* Mike Dramytinos' literary debut, his unyielding spirit shines through, daring readers to embrace life's adventures.

Dedication

This book is dedicated to all those who embrace the belief that life is an endless journey of exploration and expansion across various domains, guided by the driving motto 'vivere pericolosamente' (live dangerously). Like the author, whose life has been shaped by a commitment to continuous growth and adventure, these individuals hold unwavering faith in the principle that it is never too late and never enough. With a profound understanding that 'whatever you abandon will certainly abandon you', this dedication serves as a reminder to persist, persevere, and reap the rewards of relentless pursuit.

Mike Dramytinos

AREUS

AUSTIN MACAULEY PUBLISHERS™
LONDON * CAMBRIDGE * NEW YORK * SHARJAH

Copyright © Mike Dramytinos 2024

The right of Mike Dramytinos to be identified as author of this work has been asserted by the author in accordance with sections 77 and 78 of the Copyright, Designs and Patents Act 1988.

All rights reserved. No part of this publication may be reproduced, stored in a retrieval system, or transmitted in any form or by any means, electronic, mechanical, photocopying, recording, or otherwise, without the prior permission of the publishers.

Any person who commits any unauthorised act in relation to this publication may be liable to criminal prosecution and civil claims for damages.

This is a work of fiction. Names, characters, businesses, places, events, locales, and incidents are either the products of the author's imagination or used in a fictitious manner. Any resemblance to actual persons, living or dead, or actual events is purely coincidental.

A CIP catalogue record for this title is available from the British Library.

ISBN 9781035838103 (Paperback)
ISBN 9781035838110 (Hardback)
ISBN 9781035838127 (ePub e-book)

www.austinmacauley.com

First Published 2024
Austin Macauley Publishers Ltd®
1 Canada Square
Canary Wharf
London
E14 5AA

The English language is not the author's mother tongue, which may result in some spelling mistakes.

This is a work of fiction. Names, characters, businesses, places, events, locales, and incidents are either the products of the author's imagination or used fictitiously.

Any resemblance to actual persons, living or dead, or real events is purely coincidental. The author's views do not necessarily reflect his pragmatic considerations and are subject to the reader's discretion to affirmatively accept all issues and conduct.

In 1947, after three years, the German occupation of Greece came to an end. However, the suffering of the Greek people persisted due to the ongoing civil war. In July of this year, a boy named Areus was born. The name is derived from the Spartan King, whose main goal during his reign was to transform Sparta into a Hellenistic kingdom.

The civil war unfolded between the Greek army and the armed rebellion communistic forces. One day, the rebels entered the house of the major of the Greek army, and his mother's brother was brutally killed.

He was raised in a family residing in a peaceful suburb of Athens, part of a neighbourhood that was intended for inhabitants tracing their roots to the glorious years of the Byzantine Empire, originating from Constantinople and Smyrni.

During a period when hunger was rampant in Greece, his father held a good position with the British Cable and Wireless (a British company). Despite this, the income fell short to meet the family's needs, compounded by his father's daily consumption of two–three boxes of cigarettes.

His father hailed from a distinguished Cretan family that had migrated from the Byzantine Empire to Crete many years ago. Emperor Nikephoros Phokas sent ten well-known Byzantine families to Crete to civilise, refine, and ennoble the local population.

His mother, equally esteemed, belonged to an aristocratic Ionian Island family. She was highly educated with lessons at piano and was also a painter and student next to a very famous Greek painter. So, an islander from Crete married another Ionian Island girl. His mother's family lived for many years in the most exquisite neighbourhood of Athens, in the very centre of the capital city, the so-called Kolonaki.

A beautiful brunette girl and an intellectually handsome gentleman both of high-level education were the ideal couple that nowadays, due to speculations of conveniences, both sides striving for interests tend to almost disappear. His father, as a deeply knowledgeable person, with quality humour was known as a kind of philosopher, a plain-faced intelligent man having the advantage to manoeuvre and manipulate the conversation very easily. This was his power and his upper hand versus any other co-speaker.

Everybody wanted to meet him and hear his wise theories, either in politics or economics, but focused more on politics. He had such convincing and eloquence in his influential speech with arguments and persuasive ability that he was able to turn anyone from a fanatic communist to a rightist or at least convince him that socialism is what he has to vote for in the next elections, or vice versa. That was his actual beloved habit—to turn things upside down with an activating figurative language and a unique, convincing talent.

His characteristic humour was teasing but also sophisticated; he remembers one day his brother came home with one of his friends, who was known to be a fastidious kind of squeamish. His father knew that, so after dinner, his mother brought a plate with nice figs. That fellow, named Petros, he greedily ate more than six of those figs, declaring that he never in his life ate such tasteful figs. His father grabbed the chance, telling him, "You know, dear Petros, the reason these figs are so tasteful? Look at that fig tree in the garden; the roots of this fig tree end down to the sewage tank." Petros remained stunned and almost ran away to vomit.

As said, his father was a heavy smoker; he needed by all means to find cigarettes throughout World War II and after the civil war in Greece, which was even worse than the war against the Germans, a full of hatred and harsh war between communists and democrats. His father had to walk many kilometres to find someone who was selling cigarettes in the black market and at a very high cost.

The war, the hunger, the misery, and his smoking brought health problems, and his father got tuberculosis, and that passed over to Areus and his four-year-older brother, both rather mild. This said, that time almost all families suffered from that disease. The doctor suggested that the whole family should move from the southern suburb to the countryside to have fresh and clean air in their lungs, and so it happened.

They moved to the countryside in a very humble home with a fantastic view over a forest and a small river that during heavy rains brought a flood to the whole flat valley. His mother had to work hard with her chickens and a goat to get eggs and milk for the family.

She had to carry two big metal bins of drinking water with her small hands and arms, which became quite strong and rough, from five kilometres away. Areus owed a lot to his mother's and father's advice. His mother was always telling him, "What you can do today, do not leave for tomorrow," or "Do not keep looking at the water faucet to fill up the big tin bin but do something else by side until the tin bin is filled up," or his father said, "Never be late to the appointment, be a gentleman and be there even little before and never let a girl or a woman wait for you at a date; you must be there before her," or "Be whatever you decide, for example, a garbage collector, but be the number one garbage collector, the best." Such advice was the cornerstone and the backbone of his later success in business.

His mother was good at languages, especially English; she was among the few Greek girls to live a long time in London. Her family sent her as an 'exile' in London so that she would forget the Cretan young man, her affair. But he was there at the airport when she returned after two years, with flowers in hand.

His mother also spoke French, and she was teaching first him and his brother, but mainly him, as his brother left their home early to go to a school, where he stayed there almost for a whole week, coming home only on Sundays. His mother was also teaching English for free to all boys and girls in the neighbourhood. Every third Tuesday, she had a hair-cutting machine to cut the hair of all the boys so they were clean to avoid infestation of lice.

So, at the age of seven, Areus was already speaking English and French, and not only this but he managed to gain a few Drachmas by teaching a five-year-old beautiful girl who lived on the floor above. Those lessons started turning into a sexual update, telling her that a boy has a different peeing organ. That made her eyes widen, asking, "How come we all have one organ to pee?"

So, he showed her the difference between a boy and a girl, showing her what he had between his legs, calling that penis, and asking her to show him what she had between her legs. It was nice, and both enjoyed that, but that was all—no touching. One day, wanting to impress the two girls on the second floor, he climbed to a high tree, just next to the house; that tree was somehow bent, and so he managed to reach the top with the air of a conqueror. The two girls came out of their balcony, and he was so proud of his achievement. But that turned into a fiasco as he could not get down.

There was a tree branch that made it impossible to step down. So, he stayed there for many hours until the neighbourhood heard that he was unable to get down, and they all gathered under the tree to help somehow but with no success. His father was called, and he returned from his office in a panic.

Finally, the brother of his friend, who was a marine engineer, managed to climb to a certain point of that tree, and Areus with his leg stepped on that guy's knee, and so at last he managed to get down. Obviously, instead of triumph and admiration from the two girls, he succeeded in getting only laughter and humiliation.

Something happened that left unexplained tracks in his memory. His grandmother was living with the family in her own small room. She was 95 years old and very ill, maybe in her last days. She was a good Christian and a woman who cared more for others than for herself. In her life, she helped a lot of people as her brother was a very wealthy man, owner of all the casinos in Greece, who unfortunately died poor after losing money in his own casino. She helped many poor people, and they all loved her for her philanthropy.

The very last day before dying, he was out of her room crying. His mother called him as his grandmamma was asking for him; he was her beloved grandson. He approached her bed; she held his hand, then a kind of miracle happened. She, for many weeks, could not move at all from that bed, but suddenly, she found inexplicable strength and raised her body, stretching her hands high up as if she were facing God, saying loudly, "God take me," and she fell back and died. That incident would never go away from his memory.

At the age of seven, he was the only boy in the area who managed to have an erection by caressing his male sexual organ, obtaining hardness; at that time, he did not know that this was called masturbation. They were down to the dried river, and they were demonstrating each other's penises, and he was the only one to demonstrate erection with a hard male sexual organ. So, he was admired by the other boys, having the proud look of the rooster of the neighbourhood. In other words, he was the only one to be sexually upgraded.

There was a wooden bridge to pass over the river from one side to the other, and he was staying under the bridge, peeping at the girls that were passing and by seeing their panties and some even without to save the cost, imagining which one he would choose to marry. Many times, with a water gun, he was uplifting the skirts of the girls, wetting their panties and enjoying many such toys and tricks, but always the girls were his preferential target.

The time passed, and the family moved back to the southern suburb of Athens.

He never forgot those two girls who were on the floor above his home, and many times in his teenage years, he masturbated about having them as fantasy.

His brother, in the meantime, being a very good student, won a scholarship, and with the recommendation of their uncle (cousin of his mother), who was Air Force general and the second in command, next to King Paul of Greece (he was the same uncle who later helped a lot for Areus career), to the most prominent school in Athens. His brother was in the same school as Prince Constantin, who later became King Constantine.

Back to their previous home, he went to one of the best schools, a famous school that time and still is, where he started quite well as a good and consistent pupil. After the third year, he discovered the cafés where he could play pinball flippers and also French billiard.

Areus stopped studying, and he was all the time there spending his time despite his mother's strong daily chase. He recalls and still laughs that he had a ceramic money bank, and his father every third day was putting inside, the silver those days 20 Drachma coins, so then shaking this, they could hear that there were plenty of coins inside. He smartly discovered a method to take coins out of this without breaking it, and every time his father was adding one new coin, he was taking out four.

One day, he needed to play the pinball flipper game, so he took out 10 or 12 coins; his father the same night called him, and he was so proud to put one more coin inside. His father then took in his hands the ceramic money bank and shook it, and what they heard was just one single coin moving left and right inside. Then he was in trouble not only with his mother but also with his father.

He had close friends (one of them was from a communist family while his family was always democrats or conservatives) and was there so often playing billiards and more games with less school attendance.

The wife of the coffee house owner, a blonde marvellous woman, was there all the time, and they brought masturbation work at home. The masturbation was almost a daily hobby of all boys of that age; those days, there were not any Playboy-type magazines, so a photo with the bare knee of a girl or woman was enough to activate the desire for onanism.

He was 16, at the peak of his adolescence, and he needed a woman's pussy, so his brother took him to a brothel. There was a bad, unpleasant smell permeating in that waiting room; he probably thought that this was the peculiar odour of women's vaginas. There was a curtain, and there appeared the lady with big breasts; she even jiggled those big tits to provoke all who were in that waiting hall, quite a huge woman for him, probably around 40 years of age.

There were five to six men waiting; she asked whose turn it was, and it was his. His brother pushed him with a 'Go'. He was somehow frightened but had to go; she took him by the hand, and in the bedroom, the smell there was even more intense, which created an impact on his incredible wish to perform well for the first time sex with a woman. She had a lot of experience and knew how to handle such situations. She took off her see-through gown, and for the first time in his life, he had in front of him a naked woman.

She nodded to him to approach and with her hand asked him to come close to her and get undressed. She asked him if this was his first time; it was obvious to her, and he said yes.

"Well, I see you are a hunk boy. I am here to help and give you the first sex experience. Don't worry."

"What you have to do is follow my motions," she added.

She took in her hand his cock, which was still soft, and this was only because he was shy and shocked. She started softly and skilfully to masturbate him, and then the reaction was immediate, and he was there standing with a hard phallus.

When the penis's length reached to the peak, she reclined, opened her thighs and took his penis in her hand and drove it to her pussy directly.

He believed that her vagina canal was wide, but it was not. Anyway, now he was inside and tried to find out what he had to do.

Merely nothing as she did all; she started moving and guided him to do the same, and this was it; he simply followed her. She pretended and showed to him that he was a good sex performer to motivate him to come fast as there were five more men waiting in the hall. He did all he could, and at last, it was an unbelievable moment to ejaculate inside the vagina of a woman.

Needless to say, during those times, no condoms were necessary. She congratulated him, and she washed his phallus with a kind of reddish liquid to protect him from any kind of aphrodisiac disease. She asked him to hurry up and get dressed, and she left him alone in there. He, with his agony, could not find the way to put his trousers on and even forgot first to put on his underpants, so what to do? She was there again and repeated to hurry up, so he put his underpants in his pocket and went back to the hall.

When he stepped out into the hall, his brother asked him, "What do you have in your pocket?" He told him silently that they were his underpants. He smiled, and they left the brothel, feeling that he was now an experienced man and having a proud expression on his face. He walked the streets like an adult man, having the feeling that around him people, especially women, were staring at him as an experienced lover young man.

Indeed, from that day and at the ripe age of 16, he was visiting at least two times per week to the brothels, meeting different women each time to meet different sorts of vaginas. He was even proud in his classroom that he was the first to have a real fuck, and many begged him to take them there too, and he did, always being the experienced leader and mentor.

The brothels street was in Piraeus, and the girls there all knew him well as he was a frequent customer, and not only this but they knew that he brought with him several other boys, and being out of their windows and balconies, they were calling him to refer them to his friends.

"Areus, come to me. I will give you extras and more minutes and even a free one; bring your friends to me."

One of them even proposed to give him a commission to bring his schoolmates to her, but he, of course, refused to become a brothel agent (a patron).

The years were passing; he managed to proceed through the school classrooms with mediocre records until the last two. His mother went to the school director to check on his progress.

The director said to his mother, "Yes, your son came the first day to the school, but since then we did not see him again."

His mother was shocked and in an alert situation; she had to find a way so that he would not lose his schoolyear. But during those times, it was not easy to change schools unless there was a real reason. So, she invented a story that his father comes home every night drunk and her son must change the school environment for psychological reasons (his father did not drink in his whole life, maybe more than four bottles of wine in total).

So, he moved to a private school where he managed to finish the gymnasium and where also the girls were there, but what he only managed was just to fool around by touching their asses or tits, supposedly by 'accident', with them protesting, one even with a slap, but who cares, touching a girl's ass or tits had value and made the slap worth it.

Those times were the times of running after foreign tourist girls. He had the advantage of speaking two languages already. So after chatting and having fast food (souvlaki), he managed to get quite a few tourist girls. With most of them starting with kisses on street corners as the first stage, then bringing them home to continue there with amateur kind of sex.

Many times, they did it all at the beach at night. Those beautiful girls liked to have sex in the hot weather and under the full moon. That made it necessary to get naked under the moon and swim naked in the hot waters, which excited them. They rushed to return on the sand to fulfil a good sex and, in some cases, also in the sea waters, but that was rather complicated and a difficult sex process.

There was an Israeli lady around 45 years old who liked him a lot; should say that she rather ran after him than was the opposite. She offered him an expensive dinner at a good restaurant and then invited him to her room in one of the best and most exclusive five-star hotels in the centre of Athens.

In the room, there was an unpleasant surprise waiting for him; her old husband was sitting on the sofa and wanted to watch as a real voyeur the whole of it. He was embarrassed at first; he could not have an erection as he could see that old man staring at him rather with pleasure that his wife would spend nice time with him, desiring not to miss anything.

Many times, that old husband stood up with difficulty, due to his old age, to see, in case they were on a side sex position, how he could better observe any and all single motions, how his penis was moving inside his wife's vagina. She later confessed to him that he was her timekeeper; he counts how many times during the whole night she has an orgasm and keeps a record.

She helped him to overcome that as she had the experience probably with other boys, so he passed the first shock, and there it was a rather wild sex with her to care for all initiatives. That night, she did not want to stop having sex, with just a few minutes' break to smoke cigarettes and then back to business, where she taught him more about sex than he ever knew. Her husband fell asleep at 03:00 and probably lost the orgasms' counting, so it was easier for him to perform better.

He after all felt wiser as that cheater woman enriched his sexual 'hors d'oeuvres' that turned a woman mad. Adding tricks, with the tongue as protagonist, to his sex performance menu to be used for the next to come intercourses. As such were licking the vagina, putting a finger impaling her anus when she was on top, or his thumb in her ass when she was on all fours, and several more 'unlocked tricks' to spice up a memorable sexual intercourse.

When he left her in the morning after she ordered eggs and bacon, he was dizzy and tired from the whole night full of a variety of sexual activities.

He could not even walk to reach the bus station to return home. It was funny to see when he reached down with the lift in the lobby the receptionists laughing as, probably, they had seen this happen many times before. Indeed, that woman was rejuvenating herself by sucking the youth from all the boys she brought up in her room, boys under the approval of the peeping cuckold old husband.

When his mother saw him so tired, she was worried and gave him milk to drink to recover as she could only imagine what happened the whole night.

He will also not forget what happened at a nearby Athens tourist resort, where for years his parents spent their vacations, in a hotel that was also, many years ago, a casino. The owner of that hotel casino was the closest relative to his mother, and she was the only heir, but he lost all his money. He even gave a lot of money to the girls who were helping to clean his house and cook so that they could get married well, but after he was broke, he left nothing to his only heir, Areus' mother.

So, arriving at this resort small city, already from the very first day, he ran after the tourist girls while his other two friends, who were there already a whole week and could not manage, even though there were many tourist girls available.

They were all waiting for him to arrive, being the expert in that sort of 'chase', which in Greek slang is called 'kamaki'. The very first day, he approached three awesome Austrian girls.

So, that very first night, after having a simple tavern dinner and always sharing the bill with the girls, there he was performing sex already with a gorgeous blonde girl with golden hair around her pussy. He left the other two girls to his friends, flying in the sky with happiness as all three girls were very beautiful.

With his blonde girl, the best of all three, he was bathing nude at the very end of the beach where nobody was to see them and near the rocks that made the whole thing more romantic. They were rolling in the sand. Her divine breasts were covered by sand, but the nipples were emerging out of the sand, giving the allowance to be nibbled and sucked until it became rock hard. She had a perfect body. Despite her soft denial, he licked her pussy smelling like sea; he had in his mouth the taste of salt.

They made romantic love, but what he found after he finished was shocking. Under her back, there was a stone that was surely hurting her back, but she did not want to stop him from making love to her. She probably liked him so much that she ignored the suffering pain under her body and pleased him to reach his climax.

That girl told him that although she had enormous sexual appetites, she never had any satisfaction at all and never ended with an orgasm. He took her with him to Athens to show her around Acropolis and Plaka and ended up at his home, where his mother welcomed her with an open heart, appreciating the beauty of the girl who will bring pleasure to her son but also, and that was important for his mother, to help practice his languages. She was so beautiful that his mother was so impressed, she told him that of all the girls that he brought home, she was by far the most beautiful. "Be gentle to her." He tried all the ways to make her come to orgasm; he wanted this desperately so that she felt the pleasure of the climax, and this he desired to happen first with him.

The orgasm was impending, and this at last came at 5 o'clock in the morning after him excellently performing with so many attempts. He felt so nice with her giving an appreciative sigh from underneath having her on her fours; she was so happy, smiling and kissing him and thanking him for at last, at the age of 19, she felt the orgasm and the sheer satisfaction that followed it.

The next day, they continued making love, and this time, she kept coming and coming. They were both in a perfect mood; he wanted her to look and feel happy. When she left Greece to go back home to Austria, she was sending him letters every day, telling him how grateful she was for him striving with great efforts to make her at last feel like a real woman and that she misses him so much.

Back to the chapters of his childhood and schooling, he did not have any best records; there were family discussions about what he would do and what profession he would choose after finishing the gymnasium.

His other uncle was a bank director who married one of the sisters of his father; the other two sisters were never married despite being the two most wanted girls in Crete due to their beauty and deep education. One of them wrote books about the civilisation and the local songs of Crete. That uncle was not particularly friendly with him, and he suggested opening for him maybe a small shop or rather a kiosk selling cigarettes and newspapers, but unlike his father, who was always saying that he trusts his son.

"One day, you will all see what he will become and make us all proud."

Indeed, he was not the first pupil in school, but at the age of 18, he was the only one speaking English, French, but also German as in the neighbourhood the daughter of a lady friend of his mother was married to an Austrian pianist.

That real intellectual pianist liked him a lot because of his polite attitude he had from his family. That gentle way of communicating with people and always respecting all, especially older people so he always gains their sympathy with his courtesy. The Austrian pianist volunteered to teach him German, and he was also keen to prove to all that they have to trust him and his future choices.

He grabbed the chance, and in a few months, he started speaking with the pianist, not in Greek but in German. He had that gift to learn languages fast and not just speak the language but write the language with the proper and deep knowledge of the grammar. His mother always has him on her mind wanting to prove to everybody that he is a boy who will one day become someone important.

She cared about how to improve his languages.

She was always visiting small islands with her pallet to paint small harbours, island houses, and fields, and there once she met two boys from Germany.

She invited them to come with her to their home and offered them bed and meals, aiming to befriend them to her son. They were heartily welcomed to his home, offering a friendly bed and all meals and speaking to him in German so that he could improve his German. Those were very friendly boys, one his age the other two years younger. Martin and Peter were their names; they were all the time together, enjoying a profoundly created solid friendship. He showed them all Athens, and his German was getting better and better. They left to go back home to Germany, and one day, he got a phone call a little before Christmas, inviting him to go to Stuttgart and spend Christmas holidays at their home.

Indeed, with the permission of his parents, he took the train passing through Yugoslavia to Germany and stayed for the holidays in their very luxurious home. They were all very hospitable, taking care that he was happy being far away from his family for the first time. He was at the age when girls and ladies turned him easily on. The mother of the boys was approximately 50 years old but a real woman with a beautiful, curved body with great tits, and at night, he dreamt of her, having uncontrolled ejaculation in his bed.

When in the morning she came to fix his bed, she noticed what happened on the sheets, and she inwardly smiled, knowing what that was and asked him to give his underpants to wash right there in front of her; he had a boyish and shy face.

She said, "Come on, I have seen my boys naked, so it does not matter to see you too. I am like your mother."

So, he, in front of her, took off his underpants and gave her while she cast a glance on his penis that was semi-erected, but this time with a new brighter smile. The problem was that when packing his luggage, he forgot to put any second underpants and now she took the only one to wash and probably she will return in one or maybe two days.

The next day, he went to the bathroom before sleeping to masturbate so that it would not happen again during his sleep and sully the sheets and avoid embarrassment to both him and the mother of his friends. He noticed that when she discovered the sperm spot on the sheets, she rather looked at him pleasantly, not with the look of an angry woman for staining her bedsheets.

One day, the two brothers left for their school as they had a special before Christmas gathering at their school; the father also went to Hamburg for a business meeting, being the CEO of a big multinational company. Areus stayed home with his Greek-German dictionary to learn some new German words.

He always learnt the languages with the help of a dictionary. He was on the bed with pyjamas on, studying, and she was cleaning the living room, having shorts on to make her motions easier but also, as he later understood, deliberately to allow her thighs to be seen, and under the top of her shirt her tits with not any bra were moving provocatively. He was getting horny and was trying to hide his erection.

She came close to him, asking him if he could help her with the clothes to take out of the laundry and stretch the bedsheets to be ready for ironing.

He told her just a moment to change the pyjamas and put trousers on; she said there was no reason to do that; it won't take more than three minutes for the sheets' stretching. They indeed went to the toilet where the laundry machine was, and she bent down to start taking out the big sheets. He watched her big and well curved ass that caused tremendous impact to his usual erection, which was impossible for him to hide as the pyjamas were of a simple, soft cloth and this enabled the hard penis to be seen like a flag pole with the dick's head to grow and tingle unbearably, given that he had no underpants on at all.

He did not know what to do; it was very impolite from his side to ask her to help, and he adored her ass to get an erection to be seen. He turned around the moment she got a sheet out of the laundry and asked him to hold the other edge. With him looking the other direction, she asked him to turn around and hold one edge of the bedsheet to stretch. The damn erection was uncontrolled. What to do? He turned around with a blushing face, and she noticed what was there under the pyjamas, looking like a camping tent.

She softly smiled and told him, "What do we have here, young man?"

He was almost ready to faint. She came closer and touched and grabbed his penis; she was impressed how hard it was. She again smiled and took him from the hand, like a teacher gets the pupil from the hand to punish him for bad behaviour. But there was not any bad behaviour, on the contrary and by all means, a wanted erection. He felt that he lacked the power to handle a woman like herself, but he had to push aside any hesitation and focus on what was up to enjoy and experience.

She guided him to her bedroom; they both sit next to each other, and she murmured in his ear, "Are you a virgin?" He nodded positively despite the fact that he was several times with prostitutes but also for non-paid sex with tourist girls. Yes, he confessed that he was indeed a virgin.

She was happy and intrigued to hear this. Later, she confessed to him that her fantasy was to have sex with a virgin man, in this case, a boy, so even better. At the same time, she told him that she was suspicious that her husband had an affair, being most of the time on 'business trips'. So, to say having sex with him was not only a mature woman's dream but also a revenge action having lesser and lesser sex with her husband.

She told him, "You have nothing to do; I will teach you all," and asked him to stand up, and she removed his pyjamas so he stood there only with the hard penis always up and facing her seductive, brilliant face, which seemed to be exceptionally tempting for her eyes. She also stood up, and she took her shorts off and what he saw was that she had no panties on.

A bush of hair around her pussy and on the down part the clit was to be seen very obviously. She told him that the first that he had to do was to make her wet by caressing her clit gently with his fingers; she took his fingers, and there he was fingering her pussy, reaching even near her anus. She never left the penis from her hand, just holding but not masturbating.

She was clever and well experienced. She did not want him to come before he entered inside her, and then she would masturbate unless he relieved his load in the deepness of her vagina.

She bent lower and licked his penis, kind of a blowjob, not any slutty blowjob but sort of smooth, adorable kissing and tasting of the penis head's moisture. He felt her pussy getting wet and that wetness increased her moaning and snorting. She told him, "Now you have to act like a real man and lose your virginity with me and not with any other girl of your age."

She laid at the edge of the bed with wide opened legs; the sight of her pussy was a marvellous image. She took with her hand his hard penis, and she led it straight to her wet pussy, and that was fantastic; the slippery sound of his penis driving inside her as deeply as possible created a great tense in that bed; her pulse had quickened, slide in and out slowly and incessantly and then faster like a piston, while at the same time, she was swaying backwards and forwards. He felt him inside her jammed and as a captive in a hot, hospitable, and extremely tight vagina. A woman of that age having two births already and still keeping that narrowness was quite strange for him.

She asked him to move back and forth with slight motions, and he felt the sliding in and out; she was always looking at him, telling him that for a beginner he was doing great. She suddenly stopped. She told him that this was the first position and the next one will be different. She moved his penis out; she took her shirt off and what great tits he had in front of him, asking him to kiss and suck her nipples so he could feel how hard and rose became while she with one pointer finger was just caressing his penis looking at the wet and gradually purple penis head.

He crouched down to be on the same level to her vagina at the edge of the bed; she turned around, having in front of him her whole back body and her huge ass. She asked him to hold her breasts softly from behind, and he was feeling two big, soft, desirable tits in his hands, and with her hand under her legs, she took a hold again of his penis and led directly to her even more wet and anxiously waiting damp pussy.

Now it was her turn to move front and back. Exactly opposite was a big mirror, and he could see her leaned down (later he heard that this is called 'doggy' and became his favourite), his hands on her breasts a he could see and adore all this image, him behind her and she moving from slowed down to accelerating motions. She tilted back to see him and ascertain that he enjoyed. At the same time, her two hands stretched to get a hold of his two buttocks and yanked him to pull him even closer.

The mirror enlarged all; he looked not as a boy but as a strong man, as a wrestler. He counted the in and out driving between 30 to 40; he also noticed that she started gradually but with lust and desire to close her eyes, a warning that showed to him that she was approaching the climax, a woman's climax that he will experience first time as those whores never arrived to any orgasm, neither the tourist girls showed that so vividly.

Her face, in the big mirror, became sweet with a characteristic calmness before an eruption that was to follow. A fiercely accelerated breath succeeded the calmness; she turned around and with a gruff whisper said, "Now hard, harder."

Indeed, she came but with a combination of moaning and happy smiling, the smile of satisfaction showing that she fulfilled her dream to have sex with a virgin boy and steal his virginity before any inexperienced girl. She kept there moving; he also increased the speediness of his movements back and forth as he could feel that in seconds he will come, and in fact, he did, but she did not allow somehow to remove his penis out of her vagina, and he obligatorily ejaculated in her vagina.

She enjoyed him ejaculating and falling his head on her soft, spotless back until he unloaded all his sperm and with more than 10 spasms; she never forced him to stop that at all but let it go to the very end. When she felt that the penis started to go limp, she released his penis and turned around; she looked at him with passion and affection; she kissed him and she told him, "Now you are certainly no virgin anymore, and I bet you are from now on best in bed and satisfy many girls; something is destined to be different for your sexual life, my beloved boy lover."

He was touched hearing this from her, but at the same time, it was for him a question mark why she allowed him to ejaculate in her; he thought that probably she was already climacteric so no consequences.

Then she said, "It is our love secret, and as long as you will stay with us for another six days, I will find a way while all are absent to teach you more positions and erotic magic tricks."

But it did not happen so; she was super-hot and, already the same evening at 2 o'clock, she came to his bedroom silently, risking that her sons would hear her walking to his room; luckily, his bedroom was far away from the two brothers' bedroom.

She got under his sheets, going straight to his penis, licking from up to down his testicles and also close to his anus, and there the third position both being in bed, she turned around on her side, and he got his penis this time by himself in her pussy, and a silent performance started and ended this time without a least of moan or sound to avoid to be heard and reveal what was going on in his small bedroom.

She kissed him and ran back to her bedroom. She whispered into him, "Tomorrow again, now wash yourself in the bathroom and sleep." The lady was a sex machine. She found many ways to have sex with him: in the toilet, even on a hidden part of the outside balcony, until the time came for him to leave for his home. The goodbye with both the brothers and the mother was not easy at all. She bent over his ear and told him, "Thank you, my beloved boy. I will never forget you. I hope you do the same."

While on the train, he had some thoughts what if when he ejaculated in her and who knows what if she gets pregnant because she did not rush to go to the toilet to wash herself off his sperms; anyway, he would never know this.

He stayed there for 12 days and returned home with his German almost near to perfection; he was an easy and fast learner of languages.

So, again, the family council, what will he do? He was very versatile speaking three languages.

What is a profession that requires languages? In that same family of the pianist was an uncle who was teaching at a school of tourism and hotels on a Greek island. So, this was it; he suggested that this was the future of his hotel business, but aiming high to hotel management and not become a waiter or a simple receptionist.

So, this was it; there at the hotel school, he changed from a bad pupil to the leader in that hotel school. They even chose him to carry the flag of the school at the National Parades. Needless to say, there were many girls, mostly not from Athens but from many villages and islands who loved to have an Athenian boyfriend feeling, somehow as second-ranked girls in competition to Athenian girls.

He was not only a handsome boy and a hot stuff lover but an athlete and mostly the leader of all sports, so all the girls were around him all the time, making him feel great with a proud smile. In the school's theatre, he had the major role; the lady teacher painted his temple hair slightly silver, as the role of the first prime minister of, after 300 years of Turkish occupation, free Greece, demanded to have white hair at the temple, and that gave him an additional gentle and handsome appearance.

The teacher herself looked at his attractive appearance and said that she wished to be younger and have Areus as her boyfriend, and they all laughed. He, of course, already had love affairs with two ladies of her age, and he could, for sure, please her for all her sexual appetites. He did manage to proceed with some and only with the best-looking girls in an advanced stage of the relationship but not without any final end at the relation (sexually), just nipple sucking and the girl masturbating him. With one of them, he was close and seemed she was also ready for an erotic encounter as she was touching him with meaning and so did he. She was quite a cute chick, so they fixed the date, and they went to the cinema.

When he approached to kiss her with an enormous hard cock ready to explode, he felt an upsetting bad smell from her armpit that made him not feel well as he liked the girls and later the ladies to have nice odour, but he thought, *Well, what the hell, I will not fuck the armpits.* In that cinema, he took her hand and brought to his hard dick; she turned red-faced but kept her hand on the hard penis, and his hand was under her skirt reaching the clitoris; his fingers were sucked inside her pussy, gathering her wetness.

He turned to her, ignoring her armpit smell and kissed her on her neck while squeezing his penis with her hand that she never removed from there. They almost ran to a nearby cheap hotel, and they did it there the whole night. What that was meant to be was just an amateur fuck, but he activated all his knowledge, all the positions he knew, and she was amazed as she had some kind of sexual orientation before but nothing to compare to what he abundantly revealed to her. He even did something that he never did before and fingered her anus; she denied that, but after insisting, she accepted and liked it a lot as the finger went all the way inside, widening enough to accommodate his.

What made him a peculiar impression was that she insisted that he comes inside her vulva as if she wanted to conceive so as to oblige him to marry her. What a cunning way to tie him up with an unwanted marriage. He, of course, at the right moment as she was on her four pulled out, despite her protest and her frowned face, but he automatically without losing the momentum went 1.5 inch higher to her still wide anus; she figured out what was to happen and took a sharp intake of breath, allowing her opened arse walls to accommodate him; the penis was gradually sliding inside her anus.

He believed that the more he went deeper, the more narrow it will be, but to his surprise, that did not happen, and the penis slid deep inside her anus canal with not any extra effort; she then with backwards hip movements accelerated his already randy cock, with a loud orgasm let all his seeds go in the deepness of her arsehole, with a glorious satisfaction and without any unwanted consequences.

She was one of those girls who cannot keep their mouths closed, and she spread around that Areus fucked her for five hours and with all possible ways and even from the anus to intrigue all other girls. She wanted to give a bigger dimension and emphasis to their whole sex limitless orgy, most of them had not even seen a penis in life so were stunned with perspiring faces.

The rumours and banters went around like a fierce wind and sparked a serious annoyance but also desire to know more details.

The lady chief teacher called him to her office and asked him to tell her what exactly he did to that girl, Annie, which was her name. What could he answer, so he told her simply that they had sex. She said, no, I want all details, a full report as to what happened in all those five hours.

"Cannot be just a simple sex engagement. I demand blow-by-blow description in explicit details," she said.

She used that word that meant she tenaciously wanted herself to get turned on. So, he very graphically described all positions and acts he offered to Annie, adding also a lot of 'dirty' tricks that, in fact, did not happen so as to bring her in a sexually aroused situation, grabbing her mouth in a shock and awe.

She even asked him, "Is it true that you made sex to her from her anus?" Saying this, she was almost ready to jump on that desk and open her legs, but she hardly controlled herself.

He, with a stammering voice, confessed that he did, but he regretted doing that as she had that backdoor virgin and she suffered a little, that was the zenith of his description that even more inflamed her excitement. She wanted to punish him and ask him never to do this again with any other girl or she would be obliged to activate sanctions on him, even expel him from the school, needless to say that all this was an act; she wanted for sure to be at Annie's place. Most probably when he left, she ran to the bathroom to masturbate as she was blushing as a young virgin but ultra horny girl.

There were many girls at that hotel school that were surrounding him especially after the even exaggerated details given by Annie, and for sure, they fantasised him, being the superstar of that school, on top of them or behind them; they enjoyed secret masturbations in their beds. He took one of them on an 'excursion' to a nearby small hill forest.

They played stupid kids' kind of innocent hide and find games. When he found her hidden behind a bush, he grabbed her from the overhang of her buttock, touching her ass with his hard dick. She turned around angrily, showing that she did not want any sex; he begged her taking his penis out of his trousers, showing to her how hard and swelling it is, telling her a 'story' that if he will not get rid of his sperm from his testicles this might have bad impact to his health with headaches. She looked curious but at the same time seemed willing to cooperate as in no case wanted to create any health problems or headaches. She asked then, "What shall I do, then?"

He asked her to get a hold of his penis and play with it. He was not sure if this girl had touched any penis before. She indeed did this, with her eyes wide open, observing his hard organ starting slowly but clumsily to play with this; he helped her to show how the handjob was to be done, and at the same time, he with his hand went under her skirt and started caressing her pussy.

This time, she was hot and allowed that, following his advice on how to masturbate him; he had a supreme ejaculation in the palm of her hand at the same time she also had kind of a climax and felt ashamed for this.

Driving her back to the school, she was silent, thinking that she made a sin as she was also from an island where they were very religious.

He managed quite some other girls to bring to the same situation, but they did not allow him to have sex, but at least he kissed them and sucked their tiny nipples, and as sex was not allowed asked them to masturbate him, and some also did a little of licking but obviously with a blowjob of an amateur.

The school finished, and he got the diploma at the highest degree, which made his parents feel especially proud and justified for their son.

He was always thinking big. He wanted not to go and get a job, like all the rest of the students did, but continue his education in this profession where he wanted to learn in depth and in all stages and at all hotel departments, because only then he could one day become a good manager.

Here comes his good uncle again, and through the general secretary of the Greek National Tourism Organisation, they found for him a five-star hotel in Nurnberg Germany to make his practice. So, he took the train to go to Germany.

He recalled with him in the same compartment of the train a Greek guy who was telling him all the time how anxious he was to reach the Yugoslavian borders. In those times, there was one and a big Yugoslavia and not as it is now, split in six smaller countries.

Those days, you were not allowed to bring dollars out of the country unofficially and only from the Greek Central Bank, so what that guy did was hide some dollars in his Zippo lighter. When the Greek border police were checking all their dresses, pockets, and luggage, they also checked him, and they found the Zippo, but that Zippo was not working, so they opened and found the hidden dollars. The poor guy, they took him down, and he would have been in real trouble.

What a bad experience, travelling by train through Yugoslavia where Yugoslavians brought in the train their chickens and goats, what a dirty and bad smell.

That trip through Yugoslavia, of course, brought also troubles to him and his body when he arrived to his room in Nurnberg, which was arranged by the hotel staff department; he had to shave all hair on his body as it was infested by the so-called pussy lice, with horrible itching, and those midges suck blood and were not easy to remove. He remembered he was sitting in the middle of the room that he rent but forgot to lock the door, and suddenly, the old house lady opened the door thinking that he already left to go to the hotel, and she saw him naked with the razor in hand, and obviously, she was shocked, probably thinking to what a guy she rented her room.

The hotel that he was to spend the next eight months practising in all departments was the Grand Hotel, a very famous hotel in all of Germany. That hotel was neighbouring the place where took the famous Nurnberg trial of the SS among them was Rudolf Hess, Goering and Goebbels and many more high-ranked officers on the side of Hitler.

He started from accounting to see how the control system of a hotel operates, and then he moved to the restaurant as a waiter and then to the reception, getting an overall extended experience. They all liked him with the way he worked hard, and they all could see his future and that one day he would indeed become a manager. They were all addressing to him with 'Herr Areus' or 'Mr Areus'' and not just Areus as he oozed kind of respect, while all other waiters were called simply by their first names. This was a notable sparkling sign, proving that he would one day become a director.

He recalled one day that he was a waiter next to the head waiter. They had a very rich frequent customer about 80 years old with the title of a Von (Von—title of honour—can't remember the surname), who always was ordering expensive wines and giving big tips. He was a characteristic exhibitionist. All waiters were after him to please all his wishes, sometimes also his extreme demands.

He always reserved a nice corner table from where he could see all the restaurants, and also all restaurants could see him. In the restaurant, he was always accompanied by a lady of maybe 45 years old but unusually impressive in all aspects, a real lady with a huge 'L', probably his wife and who probably aimed to get his money after he passes away.

He asked for the wine catalogue, and he chose the most expensive one (costed a small fortune of money) if he remembered well, which was kind of Grand Cru Cote de Beaune. He asked the headwaiter where this wine bottle was and to go and bring it. He told him, "Take this key (a kind of key that opened old type of money safes) and go to the third basement cellar. You will see a metal door that looks like a bank safe; open that but do not turn on any light; take a candle that is next to the door and try to find that very rare and expensive bottle of wine and take care not to let that bottle fall from your hands as that will cost seven months' worth of your salary."

It was difficult as the light of the candle was very dim and that special cellar was very small, maybe two square metres, with dust and spiders. After a long time, he found it. It was the very last bottle of that exclusive year, but the bottle was full of dust and spiders. How shall he present it like this? One could not even read the label. He took a soft cloth, which later proved to be a wrong decision, to clean the bottle from dust and spiders, and he brought it to the restaurant.

He proudly and professionally presented the bottle in a wicker basket to that best, old customer so he could read from the label that this was the 25-year-old wine that he ordered. He turned red-faced and angry, shouting loudly, all could hear him in all the restaurants, and they were fully booked, not a single empty table as it was a Friday. He angrily said, "Where is the dust? Where are the spiders? I do not want this anymore, so to take it away."

The head waiter was very angry with him, but how could he know? No one explained to him how to serve a more than 25 years old wine and leave it dirty with the spiders and dust.

At that same table, as he mentioned before, was with her back on the wall that amazing mature and very noble-looking lady, who made clear that she loved to be looked at, with tits that turned him crazy. He could not take his eyes from her half-exposed tits; he was almost ready to ejaculate in his trousers, but that was a shameful action. The lady noticed that he was staring at her bosom and seemed to him that she liked this by throwing a glance to him with a hidden but with a meaningful grin.

In those times, a slightly darker skinned, suntanned guy was always bringing the attraction of both girls and also middle-aged ladies with the fame of the Latin Mediterranean lovers. He went closer to her to serve, but behind her, there was not that much of space, and albeit she knew that, she did not move her chair, so he had to squeeze himself behind her chair, and with the left hand, he had to remove the used dish, and at the same time, with the right hand, he had to serve her the new dish with the ordered filet mignon, him always looking deep into and between her tits. She was aware of this, and all of a sudden, she put her hands behind her chair, pretending that she wanted to move her chair a little to allow him more comfortable serving, but consequently and probably intentionally, she softly touched his erected penis.

She smiled again and made a peculiar nod to the headwaiter, a nod that was hiding something that only she and the headwaiter knew. Here, he had to mention that this head waiter was a huge man who took part in the Nurnberg Trial Movie; he was the guard jailer of Hermann Goering.

He certainly was aware what that nod meant, and that was not other than to give to young Areus her telephone as she was always the one to make the reservations, and her telephone was known.

The old man who was angry with him because of the wine situation left, leaving not any tip as he usually did, but when he moved to the exit, she stayed a little behind and gave a good tip, looking at both the headwaiter and him, but with a different glance to him than that to the headwaiter.

The headwaiter blinked his eye to him saying, 'Lucky you' and passed her telephone to him. A blonde, middle-aged goddess and, for sure, a master of sex of 45 years, what she wants from a 'supposedly inexperienced lover'? The headwaiter because of this lady's desire to pass her phone number to him and the good tip she left and this was done due to Areus, he forgot the unlucky moment of the wine bottle that was returned due to his inexperience to polish the bottle from the spiders and dust and handed to him to return to the cellar.

He never, of course, asked, and she never told him her name; that was top secret for her; he even searched the reservation that was supposed to be on her name as she was always doing the booking of the table, but there, he found just the name of that VON…Full secrecy as if she were the companion of Hitler, Eva Braun, so for now on and in the next to come compelling narratives, he will call her 'Eva Braun' or maybe 'Artemis', the goddess of chase as she was the one to chase young men with her erotic bow.

The whole night he could not sleep, squirming around, needless to say how many times he dreamt of that lady with the hefty consequence of plentiful masturbation. What shall he do? He was kind of timorous. Should he call her, and what if this is a trap and they will catch him and he'd be in trouble? What shall he do: take risk or not?

That was a big question that needed to be answered. He took the decision, and he called her; she was happy to hear that he called her; maybe she had also dreamt of him. She told him, "Come to my house," and gave him the address. He told her that today he was on duty and cannot come and that he can come the next day. She said, "No way; either you come today and now or forget it."

Oh my gosh, what a dominatrix, probably she was so horny, that was the reason hidden behind this. "Now." He did not like this, but he was also so hot hearing her warm and hot voice but, at the same time, commanding voice. "I need you now." He had, even though this was not professional, to call his headwaiter to tell him that he felt sick, and he couldn't come today.

He sounded as if he were aware of what was happening and he told him, "Yes, get better, and do what is needed to feel good and come tomorrow."

He felt not nice as his words were as if he knew what the special lady wanted and wanted now or never. He felt bad because he did not tell him the truth. Anyway, the decision was made to go for this adventure, and he went to her house, which was nothing of an ordinary house; it looked more like an old castle than a house, an old impressive building with a huge black metal arc-shaped gate. He pushed the antique-looking bell; the door was immediately opened as if she were behind the bell, waiting.

He walked quite some metres to reach the building, and the door was opened; he needed just to push, and there she was sitting on a green velvet sofa with a red robe de chambre, and as he noticed, on a metal golden side table was a champagne, and from the label, he could read that this was the famous and very expensive Louis Roederer Cristal champagne, in a silver ice bucket.

He imagined that there was nothing under that robe de chambre, and the junior guy in his underpants with a prickly sensation was stiff, already showing visibly his presence inside his trousers.

Everything inside the house was an antiquarian with two pianos and three bedrooms. Out of them, one was the master bedroom, and then he later found out that there were also two bathrooms, one like the modern jacuzzi but was not a jacuzzi. She kissed him on the cheeks and told him, "Of course you know why you are here?" He somehow nodded affirmatively and, at the same time, turned a bit red-faced.

She said, "Sit next to me and have a glass of champagne." And so, they did both and impatiently as they both knew what was soon going to happen. She never took her eyes away from his trousers that were looking like a camping tent that hid an obvious hard-on.

"Well then," she said in an authoritative manner, "go up the stairs and take a hot bath."

He said, "No need," Telling her that he had a shower before coming. He does this every morning.

She said in a strict way, "Forget your morning shower and take a new deep bath upstairs." Probably, she smelled his sweat as he not only walked quite a distance to reach her home but he was also sweating with only the imagination of the great sex that was to come.

He was sweating because of the anxiety, envisioning what he was up to enjoying or rather to explore what unimaginable sex moments she was to reveal to him.

So, she repeated, "Forget your morning shower, and the hot bath is expecting you upstairs; go and rush. I don't have plenty of time." She made it clear with a non-negotiable insistence. "Use all foam soaps," she said. "Also, use perfume, but it should not take long." He had indeed taken a shower before coming; he always does that if he was to meet a girl, just in case. He even took showers before he goes to a brothel to a prostitute and not only take shower but spray his body with deodorant, perfume and also chew chewing gum so he had a pleasant breath, and as he said, he needs to respect even a whore in a brothel.

He went up to the bathroom. The bathtub was filled up with hot water and foam, only the leaves of roses were not there.

He will never forget that while bathing he felt like a prince. His body had the smell of an aristocrat; in fact, he was as such as his whole family were aristocrats descending from the glorious families of Byzantine. That aristocratic attitude was innate, and that always added an extra attractiveness to girls and ladies and later as a hotel director and a respectful businessman.

She told him that a big towel is expecting him and asked him to wrap his body with the towel and come down but fast, making obvious what a horny status she was in.

He asked her, "Where is your husband?" She said he was there next door, sleeping. He asked her, "What if he wakes up and comes into their bedroom?"

No problem was the answer; her husband might be in the other room and come in watching her having sex. He felt uncomfortable as this was the second time in his life that an old husband might watch him while he was on top of his wife and she was working to envelope him inside her. He protested saying this would make him feel embarrassed; she said do not worry she will make him feel relaxed he had done this many times; she cuckolds him with his absolute approval and delight.

She even told him that many times her husband comes in but also many times does not, but if he comes, he sits on that big armchair, watching the whole sex ritual, if what he sees he likes, he leaves on the bedside table 500 Deutsch Marks as a tip to his wife's lover. She told him, "He knows that you will be in my bed, and he is still angry with you because you destroyed his show off at the Grand

Hotel restaurant with the wine that you wiped off dust and spiders from, so most probably, he will not come to watch the sex activity."

She made it clear to him that they have to hurry as she has to go to the opening of a gallery. So, he wrapped himself with that big towel and went straight to that huge bedroom, and there was a side room with an opened door. He did not see if the old husband was watching or he would do it later. She asked him to remove the towel and lay completely naked on the bed.

She sloped out of that robe entirely and revealed kind of the nowadays Victoria Secret red bras and panties, and she started taking off piece by piece her underwear. Her marvellous nakedness was a piece of art, a contemporary nude Venus, which was despite her mature age. He was almost ready to experience physical orgasm without even touching his penis, as it happened in his sleep with wet dreams in his teenage years. The bedroom itself was 'flooded' in an obvious erotic atmosphere.

But he thought, *No, you must not; you must offer to this lady pleasure and not ejaculate fast.* But how could he manage this? He, as he usually does, started thinking of other things, like his career so that he forgets for a moment what is going to happen, so he holds his erection down.

Now he was in front of a fabulous lady's body, fully naked with body curves in full harmony and a very wishing face for hard sex, that she needed it in despair. She was looking at him with full lust; he was completely at her mercy.

Now he knew why she asked him to take a deep bath; she noticed with satisfaction he was in full erection. At this point, he had to say that this was his advantage that he even before the girls, or ladies, or even prostitutes take their clothes off. In fact, he does not want to call them prostitutes as they are not; they get paid to make love, especially the Russian escorts in luxury hotels as they are pleased to do this not only for money, so what he wants to say is that those ladies were so happy to see that he had erection right away even later at his 60s+, so they needed not to try hard to obtain erection, but at the same time, they enjoyed real orgasm and not any theatrical fake orgasm.

Those high-class escorts, many years later, were telling him what they were obliged to do many times and this was tiresome, and even with young men of 18 or 20 and 25 years old, they have to work hard to get those guys with erection, and sometimes even they never get. At this point, he wants to point out that a man little plus or minus 70 is not at all a man resigned from sex. No, if a man keeps his penis busy in all possible ways, a man can go over his 80s and still be able to offer good but, at the same time, experienced quality sex because the good sex that girls and mature women miss is the altruistic sex that an experienced man knows what a woman needs to have one and more orgasms, and can offer that.

Anyway, back to his goddess lady, his 'Eva Braun', 'his Artemis'. The reason that she wanted him to take an overall bath was now crystal clear to him.

She 'threw' him to bed and turned him around and asked him to uplift his ass a little, and she started, oh God, she started licking his anus; this never happened to him before. That was so nice, having at the same time her hand playing with his balls; she was licking and putting her tongue deep inside his anus and licking his testicles with him almost ready to ejaculate, but he had to hold.

She possessed the know-how; she did not allow him to experience orgasm yet; she started talking to him about his plans for the future, just holding his penis but not masturbating it so that she will slow down his erection; she was so clever, and she managed to hold his ejaculation back. When that happened then she turned her ass around him to take her from behind; she was there at a 'doggy' position. At this moment, he heard a sound from the other room; maybe that old husband was there hiding and watching.

He could not resist having in front of him a divine arse, nice and smooth; it was the first time for him to see that she was fully shaved, not any single hair, nothing but smooth, soft vagina lips like a baby. Maybe she used wax to remove any single hair from there and offered an extreme soft pussy that mounted the desire and the lust to super heights. For him to satisfy this sex mature remarkable woman, he needed a 'fucking black belt', but it was worthwhile to give all and make her melt into bliss with quality diversified sex.

He held her from her waist, and his desire was such that he mixed the holes and went straight to the upper canal. She made a small but sweet, light scream, but she turned around showing to him with a wide smile that she likes this, but that was not the hole to start with.

She put her hand from under her legs and directed his tingled penis to her pussy.

Her sweet, hot vagina was ready, eagerly waiting to feel the prolonged tip of his penis to her pussy entrance, and that was it, easy sliding penetration as she was so wet; she thrusted back, forcing him to go deeper into her. The huge bed started creaking, and she needed just three minutes to burst with a loud orgasm that would not only wake up the husband but also the big dogs that were outside in the garden as guards ready to attack the guy who intends to harm their lady master.

The ongoing process continued, but when she felt that he was approaching the climax, she gently and, dare to say, professionally took the penis out and asked him to join her with a glass of champagne, which she moved from the front sofa to the bedside table. He was crazy. Champagne again? He was almost there, and she stopped him to bring his penis back to soft condition; the hard-on was gone.

What a velvet excuse of a woman to bring her sex partner's sexual organ down and in idle. She wanted incessant sex, so after drinking the glass of champagne, she again took the upper hand and brought his penis back to life, and this time, she guided directly to the correct position, allowing him not, because of his anxiety, to make the same mistake, to aim the wrong hole.

She moved in such a way to allow him to hold until the right moment, her hot breath on his neck became louder and deeper and the steaminess could even fog up a window if they were closer to that, and she came with a sweet moan and him being happy that this was the so much wished relief; he witnessed the zenith of her erotic expression.

He then took the initiative and asked her to sit on him, and she bent so her lavishing nipples pressed his chest, playing and flirting to a gorgeous nipples' dancing. She had new orgasm, and after the second climax, she said now was the time for the intact for that night anus, always keeping him in a sex combat effectiveness.

She had next to her bed a small jar with something white in it, probably face cream, and with this, she rubbed her anus, slowly circling her symmetrically wrinkled asshole entrance; she not only rubbed but she also put her finger deep into her anus so she cautiously made her anus very slippery, a so well-shaped and anatomically cute backdoor. She turned around, and with an indicative sign plus a big and sweet smile, she asked him gently to go ahead. So, permission was granted. The penis slipped in the passage of her anus canal this time so easily, no groan, just pleasure from both sides.

He had to go deep in and out maybe 15 times while she, with two fingers, was caressing and rubbing in circular way her clit; then he heard her coming for the third time, but this time with less loud voice but still a sweet sigh, and there was the time for him not to hold anymore but to ejaculate inside the cave of her anus.

What a relaxing and unforgettable moment. She squeezed her anus; the tiny hole clenching and unclenching as if she wanted to tell him to stay there inside until the penis gets soft and then only and slowly drove him off from her hospitable, majestic, narrow arsehole.

Not to forget to mention how she was acting the blow job between breaks, the licking that was a piece of art, what a tongue what a way that she was staring and observing each centimetre of it with eyes wide open, not to lose any curve of his cock. She was licking and sucking, but her glimpse was shared between the penis and his eyes.

She touched so gently his testicles and kissed them both, also sucking and getting one of them whole in her mouth like a caramel, and some times, her hand was under his testicles; she was fingering slightly his anus. What a woman! How much of 'expertise' was assembled in that marvellous lady!

Her astounding sex artwork through the use of richly imagined sex positions in all extend of the words was impossible to be forgotten. She knew all sorts of expert angles, her hands and tits never fumbling, going over his whole body to locate and dedicate herself to the hard 'fellow', as if the penis were to whisper to her the words, "Yes, here I am."

To his regret, as he hoped to have many repeat encounters, but it was not so; she told him what happened today will not happen again. She said clearly the men she gets in her bed are always for one time use, so kind of disposable. She, with rather sorrow, told him that he had to forget their explosive love moments or rather hours; she had a name in the local society and must not spoil her image and reputation as a nymphomaniac absorbing the youth of young men.

She revealed to him that she did not pick him up by chance or his masculine appearance, but she watched him two times before in that same restaurant and was obvious that he was from a family with good upbringing, well educated, serious young man who she could trust to hide her adventure with him from gossips and rumours that could harm her good name.

She advised him that he had to look after young girls around his age and be altruistic in sex. She told him that today he learned a lot how and what a woman needs to offer to her pleasure.

He had to use the knowledge he obtained that day to make more women and girls happy because, as she confessed, he possesses the demanded standards. She even gave him a gift, a golden comb although he did not have long hair, as those times was in fashion, no long but black hair; she especially liked and kissed many times his chest with the black hair.

Well, after not many soft amateur experiences with young tourist girls in Greece, in addition to the special sex seminar of that 50-year-old great woman in Stuttgart, the Israeli greedy for sex lady, plus the relentless sex knowledge he acquired from that extreme sex bomb 'Artemis', he, so to say, was 'the sex expert' or better 'the sex mentor'.

In Greece, you should promise an official engagement to girls and then only you are allowed to see part of their thighs and nothing more. The virginity those days was a taboo; some of these girls noticing that he suffers with a horny penis they offered him a masturbation with their soft hands and, in exceptional cases, a blowjob so that he demands no real sex.

After that sex torture with girls protecting their virginity, he all of a sudden found himself plunging in uncharted waters in an extra big bed with expensive satin sheets next to a perfectly shaped body of a Lady with big L, a real 'femme fatale' who could be a dream and fantasy to millions of men.

As mentioned, he never trusted her actual name, so he had to invent a nickname so that he can recall her to his memory. He called her with a Greek name Artemis, the goddess of hunting, as indeed she hunted him without a bow to chase wild animals but a bow of desire and lust to hunt a young and hot man.

It seemed to him, according to her husband's attitude that maybe he was a fan of the Third Reich so maybe the name of Eva Braun was more to fit her. If he put numbers of perfect sex and comparison between 'Artemis', the Stuttgart lady, the Israeli greedy lady, and the school girl, Artemis gets a 10, the Stuttgart lady an 8, that school girl 4, the tourist girls no more than three except that Israeli one, who gets a 6, and this was because she was extremely dominant, addressing to her fucker as if he were a pawn with penis.

In Nurnberg, he had a Greek friend who was working at Siemens. One day, he told him that he was the member of a club 'Protect the Nature' where many girls were members and they organised a weekend excursion to the German part of the Alps. He joined to participate, hearing that many girls would be there and hoping to have the chance to get a permanent girl for the rest of the months he was to stay in Nuremberg. The bus arrived the very morning of the Saturday and drove the group to the Alps' German side. What he saw in the bus were 10 boys and 25 girls, among them 10 were very beautiful. He thought, well, here are many chances and very many choices, but it was early, and he fell asleep throughout the bus drive.

They arrived in the Alps to the top German side of the mountain, where there was a big hostel with a huge eating place. They all had to sleep there one night, but first before that, they had to go down to the dining room. The huge place was filled with more than 300 boys and girls, who all came from all over Germany for the weekend. They all sat down and waited to be served very simple food, soup and Wurst (sausage) with Sauerkraut (sour cabbage), which was needed as they were all hangry from a long bus trip, and such hot meal was more than necessary.

Then happens something that will never be forgotten from his life's memories.

The kitchen door opens and a blonde waitress appears with a tray in her hands.

She had an Aphrodite beauty; he never saw anything more beautiful since then; he was magnetised by her beauty and her amazing blue eyes; he was looking at her so stupidly, almost with his mouth open, while stepping towards his group's big table.

He stood statuesque staring at her, but what paradox happened; she did exactly the same; she also stopped walking, and standing there like a salt pillar, she was also looking at him straight into his eyes. The love angel's arrow had hit them both.

So, there was him standing and staring at her, and two metres away, she was also there, staring at him, both the one looking at each other's eyes with admiration; the tray almost fell off her hands. What happened in the dinner room was difficult to describe. It was unbelievable how they all, maybe 300 boys and girls, stood up applauding this scene as if it were derived from a movie film as if he were kneeling and proposing marriage to her. They saw one black-haired but handsome and strong looking guy and a blonde princess, because this was the correct description for her beauty.

She came closer, and they did not move their piercing looks away from each other. That was a moment of sweet embarrassment. Both became all of a sudden enamoured with each other, feeling something that they never felt before. The applause was kept for long as if it were a love scenery not often to be seen.

He touched her hand the moment she put his dish in front of him; she was kind of trembling, and he grabbed the moment and arranged to meet her when she has her day off after two hours.

She came, but this time with her Bavarian kind of dress, so sweet, cute and impressive. They touched each other's hands with a small kiss as more people were around, and they all knew what happened in the dinner room and wanted to see the continuation of what took place inside.

It was pure romance; they managed to find a peaceful corner on the back of the wall of a small house. They gave each other hundreds of kisses without each one knowing what her name was and what his name was.

They stopped the kisses for a while and walked on the snow, playing a little with the snowballs. What a sweet girl; he wanted that this to last forever. She told him that she was one of the champions in Munich for skiing and on the weekends she worked there to make some small money without needing this but just as a routine change and also to show to her very wealthy parents that she does not live exclusively from their money.

She told him that she has a small apartment that could accommodate their love, and she begged him to leave Nurnberg to go to her. They were so enthralled by the romantic moment and there was not even a thought of sex as sex would maybe ruin those imaginary moments there on the Alps in the snow.

It started to get darker and colder; they were freezing; they came so close to the other to get warmer, her breasts against his chest, a marvellous touch, and she, of course, being both like one body, noticed that between her legs there was something stiff; she smiled but also turned blushing; something that made him also not willing to destroy this romantic moments by asking her anything more in the snow.

He only managed to kiss the top part of her fantastic bust, between her fabulous breasts. She repeatedly begged him to come to Munich and have their own small love nest apartment; she gave him her phone number, and he promised that he will do all to go as he made it obvious to her that she was the unique true love of his life.

Later when they were back, he had to decide what to do: keep on his career that seemed to go brilliantly well or obey his heart with this pure and virgin love affair.

He decided not to call her and stay with his job. So, from the professional sex affair with the 45-year-old lady 'Artemis', which he could in no way forget, to the romance of the 19-year-old beauty, which was deeply engraved in his heart.

In the bus, all the girls that were ready to come close to him from the very start and the initial inviting glances turned to angry and showed offence that with this love episode with the Alps girl he did not flirt with them, so he lost a good chance to get a permanent girlfriend for the rest few months remaining in Nurnberg before going to Heidelberg.

One day, a disease occurred at the hotel, and 12 people that worked at the hotel had to get hospitalised; he was among them too. Probably, it was a chicken salmonella. He stayed there for 10 days. The Greek Embassy Consul, after phone calls from his uncle, came to see him.

It was funny, and rumours around his hospital department were spread concerning the hot Greek guy. The beautiful young and less young nurses came every day and in the very morning, where they all know what happens to young men when they wake up. They came with a wet towel to clean his body, and they noticed after lifting the bedsheets a hardon that he could not hide despite his efforts.

Amazing was that every morning this happened with a new nurse to come to wash him with a wet towel; they were all snickering by themselves in the corner. Usually, they have plastic gloves, but especially in his case, they were not using gloves, and all of them, with not a particular reason, were holding his penis to wash around it.

Most of them squeezed it and noticed a desire in their eyes, stupidly, which he always regrets for this, he was unreasonably shy and did not ask for their telephone numbers, especially the one that usually was washing him 10 minutes longer than the others and asking him to turn around and washed smoothly his buttocks and often her fingers touched his testicles, probably this was discussed between all nurses who will make the next step first.

It was obvious that all this could not stop him during his sleep and his dreams to come, and his sperm was always there on the sheets, having the nurses change the sheets with a smile and "You sweet, sexy boy, what shall we do with you?"

Three days before he was to leave the hospital, in the morning, the elder nurse, maybe 40 years old, came to do the usual body wash, but she closed the curtain so no one could see, but he managed before the closure of the curtain to see and hear that there were four or five nurses outside, waiting to hear the good news and in the midst of a certain soundless commotion with plenty but hidden laughter were all of them eager to know that they won the 'bet'.

She went directly to his morning hard upstanding penis and started a sort of masturbation at the same time with her eyes asking for his approval to keep on, and that OK head motion was given. It did not take more than two minutes; she bent closer to watch the head to become moist and kind of purple; she seemed to enjoy very much, but she was so close that he could not hold, and he ejaculated on her face with an unavoidable scream of relief being for long with not any sex.

She was not at all offended; on the contrary, she liked it a lot; she even was prepared, having a tissue paper in her hand to wipe off her face. But yet what happened with the five nurses from outside? They silently applauded hearing his scream of relief. Indeed, there was a bet between them.

It was maybe the best ever morning of his life.

A bad moment that left a bad taste to him and many days to go was when he went to a supermarket to buy cheese, and all of a sudden without any intention, he found himself at the exit, thinking what to do; he walked and he still felt that they were chasing him for that piece of cheese.

The nine months of practice at the luxury hotel came to end, and as he had decided beforehand, he had to travel to Heidelberg to go to the highest hotel management school in Europe, on a university level that prepared only hotel managers to graduate. He arranged a goodbye dinner at a German Stube tavern with his friends, and there it happened for the first time in his life to get drunk.

So many beers were drank that he had to go to the toilet to vomit. He recalled that his close friend came after him to take care of him; he threw his wallet under the toilet door asking him to pay the bill.

Between the nine months of the Nurnberg Hotel practice and the Heidelberg School, there were 30 days. The program was to go 30 days earlier to the school to see around, maybe meet some friends and, of course, the always much-needed girls.

Then an idea excited him: why not call that Munich Ski Champion (her name was Anabella), that blonde goddess and see if she was still in love with him. So, he called her; she was silent for a few seconds; she could not believe that he would ever call her.

Anabella, he could understand that after hearing him on the other line, jumped up in the air with immense happiness. He asked her if she wanted him to visit her; the answer was not just yes but maybe a hundred yes. He asked her to find for him a small, cheap hotel to stay as he was with not that much of money.

She answered, "What hotel are you talking about? You are more than welcome to stay at my cute apartment."

He rushed the first train from Nurnberg to Munich, which was not a long distance, and was to arrive at 2 o'clock in the afternoon. The train arrived slowly inside the famous, old but impressive train station of Munich. The train stopped, and oh what a divine creature was there to wait for him at the train station. They embraced one another and stayed tightly for almost two minutes. She was such a joyful, open-hearted girl who he felt never before better than that moment.

They took a tramway to her home, a cute, little, warm home very well furnished with many adornments and plush toys, bears, lions, and bunnies, and in a glass cabinet were many medals that she had won at skiing championships, and there was also a very friendly white cat, who caressed his legs as if it knew that Anabella loves him.

He was always fond of cats, so became friends very fast. Zizel was the cat's name. She told him that her parents live only 100 metres away, but she wanted to feel somehow independent.

She was so happy that she did not just move around in her room; she was almost dancing full of joy and harmony. He was tired after having little sleep and also drinking heavily the night before. She showed him around although there was not much to show as her bedroom was not that big and very close to the living room—a real lovers' nest. He let him be well accommodated on the sofa, together with the plush toys and the cat at his feet and him without knowing how he fell asleep.

It took four hours when he opened his eyes. The room was dark; she was there at the edge of the sofa for many hours with the white cat on her lap, staring at him affectionately in the dark to allow him to sleep. He felt bad having her to wait for him to wake up being in the dark without moving to disturb his sleep.

He woke up with kisses. The cat was also there desperately looking for his caresses. He did not know whom he had to first caress and hug.

Anabella, in the meantime, opened his luggage and took his trousers and jackets as well as his underwear and put them all in the closet, well folded and hanged and all this in the dark with only a small candle.

She suggested going to a nearby small, but her favourite, Hungarian restaurant.

Indeed, they went there by foot, holding each other's hands. When entering, the lady who welcomed them looked surprised to see, for the first time, Anabella with a young and slightly dark-skinned man. She explained to him later that she was going there either alone or with her parents, who, as said, lived only a few metres away from her small apartment.

The dinner was a really terrific experience; he never before had such a soup called Goulash, a hot soup that was absolutely perfect for the cold winter in Germany, a soup that also wakes up sexual appetites and desires. They had then a big sirloin steak with a great red wine called Bikaver (she told him that this means the bull's blood). Then as dessert, they had the famous German, or rather Austrian, cheese strudel.

They discussed during the dinner; she told him that her parents live in a big house near her small apartment, are of excessive wealth, and her father is a famous doctor in Munich, and in fact, there was no need for her to work, but she does from time to time going up to the Alps, the mountain that she loves.

There she meets people and at the same time makes some pocket money to feel that she contributes for her own expenses. She also told him that her parents knew that he was going to come and that he was going to stay with her.

They were not that happy with this, but as their daughter seemed to be happy, they did not have persistent objections.

She paid the bill, allowing him not even to put his hand in his pocket. Outside, it was snowing, so they kept tightly close to each other and rushed to their nest. Now they were in her warm, nice home with the cat always looking at him, so he took the cat into his hands and lap.

Anabella asked him to feel at home and that she would put something more comfortable, but her closet was at the corner of the living room because the bedroom was small, and there was room only for her big bed, so where was she going to change? There, in front of him?

She sweetly asked him to turn around, and he did, but there was a small mirror that could give the perfect reflection of the undressing, which she, of course, knew. He was watching that blonde tall girl with the body of an Aphrodite removing one dress after the other, and there she was with her panties and bras. What a snow-white body but at the same time also an angel's body, kind of white pinkish, like the skin of a baby. He was not as usually horny but kind of respectful and overemotional for this exceptional girl. She threw on a nice velvet gown, and she indeed looked angelic.

She asked him to put on something more comfortable, but he didn't have anything other than his pyjamas, so he went to the toilet. He didn't want to change in front of her, so he put on his pyjamas. When he came out of the toilet, he was looking rather funny. She laughed seeing him in such pyjamas, looking either as a jail prisoner or as a clown, but she came closer and kissed him. She told him they would go to the Kaufhof department store tomorrow to buy a nice bathrobe.

He rather lightly protested, declaring that he had not enough money, but she again made it clear that she would buy this for him as a welcome gift. They drank a kind of mild brandy; she turned on her pick-up with soft music, and they danced cheek to cheek; the relaxed vibe was quite heady. The dancing bodies were so close, how could he hide his erection? She noticed, and she turned red-faced and seemed to him to be a girl of principles and not any girl to run after sex. He excused himself, saying, "Sorry, I can't help it." The little guy down there was between her legs.

The music stopped; they still stood there facing one another. The pyjamas were so light in cloth thickness that his erection was evident and extremely noticeable.

What a sweet girl! She bent her head to his shoulder and she told him, "I like everything about you." Obviously, including his erection. He was not feeling comfortable being unable to control his passion and feelings for her, but why did this had to happen through an erection? He tried to think of other things, such as count in his mind what money he had for his career's continuation so that he forces the refusing to obey penis to relax, and he slightly managed.

She turned the light off and lighted up two candles, turning the ambience really romantic, and it also made him feel cozier and convenient, but that erection again appeared, offering a funny picture under the pyjamas. Time was passing, and inevitably, they found themselves on the bed, both still dressed in pyjamas and a gown.

They were kissing passionately, and he started to touch her erect nipples, proving to him that she was ready. The chemistry between the two in that room was ideal.

She charmingly took all off except her panties, with him also doing the same. Her soft breasts were against his chest. What a pleasurable touch! He could not resist gently kissing and sucking her gorgeous nipples, and automatically, he was removing his old underpants as the situation was ready like a volcano to erupt.

His penis was between her legs, touching her pussy, but she still had her panties on.

She looked at him, having a calm adorable face and smiled, and again in a graceful way, she removed her panties. The sweet, wet vagina was ready and fit to receive him. They had nothing to do; not one of them needed any hand to guide the one's penis inside the other's vagina. His penis slipped in her rather tight vagina, finding the way automatically, and the tango started.

He was praying that he stays hard and make her come; he wanted so much to hear and feel her climax; he wanted as never before to give to this angel the pleasure, so he was moving inside her smoothly and synchronised, and that was indeed an art.

Kisses never ended; the kissing and sex ceremony went side by side until he felt the sound of her breathing on his ear accelerating and so also did her rhythmic movements; she meandered up her thighs towards his hard penis until a deep relief came; she did not moan but showed in a magnificent way that she was silently coming and kept coming, squeezing her vagina; her angelic face was shiny, and her face glistened with a gracious tenderness.

He kept back his orgasm without any special effort as he was after so many enthralling intercourses trained to prolong that pleasure. Now it was him, proud that he kept his promise to himself to hold until she fulfils her total relief and happiness. His whole torso was on top of her and never changed position. He wanted with this girl no tricks to be deployed and advanced sex secrets but an orthodox and traditional sex action.

It was easy for him when he was just about to come to move himself on the side and prevent to ejaculate inside her. He also tried not to make her sheets with sperms spots so he released his sperm in his palm. She was on his side, and he watched with immense satisfaction that she still and for 10 more seconds had slight, cute spasms.

He rushed to the toilet to clean his hand and his penis; when he returned, she was still naked with a face of absolute relaxation. He laid down next to her and turned to her so that she also faced him. She thanked him many times for what quality of pleasure he offered to her; she kissed him several times and told him her sex had been unpleasant in the past, not to forget the cat was always at the corner, showing her happiness that her boss was in a high joyfulness, and at the same time to inspect and be sure that he was doing the correct job and was treating her gently.

She, at the age of 17, had to have sex with a German boy not because she was in love or because she wanted any sex with him, but she was the only one at her school class who was a virgin and she suffered from bullying from both boys and girls. That first sex intercourse by her late teenage was a horrible experience as that boy's only aim was to be the one to steal her virginity and crawl like a rooster and tell others that he was the one to steal the virginity of the most beautiful girl in that school.

That frustrating bad experience followed her with two other tries with almost the same unpleasant experiences. While what she experienced with him was a superb sex experience that she missed so much and always dreamt of. They both slept heavily and exhausted.

The next morning, she was up before him to prepare breakfast, and they went out shopping. He felt really uncomfortable as she was buying only for him; she wanted him to look nice and gentle not only for her own eyes, as later, he found out that she wanted to present him to her parents. She dressed him elegantly; he was rather looking like a lawyer, and at the end, the result was great. He was looking at himself in the mirror, and he could not recognise himself.

She did not only buy a suit, shiny leather shoes, and nice but not shiny ties but everything necessary to complete his external outlook. She also bought him an underwear, a bathrobe, and slippers. How to thank this girl? Words were not enough. The best she could hope from him was to stay there with her forever; this was why she intended to introduce him to her parents soon. Her father was a famous doctor but, at the same time, very conservative or, better to say, an old-fashioned gentleman; therefore, the purchase of a suit for him was essential.

The days were passing, and the nights were all for her a new sexual surprise; she started to be free from any complex of the past, and she enjoyed unlimited sex. He started to exercise one by one all what lady 'Artemis' had taught to him.

It starting by kissing her so sweet vagina; she at first did not want, feeling that he gets humiliated by licking her there; he made her understand that he liked this more than anything else, so he bent her first reaction, and she adored it, and she came twice, him feeling like the man to offer happiness, activating many magical sexual features.

Next, he asked her to do the same to him, but she did not have the appropriate experience for a blowjob, so he had to tell her how, and she gradually started to do this perfectly well, doing this with exceptional love and not as an obligation or another sex variation. Next came the 69; she was amazingly happy to do this and do this so well that he lost his self-control and could not manage to pull out his penis from her sweet mouth and almost ejaculated on her breasts.

He apologised, but she did not mean at all to be annoyed by what he did as she wanted this to happen; on the contrary, she smiled and went to the bathroom to wipe her off. So, they did almost all but one, which he dared to perform after three weeks or one week before leaving and that was the sex from behind.

But how to tell her this? How to ask her for this? He was explaining about sex and Kamasutra positions, and that the French girls do not end the sex process unless they get it from their derriere, the small and narrow cute cave. She turned, blushing; she could not imagine how this can be done.

She told him that if this would make him happy, then she would also do, but will she not have pain? He told her that this gets solved either by Vaseline or by a cream like Nivea. She jumped up and went fast to the toilet and brought with a big smile her night cream. So, she told him, "Go ahead, do it the way you think, and I do not care if that will be a little painful."

He asked her to roll over and pushed her beautiful arse a bit higher and put a pillow under her waist, and there he faced an angelic anus, anatomically perfect (there are many ugly assholes, some even with undesirable lousy haemorrhoids). He kissed her there; she pulled back; he explained her that it was for him a unique pleasure to kiss that beautiful part of her body, so she accepted, and there he started kissing and putting his tongue inside her as deep as possible, but with his other hand, he stroked the stem of her clit, and her whole body started shivering from explosive passion being in highest possible libido.

She had, so to say, a kind of bodily tic twitch when he touched or sucked her clit, and that gave him extra excitement to do this; it was very arousing. He then applied the cream and fingered her smoothly and gently; he felt that she was ready to accept him.

He asked her to turn on the side and lift up one of her legs so to allow easy access and started penetrating as smoothly as possible; she felt the touch and the smooth slipping; she lightly had a small but a pleasant moan until he was deep in her, staying there with not any motion at all; he just asked her to squeeze so she will feel very well what he was inside her and then started the process in slow motions, always with his other hand touching and feeling her clit, in other words masturbating her but gently and with passionate love.

Anabella was on fire; she came with such grace; she turned around telling him sweetly that she wanted him to come inside her, and he did, and they both were like an active volcano. Well, this was four weeks of extreme passionate love, real love, not any primitive or savage sex, but all was done with charm, finesse, and respect.

The chemistry between them and the sexual communication was the perfect match; this was derived only if there is formidable love between lovers and not just sexual desire for intercourse.

As mentioned before, dressing him like a lawyer, they paid a visit to her parents. A nice house of elegance and impressive furnishing. Her father was a nice but serious man, who despite the fact that his daughter told him that he is studying in Germany and that he is from a well-educated family, he looked worried and sceptical, and this was normal; their only daughter to love an unknown Greek guy was not easy to approve of. Her mother was as sweet as her daughter.

She welcomed him with a kiss on his cheek. They had dinner, and the doctor was asking him hundreds of questions that brought him into an embarrassing situation.

The doctor indirectly in a clever way wanted to discover what plans he had for his daughter. He tried as best he could to tell him that his relationship with their daughter was very serious and just as important as his career. He tried to avoid giving promises and engagements although his heart was saying that this girl could be what a man could ever dream as a wife. She was from an affluent family, extremely beautiful, and she loved him; he never felt before such a pure, frank love.

The day came that he had to take the train and go to Heidelberg. He wished that he never lived such a separation…Both were in tears, kissing each other; she was holding him so tight as if she wanted him not to step into that train. She whispered into his ear, "Please stay, please stay with me."

He had to say that he must follow his career and that he will return. The train started. He was at the window in tears. She was a wreck, ready to crash down; it was a lovers' split that reminded a Greek tragedy, but unfortunately, not all good things last forever.

He begged God to have the train leave faster as he could not bear his love standing there shedding many tears, and the train left, but his heart stayed there behind.

That journey was a torturous one. He was thinking of her, and he was in a big dilemma: what to do, follow his heart and eventually embark on a new page of his life or follow his professional career? It was a real deadlock. He decided to keep on with his career, finish that school, and having a very advanced education, he could maybe find a good managerial post at the big hotels in Munich and marry his darling.

The train arrived in Heidelberg, which is supposed to be the nicest city of Germany, where a song says, '*ich habe mein Herz in Heidelberg verloren*', which means, 'I lost my heart in Heidelberg.' But his heart remained in Munich unless this would happen again and he loses his heart in Heidelberg also.

In that school were six Greeks among the other 300 students. These Greek guys were at least 7–12 years older than him, and they were not in the hotel business at all; the reason to be there was to obtain a diploma so that they get a hotel manager's job in smaller hotels in Greece and so indeed happened when they returned to Greece.

One was studying in Graz as an engineer for many years but never reached the diploma as he married an Austrian girl and had a daughter, so his plans changed; the other was a musician; he later married a rich German woman and stayed in Germany, and the third was a waiter in a tavern in Manheim. There were also three others who just came but never continued.

These three guys were good men, and they very often gathered at the house of the one or the other together with a guitar, singing Greek songs; the moment he writes this, they have all passed away.

He was working hard at school. He wanted by all means to finish and get his diploma. He even won a distinction as he solved a very difficult contest that only two other Germans managed to solve.

It took long for him to get to know a girl. Was it because his heart was always in Munich? But he had to find a girl as he did not have sex since he left Anabella.

In fact through a courtship, he came close to a girl at a dancing club; a beautiful girl, as she told him she was a fugitive from east Berlin; her name was Johanna.

He noticed she had a great body and was very athletic; she told him she was a champion in east Germany for rhythmic gymnastics, so it was easy for her to jump over the Berlin wall and escape.

He recalled in summer when they went to the swimming pool how the German guys were looking angrily but also with jealousy at him, seeing as a '*Gast Arbeiter*' (foreign worker) was the boyfriend of such a beautiful girl, but he was not any Gast Arbeiter; he was studying there and bringing money to Germany and not taking money out of.

At that swimming pool, his new, beautiful German girl, Johanna, was showing her athletic skills on the grass, doing impressive exercises, and all those German guys became even more jealous of him, thinking that he was her lover; he, on the contrary, was proud to have her for himself.

It took a long time to enjoy sexual intercourse with her; for the one or the other reason she wanted first to know him better and then make the second step, a step that he desperately needed. The first sign that she was ready and also in big desire for proceeding was when he accompanied her to her small apartment up to a small hill, where there was a small forest. They went there to enjoy their love, far from the eyes of others. Kisses and more kisses and again kisses. Kissing each other and being so close to the one another, he evidently could not avoid having her body come in touch with his hard dick.

She looked at him with a smile, showing that she liked that; she turned really hot and surprisingly got down to her knees; she released his fly, approaching one breath away from his penis; she took it out and licked it with plenty of passionate love. What she was doing was not the usual blowjob but a pure penis licking of the man she had in her heart. It did not take more than a few seconds for him to explode and experience orgasm, and, of course, away from her mouth on the ground, he left his 'kids' there in that small forest.

He started to think what a bastard he was; a few weeks ago, he was madly in love with his Anabella, his blonde princess and their perfect chemistry, and now he finds himself in love with another divine girl; a new heart-wrenching romance was ahead.

The beginning was done; she told him that he can spend Friday night at her apartment, but must come late in the dark and leave also early next day in dark as it was forbidden by the lady owner of the apartment to bring a man because she had two daughters and would not like them to hear sex or whatever sounds coming from the next door and the thin wall in between. That first sex contact with her was really pure lovers' sex.

After a soft music and a romantic dance, she noticed the obvious hard penis in her legs and kissed him softly, whispering into his ear, "Now is the time to enjoy my body." And they both steered themselves to bed.

Johanna asked passionately, "When I am back from the bathroom, I want to see your nude body lying on the bed."

Indeed, and obeying the girl's desire, he was lying in bed, naked and waiting for her to come from the bathroom.

She came wearing a see-through dress, a negligee; he could see the marvellous body and the well-formed and rich natural tits and her horny nipples. When she took off the see-through gown, allowing her strong legs and muscular thighs to be projected, she lay down on top of him, kissing him. Areus felt her breasts on his chest, and what a beautiful moment that was! He expected this moment to come for almost 20 days. What a feeling it was having his athletic girlfriend's body at his entire disposal to show to her his endless sexual abilities.

They made soundless love although that was difficult, especially for her, but they managed. She slowly rotated her hips, 'arresting' inside her his defenceless penis. He gripped a pillow to help hide her relieved groans from piercing the thin wall of that ugly neighbour lady owner; a silent orgasm for a woman was not the perfect orgasm, but that was a necessity. With that unforgettable girl, he had sex several times on the bed, on the couch, on the sofa, on the kitchen table, under the shower, in the toilet, and their starting point had been that small forest where he had 'planted' his children.

Many times with her athletic muscles surrounding her pussy, she squeezed his penis in a snug fit and in a unique way to feel that he was in her very narrow, small, sweet nest, obliging the head of his tennis to grow like a mushroom inside her. He was scared what if that stays like this in a hard-on situation and cannot get released and have a situation like dogs where they are tied together and need a doctor with an injection to separate them. What a bad comparison occurred to his mind. She did this pussy squeezing in a magnificent way, and he had his penis inside a pussy captivation, feeling at the same time a certain loneliness inside that sweet channel and was absolutely surrendered.

Usually, one can feel the narrow walls when entering from the anus but not from the wet pussy. They both enjoyed themselves, but it seemed that her apartment owner found out what was happening, and she warned her that she would throw her out if this was to happen again. So, they had to move to hotels. but she did not like this to happen in Heidelberg hotels. So, they took many times the train, going to nice hotels in the nearby city of Manheim.

They were also there like tourists, visiting museums and landscapes. One day, she called him and said that she had a delayed period.

He was shocked. It was 11 o'clock in the night, and he was sitting crying on a bench in a small nearby park, thinking that he had to marry her as he was responsible, but this would abruptly stop his career and leave a nice road of success in the middle. He had tears in his eyes, and then he saw a shadow coming; it was one of the three guys, Nikos, the one who had studied in Austria and was already married to an Austrian girl.

He explained to him what his problem was; he told him, "Do not worry; we all had the same stories in the past. In two days, she will call and tell you that she has her period." And so, indeed, it happened. They were together for quite a long time, but her company sent her to work at their subsidiary in Dusseldorf, so consequently, a long-lived love came to end.

Not two days passed, and he had sex with a waitress of a stube/tavern, but it was nothing to compare with the love he enjoyed with his previous girls, Anabella and Johanna; that sex was just to substitute for a hand job.

He moved to a cheaper room that was closer to his university school. There, he had an unforgettable experience. The old lady house owner had a 35-year-old divorced daughter with a young son of the age of seven or maybe eight years old. It was summer, so he took the boy many times to the swimming pool. He remembered when they were at the changing room to change their swimsuit, the boy noticed that obviously he had a much bigger penis between his legs than his, and he told this to his mother.

Probably, the 35-year-old girl, who was quite a woman, was somehow intrigued, and her thoughts tormented her mind for the sex that she missed for quite some years after she got divorced. One morning, he woke up having his balls full and had to run for peeing with just his underpants to the common toilet; the door was slightly open, and him almost holding his penis, he pushed the door, and what he saw was that there was the 35-year-old mature woman sitting, also peeing; he could not hold his peeing; she kept staying there, her nice curved arse embracing the toilet. Without any second thought and instinctively, he could not hold the pressure of his balls; he took his cock and started peeing in the lavabo (washbasin), feeling a great relief.

She was surprisingly watching without any sign of being uncomfortable and kept smiling and laughing; what a beautiful laughter! He adores women with a kind of musical laughter. Was that maybe a provocative sign? He said sorry and kept peeing all over the lavabo because having simultaneously the morning erection and need to pee and actually in the lavabo was not easy, so his pee reached even to the mirror; he felt so bad, and he turned to apologise, saying, "Sorry can't help it."

She was holding her mouth to hold her loud laughter at what she was seeing; she told him, "No problem, young man, keep on, and I will clean it all." He was seized by a sudden impulse to get his cock into her mouth as she was still sitting on the toilet, but he held back as he was not sure if that was appropriate and maybe too early and too fast; better let it come, if it will come, spontaneously from her side. He ran to his room and exercised a gorgeous masturbation, shouting so loud when the orgasm came, which, for sure, was to be heard in the whole floor and not only in their apartment.

Someone knocked at the door; it was her mother. "Mr Areus, is there any problem? Are you OK?"

He could barely answer as he was still in spasms. "Yes, Mrs Gerhild, I am OK. I just knocked my knee on the side table."

The same evening, he was invited by the boy, probably she was behind that invitation, to play some table card games with the family. There, it started when he was watching her. She liked his company. She was teasing him; she told him with a sly smile what her son told her, which turned him red-faced. She added, "You naughty boy, are you not having any girl these days?"

He giggled but found the courage to intrigue her the same way she did to him and answered, "Yes, it is true, and I have to self-satisfy myself; you know what I mean."

She blushed and took her hand under the table, caressing his bare knee with her soft and hot hand; her thumb came in a slight contact with his bulge under his shorts. That caress hid double intentions and as if she wanted to tell him, "Well, I will also want to see your penis but hard and not soft as my son saw."

Leaving the living room, he took the courage to ask her to come to his room to show her some photos of Greece and lovely Greek islands. He felt surprised but happy to hear knocking on his door at 11.30 when her mother went to sleep and so did her son. They started with photos, but he noticed that she showed rather less interest in the photos, and she was after other pursuits. She put her hand to his lap at first and slightly moved up to his penis. She caressed it softly without any violent grabbing of it; with the outer hand, she started unbuttoning her shirt, and there were no bras but two marvellous tits.

She took his hand and inserted it between her two tits, feeling that adorable warmth of the woman's body. She smiled to him with that same smile when she was watching him peeing at that washbasin, showing or rather telling to him why you stand still, go, get a hold of these gorgeous tits, squeeze softy, the nipples are ready to be sucked. She whispered into his ear, "Don't be shy; I am here not to play chess but need a good sex; after all, I have been with no fuck for the last three years, so I want all now and catch up on the three-year-long missing fuck, you understand?"

"No shyness but good fuck, I will help with this." He furiously took all off in two seconds and was naked in front of her; she was sitting on his bed and he was standing up, projecting the hard penis, reaching the highest point of length, as if he were telling her, "Suck it, why do you hesitate here? It is all yours." He guided her onto it, and she obeyed without waiting and took it direct into her mouth and started licking and sucking wildly as if there was no tomorrow, as if this was her last sex and had to exploit it all the way long. While his penis was growing bigger and bigger inside her mouth, she wanted it all the way through, reaching almost her throat.

He asked her to stand up and turn her around facing the wall; with both standing up, he lifted up her skirt and pulled down her panties finding himself in front of an ass in full desire, an ass and a pussy, a sex-starving vagina, or better her honeypot. He braced his hands against the wall, clamped and hooked her legs to enable him to drive deeper; she crouched even more to have better access, and in one second, he was in her full depth; he could not go deeper, until in that vagina canal was nothing else than a cock; she still thrusted into him. What a desperate woman for a so much missing fuck.

Both were enjoying the delightful sex with intricate manoeuvres and the in and out back and forth in steady tempo with harmonised and very competent motions until the moment came for her.

It seemed that she needed a little more 'ferocity', conducting the movements less rhythmic and harder and harder, deeper and deeper, so desperately needed to burst to come having a real penis inside her after so many years abstaining from sex, besides from eventual masturbations, or use of a vibrator, or a dildo.

She was the type of woman who when they come, they cannot hold their groans and moans. He tried to gently close her mouth while picking up the pillow so as not to wake up her mother or son but with little success. A 35-year-old woman in the very middle of her maturity, going three years with no intercourse, it was natural to live it vividly and enjoy every single moment.

She came first, and then he came as well, and right after, she begged him with kisses to stay in his bed for a few hours and repeat the sex after two hours of a short sleep. She had colossal lust; she wanted to catch up all the three years away from any sex in one night.

A woman of almost double his age begging him was an honour, a command to him and so it happened. After two hours, she pushed him sweetly to wake him up, kissing him, and there, they did it again on the bed and side by side with her back in front of him that allowed a rather relaxed penetration and soft balanced movements; they came almost simultaneously, pulling him off right in time while she still was moaning with splendid spasms. She kissed him many times, and right away, she took her dresses in her hand and ran completely naked to her bed but turned back to give him three more kisses and ran to her bedroom where she slept with her son.

This continued almost every night except the days of her period, but she still was there for blowjobs and soft handjob for him. She probably thought that if this hot Greek young guy was with no sex for four days, he might then look for another girl.

So, she was urging to end that period to go back to his room, but this time, with actual sex, no hands substitutes. One night, they got horny and did an unforgeable 69; it was so wild that she came in his mouth, and he came in her mouth in a culminating orgasm outburst.

In those old times, most of the girls and ladies did not shave their pussy except for that 45-year-old lady of Nurnberg, the unforgettable mature Artemis. They repeatedly did it as they both liked the 69, having her pussy in front of him, pushing her ass down and her clit touching his lips. What shall he do? Nothing other than go ahead and start something that made him later to be the professor of the so-called preliminaries.

So, they were licking each other, and he started to enjoy this even more, sucking her clit, and he heard from the other side, resembling like music in his ears, her moaning with colossal pleasure; she gave him a lesson to always activate the 69; following her advice he appreciated it for the rest of his life. Well, this was the start of a new sexual experience that he never even stopped it, but he always started with this, making mainly girls and also ladies happy with orgasm before even penetration.

Every night, their love story kept going; an image passed by his mind. One time, she was in such a sexual ecstasy that she kind of stylishly, but also cheekily, asked him and right after that turned better to say, begged him to squirt/pee on his swollen dick; he said, yes, why not, and that was one more new experience; her drenching with her fluid that came from her divine clit.

He believed that her mother did find out what was happening in his narrow bedroom and that she was rather happy that her daughter was joyful after so many years.

Her mother when her daughter was away for her job was offering him every morning very rich breakfast with two fried eggs and bacon and small sausages, as if she wanted to tell him, "Eat and get strong to satisfy my daughter."

In the meantime, he found another room in the centre of the city and close to coffee shops, fast food restaurant and clubbing, and also that room was big like an apartment and even had his own bathroom and shower. So, he told them that he will move there, and said goodbye to the whole family, all with tears in their eyes, including her son who liked him as his brother or father.

She whispered into his ear, "Stay, and I will not ask you for rent." But he had already given a deposit to the other owner and had to leave anyway.

So, he moved to his new apartment on the ground floor with a big window on the street and in the centre with his own bathroom and not sharing with anyone. Next to this apartment was a butcher, who made great sandwiches and so he had the chance to get fast and perfect sandwiches.

It was *Fasching* (Halloween) in Germany, so he and his three Greek friends went to a German tavern with local music to enjoy that special night. There again, he found himself in a situation like that of the Alps. He felt embarrassed when a very young girl of a rare beauty, 16–17 years old, came to his table, asking him to dance with her, and it surprised him as it was usually the opposite. He was stunned, and right away, he found himself in love at first sight. She was so sweet, so beautiful, and still well-formed as a woman.

Her father noticed with not an agreeable manner that his daughter was repeatedly dancing only with him and sweetly resting her head on his shoulder and also cheek to cheek. Her father stood up and brought her back to their table. She again ran away and came to him and kept dancing; she was admiring how hunky and well-built he was, with his sunburned skin and black hair.

Her father was angry and nodded to her to get back to their table; his reaction was very irritating and unjustified as Areus looked elegant and gentle, which was why his daughter was so much attracted by his whole appearance. Even his dance had an imposing and genial consideration to this girl whom he was dancing with.

He decided to go to her father, who had a scrawled face, and told him, "Sir, I am not a Gast Arbeiter, not a working foreigner, but a student with a brilliant future. Give us the chance to know each other, and I give you my word of honour that I will not to touch her." Somehow, her mother was touched by this small speech and also looked at her daughter to see how delighted she was.

The mother supported her daughter and asked her husband to give his consent, and so they managed to bend his objections. They fixed a date, but she never came, that story left a deep wound within him; he always tried not to delete from his memory her angelic face and blamed himself that he did not ask for her address or her phone number, as he was sure that she would have come, but probably, her father changed his mind.

He only had her name, Henriette; even this name hid virgin beauty. His carelessness not to ask for her address and phone number sacrificed a much promising serious relation with a fabulous person.

His beloved Anabella was calling him all the time, asking him to come to Munich; he was promising that this would happen in maybe one or two weeks, and she was so happy. He told her a bare-faced lie as he had to return home after two months for his obligatory military service.

In fact, the big love fire he had for Anabella slowly became paler, as in Heidelberg, he met quite some beautiful girls, and although she was by far the most beautiful one, the several girls he made love with, made him less soft as he was when he first met her and spent 30 days with her. Nevertheless, that girl will never go away from his memory, and he wished she would find a good man to marry as she deserved a gentle man.

But, as if she knew that he was thinking of her, the next day, he was shocked; his sweet girl from Munich (Bavaria), Anabella called him. She told him that she will come to Heidelberg. How could he say no? How? This was impossible; he wanted to see her as nothing else in this world. He asked her what train she would come by, but she told him, "What train will I come? In my father's car, the latest model of Audi?"

She said he wanted to see all of Heidelberg and the nearby graphic villages and also make some excursions to nearby cities and graphic villages. He had no worries in having two girls at the same time and get the one to meet face-to-face with the other as with his previous athletic girl, Johanna, they had an obligatory separation due to her moving to another city for her job's needs, so one headache was over.

He tried to clean his apartment as best as he could so she will have a relaxed stay, and then he went to meet that regular waitress and lied to her, saying that he will be away for more than two weeks, so as to avoid her to come to meet him for one more fuck as she came almost always uninvited in his apartment.

The day came, and his most cherished girl arrived in a black huge Audi, and his sweet love was just there in front of him. What a girl indeed! He was not sure if such a beauty will ever pass again from his life. They embraced and kissed sentimentally after quite a long time to get together. He asked her to get her luggage to go to his apartment. She said, "No, I have booked a suite at the best Heidelberg hotel with a spa."

So, she asked him to get his stuff to move there as an almost married couple. He said that the suite costed a fortune. "Well, so what, and keep in mind that I am from a wealthy family." Her father always wanted her to have a nice time. He packed mostly those things that she bought for him when he was in Munich. She told him there was no need for too many as she had bought him new ones. What will he do? She wanted to dress him again, but sportily this time. He does not like and he is not used to a girl, even his beloved girl, to spend so much for him, but what was done was done. He indeed made one luggage, and they went to that ultra deluxe hotel and to their suite.

God, that was indeed a luxury that one had to live at least one time in their life to feel like a tycoon. A huge suite with a bathroom, all in marble, the bed extra double that could accommodate two lovers comfortably. She was to stay one week in Heidelberg—the first time for her to be there. It was for him an escape of possible troubles by staying in the hotel because if he were to stay in his apartment, there was always the eventuality that all of a sudden that waitress would arrive just to check if he was there, and he had lied as they used to have sex twice a week or maybe the 35-year-old previous room owner could come and knock on his door as he heard that she was at the school asking everybody if they knew his address. Or any of the girls that he had a one-night stand with.

They unpacked, and she showed to him what she bought for him. This time, she got not any suit but casual or rather sports dresses that he liked a lot. She was hungry but also tired, so they went to the hotel restaurant, with him dressed in suit and tie as that restaurant was a high-class restaurant; she was also dressed so impressively that he felt so honoured to accompany a real lady this time and not just a 19-year-old girl. The dinner was an unforgettable bon biveur's dinner, a gastronomical gourmet meal.

He ordered smoked Scottish salmon and then the famous small Nuremberg sausages with Sauerkraut (sour cabbage), and, at the end, cheese cake. She ordered prosciutto to start with melon and as a second, a sirloin steak, and also a cheesecake. She had a glass of good French red wine and him a Bitburger beer, so the dinner was over.

Somehow, they rushed to finish the dinner to run to the suite to continue their love there but for new and updated episodes. A Veuve Clicquot champagne was waiting in the room ordered by Anabella to be there an hour later after they left the room together with white cheese Brie and camembert and strawberries—all done *comme il faut* as the French say.

They drank two glasses each of the champagne and bites of cheese, and the sweet dizziness hit their heads.

In seconds, they were naked in that royal huge matrimonial-type extra-soft bed, and there, they exercised all that they did seven months ago in Munich—those unforgettable 30 days. So, it was a long night of sex in all variations; it was an overall complete lovers' sex intercourse and not just another sex performance. All movements had unique and rhythmical grace, style, and above all, finesse. The sex duration was not too long as he felt that she was tired from the driving.

They woke up rather late at 10 and ordered breakfast in the room. She arranged that at 11 they would go to the spa of the hotel and enjoy the nice ambience and also the professional massage. Two nice ladies were massaging them together, the one near the other. Anabella seemed a bit jealous when she noticed that the hands of the massage lady were approaching under his waist, but the massage lady knew as a professional masseuse how deep she could go.

Both massage ladies were telling them how the one fits to the other, both having nice bodies, blonde and white soft skin, or, better say, angelic pinkish, and him with darker Mediterranean skin and black hair. It was nice and relaxing, and they went back to their royal bed to continue last night's ecstasy.

The next two days were rolling at the same tempo. He took her for a walk to the Philosophen Weg (Philosopher's Walk), where university professors and philosophers used to walk. That forest was a known romantic walk for lovers; he also guided her to the famous and impressive Heidelberg Bibliothek with the Greek Manuscripts, and they also visited the famous zoo.

The next day, her wish was to pack again and travel in the car to Schwarzwald (Black Forest), near France. It only took two hours' relaxing drive while enjoying the scenery. First, they were in a nice mountain hotel with such a nice view, forest, and lakes. What a nice choice for lovers. They spent two days there, and when returning back, they stayed in Baden-Baden, an equally nice hotel and nice stube (German taverns), and also they visited the famous casino.

Then they were back to Heidelberg for two more days to the same hotel and spa. The days were approaching the end, and they inevitably had to talk about their future. She wanted him to come to Munich to get engaged and married. He said he wanted this more than her, but what shall he do there professionally. Her father was a doctor; he was not a doctor and she was also not a doctor, then who will continue the father's doctor office? There was family money, but he did not feel nice living with his wife's money.

He said it was better to continue his career, get his diploma, and then come to Munich, and maybe, work in a hotel at a managerial position. This sounded as a nice pat in her ear, bittersweet but anyway still good as there was a logic in that, and they agreed to this as planned.

The next day, she was to leave and again the tears ran like a stream; they kissed and again kissed. She sat in her car and drove with tearful eyes. He stayed there, thinking that maybe he would never see her again and returned to his humble room.

There were only two–three weeks before leaving Heidelberg to go back home for his military service. One night, he had that waitress in his room for the routine needed sex. Late at night, someone knocked on his door. He looked at the clock it was two o'clock. The waitress girl was deeply sleeping after the usual easy sex, so he opened the door, and there was his previous room owner, his 35-year-old lover woman.

She told him she couldn't sleep because she refused him to take her from behind, so now she wanted this more than anything else. "Please make love to me now. I beg you look at me. I am on my knees." She even hastened to tell him that she lubricated her anus.

He was shocked. "Please get up. I cannot see you on your knees. I do not allow myself to see you begging me in this way; you were and are for me a beloved person; you don't need to beg me. I am the one to beg such a beautiful woman." He said, "I want you and you want me now, but look, there is a girl sleeping in my bed."

She said, "No problem, let us go to the bathroom." She was so crazy; he would rather say she was hungry for sex and specifically from the backdoor.

They did go to the toilet and made a real goodbye sex, her bending on the washbasin and him to come from the back and inside her easily accessible anus while she was masturbating, same time asking him to ejaculate in her asshole, and so it was done, and they concluded a not-easy-to-forget sex process. He told her that in a few days he would leave back to his country. She cried with heavy tears, and to be frank, he also did, as he had spent so many beautiful nights with her.

One week before leaving Heidelberg, he went to the post office to send a letter to his parents, telling them that he had graduated and that he would be back soon with the diploma in his hands so that his father was justified in trusting him. Going to the post office, he noticed a tiny (mignon, would rather say) girl; he looked at her; she looked at him; they crossed each other, him heading to the post office, and then he said why not turn around to see what she did, and there she was also stopping and looking at him from the distance. A new but for a short period affair was to begin. He was fascinated with her mignon look.

They immediately felt very close together; one liked the other admirably. Due to her Hoch Deutsch (gentle German language) and her good knowledge of the English language, she was working at the famous during those times Radio Luxembourg, and every Sunday, as a hobby, she was falling by parachute. Her name was Julianna.

She told him that she was invited by the parachutist's club in Greece, and he gave her his address, just in case. He managed after one week of many kisses and caressing and overall touching each other's body, to bring her to his home, where they could not even reach the bed and fall down to the wooden floor making wild sex.

He was to wake up at five o'clock in the morning to go to the train station, but he never told her; having this in mind, he could not perfectly operate his sex with that amazingly beautiful girl, who looked like the famous Madonna singer, and he came unexpectedly fast. She was angry; she was beating his chest, shouting at him many times. "Why, why, why? I was about to come and you came before me, why?"

He will never forgive himself for this. It was the first time that he left a girl, and what a girl, unsatisfied. He calmed her down, and as a compensation, he promised that tomorrow they would do it again, and he would be sure, this time, he would control himself. She became cool and sweet as she always was, and she kissed him many times; she indeed loved him. They fixed a meeting for a coffee the next day, but that never happened as he was on his way back home. He felt very bad as this was against his father's advice. "Never let a girl or a woman down."

He had to take the train back to go home for his obligatory military service, which was during those times for 24 months.

Again, here, his uncle helped so that he spent most of his military service near Athens, or rather in Athens, not far from his home, where he always slept most of the nights, unless those nights when he was an officer in charge and had to sleep in the office.

Normally, one has to go far away to the Greek borders for the bigger part of the military service, but with the pretext that he was a linguist, he got an office post at the Greek Intelligence Service department of communications, being also at the same time the officer in charge of the small squad of 10 soldiers, who were supposed to guard the building, but they were almost all kind of golden boys.

Well, there he spent easy military service, and he had some relations with two or three ladies; they were working there, but nothing like a real affair that would have remained as a memory.

Some kisses, some touches here and there, but that was all. What was better was for him to look for beautiful tourist girls—either German or Scandinavian, that was easier with fast sex ending and with no obligations.

What happened to him will remain strongly engraved in his memory. The day of 21 April 1967, he had a night shift as the officer in charge. He was sleeping on a big desk.

He was the officer in charge of the most significant office, which was the worldwide communications with all embassies. Around 3 o'clock, the in-charge chief of the telex department woke him up, telling him that they have not a single connection nor a single telex communication. He told him, "Fix this technical problem. I am not a technician; you are the experts, not me. I am in charge of your security."

Still, they came back saying there was nothing to do. There must be a serious problem not there but at the big building of Greece's communications organisation called OTE (his father had worked there before he retired). He called the military infantry regiment to whom his little squad belonged to, and he heard a commanding voice from the other line, "Do nothing; stay there; do not move." He gave him his name as a major, so he had to obey and shut down the line.

The whole system was down; the whole team came to him, asking him to do something as he was in charge of the military part of the department.

So, he said, "What the hell! I have such an enormous responsibility, and that major tells me to stay and do nothing? No, no way. I have to do something and ignore him." He woke up a soldier driver and took a military jeep to go to the central communication building to see why they have no connections.

The jeep ran for two kilometres, and they found themselves in front of two huge military tanks. He was shocked; what the hell is happening? He told them who he was and what he wanted, and they told him to just shut up and get down from the jeep.

He was angry by how they dared to talk like this to an officer in charge of such a crucial and important military secret agency. They did not care who he was and what was behind him, just took him down and with force, better to say.

So, finally, after some internal talking between the two sergeants in charge of the two tanks, they took him, walking and leaving the jeep behind with the guns in their hands. It took 30 minutes to reach the communications tower, and all those 30 minutes he was seeing jeeps, big military trucks, and tanks moving, stopping any cars' circulation.

At last, they reached the telecommunications tower, and what he saw were thousands of cables all cut in pieces; there was not a single cable that was not cut. On the roads, tanks and military cars were running in the dark as the road lights were turned off too.

What shall he do? He knew the home of a colonel who was the head of the Intelligent Service and asked another soldier who was there in front of the building with a motorcycle; he explained to him who he was and for what he was responsible, and he was also not knowing what was going on as he did not have any instructions; he agreed to carry him to the home of his head officer, the colonel head of the Intelligent Service for Communications. It was 4 o'clock in the morning; he was lucky that not any tank or any soldiers' blocks stopped him.

He knocked on the door of his chief, and there he was in his robe; he did not know what to tell him; he just told him, "Sir, I believe there is a revolution going on."

"No, my boy," he says, "this is not a revolution (personally he liked him a lot for his good services); this is a coup, the seizure of democracy; this is a dictatorship." In fact, almost three days later, they sent him to retirement as he refused to cooperate with the junta.

The next few days, they all knew well what happened in Greece; no democracy anymore but dictatorship, which brought all politicians in prison and in exile to small uninhabited and isolated islands with bad human conditions as prisoners.

The worst of all was that one could not speak and talk to the neighbour or even to a friend as the dictators and all their secret service had ears everywhere; this was the most unbearable part of a dictatorship—the restriction of the freedom of speech.

He had two more months to the end of his service.

So, now he had to continue his life. It was August and very hot, so the only solution was the beach, and there he met a Danish girl, not a very beautiful girl, but the aim was to get her to bed, which was needed heavily even if she was not the most beautiful girl he had ever met. She was the *au pair* (babysitter) of the children of the Danish ambassador.

Denmark was the black sheep in the system of the dictators as Denmark denied them as legal governors. He was entering the ambassador's home to have sex with this girl almost every day.

All in his service were telling him to stop going there as this was crazy because for sure the Danish ambassador's home was closely watched by governmental agents. He took the risk as he needed the easy sex.

The girl was telling him that she worked before coming to Greece at a lunatic asylum, a well-paid job. He needed to gather enough money to later continue his education in his hotel manager career. He asked her to communicate with them and get him a job there as in a few weeks he would finish his military service and needed a job. Indeed, she wrote and got back the invitation for him to work there for one year as the patients' carer.

To go to Denmark, you needed a visa, and the visa was not at all easy to get, as Denmark was always a hostile country to the dictator's government of the three colonels who did the coup.

How then could he go there? His parents were playing cards in two friendly homes, and in one of those homes was also one ex-officer who was with the system and had good connections with the junta regime of colonels.

He managed, especially helped him with the experience he had by having his military service with the intelligence service, to get the visa as if he were one of them and on a mission.

At this point, he couldn't forget another life's experience. That ex-military officer was married to a 20 years younger German lady. He was 65 but always somehow with a non-healthy body, and he walked crookedly. His German wife was not participating in the cards playing table, so she was obviously bored. His mother noticed that she was not that happy doing nothing, so she kindly asked her to move to the next room with her son and speak in German so that he exercises his German after two years of not talking German as much. She had no objection; on the contrary, it was for her a relief to leave that playing cards room, where she was pretty well bored, and they went to the next room.

What legs she had and what a broad chest she had; she should be around 45 years old. She crossed her legs many times; he believed probably deliberately, and he could almost see her panties. They were talking about the life he had in Germany and his career, and he also intelligently told her about his sex moments, especially with those 45-year-old lady (Artemis).

Her gaze looked at him up and especially down, giving him a warm glow to add spice to his narration. She liked that catchy story so much she wanted to hear all the details as she noticed that, at first, he was reluctant to reveal all details. He also could see that she was a deprived woman with that handicapped and much older husband, most probably with no sex at all.

She was asking how you did that, what you did then, what she did and how, asking him persistently to tell her more about his sex with that lady without any shame or hesitation; she wanted all the details. What? How? Where? He was cleverly bringing her in a hot sexual desire, especially when he told her that the 45-year-old lady even licked his anus.

He noticed her biting her bottom lip and her hand closing her mouth as if something she heard was unbelievable for her, or better, she felt sorry that she never tried this with any man and, of course, never with her husband. She kept crossing her legs and touching her massive breasts, putting one hand to erotically squeeze her nipples under her shirt. She could not control anymore; she was sweating. She was quivering a little; he could rather say shivering.

He could notice she was in full desire and extremely explosive passion as if she were about to have an orgasm there sitting on that sofa.

She found, or rather discovered, an excuse to go to the bathroom; she did not just go, but she almost ran to the bathroom. What was weird to him was why she took her bag also with her to the bathroom; there were two options: either she had always in her bag and just in case, a vibrator (having less or even not any sex at all with her husband), or her underwear was so wet that she had to take it off and put them in her bag and stay with no panties, so as to be more easy to rub her clit for a heavenly masturbation.

He was more than 100% sure that she masturbated there because she came back after more than 15 minutes in the bathroom with a fresh, relaxed, and familiar face of a woman after a climax.

She asked him if there were more experiences to recount, and she changed twice the crossing of her legs, and there it was, no panties just the pussy. He told her many stories like that of the Israeli woman the same age as her and that he had to perform sex under the watching eye of her chuckhole older husband. At that point, he noted that maybe he had given her an idea. She was so clever and hot, and she asked him, "Are you also not going to the bathroom?" With a meaningful smile and a wink of her eye.

At that moment, he could not understand why she wanted him to go to the bathroom, but he obeyed to her for that moment's motivated advice. He went to the bathroom; he was so horny that he also started masturbating and only with the erotic fantasia that there in this same bathroom only a few minutes ago that mature, but horny, lady masturbated with him as her fantasy, while he did not lock the door, hoping maybe she will follow him to the toilet.

He was sitting in the toilet, and his trousers were down; he was in the process of handjob, but it happened; she, without any knocking, entered and locked the door behind her; she came close, knelt down as low as her to be able to get his penis in her mouth; her tongue was soft and wrapped the penis all around; her hot lips started licking it overall and unstoppably in a steady magnificent rhythm. She was such a revelatory, with lusciously curved hips, a real lush woman.

He slipped both hands under her shirt to grab her breasts. She was in such a situation that she did not care if any one came to use the toilet and see that it was locked and understand that he and she were certainly inside.

She got up; they went to the lavabo (washbasin) and raised one foot onto the lavabo with her hands on the edge of the lavabo; she lifted up her skirt, no panty under it, and she shouted with a loud voice, "Come, come, come, do to me what you did to those 45-year-old nymphomaniacs." And, of course, without hesitation and in seconds, his mushroom-shaped penis head touched the entry of her rectum, feeling her moistness and slid easily inside her, at the same time holding her soft and massive breasts that were hanging like mangos.

She moaned; she was moving her ass left and right in a new for him motion, trying to get it all deeper and deeper; she wanted to feel all of it 'her way', that sex position succeeded deeper narrowing the walls of the vagina; she was in a way in another world, and he guided her to a pathway of sexual eruption; her impending orgasm was on its way.

Not too late after the penetration, she came and came and again came as if she did not have sex for years. He could not manage to count how many times she was in a merely continuous climax. She turned around and started a divine blowjob when he was to ejaculate. She said, "Stay, I want to swallow all of it," and so he did.

That unfortunately did not happen again as he had the visa, and he had to go to Denmark, but that sex, that blowjob, and that masturbation was maybe the best he ever had, knowing that few minutes ago that fantastic woman was masturbating upon his sex recital and narratives and was impossible for her to limit her sex desire with just a masturbation.

Finishing all and knowing that he was to leave for Denmark, she said in his ear, "I know where to find you, and I will come for you in Denmark even if I need to get a divorce." Her name was Alexia.

So, now again, he found himself in that horrible train experience, as he had taken that train many times before. It took three days to reach Copenhagen.

Arriving in the main train station of Copenhagen, he took a train to that small Copenhagen suburb in the northern part of Denmark and near Sweden where he was to work. He walked 30 minutes from the train station to the hospital, and there he was in front of the gate of the installation of the lunatic asylum, but what a lunatic asylum was that?

A heavenly environment, looking like a super impressive and clean clinic for retarded men, women, and kids in the middle of pure nature. Here, he gained a life's experience only in one year working and taking care of crazy people, who in many cases were not as crazy as they were meant to be. If you just cared for them and handled them gently and friendly, they behaved as ordinary people.

First thing to do was to eat something; he was starving; it was lunchtime and at the asylum's restaurant were more these 200 nurses, girls, men, as well as doctors. Blonde beautiful girls who stared at him with curiosity as those times black-haired men with slightly darker sunburn skin were seldom, plus the fact that he was handsome and strong-looking. The menu was spaghetti, so at that time he cared more for the spaghetti than for the almost hundred beautiful girls who were there. He had to walk to the buffet table where the spaghetti was and with his dish filled up to the very top returned to his table, where two other Danish guys were eating.

He was very hungry, so he walked back again to fill up for the second time. There, he heard a little laughter. Shit, what shall he do? He still had quite an empty space in his belly. Well, fuck the laughter, and he went to the buffet for the third time. Then in the whole room was a big laughter from all 200 nurses and doctors; they stood up and were staring at him as if he were from another planet where all were starving. That was the first picture of his appearance there.

They took him to his room where he was to stay for a few days until he finds his own room in the small town. There was a girl who took care of him, beautiful as they all were, speaking good English. She was in charge of showing him around. In fact, all Danish speak either English or German, so he had no communication difficulties.

After she showed him where he was to sleep, she also took him fast to see where his department was to work so that he knew how to walk to go there the next day.

He kindly asked her to take him to the centre of that small town to buy some necessary items, such as toothpaste and a razor. She was a very polite, sweet-looking girl and agreed with no hesitation. After he installed himself in the room, he managed to take a nap for an hour. She came this time dressed not like a nurse but with a nice and attractive dress, allowing him to see her beautiful body.

While walking out of the hospital to go to the, town he noticed other nurses' glances showing jealousy towards the girl who volunteered to show him around. He was happy to see that this was a paradise for him, surrounded by numerous and all beautiful girls.

So, they went to town. She was very friendly but also showed a sort of desire to be with a Mediterranean guy, showing pride in having him next to her. In those times, Mediterraneans were seldom, especially in that small town, and, of course, there were not any black boys or other far-east guys, who are now plenty in all of Scandinavia.

She showed him around and suggested him to come at six in the afternoon to take him to Copenhagen to show him more of the capital city. Indeed, they went there and ended up at a dancing club.

They danced and came closer; needless to say, what happened down there with his penis always obeying the messages and never failed to arouse especially mature ladies. She, of course, noticed that but showed no surprise. She knew well that she had the gift to turn the guys on.

They ran to catch up the last train back to the small town; in the train, kisses took place and hands were playing over zip flies and under skirts. Passengers on that train were shocked to see that erotic scene between an excited Danish girl and a southern European handsome young man, trying hypocritically to turn their faces away, but they could not succeed as they adored with jealousy what was happening there.

She was so hot, even more than him; passengers were also turned on and could not hide it, deep in their fantasy desire to join. Most probably, the husband or wife will benefit from this erotic scene in that train when they reach their homes and will copy what they witnessed a few minutes ago.

Especially after four days of an exhausting train trip in an unbelievable sexual desire, she was happy for this and obviously showed it. They 'ran', when he says ran, they indeed ran to reach his room as fast as possible as they were both in an extremely horny situation.

They entered the room, and one was undressing the other rapidly. What a body she had, completely naked, ready to penetrate, but she stopped him. She told him that in Denmark abortion was not allowed and as the sex was done with no condom, she could not take any risk but to take protective measures.

He suggested the French way, in other words, from behind, but she definitely denied it, feeling strange that he asked her such an abnormality.

So, there was no other solution, and according to her guidance, his penis to act a rubbing over her cute clit, up and down in fucking motions but not inside; she was so pleased for this clit pat and came fast with a calmness and brightness in her face filled up with satisfaction leaned down to the bed holding her eyes shut tight to enjoy all last spasms.

This scene always makes him happy as an altruist he was to feel that he, as a sexual genius, offers happiness to all his erotic partners. She took over for a rather clumsy blowjob, doing this under the effect of her still ongoing climax, but he told her to stop as he wanted her to come again for a second and why not for a third orgasm.

She was startled; local boys never asked for a second time, or give one more chance of happiness to the girls. She was happy to hear this, and she asked him how this time, so he told her 'leave it to me'. So, he exercised the 69, him licking her pussy, and she did the same with his penis.

He was 100% sure nobody before had licked her vagina; at the same time, his finger was exploring here anus, just a finger she allowed, and this was an enormous happy experience she came again and again and, of course, him twice, and one and despite his avoidance on the small 'river' between her two gorgeous breasts.

She kissed him many times, thanking him for the satisfactions he gave her, telling him that this happened to her for the first time to have three consecutive orgasms. She will dream again and again about what happened unexpectedly to her today. The sight of a woman who leaves his bedroom with such a happy smile on her face always gives him the motive to offer with playfulness his erotic 'services'.

The next day, they took him to the department where he would work. That was the special department where the patients were not fundamentally lunatic but half disturbed. Means, they knew they were not normal, while those that took care of them were normal and mentally healthy, and this made them exceptionally dangerous. Especially to him, they showed additional hatred for another reason that a darker skinned guy, who they never saw before, came suddenly to their department.

He was very nicely welcomed by the lady in charge, all staff, all nurses, and a leading kind girl of approximately 23 years of age. A tough girl with a proud walk, but with an absolutely great ass and enormous, strong, natural tits that could easily grind on his chest when and if the time comes.

She was engaged that time with a German boy, so he could not try to touch her yet, but he started his usual way to bring her around. She was telling him that her fiancé was not expressing his sentiments and has sex very seldom; they had sex, but he was rather ignorant and selfish, or he made sex just as routine and an obligation, and she never enjoyed this.

Here, he found the opening, and he, as a smart fox, took the chance to tell her that for us Greeks, their girl or fiancé is their queen, or, better, their princess; they deal with her as if she were a real princess, and even the sex is a respectful and altruistic ceremony and not any rough encounter. All these stories touched her, or rather sounded to her as supernatural.

One day, they were both working to fix one patient's bed; while doing this, he deliberately touched her hand, and she responded by squeezing hard his hand.

Without losing the momentum, he took her friendly and gently by the hand and led her to an empty room at the very end of the corridor. He started with no loss of time to kiss her in full passion—something that was unknown to her.

He had enormous stiffness down there; he took her hand and smoothly put her hand on his hard penis; she blushed, but she liked; she squeezed feeling that was something that she maybe had to avoid being engaged, but she felt a desirable lust when touching his penis. They were processing, and he started to unbutton her shirt.

Unfortunately, that institution was all around with big glass windows so one could see the next nearby department, and this is what happened: five nurses were there on the opposite department watching all their pre-sex approach, with him ready to put his hand under her skirt and caress her pussy. Those nurses on the opposite window attending the whole show was unusual for them, but at the same time, a total sex pleasure clearly was to be seen on their horny and jealous faces.

One of them was even masturbating herself to the incredible for her, those times porno show; he spotted who that girl was for the next girl-hunting.

So, they had to stop. What a pity; he was there to make one more girl happy, and this time a tough and self-controlled-looking girl.

But it happened one night when they both had a night shift with her and him. He was looking forward to the patients to go to sleep, but there was a bastard called Axel; he was a big guy, and he knew that there was something to happen, and he denied going to sleep; he was going up and down the long corridor with the sound of his clogs that penetrated brains, creating a kind of block to what they were ready and extra hot to start. He had to go to the pharmacy and take an extra pill, adding to his night pills, and that was the way to make him fall asleep.

She took his hand, and they went to the big bathroom, where they bathed and massaged the patients as that was the only room there with no glass windows.

What happened there was difficult to describe; there was no other way than go down to the floor, unbuttoning each other; she never took any penis before in her mouth, and obviously, she did not know how to make a blowjob. That German son of a bitch was entering in her, finishing, and was doing nothing else, with not any *hors d'oeuvres* (preliminaries, as he used to call).

He took her around for 69. Her pussy was hidden in a big bush of hair, which he did not like, but he had to provide her pleasure by all means; she needed it desperately.

That licking made her come in two minutes; she shivered while coming, and she was in such ecstasy that she even bit his penis, of course, with no intention. The rest was easy. He asked her to bend over the bathtub, allowing that big but beautiful whole ass to be in front of him.

He put a finger in her anus, but she did not want that, so he let the anus to go down to the main hole, where he tried to stay in as long as he could, so she came again and again, and indeed, she came, always with a sweet sigh, not that loud for such a big girl, but a sweet erotic voice that was telling him all.

When she finished, she took his penis out and masturbated him; the same story that all girls were afraid of getting pregnant as no abortion was allowed. She was offering him a handjob doing to him what she did not want him to do to her; she also put a finger in his anus, and frankly if this brings her joy, he allowed her and let this to happen.

When he came, she went down to her knees to ejaculate in her mouth. She thought that this would make him happier, but he did not like this. He does not like seeing a nice girl's or lady's face full of sperm; no, this is a disrespect to his sexual partners and never allowed this even if they asked for it. He ejaculated but not on her face but in the bathtub.

She was living very close to his place, and she quite sometimes came to his room and had divine sex; she started learning tricks of sex that he had learned before from other ladies, and so they enjoyed it.

One night, she came to his room with something well wrapped. He asked what this was. She said it was a gift for him; she unwrapped, and what was there was a small jar of Vaseline. She said, "Well, tonight, I will allow you to do to me what I denied you the first night."

So, the upper hole, when she was on her fours, was conquered with little of the suffering and moaning from the girl, but she was happy that she also had that experience in her sex menu that until then was a blank menu.

He wanted to buy a car, so he took extra working shifts and many extra hours, and so he was making quite some money, especially taking night shifts that were paid double.

His only trouble was that bastard Axel, that tall, half-mentally ill guy who was aware that he was not normal while he was normal, and then he could imagine what was going on with him and the 23-year-old nurse. He hated him because he was watching him talk and flirt with all the nurses, and he was kind of jealous that a foreigner would sooner or later get them to his bed.

He will never forget what happened when he took the Christmas night shift, which was a triple-paid shift. It was late at night; all was peaceful. He was watching TV with all the patients sleeping except Axel.

All was very peaceful as a nice Christmas night, but then suddenly, he heard a whistle kind of sound; without knowing what this was, he crouched his head, and that bending saved his life. That bloody Axel dashed a stainless steel heavy and sharp lid of a casserole aiming his head or neck; he sent that straight to his head, and if that was to meet his neck or head, he would have been right there dead.

This lid finally ended up on the TV, breaking it into pieces. The next morning, he reported what happened, and they sent him to another much stricter department where he was not to have as many free behaviours as he had till now.

Among others, he also had a pleasant experience; this time, let him call it a medical memory. There was among the patients also a boy called Ule, who had kind of Down syndrome (a spastic boy) and never spoke a single word. From morning to night, he was only moved half way up and down his head all day sitting on a wheelchair, always with a smile but never any word. He was close to him and often took him out on his wheelchair. He wanted those promenades a lot as he thought that other nice girl nurses were also carrying patients on a wheelchair, having many chances for dates and whatever will come out of it. He liked Ule, and Ule liked him a lot, so he started trying to make him say one single word, and in fact, he succeeded.

At this point, he could say that after three months, he was speaking almost very good Danish, which helped him a lot to get girlfriends who spoke no other language, and they were especially low-educated nurses.

So, all day, he was asking Ule what his name was. (This in Danish: *hvad er mit navn?*) He asked him thousands of times, again and again for many months. "Ule, what is my name?" He was trying, but unsuccessfully—until after three months, one day, he asked him one more time to call his name that he knew as he heard the nurses call him Areus.

He bent down, showed his hand up in the sky, and said loudly, "Areus," with a big smile and showing pride that he was able to talk. That was a miracle written in the books of the hospital with golden letters, and all respected him even more, wanting to have him as a friend and girls as a lover as he was the guy of the year.

The doctors came and asked how he managed to do that. He simply showed him love and patience—no medicines or pills—and showed him pure, not plastic love, and so he did it. Since that day, from morning to night, with a big smile of happiness, Ule has been loudly saying 'Areus' hundreds of times. He, as a self-taught healer, tried to perform a type of healing on that mentally ill child, and he did so successfully under general recognition.

During those times of his glory, his name became known from the one corner to the other, and with Ule on the wheelchair on the usual promenade, he met a fantastic, beautiful nurse, whom he had spotted for a few weeks, managing and following her route with her patient on the wheelchair, and 'coincidentally', their wheelchairs met.

They got to know each other, and she told him that she was married, but that was not that much of a problem for them to have an affair; after all, her husband also had his affairs, but with a man, proving he was gay.

So, that was it; on their first date, they met at a café. They drank the coffee fast and then she told him, "OK, let us go to your home," simply and naturally and without any reluctance. He was astonished he never got a girl in his bed so fast. Entering his bedroom, she took off all her dress right away with no excuses and laid on the bed with wide open legs, telling him, "Come, my pussy wants you; heal my passion the way you well proved to know." And that was it; after doing it as normal sex, she wanted his favourite to gently get her down on all fours style, and he enjoyed that, she also did profoundly.

This time, no 69, or blow jobs as he had intended, and as he was always asked to pull the penis out when the right time was to ejaculate, but she squeezed her pussy, allowing him not to take it out, so he came in her hot and fully wet pussy, and she did not object at all; she wanted to merge with him, who knows maybe if he has a son or a daughter left behind.

One day, he was off duty and in a good mood, he turned the radio on, and it was rather loud as it was only 11 o'clock in the morning so he could not disturb anyone.

The radio was on with rock n roll music—quite modern music. He heard someone knocking at his door. He first thought that someone wanted to protest for the loud music as it was 11 o'clock in the morning.

He opened the door, and the married beautiful girl of the first floor with very sexy attire rushed in, went right into the living room where the music came from, and like a professional dancer, or rather a wild pole dancer with a perfectly chiselled body, she performed an extremely erotic and vigorous dancing; when he says erotic, he means real erotic that would make a dead man rise up from his grave.

There was a lot of suspense in the living room as she performed an unbridled sensual dancing, adding superior movements with fluidity. Many times, her skirt raised up to her navel, and from her tiny panties, he could see part of the lips of her shaved pussy, without a strand of hair. She looked astonishingly beautiful, never before he was in front of such a crazily dancing woman. That unique session and image brought his wild imaginations to life, feeling pressure under his jockey.

He was crazy seeing her lying down on the wooden floor with her legs open, moving at the rhythm of the music; he moved in and tried to get atop of her, but like a snake, she managed to escape, laughing loudly, feeling good, and continued dancing more and more nimbly and crazily, making him feel unable to reach her with the incredible flexible and ethereal movements of her vigorous dance.

The music stopped as there was an advertising break on the radio. She leaned flat down, dazed with dripping sweat all over showing obvious tiredness; this woman's instinct made it clear that she was committed to go further with no hesitation, and second thoughts such as 'cheating opportunity' will not appear again.

He adored inhaling the woman's sweat from the body; her total submission intoxicated him, and he started licking her sweat from her face, her neck, and started unbuttoning her shirt to continue licking her breasts and the already aroused nipples until he reached the sweet pussy.

She was exhausted and absolutely surrendered to his unstoppable desires. This sensual dance enticed him to implement all the experiences and skills he obtained from all his girls, especially from the ladies; he managed to gather all the intriguing past years. All those sex methods and tactics as well as positions were completely new to her; she had never felt it before, as she later admitted, with her husband. So, it was a sexual stream that slowly became a huge, flowing Niagara Falls.

He kept licking her completely naked body, a perfect body that one can see at the strippers around the metal pole bar dancing.

She stayed there on the floor, making not a least of motion or hesitate to accept all that his tongue was driving her mad and deep in her hyper-flexible and perfectly shaped vagina; she helped by raising her hips to meet his tongue's impels even deeper.

Many women do not possess such flawless vaginas; there are many sorts of pussies; there are also not beautiful-looking vaginas, but hers was absolutely superb, and her clit was a piece of art, golden blond clit; this is the colour of the clit he likes most and less the black clits; her intact asshole was impeccable. God was in an optimal mood when he created her.

She was out of control. She jumped up, took his trousers off, and here the real erotic action started; she allowed him to go inside and penetrate deep inside her; he asked her how come as all the previous Danish girls were very reluctant to let him go inside and get to finish inside them. She said, "Go ahead, do whatever you want with my body, penetrate wherever you want, get inside me as deeply as possible with no consequences."

She had a doctor's report that she cannot get a baby. So, having the approval liberated him from any precautions and started thrust by thrust while at the same time her bobbing down and up on his penis got faster and more impulse. They made sex that was an Oscar sensual performance. Using all the previous experiences he had, he made a happy woman, a woman who probably never before felt so nice.

The 'wherever you want' gave the green light to go also from behind, which was slightly painful, but she adored that, and with a hoarse voice, she turned around whispering, "That I wanted as nothing else, but I was ashamed to ask you; please wear me out." And there was the 'Grand Finale'. A monumental erotic theatrical scene came to an end and 'the curtains fell'.

To his regret, they did not do it again; she told him that she only wanted to instantly punish her husband for obscene or excessive masculinity that she was constantly demanding from him but unsuccessfully. She did not want to cheat on her husband anymore as that was the first and last, and that sex intercourse they had was for her a delight that filled the gap she had in her sexual married life.

She added, "In fact, my dream came true as I wanted as nothing else to have sex with you, watching you through that small door peephole, coming up and down the stairs and having you as fantasy, I made exceptionally better sex with my husband; now this dream is accomplished, and it is over, and I thank you."

In the meantime, that Danish girl who found the job for him in Denmark came back, but he told her clearly that he did not want her anymore, as he heard from Greece that she fucked both his brother and a close friend of his. She cried and showed how she felt guilty for what she had done and in order to hold him next to her, she rented a big apartment with two bedrooms and asked him to move into one of the bedrooms, and they agreed that he was allowed to sleep with any girl he wanted in his bedroom. She agreed, so he stayed there; at least, she knew that he was just there even if there was no intercourse.

His brother was a seaman, going quickly up the ranks to become the first sea captain. From the letters he was sending him, he could see that his life in the sea was not that amusing at all. Being a long time at sea and when they reached a harbour, what was there, just harbour dirty prostitutes, so Areus took the initiative to ask the clinic director of the hospital. After being so happy with him, they accepted his brother also to work there for a certain period.

He told him, "Come here, take a break, and live like a normal man." He was a very handsome and strong man with muscles that would turn on the Danish girls lusting for such men.

He indeed came, but when his brother came, he was hospitalised. What happened was that he had been suffering for the last few weeks from haemorrhoids, and that was going from bad to worse; he could not sit on a chair. He decided to go to a Danish doctor.

He examined him and told him, "Look, Mr Areus, you have no haemorrhoids, but what you have is that you got a very small anus, and you have to get operated on to make this hole wider."

He said, "Are you kidding me?"

"No, this is a very simple operation," he said that with a seldom face, but he guaranteed that he would never suffer again.

He laughed, but he decided to follow the doctor's advice to do this small operation. He then went to the hospital. He opened his legs like a pregnant woman, and he noticed that there were seven doctors there who watched as this operation had never been performed before in their hospital. Among them was a black guy.

He asked him, "What the hell are you doing here?"

He said, "I make my practice."

He said, "You will practice with my asshole?"

They all laughed. The operation was done easily and fast, and the next day, his brother came to see him and took him with a taxi back home. The brother was to sleep in the same bedroom with his ex-girlfriend; she had not any objection, and on the contrary, she wanted someone to fuck her and not him anymore as he had many other more beautiful girls at his disposal.

His brother was to work in another department of the lunatic asylum. He was in the most dangerous department with 18–22-year-old boys, who, if you forgot to give them their pill on time, were able to break down a wall with their heads and still laugh loudly as if nothing had happened.

He was locked inside the room where the mentally disturbed but strong guys were inside, and he was working with them to teach them discipline and obedience, which he did in his own way.

He will come back to this later for an unbelievable matter that happened in his department.

Himself at his department, he was taking out with the wheelchair a Norwegian very short fellow, who believed that he was an SS during the war, and he was saluting all the time with a 'Heil Hitler'.

While his brother was there, they decided to go to a judo school. They had lessons, and they were advancing well. One day, the instructor wanted to show everyone a judo exercise, and he asked for a volunteer. In judo, when one of the opponents is in a bad situation, risking his life, he strikes the floor with his hand so the other one releases him.

His brother volunteered, and the 'fight' started. Indeed, the instructor managed quite sometimes to drop his brother down, so he got angry, said to hell with judo grabbed the instructor by the neck, brought him down, and the instructor started striking in despair on the floor. Well, that, of course, was not judo but Greco-Roman wrestling.

During promenades, he several met nurses and had most of them the next day in his bed, making sex. He remembers one time while he was in his bed with a girl, and at a doggy process of their encounter, someone threw small stones to his window; he believed that this was probably her husband or any other girl who was there in that room before.

He discovered later that the one who was throwing small stones on his window was the 23-year-old nurse of his department with whom he had already made sex before in the hospital bathroom and in his bedroom, but she felt horny and keen for a good sex, but he could not open the door for her as there was other girl enjoying sex in his bed.

The next day, he had to go to Copenhagen to the Greek Embassy, as they were looking for him from Greece.

Here, he was in real trouble; the reason was that when he decided to leave for Denmark, he needed the visa as Denmark for junta was a black-listed country. As he mentioned before, that limped major helped him to get the visa. At the embassy, they handed him a classified letter. He opened, and he was shocked seeing there were no names, just contact codes and protocol to be followed, asking him to watch over the Greek students that were studying at Danish universities and give names of those who took part in several protests against the junta.

He could not do that, of course; he was not a spy or a snitch. He never answered them, but then a new letter came, and they were angry this time with him; they even called his father asking why his son was not obeying their instructions.

His father was in panic—a peaceful and real democrat man felt that they were threatening him. His father called him, and he assured him that he will soon leave Denmark so they would lose his tracks.

He told his father that if they call him again, tell them that he was somewhere, probably in Europe, but that he does not know where.

When returning one day on a train, he met a German girl, who was happy to meet him as she had a Greek boyfriend before. They arranged for a date, and the result was them having sex in his 'famous' bed, but it seemed that girl was not that a super virgin girl, and she passed to him her gonorrhoea.

He went to the doctor; he gave him the appropriate medicines, and he obliged him to tell him which girl he had sex with the last 10 days, but that was the German girl. He explained to him and later to the police that he met her on the train; he only knew her name, which was Gerhild, and, of course, he does not know where she stays.

To his department came a Danish guy who was also a caretaker like him or rather the correct word of the duty for a man was not nurse but a man who cares the patients. His name was Lars. He liked him; he was a very nice guy. He asked him to come on the weekend to his country house and enjoy the Saturday night dinner there.

He had, at that time, his own car, a Volkswagen that he bought going for one day to Hamburg, which apparently ruined the engine as he was driving all the way from Hamburg to Copenhagen with the handbrakes on and on the first gear. He had to change the engine when he arrived in Denmark. His friend's country house was quite a long way away, so he took with him that ex-girlfriend, with whom he was already with in Greece, and was staying in her apartment, to guide him to his friend's country house.

They drove to that country house, which was a really beautiful, typical Danish country house. His wife was an impressively beautiful woman of 30 or 35 years old. The night with candles was going well. They had a nice dinner, drank wine, and there was also nice, slow music that invited them to dance.

So, they danced, his friend with the girl he mentioned before and Areus with his friend's wife. He noticed his wife while dancing. She had a deep breath on his cheek, as if she wanted to show him that she needed something, and by 'accident' sometimes, she touched his penis with her knee, telling into his ear, "Oh, I am sorry."

They danced and sat down on the sofa. Lars came asking him to follow him to the kitchen. In the kitchen, he told him that he likes that girl he came with, and if he likes his wife, they can swap girls and sleep overnight in separate bedrooms.

He told him that he cannot fuck the wife of his good friend, but as far as he suggests this, then he will do it, but against his principles, which, of course, didn't make him less desireful to get that horny wife satisfied.

He approached the girl he came with when they returned to the living room and told her the swap story; she had no objection because Lars was a good-looking man. He took his girl, and they went to the one bedroom, and he stayed alone in the living room with the wife.

She told him to dance one more time and then go to the bedroom. He was astonished that this girl's swap was pre-planned.

They danced, but this time, there was not any 'sorry'. His knee was between her legs, and then her knee was touching his hard dick. She grabbed him by the hand, and they went straight to the bedroom.

That woman was a volcano ready to erupt. He did not think that his very sympathetic friend as husband was a bad sex performer, probably the marital issues after some years refraining the desire and finally it all became a routine so a variety was necessary to energise and revitalise the lust for renewed sex. She wanted everything, when he says everything, he means it, and he had so much to give her.

The woman eagerly seemed to absorb all his tricks and exclusive extras he offered her in abundance. They fell asleep at four in the morning after 'uncontrolled' sex, and she asked him to spank her bum until it became kind of pink; among others, she was masturbating his penis inside and between her beautiful tits.

It was a rough hard-core sex as this was what she desperately wanted, a good sex that she missed for probably long, the ultra-exceptional for her was the anus fuck even without any Vaseline; she wanted that even if there would be pain during penetration. How could he deny such gorgeous anus?

While slipping inside her tight anus that she was enjoying the fullest, he felt the raising of her heart rates and the shivering of her already fully sweated body until one more relief, but this time with an extra loud orgasm that broke the silence of the night, not caring or even thinking about what loud scream she might produce.

That loud screaming, of course, was to be heard from the other bedroom where her husband was also in a fucking full action; maybe that loud scream added extra motive to that other couple. In the morning, as if nothing happened, they all were happy, ate the typical Danish breakfast, and they drove back to their apartment.

With this friend, it was fun to take his car and drive north to Helsingor, a port city in Denmark, having on the other side the Swedish Helsingborg. In those days, snaps and alcoholic drinks were not allowed after nine at night.

So, many Swedish girls were taking the ferry boat from Helsingborg to Helsingor because on board snaps were allowed. So, when they arrived on the other side in Denmark, they were almost drunk, and it was easy for them to take them to the nearby hotels and enjoy easy and nice sex. That was a nice trip with always successful outcomes, and they did quite often.

One day, he heard on the radio that in the village not far away from their place, they had their village dancing night. This happened in all villages. His car was again at the service garage, so his brother and he took two bikes and went there.

It was a small village, but the dancing place was big, having two big dancing rooms with different music to each dancing room.

When they both entered, they felt that there was an agitation, a female nervousness and slight admiration, and at the same time, from mouth to mouth, it was spread around among all the girls that two handsome sunburned-skin men arrived to their village dance party, which seemed to have either seldom or never happened before.

He noticed at the end of the room, there were pinball flippers, and in such electronic games, he was an expert. He started playing, and suddenly, he felt two hands touching his buttocks. He turned around, and what did he see? A black 'Aphrodite' girl asking to dance with her, and this she asked in a rather demanding way. "Dance with me now."

He could not deny such a divine black lady, and they danced, but it seemed that dancing was not her goal as many times she took one of her hands away from his neck grabbing his penis, without caring that everyone could see that. She whispered into his ear, "I want to fuck you, and I accept not any denial," with a dominant voice; that was a ruthless sexual harass.

My God, that woman probably was the woman who all Danish men craved because of her black body, and she thought that all must obey to her commands. There, he did the gross error of his life and lost the chance to fuck a black girl and not any girl but a real black beauty admired by all present men, and probably, she was spoiled after having all men in submission to her.

He right away brought in his mind her naked with opened legs and what he saw was a black pussy with the red clitoris like the crow of a rooster. and this image kept him behind, thinking why go with a black girl when there were so many equally beautiful Danish blonde girls, and so he refused her invitation, leaving her with a big surprise and in deeply humiliate status as all Danish men were eager to get her to bed but him; he stupidly rejected.

She left the room as fast as she could, not imagining that a man existed to reject her sex invitation. The Danish girls there were many and were showing him their vivid interest, especially after seeing that scene where he said no to the black Aphrodite, whom all Danish girls somehow hated as she could do whatever she wanted to all their boyfriends, but she, the black girl, wanted him and 'now'. He somehow felt proud. *What the hell? There are so many blonde girls around, why would I go with the black one?*

He never stopped regretting that bad decision as it would be hypocritical not to admit that she was a real black beauty, a black puma. He will never forgive himself for losing such an experience (this experience came in Sudan, but nothing to compare with that black 'femme fatale' and very later in France that he enjoyed in all senses).

Needless to say, all the Danish men were there chasing her; they were angry that among all she chose him; he made her horny but not those blonde and handsome white Danish young men. They were all crazy for her, but she was crazy for him, maybe also to demonstrate to all those blonde girls who were after him that she would be the winner, but in the end, she not only wasn't the winner but his stupid rejection also made her lose face, and she left the dancing hall, showing how angry she was and with an obvious bitterness in her shadowed face and horribly ashamed. That was for her maybe the first time to happen, such a humiliation as no one ever rejected her so obviously and let her down in front of all her 'Fan Club'.

On that dancing night, he managed to have one girl in one room and another in the other, and finally, he took a third one to his home.

It is funny, and he wants to mention that when they were in that dancing hall, many girls surrounded them, and the Danish guys seemed to be annoyed. Two of them approached tossing threatening words such as 'you bloody spaghetti guys, you want to steal our girls?'. They probably thought that they were Italians. He was more quick-tempered than his brother, so he threatened them, telling them, "Get lost before I get angry and punch you."

There, his brother intervened and said, "Well, let us all calm down and let us shake hands as friends; there are many girls here to share." So one of them gave his brother a handshake. His brother, with his very strong hand and always smiling in full calmness, squeezed his hand and slowly made him kneel down until he collapsed and screamed enormously due to pain.

So, they understood that there was trouble, and they left them alone to keep dancing with several girls.

He watched his brother, the seaman, who fucked while on sea only dirty harbour whores, and there he was at the bar having two girls on his laps, fighting with each other who was the one who first saw him. What a tricky story: two girls fighting over who was the one to first locate him when entering the club, claiming priority and almost ownership.

He had such a big smile of happiness; he felt happy for the first time after so many years in the rough seas to find himself surrounded and claimed by many beautiful girls. Areus, later in a taxi, took one girl with him to his home, leaving his brother there still dancing with several girls. He was doing his sex routine with the girl he came with, and there his brother came alone. He asked him. "Are you alone after so many girls wanted you?"

"Yes."

"But why?" he asked.

"She did not want to come on the bike."

He said, "Are you crazy? You wanted to have the girl come to your home to fuck her and you asked her to jump on your bike? Leave the bloody bike there and take a taxi. In Denmark, the one uses the other bike so their left bikes someone will use, and they find other bikes of other people to go home."

In that dancing club, he met a beautiful girl whom he did not want to take from their first dance to his home as he felt differently with her, and he wanted a more serious relationship, and so they arranged for a date. Her name was Mathilde.

She was not of any extraordinary beauty, but she was sweet with a nice, happy smile, and always pure, maybe even naïve, eyes. She told him on the first date that although her father was a rich industrialist who was working as a hairdresser, she was always saying the man she would marry would take over the factory, as she was not capable enough to run it. Here, he was again with another indirect marriage suggestion for him to take over a big factory.

Again, a girl who he dated was a champion; she was on the Danish National Team of Badminton, so another sportswoman was added to his list. First was the East Germany champion in rhythmic gymnastics, then the parachutist, then the champion of Munich in skiing, and now the badminton champion girl. Well, then, he can add to that that he was also a champion, but in sex.

With this girl, he fell indeed in love, and they were doing very nicely together, and they also had a harmony in sex, but a man is a man, and when chances appear, he cannot allow these to go to whatever objections of his heart.

He wanted to make more money, so reading the jobs list, he found out a factory was looking for an eight-hour night shift. That was a quite big plastic factory but not with easy access as he had to cross a valley to reach that factory, and in winter, that was not only difficult but also dangerous.

They, his brother and him, decided to share that night shift (4-night shift hours for him from 12 to 4 a.m. and 4-night's shift for his brother from 4 to 8 a.m.). That was quite a distance from their home, and that was during winter and heavy winter with thick snow that covered more than 50% of the bike. His car was always having problems, so they had to go on bikes.

At 3 and 4 o'clock, it was real deep darkness; the only light was the northern lights flickering over the dark sky, like thin shimmering veils of green and yellow breath. It was like the breath of the sun doing light dancing with the soul of the earth.

There were plenty of beautiful factory girl workers; there were many options, and he did not lose any; he had sex with quite some either in the locker room or even in the toilet, and only one time he took one of them in his room, which proved to be both fortunate and unfortunate.

His brother after living in Denmark for four months and having a lot of sex affairs, he had to complete in sea five months service to his second captain service so he will be upgraded to first sea-captain, so he left Denmark.

One day, he had a day off, and he got an unexpected visit from that factory girl, the only one that slept in his bed and knew his home.

She came with her girlfriend, probably because she wanted to kind of show off by introducing her Mediterranean boyfriend. He must say, her girlfriend was much more beautiful.

Well, they started talking, drinking coffee, and then that other girl told him that after many attempts it was officially approved by the state that she would have abortion as she was at the very first phase of pregnancy.

He grabbed the info, and as he could see that she was always looking down at his penis, that gave him a signal that she was aiming to do that. He told her, "Well then, why not have sex today as far as tomorrow you will have the abortion? And then if you still feel not that comfortable, there is also the just little less than four centimetre the anus door that hides no consequences but plenty of pleasure and enjoyment. Let me show you; I am the expert of the arsehole."

She laughed as if that were a joke, but at the same time, she seemed to like the idea. But in any case, he told her, if she was afraid of any pain from behind then go for the pussy; he was an expert, and at the right moment, he would pull his penis out so that it would be no problem for her. All this was going on while his factory girl went out to find a kiosk to buy cigarettes.

He took her hand and put that to feel the hard erection he had.

She turned a bit red-faced, but she squeezed it, and this was it; they started unbuttoning each other until they were completely naked, but then the other factory girl, whom he had sex one time before, returned with cigarettes in her hand. Seeing them naked, she blushed and got angry. "What the hell are you doing there?" she addressed to her girlfriend angrily. "I did not bring you here to fuck my boyfriend."

He then stood up already naked with the erected penis. He took her hand to hold his penis to feel the hardness, and with the other hand, he brought her to the sofa where also the other girl was already nude, and that one was already in the peak of her lust. He slipped her hand between the two bodies where his cock was pressing the belly of the factory girl. She, in seconds, got rid of all dresses, and the gorgeous nudeness was to his avail.

What a sex was like having one girl sitting on top of him and his head under the pussy of the other sucking her clitoris that made her feel great while the two girls were kissing each other, thrusting their tongues inside their mouths with enormous passion.

He got the feeling that they were not doing that for the first time; probably, there were several lesbian actions before, but the first time with a penis to be present. That was done several times having the girls changing positions with each other, and both pussies dripping wet.

Then he asked them to sit next to each other and turn around sitting in a doggy position on the sofa, showing him their two asses side by side the one better than the other. What a dream image having two beautiful soft and so well curved asses inviting him; he could not make the difficult choice from which ass first to start with.

He was penetrating the one and fingering the other in rotation, satisfying both. It was all going so well until he heard someone knocking on the door; he said to the girls stop making no sound.

It was his good serious relation Mathilde, who was calling his name, knocking forcefully on the door, and shouting, "I know you are there!" She had seen his car outside. Unfortunately, one girl right at that very bloody moment to come to a loud orgasm, and she could not stop her coming; he tried to shut her mouth, but too late, she was in heaven that very moment. How to stop her loud screaming?

His good girl, Mathilde, heard that, and she knew what was happening inside. Since then, as he heard from her close girlfriend, she was so sad, crying day and night but could not tolerate such cheating behaviour from him, so she decided, although she had initially cancelled this, to finally join the badminton trip on a 10-day tour so that she would try to forget him.

He was also very sad, and he went to see her closest girlfriend to her home, telling her how sad he was. She had a big sofa, so they sat there, explaining to her that what happened that day with those two girls was a one-time bad moment that was never to happen again.

Recounting to her the so many love moments they had being together with Mathilde and the total sex they did with all possible ways from only the front door and never from the backdoor; he wanted to keep that at their official engagement as an extra gift.

It was funny; he described to her an unusual intercourse he had with Mathilde, making love to her on her three-wheel children's bike. It was difficult for her to understand how this could be done. He tried to show her, and the previous minutes of sorrow turned to fun and laughter.

The time was getting late, so she offered him a glass of wine and a very strange Danish cheese. So, when it was time for him to go home, he stood up and the bulge on his trousers was more than obvious, and he had to adjust his penis, as it was jammed in his boxers.

He kissed her on the cheeks and reached the door; she stopped him there. "It is late, and there is snow outside; it is dangerous to drive, so sleep here. My bed is big and more than comfortable for two."

So, while they were in bed, he noticed that she was kind of a big girl, the complete opposite of Mathilde who was petite and cute, so to say mignonette.

Inevitably and with innocence, the two bodies touched each other unintentionally. That said, he was always having an erection in seconds, so his penis already in the underpants touched her butt.

She noticed that something hard was contacting or rather was pressing her buttock, and unconsciously, she, with her hand, still looking the other side, searched to see what that hard object was.

If it was at all possible that she did not know what this was, just pretended that she did not. Her 'searching' hand touched his penis. She turned around rather angry at him. "How dare you? A few minutes ago, you were crying for Mathilde and you now have an erection? You forgot that Mathilde is my closest girl friend?"

He felt bad; he apologised saying, "I am so sorry, I can't help it; even if I see the bare ankle of a woman who is wearing trousers, I get hard."

She added, "Yes, I know. Mathilde told me that in the car either she drives or you drive. Your cock is always up, and many times while you are driving, she flipped off your zipper, got your cock, and gave you a mouth job.

"So, now calm down, control your erection, and go back to sleep." She turned the other side, but the hard penis was always there untamed, and as he was wearing boxers, the penis found its way to get through the peeing boxer's opening.

After a few minutes, he felt her turning her body behind him, and her hand slowly slipped into his underpants while the hard penis that was already exploring the new environment and the warmth of the bedsheets and blankets, she easily grabbed the hard cock. She took a hold of his penis, feeling not at all guilty this time; she was incredibly hot and wet even before proceeding to the main menu.

She forcibly removed her panties and threw away something that was so damp and wet and fell on the floor with a sound of not any feather-weighted piece of cloth but soaked panties.

Now they were there, the one on top of the other. When he was on top pumping into her, she made slight grunts; when at her turn, she was on top of him, her sweat dropped onto his chest and belly.

He activated his sex knowledge to turn her crazy, never any man before licked and sucked her clitoris so forcefully. She was flying in the air. turned around for 69, and he then discovered that she even never sucked a dick; she at first avoided; she did not know what to do, but in a few seconds, him giving an oral to her pussy, she could not avoid having in front of her a hard cock, and she licked and sucked also. She came fast and twice, first at 69 and then at the real intercourse.

He turned her around at his beloved doggy position; what a huge ass he was about to come. While she was shouting there from down, he heard her saying, "Do not come in me, please, although I took some precautions, but better not risk."

He said, "I know, and this will not happen." She came for the third time, and so did he, but he was still missing the behind unconquered hole.

They fell asleep early in the morning; he explained or rather he described to her that French girls get it also from the asshole. She was completely negative; she could not imagine having his hard penis in her virgin anus that would cause pain. He told her, yes, it would, but if you have any cream, it would help a lot.

She definitely denied, but she was horny again; she having her arse towards him, he started fingering her asshole gently, with her hand removed several times, his finger, but at the end, she was bent and accepted it. Slowly and softly, his finger was sliding in her anus but still did not want penis inside her.

He grabbed her hand to hold his penis and asked her to exercise on him a lusty liberating handjob. So, he was fingering her anus, and she was masturbating him. That was very enjoyable; she liked it; his finger went deeper and deeper in her anus, then he applied two fingers, and both were warmly accommodated in her narrow asshole, so now was the time; he removed the fingers cleverly and even her not noticing that there was not two fingers but his penis to substitute the two fingers. He did it nicely and expertly, and she squeezed her anus; she felt that the whole was inside her, but she liked it very much.

He grabbed her hand again, driving it to her pussy, making her understand that she could masturbate; they came both simultaneously, him unable to remove and, without the fear of pregnancy, he left his sperm inside her deepness. Right after she headed to the bathroom to wipe her off walking with a certain awkwardness due to the derriere intrusion that she experienced for the first time.

He murmured into her ear that this he did not do to Mathilde, and she had this privilege to enjoy it. Helena, which was her name, asked him to swear that he would never say anything about this to Mathilde, even if he was supposed to never meet her again. He told to Helena that he would leave next few days for France or Greece and maybe he delays the departure until Mathilde comes back from her tour and clear things up.

Later on, when he was in France, he got letters from Mathilde, signed also by Helena. Mathilde begged him, and she forgive him for that day when she came to his apartment and he did not open the door to her as he was enjoying a trio with two other girls, and she asked him to come back to Denmark; her father wanted to meet him, but he had to follow and not sacrifice his career and get married so young, apparently his love to her was fading with the time.

He was anyway obliged to leave the country as his work permit expired, and he did not accept the invitation of the hospital director to stay for good and with a far higher salary; same they also did with his brother.

Plus, he had to hide his tracks for that spying task they wanted to put on his shoulders from that Greek dictatorship, always bringing in bad situations his father wanting to know where he was and why he did not respond to their high confidential letters.

The hospital asked them both to stay after the unbelievable achievements they succeeded. Those optimal achievements were known; they all knew what best job he was doing and they all knew that he was the one to make Ule speak even just one word; additionally, because his brother also did something that would remain in the history of the asylum by controlling his extra hostile patient Ule (most of the Danish guys have the name of Ule).

What was his brother's achievement? He had his day off, and one of his patients, a boy of 19 years old and 1.95 of height and an exceptionally strong boy, coincidentally and ironically, also had the name of Ule, but the carer at his shift forgot to give him his pills.

He broke down the door very easily. He went outside and stayed there, having his back on the wall. He was standing there, and no one dared to approach him.

Doctors came and started with different scientific approaches with words and theories to calm him down, but he was like a wild animal. Areus called his brother and told him, "Come here as Ule is in a crazy situation and out of any control."

The doctors kept trying but could not get close to him. Ule was in panic, and it was extremely dangerous; they were trying different methods to calm him down and avoid him hitting his head on the wall and dying on the spot or even breaking down the wall with such powers he possessed. His brother arrived, and right away, he applied his intervention and 'his way'.

He got very close to Ule, almost touching him. The doctors said, "No, do not go so close; he will hit you." Ule suddenly got all idly face seeing his brother so close to him. Ule then started speaking the word 'Pouli—Pouli—Pouli'. He called his brother Pouli, although his name is George.

His brother, pointing angrily with his finger at Ule's face, asked him to kneel down slowly, following his finger, and indeed, that big rock, enunciating 'Pouli—Pouli', knelt down, not scared but with relief, looking at him with complete obedience.

George, his brother, asked the doctors to give him the pill that the in-charge caretaker man forgot to give him in time. He smiled at Ule, who was down on his knees like a peaceful sheep and asked Ule to swallow the pill, and this was it.

A big applause from all staff, nurses, and doctors. The doctors failed, while his brother succeeded with his own convincing way. In the meantime, the hospital director also arrived and saw all this performance, and he was also impressed.

Not to forget that before leaving Denmark for France, there was an advertisement in the Danish newspaper that there were well-paid jobs for reforesting and rewilding Greenland, at the south part of Greenland. As it is known, Greenland belongs to Denmark.

He wrote a letter to that Greenland address, and they told him that the response was so big that the needed jobs posts were closed. That would have been a great adventure, working there and drinking ale at the traditional 'Viking' style wooden tables surrounded by waitresses.

Most of all, he desired to have sex with a 'wild Viking' Greenland girl after she was bathing him in a wooden bathtub. He had been with girls from almost all European countries and later as well as Asian girls (Japanese geishas, Philippines, and Thai girls are true sex experts), so adding a 'Viking' rough girl would have been ideal.

After five months, a second letter came to the address Denmark address, telling him that new job openings were available and accepting him for that job, but he was already in France, but that letter was sent to his Greek home address, and so it reached him too late.

He, before going to France, with his car that was finally fixed for good to return for a few weeks back to Athens. He was also in tears to separate from that girl Mathilde, but thinking later wiser, he knew it was better that way for his future, because staying there he would get married, and all his future that was to follow would be stopped abruptly.

So, he drove back to his home in Athens to see his parents. On the way home, when he was approaching Heidelberg, he found the phone of that splendid parachutist girl (Juliana), and he made a stop and called her. He explained to her who he was after three years. She was so happy to hear him and fixed a date for the next day. He was supposed to stay overnight in a hotel, but he was such a bastard that he stood her up, finally deciding to continue his trip back home and let her wait. What a shame for him.

He will never excuse himself; doing such a bad action was against his principles. He stood up this same girl twice, what a bad character he was. One of the reasons that he did that was that he still had in his heart the Danish girl who he left in Copenhagen and ran away during a night after she returned from her badminton tour, and the second reason was that this parachutist girl was another very cute girl, mignon as he likes most, with a big possibility of ending up later at an official engagement.

So, he decided, with pain in his heart, that it was better to go than face Juliana's beautiful eyes and that adorable smile and maybe find a job but not any managerial as he aimed to, and stay for good in Germany. That girl whom he promised next time to provide to her a sex with long duration and not leaving her two seconds before she was to come, he stood her up again, what a bastard he was.

He arrived home after a bad experience and some almost fatal accidents due to the heavy and, at the same time, bad driving traffic with many old vehicles on the roads like Wartburg and those East Germany's clunker cars circulating on the horrible roads of Yugoslavia.

At last, he was back home to his parents, and he met his good friends from the old school years. They were all happy that one of their best friends had his own car.

They all went together to Plaka (the old town of Athens) looking after tourist girls for a one-night sex stand, most of the time with success with beautiful girls enjoying sex at the beach and under the moon at isolated nice beach ends naked and away from any voyeurs.

He wrote a letter to the director of the Grand Hotel in Nurnberg, asking him if he could recommend him to a hotel in Paris to get experience in the kitchen, and he indeed responded. He liked him a lot and sent him to the famous George V hotel, the best hotel maybe in Europe, now called Four Seasons.

So, his Volkswagen was again on the road, this time to France through Italy. That famous hotel had a huge kitchen and worldwide famous chefs, but for one or the other reason, he did not like the job there in the kitchen, and he left after 15 days. But 15 days were enough to keep wide, open eyes to see how a well-known hotel restaurant kitchen is organised and to learn how a kitchen works from the side and the eyes of a future hotel manager.

He insisted on going to France as he wanted to further improve his French, and he applied for a job as a waiter at another huge and well-known hotel in Biarritz.

All VIPs and all those famous artists that they want to gain publicity must spend every summer vacation at the three well-known vacation destinations in France, which are Cote d'Ajur, next Biarritz, and then Deauville.

He drove down to the south, but this time through nice roads, especially in France, long distances of roads with left and right big trees and endless vineyards that created a dreamy driving route.

He enjoyed that trip and meals at some French taverns, and he enjoyed the incomparable French kitchen and the numerous cheeses with the matching wine.

For each plat du jour, there was a different suggested cheese and, of course, a different wine. This was culinary art or better eating science.

Finally, the road signs show Biarritz and are installed in the nice and comfortable individual rooms, but there were common toilets and showers for the seasonal staff dormitories. Next day, work started and all the new participants made their presence, and the hotel started preparing for the summer season.

There were many learning waiters, mostly foreigners, and were all sleeping in that annex building for the staff, near the main hotel building.

The restaurant service there was a science, an art. He and a Moroccan waiter were selected by the restaurant manager as the two privileged waiters to serve the VIPs.

There were some customers who were very demanding, and were demanding because they were bon viveur, and they knew what they ordered but also how to eat what they ordered.

One of them was the owner of Mirage airplanes, a Jew Polish, a very rich man. He was eating avocado, and he wanted to add mustard, so he called and asked for Dijon mustard. The head waiter asked him to take from the gueridon (the small side table) plate where there were all the mustards. Maybe 20 different mustards, blonde, less blonde, dark brown, yellow, green, red, etc. He took a plate, and, oh God, which one was the Dijon?

He later learned that was the blondest one, so he picked the one with the small spoon and tried to serve the mustard with the spoon next to his avocado. He turned to him, saying again, but politely, not this one but the Dijon.

He tried the next one, but that time, the customer was angry, and with a loud voice, he said, "Dijon." The maître d' hotel ran close to him and indicated to him which was the one; no one wanted to displease him as he was always giving heavy tips.

There were many such incidents, but when they had a big table with ambassadors or equal VIPs tables, they, himself and the Morocco guy, offered a real serving show that they all admired the clockwise service they offered. Of course, there were also many impressive ladies with half-naked breasts, and his eyes turned almost to cross eyes. Many times, he was also serving at the swimming pool, and there he met the *optasia* (Greek word for phenomenal vision), the lady of his dreams, was the famous singer Mireille Mathieu.

A short, little beauty like the Danish girl whom he cheated and abandoned and like the parachutist girl (Julianna), whom he also let down waiting for him.

He was always serving her lobster with the German Alsatian white wine Riesling or Traminer. She was cute in appearance but very demanding and easily irritated if the service was not going too good; this destroyed in his eyes her divine image.

One day, on his day off, he put on his swim dress and went for swimming with three other guys from the hotel at the beach right next to the hotel, and there he noticed a 40–45-year-old lady, having her eyes on him, admiring him as he was throwing disc far way to the sea, and in a real impressive style, he looked like an ancient Greek disc thrower.

He came closer to her and started chatting with her, telling her who he was, what he does, etc. While his eyes fell between her legs, she was so smart, she managed to let from her under swim part of her bikini, a small part of her vagina lip to be seen, and this she managed to do while he was approaching her. He felt embarrassed, as he could not hide the erection he had under his swimsuit.

How to stand up? He would look ridiculous having a rod standing erect under his swimsuit. She knew and noticed what happened, and she cleverly showed him the towel.

So, he had the solution to tie around his waist the towel. She was a nurse and invited him to her home at 8 o'clock on the same day, and indeed, he went.

The door was unlocked; he just had to push to open, and she was on bed, completely naked, doing what she was holding a mirror and was masturbating so she could have full view of her vagina, her legs wide open and bent, formed a triangle, her feet met at the end together, smiling at him and saying in French,

"I always before getting fucked masturbate so the real fuck will be more delightful."

He kept standing there until she had a loud and 'terrifying' orgasm, and that was really good as many women try to hold the heightening of their breath and scream while climaxing. She lit a cigarette and offered him a drink of Pernod, but not actual Pernod, a different kind of liquor, maybe a special liquor to create an even harder erection. Right after he finished his drink, with rather bitter taste, she made a gesture, making him understand that he had to undress himself with no loss of time. She was already hot, or rather tremendously, hot after the first orgasm rippled through her body.

He possessed the experience to locate the horny grade she was on, but what he saw was a first-time experience. He lay down next to her, she whispered into his ear that she had her period.

He said, "Oh shit, and now what shall we do?"

Very naturally and normally, she told him, "A French woman, as well as all women, have two holes." So she gave him the message where to aim and not mix up the entrances.

Surprisingly, she had a quite narrow anus; she knew, and next to the bed table, already there was a cream waiting. She caressed her sweet hole and also added to the top of his cock's head a small quantity of cream, and there the penetration was on the way easily to slip inside a well lubricious arsehole.

He was inexplicably clumsy, having her on her fours, and mixed up the entrances. He did this same mistake twice in his sex adventures, last time with Artemis, and this time, due to his anxiety to get inside the warmth of the anus fast.

"Plus haut (more high)," she whispered, and there he was to the right one, and her muscles closed around his dick, but that happened after she took the initiative, by grabbing the penis in her hand to lead to the correct narrow-walled anus, allowing a sweet slide in. He loved it because it was narrow and gave him additional pleasure and a nice feeling of satisfaction.

She loved it, and while his penis was 'dancing' in her anus, she was caressing her stimulated clit with her soft fingertips to achieve climax; she applied a second short vibrating apparatus that she picked up from the drawer, and this on her pussy beside her anus getting fucked.

They managed with a good duration of almost 30 minutes with in between breaks for kissing and nipple sucking as well as professional blowjob to achieve the peak, so both came with a deep relief and calmness, him unloading himself inside her hot 'asspussy'.

He asked her to come after three days when her period would be over but what he got as an answer? What a bad luck! She was moving to Paris to another hospital as she was tired of being in Biarritz for almost 12 years without spectacular fucks. She said to him that she needed to keep him in mind as they had a good sex, and if he ever were in Paris, he could call her and continue the job, and this time on both 'marvellous portals'.

That was disappointing as he wanted to have a mature woman who knew what she wanted and how she wanted to wait for him every night. He returned to his room at the annex at 2 a.m.; all the other guys were waiting for him, and from their balconies, they were shouting, "Oh the bloody Greek, he managed to fuck."

Among them, was not a hotel employee, who came every day to visit another French friend. He was a sissy boy, not gay, but a homosexual, an absolute queer.

He seemed to be insufferably jealous of him, always looking after girls, and one night, he came to his room with a tiny thong brief on, asking him to make sex to him. Well, what means sex simply, he wanted him to fuck his arsehole.

He said, "Look, I fuck girls', not boys' anuses." He pulled his tiny brief down, turned around, and told him with a completely feminine voice, "Look here, what you will lose if you still deny."

He must confess that what he saw was maybe one of the nicest asses he ever saw on any girl, and his arsehole was so flawless, spotless that it was indeed an inviting 'lustful ingress'. He hesitated for a moment but finally denied and told him, "Go back to your home. I am not the one to fuck you."

He was coming all the time demonstrating his naked ass, and he was always sending him away. In that annex were bedrooms for each one, but they had a common toilet and also a common shower with two showers in the same space. He was having his shower, and there, the sissy boy appeared. He told him he also wanted to take his shower, and he obviously could not deny.

He managed to bend down and turn to him his ass, and he could see his impeccable anus, not a single difference from a girl's anus; he dared to say that his was even better, and he managed with a magic way without any special effort or better magic way to open and close his asshole, an open invitation.

Automatically still being bent lower down with his athletic body, he bent so down that his face was between his legs, and he could have a full view of him from down; the queer boy noticed with pleasure that he had a hard cock. He did not know what to do; he had in front of him a perfectly inviting arse.

He started washing his hair and obviously closed his eyes to avoid soap to come in; that was it, the sissy boy grabbed the moment, and without even holding the penis guided straight and inside to his asshole; he did it in a magical way and managed in two seconds to have the penis in his anus.

He was moving back and forth, and at the same time, the sissy boy held with three fingers his small cock, masturbating, keeping moving back and front his anus around his cock, even not allowing him to get out as he was squeezing in such a manner that the penis was his prisoner.

He shut his eyes, imagining that he was fucking a woman; he had to confess that what he did was amazing, the way he was moving his ass towards his penis. He had full control, allowing him to come deep in his anus. He told him, "You bastard, do not tell this to anyone, or else I will 'drown' you in that same shower and never again this will happen."

There were three days of vacation for five of them (four waiters, an Italian, an Austrian, a German, and a French) so he proposed to them to drive in his car to Madrid, Spain. It was a nice trip through Saint Jean de Luz, France's Basque and then through Bilbao, the Spanish Basque.

After some hours, they reached Madrid, and they went straight to find a cheap hotel to stay the night. After they settled down, they went to the old city of Madrid, something like London SoHo.

The French guy drank a little more, and he was half drunk. There, they met four Spaniard soldiers also drunk. The French guy started impolitely swearing at them, talking against Franco, and the Spaniards did the same against De Gaulle.

This took quite some time making a circle all nine, and there was tension in the air. Areus squeezed the hand of the French guy hard, and he asked him to stop this right away as it might escalate to a severe threat.

When the nerves calmed down, one of the Spaniards had a marihuana passing over from the one to the other, and so he also had marihuana for first and last time of his life. He was not happy with this; it was not pleasant at all; maybe because it was his first time, but he was obliged to smoke that not to offend the Spanish soldier.

They returned to Biarritz but with a very heavy traffic and him playing the smart; he saw there was a side road, but with the sign of do not enter. He said, "Fuck the warning and drive to that side road." He was driving fast, having on the left the long queue of other cars stuck in the traffic, and he was showing to them that he makes fun of them playing the smart guy, and then, suddenly, he saw in front of him a huge stone right in the middle of that side road that he could in no way neither stop nor avoid; the car climbed on top of that huge stone, throwing them all to hit their heads on the car roof, but the bloody Volkswagen kept going as if nothing had happened. Anyway, they reached the hotel after quite some new experiences.

At the hotel restaurant, a lady working on accounting and who was often down to the restaurant, was crazy about him. She especially was crazy for him as she thought that he was a very robust guy because he was winning everybody in the Bras de Ferre competition, even an Austrian giant colleague, but that was due to a trick he knew by squeezing his wrist and bringing the opponents on his side and in defence.

She was not a pretty woman. She was a widow and was always coming in a black dresses that does not provide any compliment to a lady apart from the fantasy to fuck a widow. He noticed after watching her going to the toilet that she had a nice body. She was around 45 years old; he was 23.

When they had no clients in the restaurant, he always wanted to talk as much as possible to improve his French, and that woman was a good teacher teaching him even French slangs.

After talking to him almost every day, the unstoppable desire for possible sex hit her mind. She started politely in the beginning but became more demanding later, asking him to come to her home; she knew that he had a car.

He was reluctant as that woman was not that pretty, but was a woman with pussy and not only that but he desperately needed after long not having sex after his nurse left. One night, after dinner was served, he told her, "OK, let us go for a drink at your home in my car." She could not hide her happiness.

She had a pretty apartment, clean and in cute and perfect condition. She offered him red Bordeaux wine, accompanied by three different cheeses and a slice of Jambon de York, a real culinary combination of cheeses and jambon.

She left for a few minutes and took away those ugly black dresses and came back in an ordinary dresses that completely changed her whole look. She was suddenly pretty, and the mood of happiness added an extra charm. He started to be pleased with the decision after long to come with her to her hospitable apartment and her equally hospitable attitude. They had a nice time eating, drinking and laughing.

She was such a different and highly educated personality, far from any other woman he met before. From that black-dressed, strict woman at work and what he had now in front of him was a joyful lady (with a real big 'L'); her laughter and her smile was so cute that soon he was high up in the sky with an enormous wish to see her naked.

Indeed, after all, the time came; she took the lead; she gently (when he says gently, he means it all the way) took him by the hand and led him to her bedroom. He stayed there speechless, watching that strict woman turn into an angel; she was so good she almost did in front of him a full-of-charm strip tease, nothing of a vulgar or slutty strip tease, but always looking in his eyes, she took off dress by dress, bras and panties by not looking at what she was to reveal but straight into his eyes. That turned him to a maximum-generated heat; electricity shot through his body.

What he saw was unbelievable. That black-dressed, non-pretty woman was finally completely naked but a complete metamorphosis. The body was perfectly a mature woman's impeccable welcoming body. She, with her finger, asked him to approach. He even discovered that this serious woman had the smile that he had never ever seen before, with a soft and sweet mouth and lips that needed to be kissed and insert tongue in that mouth and lick her lips. He approached, and he started to get undressed; she stopped him, telling, "This is my job." He totally submitted to her.

She took off all his dresses the same way she had undressed herself; she wanted to reveal every centimetre of his body slowly and, at the same time, kissing every small part of his body that she was releasing. She kissed every centimetre of his body, maybe 50 kisses, and her tongue was so slippery that it was a caress until her tongue reached the horny and rigid penis.

What she did there was a demonstration of technique, an impeccable performance, what a tongue, what a way to stare at it and kissing and licking the penis and testicles, but her eyes were always on him. The oral sex that she performed was nothing to compare with any other that he had before. She wanted desperately to come and ejaculate on her breasts.

Indeed, this happened, and he could not stop it. That was done on purpose so that he would feel kind of tired and inevitably stay there overnight. She explained to him later when he asked, "Why you did a fellatio and allowed me to finish?"

What an answer he got: "The first is for the man, but for the second and third, the man functions better and with duration, and these rounds are for the woman."

She told him to sleep well, and later, they do again the second part of the sex recital. They slept fully naked, touching her ass from behind her. From time to time, she moved the ass to see if the phallus was reacting. Three hours passed, and she woke him up gently with kisses.

There started the Oscar performance with unusual qualities. What to say is not easy to describe. He cannot talk in details about the real Kamasutra's positions. The lady was with her highest sexual hormones, and there was nothing that he knew that she did not do with him, on top, on her back, on the side; she made him discover one more side position that was pretty relaxing for both, and with manoeuvres, she let the penis go into her by not losing any single millimetre of it; this she told him later is called 'scissors position'., which allowed her to search with the finger his arsehole and play there around and slightly also inside.

Then doggy style, 69, anus, which needed not any cream was ready beautifully squeezing her anus to reach the ultimo extension so right away to take his penis inside with silky kind of side walls and penis to feel as if entering a heavenly soft narrow gallery of lust.

After two hours of sex, when they were both finished, they lit up a cigarette, and she told him that since her husband died three years ago, she never had any sex, and this justified the hunger she had for sex.

He told her that now that the season was over, he leaves France in a week's time so she asked him for recurring sex encounters all those days that he was in France, and he did with enormous pleasure. That woman gave him a lesson to never deny a not-that-pretty woman as those who are less pretty, hide a scientific sex performance.

One day, before leaving Biarritz, he took his *commis de rang* (his assistant waiter), a young, nice French boy, to offer him a goodbye dinner and drinks at a small, picturesque village near the borders of Spain, facing the Atlantic. While walking in the middle of the main street of that village, all of a sudden, three guys jumped out of the Las Vegas bar, and they punched them without any reason at all and hardly touched the French young boy, who was on his side.

He got crazy. He grabbed the one by the neck and put him down, but then he felt something hard hit his head. That was a beer bottle, and he almost fainted and also lost his eye glasses. He tumbled but did not know how he found the strength and ran like hell towards the small police station of that small village while the three guys were always running after him.

He could hear their feet tramping, and they were getting closer, but he managed to reach the police station. He entered the police station and closed the door behind him, telling the two policemen what happened and that they were just out of the door. "Go out and arrest them.".

It was one policeman and a police woman of about 28 years old but extremely beautiful; they both answered to him no way they do not dare as these guys were wild Basque fishermen that came from the Spanish Basque city of Saint Jean de Luz to get drunk, and they carry knives and terrorise everyone they find in front of them. So, he had to stay there in the police station for more than three hours.

Having nothing to do there all these three hours, he opened discussion with that police girl in a very friendly way; she was also willing to learn about Greece. She heard at the early ages at school about the Greek gods, but at the end, she focused on the goddess of love, Aphrodite.

Coincidently, in that period, the famous group *Aphrodite's Child* was in Biarritz and was topical.

She wanted to know who were the lovers of Aphrodite and if that goat-legged Pan made sex to her, and if yes, why such a beauty had sex with such an ugly creature.

He explained to her that she did not accept Pan to take her, although he had a big, sexual, crooked member that even for the goddess of love that phallus was tempting, and she found the strength to resist, but not for long, allowing that crooked phallus to explore her 'cunt' (he used that slang word to see if that police girl was aroused). Areus noticed the petite police officer to be intrigued hearing about the crooked, big cock of ugly Pan, even her tongue urged to caress her lips.

He continued the story of Aphrodite, telling her that she was married to Hephaestus, the god of fire and volcano, the blacksmith who offered generously hard and, in many times, harsh sex to her, but she still cheated him and made repeated sex with the god of war, Ares, and there, he pointed out that this is where his name Areus comes from. That was a lie just to impress her.

Aphrodite also melted under the unstoppable fuck of Achilles. He noticed again that when he mentioned the repeated cheatings and long sexual member of Pan, she blushed and that maybe he needed to take advantage but where in the police station or in the two small jails that were there? That would be a life's experience, fuck a police officer girl in a jail.

The hours were many, and the chat with her was ongoing, more on the cheating of Aphrodite's with two other gods, and as he noticed, she was wearing a ring on her right hand, trying to cover that, but the body language made it clear that she was extremely horny. She had a gorgeous body like Brigitte Bardot; blonde hair with a ponytail; this he loved and it always turned him on. She was also petite, and this was another point that he always loved, tiny girls with small, well-shaped rounded asses. The hours were passing, but it was not boring at all; on the contrary, it was with fascination, but outside were always those bloody punks.

So, they kept talking, and the conversation turned to a more or less porno narration. She was hot; she excused herself and went to the toilet, while the other policeman, an old man, was almost sleeping. Now what shall he do or shall he not do?

He decided to go to the toilet and opened the door. She was there not sitting on the toilet. She had her trousers down and was masturbating. She saw him, but she could not stop as that moment was coming, so he allowed her to get her heavily needed orgasm.

Now or never, he approached and let his trousers down, revealing his hard penis. She simply, without any second thoughts, bent on the sink, and that penis, instantly without any whatsoever objection, was in her little pussy, holding her with both his hands from her ponytail while she pushed back to get the cock well inside her. He whispered into her ear, "Imagine that the goat-legged Pan is behind you and inside you with his ugly penis."

That made her tremble and moan loudly; she had an orgasm having the mirror to show her and him behind her and both in extra hot situation as he was approaching to his orgasm; she wanted to see that orgasm on the mirror, observing how his face will change during climaxing. He pulled out to ejaculate, but that fell on her police trousers on the floor; she did not care; she wanted to watch the spasms on his face.

What an unexpected outcome! He was bitten and chased by wild fishermen, found shelter in a police station, and in that police station, he also found the heaven.

His French young boy assistant also managed to run and hide; his face with bruises, he came to the police station to find him, and with his surprise, he was holding his eye glasses that he had managed to get from the street before any car could crash them.

After checking that those bastards had left, she volunteered to drive them to the hotel for their safety; arriving there, he said goodbye with a warm kiss.

Without allowing any objections, she asked the boy to go and kept him behind. She drove far away from the hotel to a nearby forest where, already dark, no one was there to witness what was to happen.

She took all her dresses off, exposing her small, but hard like a rock, breasts; she jumped like a cat to the back seats; she put her handcuffs to her both hands, and she cried to him in French, "*Baise moi sauvagement*." Fuck me wildly.

He was shocked; he fucked her in the police toilets, but it was not enough; she wanted more and wildly. What shall he do? What she meant by wildly? He was not the man of violence. He also followed her and jumped behind. After he took off all his dress, he asked her to fill up her mouth with his balls, not yet his penis but the balls; she obeyed and liked that. She could not hold and jerk off his cock as her hands were voluntarily hand-cuffed. He could not believe that this petite but graceful police girl hid such lust and willingness to proceed to shocking sexual actions.

She was delighted with her mouth full of balls one after the other, then following his instructions asked her to lick his asshole, and she did with playfulness of pleasure. Her tongue was trying to enter as deeper as possible to his asshole. The next step was not any other than what most of the girls want but many do not dare to try, considering it as taboo, and this was none other than the anus sex.

He picked her up as if she were a doll, so petite she was, and she was more than prepared, helping to flip around. Having her stomach on the back seat, he closed down the between the two seats, armrest so she mounted on that and got a perfectly raised ass ideally uplifted, exposing an impeccable and luscious asshole, shouting, "Do it, go deep inside, and forget if I shriek." And with complaint, she added, "I begged my husband for years, and he never wanted to enter from my derriere, while most of my girlfriends did already and many times and with several men."

How could he resist such a provocation? He put his arm out to brace himself from the front seat's backrest and guided his penis straight to that well-shaped, marvellous cave of lust, and at last, she felt the asshole taboo liberation. That cute, petite, oversexed Venus was up on heaven, moaning and groaning, and the spasms of her climax with his well-coordinated orgasm moved the police car up and down as if there was an earthquake under the wheels.

It took a while to relax after the fulfilment for both erupted, and they sat side by side, still nude, with no handcuffs anymore and her wanting to tell him the story of her sexual life. She was married to a schoolmate when she was just 17; her husband was a good-looking boy, and remained a boy until the age of 28 and never a real man, later proving what the reason was for that.

The sex for him was not that necessary, until one day she caught him returning early from her police job, with a big black cock is his anus, so it explained why he never, despite her will, wanted to get her from behind. He had the complex and jealousy that her asshole was more attractive than his to the eyes of his lovers and faced her as a competitor, a strange and abnormal way of thinking, but that was it.

She was so unhappy when she heard that he was leaving in the next two days, but it was planned and could not be changed although she was such a cute girl who complied 100% with his preferences, his imaginary and ideal concept for the woman of his dreams.

While in Biarritz, he read ads that the Greek group of musicians *Aphrodite's Child* were in Biarritz for a one week show in a nightclub before going to Paris.

He was happy as the drummer was his friend while at the military service.

So, it was so nice to meet the famous later Vangelis Papathanassiou and Demis Roussos.

It was an unforgettable night; they were also startled to see a Greek to be there in Biarritz.

The next night, he was there again, but this time with five of his friends from the hotel, and they all were delighted to hear that divine voice of Demis Roussos and the flutes of Vangelis.

The after season finished; he decided to go to Rome in Italy to a special school for learning how to organise and economise in a hotel kitchen. The kitchen was always for all hotel directors their Achilles heel.

They cannot control the cooks and the economy of the kitchen, so the hotel makes money from the rooms but loses money in the kitchen and restaurant because of the lack of experience of the manager and the badly degraded kitchen control system.

It became his specialty that no chef, whoever he was, as famous as he could be and with whatever experience he had, could fool him.

Here, he was in Rome having so many credentials and diplomas; he was welcome as there he was the major ever student to come study there. They gave him his own room with a private bathroom while all the rest slept in big rooms of 20.

In that hotel kitchen organising school, he made good friendship with four Carabinieri Italian policemen, who were sent there to learn how to organise the Italian military caserna and were there to learn the secrets of the kitchen so that they know when they take over the military kitchens.

He met at the school another Greek guy who was famous among the circles of homosexual men, most rich, and in high community positions, he was the one and the only fucker of all them, but, of course, at the same time, he was also after girls.

The girls in Italy, in those old times, never allowed to touch them unless you promise official engagement to family and to the father. The official fiancé, the so-called *fidanzato*, was allowed only some kisses and maybe some caresses here and there, and in some cases, they were masturbating their boyfriend so that he empties his load and feels relaxation, but in no case intercourse. So, there was a problem and the only solution were the brothels.

The language he learned fast; if one speaks French, then learning Italian is a piece of cake. He was speaking fast like an Italian and even Romanese, which is the high language; like he spoke the German in Heidelberg the so-called 'Hoch Deutsch', which means high German speaking quality, same in Italy, the Roman Italian was the real Italian language while the Napoli Italian was rather second-grade Italian language.

He remembers they had three days of holidays; he took in his car his four Italian Carabinieri friends to go to one of them Italian hometown of Napoli.

What a nice experience. Italians love Greeks. The pizza there is a marvel and Chianti, a Greek gods' wine. It was a real two-day stay of drinking and eating with nice, hospitable people. They had the fiancée of one of the Carabinieri one day to cook for them Napolitano specialties, and the next day, his mother tried to compete with his fiancée and pleased them with other specialties.

But the bad experience that his life reached almost to the end was the return trip on the night of Sunday from Napoli to Rome.

The traffic was extremely heavy, and all of a sudden while driving, he felt that he had lost control of the car; the car drove to the opposite current of the traffic, and only God knows how in that specific moment there was not any car coming from the opposite direction. Why did this happen? Before leaving Rome, he had changed tyres, and it seemed that the garage guy did not screw tightly the screws and one wheel went off but stayed there, not working as a wheel.

He skilfully, and with big luck, managed, God knows how, to stop the car on the side. The Italian Carabinieri friends ran out of the car, kneeling down and thanking the mother of Christ, "*Grazie Madonna Mia Grazie,*" for saving their lives.

They finally screwed the wheel and returned to Rome.

On the way back, there was a Fiat 500 car that was making some dangerous manoeuvres; the Carabinieri guys in his car were angry; they passed him and stopped to make a signal to stop. He stopped, so one of them showed his credentials to prove that he is a Carabinieri and started checking. His driving licence was OK; the car licence was OK; all was OK; he even asked him to open the porte baggage (luggage ruck) to see if he had everything necessary, such as stop cone, fire extinguisher, first-aid kit. The guy had all; it was perfect. The Carabinieri got mad; he wanted, by all means, to issue a ticket to him.

He then bent to his window with a cigarette in his lips and asked him if he had matches (*fiamiferi*); he had no matches, but he had a nice and expensive-looking lighter, and he lit up his cigarette, and at the same time, the officer held his wrist, turned around to look at the back side of the lighter. He posed him the question, "Where is the customs stamp (*ce lai bolo*)?" In those times at the customs, one had to pay for expensive lighters very high customs duties, and the customer officer engraved a stamp on as proof that custom fees are paid and it is not smuggled; he did not have such a stamp, so here he was and wrote him a fine ticket.

In the meantime, his brother, who had abandoned for good the sea, followed his hotel career steps; he learned German and also he went as practicant to work at the Grand Hotel in Nurnberg, and later, he came to join him in Rome so he also follows the lesson at the Italian school (Scuola Alberghiera de Castelfusano Lido di Roma).

If he gets a diploma, that will help him one day to become a hotel manager in Greece. Every night, they went with three Greeks and a British guy, gay probably, drinking at the next-door bar of Siora Amalia, mainly Rosso Antico and many times drinking too much and getting really dizzy.

He finished from Rome; he left his car to his brother and travelled to London.

The funny thing was that his brother got his driving licence but till then he never drove any car, so he asked him to drive, and indeed, he did. He looked up to his head and saw the back view mirror and asked with curiosity as if he had made a discovery, "What is this mirror here for?" He explained, laughing, that with this you see what happens behind you.

In London, with his rich CV and especially due to the five languages that added influence to many employers' decisions, he chose to be the manager of a nice and luxurious restaurant on the same street and near the PlayBoy Club.

Being a manager and still very young, he had to keep control by being distinctive and imposing discipline on his staff that were all Swedish girls, the one more beautiful than the other, but him as manager, he was not somehow allowed to make any relation with them or he loses the respect. So, he was watching all girls leaving with boyfriends and him go home with no girl, a real tormenting unaccomplished lust.

One day, he as always dressed in the impressive suit and leather shoes that his beloved Munich girl had bought for him as a gift. He was receiving and welcoming the customers as the manager of the restaurant and for the afternoon tea time, when mostly ladies came.

There, indeed, he saw for the first time three ladies of about 60 to 65 years old, all three well dressed and looking like they belonged to the upper class of the London society.

He welcomed them and guided them to the best table available as the afternoon tea time was a very busy time.

He took their order even as a manager as he felt that these ladies deserved a high class serving; they indeed knew what the best tea was and what best cookies match to the ordered best tea. They were happy with him serving them. They were looking at him very politely. He was always and particularly gentle. One of the ladies asked him what his name was; he said, "Areus comes from a Spartan king." They were impressed by his name and also of his Greek origin.

The next day, there were all three, his Swedish assistants. They told him that they were new customers, and with laughter, they told him that they probably came not for the tea but for him.

He answered, grabbing the occasion, "Yes, you see, older ladies come for me, but you run away with other guys and leave me alone," so as to pass a message or invitation for dating, leaving the discipline strategy behind.

The three ladies were there with one voice, and all three gave him a warm greeting.

He served them the usual, and the one of the three, maybe the one that looked younger but still 60 or 65, showed to him that she wanted him to stay there with them, and as he did not have that specific moment any other customers, he stayed there next to her, always standing as he, as a professional, could not sit at the table with them. Without him asking, she started telling him that she was a widow of a rich man dealing with imports of fresh fruits from Italy and Spain.

She told him that she feels alone, but at the same time, due to the other three ladies, she fills that gap that her husband left after dying. She was happy with the friendship of the other two 'girlfriends', adding meaningfully that she takes care of her body with a personal trainer and masseur.

He tried to figure out what was hidden under her dresses, an old woman's wrinkled body, or the dress was covering a not that wrinkly body.

Anyway, that was not him to guess what an enigma was under her dresses.

The next day, they were exactly the same minute and always differently but perfectly dressed, allowing also their breasts to be seen. He gave them the secret name of the Greek mythology, *Three Graces*.

Now the other lady called him closer to her, and she said, like the previous day also her story, always calling to him Mr Areus, "Please come closer, I want to tell you something about me that is different and not boring to what you heard from my friend yesterday." She was telling him that she never was married, but she had a passion, and that was the gambling. She was telling him that she was one of the very few to have good earnings from gambling, and in fact, that was quite a lot of money. She was playing at PlayBoy Club and also at the Base Water Casino. That 'gambler' lady was fatter than the other two, but she had enormously attractive tits, and she also looked robust, probably with big arse and thick bush around her pussy; all these came to his imagination as X-rays to undress them and see what was hidden under skirts and shirts, bras and panties.

So, the next day, he was expecting the story of the third lady. As usual, 'Good afternoon, dear ladies, 'good afternoon, Mr Areus.' The Swedish waitresses were covering their mouth with their hands to cover their laughter as they knew about the 'intimacy' that was going on between him and the trio of the ladies.

The third lady was adopted from a Scottish family with an impressive tower in Scotland. She was raised as their true daughter with high education and was married to a rich Scottish man, but he died during the war, so she found herself with uncountable wealth. She, like the other three, was rich by inheriting a big fortune.

The next day, he told them that he had his day off, so to his regret, he will not be there to welcome and serve them.

He then noticed from a small distance that they were talking to each other in low voices and discreetly. So, the one, the gambler, probably the one in better body shape and the enormous but, dare to say, attractive tits, called him.

"Oh, Mr Areus, it will be for us a pleasure and a big joy if you could pay a visit to my home where we will have a special tea afternoon, tasting an exceptional Chinese green tea, and we want your professional opinion."

He was shocked that he wanted to spend his day off looking after girls and maybe go to SoHo to pay and get sex with those London prostitutes; he hardly needed any sexual intercourse, but how can he deny such an invitation from his best customers? Professionalism wins. He told them trying to find excuses, after they gave him the address, that it was difficult for him to get to that address as he had to combine subway and tram, and maybe he gets lost. Right away they, with one voice, told him, "Do not worry, we will send our driver to your home."

Indeed, they were always there, and a driver was waiting for them outside in a limo. So, the driver picked him up from his home; he was very polite but also looked at him from his mirror somehow as if he wanted to tell him, "Lucky, or maybe unlucky you."

They arrived; it was a very typical London house; they all three welcomed him, and indeed, that house was so attractively furnished with hundreds of small porcelain ornaments and golden decorations and also expensive paintings on the walls.

He noticed that all three this time were not dressed strictly formally but rather casually and, maybe he can say, also sportily, which indeed embarrassed him, but at the same time, that outfit gave them a different look for their age, which made him think, why not? Maybe? Try?

The tea arrived, but that was not Chinese; the Chinese tea invitation was irrelevant, and tasting seemed to be rather an 'alibi', a pretext to have him there among them for unknown reason at least until then.

The tea was served in rather a hurry, and then unusually, Scotch whisky followed, supposed to be from the one lady's inheritance Scottish whisky distillery, a 14-year-old, as they told him.

The afternoon turned to evening, and he said that maybe it was time for him to go, but they objected, as they had prepared a special dinner for him with, as starter, Scottish best smoked salmon, followed by Dover sole that he told those few days before that he liked most of whatever is considered as British cuisine.

White wine may be a type of British Sauvignon. He did not know how his glass was always filled up. He liked the wine, and one of them seemed to be in charge of filling up his glass again and again while staring at the other two with a strange but with full of satisfaction glance.

The dinner was fine. He felt a certain dizziness combined with funny euphoria from too much wine, looking and moving like a lost man in fog.

They moved to the living room, where he was offered a very rare brandy, which he usually does not like to drink, and he certainly was not that crazy for it; it had a strange taste. Cigar was also given; he never smoked before, but he wanted to make a show off, as being used smoking cigars, but forgot to cut the one edge and he was trying to light up the edge but with no any, of course, success.

They laughed and gave him a certain small tool cutter to cut the one edge of the cigar; he felt rather stupid than an experienced cigar smoker.

The smoke was not supposed to go down, just a little, but him not knowing this, he swallowed all the smoke, and then he started to get really dizzy and maybe fell asleep on the sofa, no idea how and where this happened.

What he remembered, and that was quite blurry, was that he was on a big bed, naked, and the one after the other, the three ladies 'graces' were mounting on his penis like cowgirls, or at least so he thought, or maybe it was just the only one.

His penis, despite too much of wine, brandy and cigar, was still hard, and this was probably because he did not have any fuck with any girl for almost one month, or they poured in his drink any strange kind of dope. Being dizzy, he could still recognise which of the three ladies was on top of him and which of the three was finally not.

The fat gambler was enormously horny; he could certainly see her big breasts going up and down with a funny but also frightening howling like a hyena. He was in such a drunk and weird condition that even that scary sex vocal sound was like if a soprano was performing only for him.

That possible dope deprived him to distinguish the quality grade of the lady who was on top of him, her knowing by experience that this female dominant position or a spooning style would delay his climax. The other two were in better shape but equally hot; indeed, what a flame and lust a 60-year-old woman can hide.

He was not sure if all were passing by his penis or only the fat gambler, but even if they did not, for sure they were enjoying touching him and maybe also masturbating him or even activating their skills with blowjobs while he was smiling without knowing why.

They knew that having a man to drink too much and in a dizzy situation and the effect of a kind of brainwash, he lasts longer to come than if he is in full clear mind. Nothing assured him that they did not add any dope drug or kind of mild hypnosis to that horrible tea that was supposed to be Chinese.

He kept having a stupid smile, having one after the other as in a parade to enjoy his hardness; he was feeling as if he had sex with Marilyn Monroe.

What happened there was better to be called a rape, but a rape under the force of the untamed and relentless sex lust of elder women. The sex desire that he probably was under dormancy for a long time, long enough to please all three 'graces', if indeed passed one by one over him, because it was not clear who was and who was not 'raping' him.

The next morning, when he woke up, a big table for breakfast was waiting for him. The ladies were so happy and never mentioned anything about what they experienced last night; maybe they thought that he was so drunk and dizzy that he even did not realise what was done on that bed of endless lust, sex positions and maybe also anomalies.

The driver drove him back to his home again, looking at him through his mirror, knowing for sure what happened to him. In the afternoon, he was back to his post at the restaurant; the three ladies were there for their afternoon tea as if nothing happened, not to forget the teasing and fun making from all the Swedish waitresses, inventing even a small song saying, "Mr Areus had a day off and so also the three ladies had a day off, what a coincidence!"

After that remarkable experience, the ladies kept coming, but not a word about the sex incident. They always brought presents for him, such as watches, pens, ties, and he was grateful to them, making him feel as their close friend and not as his customers.

One day, he was extra hot and horny, and he needed a girl by all means, so he walked on the famous SoHo streets, on a corner, he saw a hooker, but that was not any ordinary hooker; it had the face and body of a Hollywood star. He could not dare to ask her, 'How much?', But finally, he found the guts to ask, and she answered 20 pounds for half an hour.

He thought it was impossible to be so beautiful and only 20 pounds.

He immediately said OK, and he gave her the 20 pounds. She entered a door; he was watching her from behind, thinking what a divine creature he was about to fuck. She told him to go down to the second basement, and then to the right, there was a bench outside a room, stay there and she will get the key to the bedroom.

Indeed, he went down, but it was so dark down there, he could not find that bench and that room, so he turned to the left, and there indeed was a bench but not in front of any room. He was waiting. He saw ugly big men passing by, but not one asked him what he was waiting for. That was a scary situation. He took the money he had on him and put in his socks to hide, just in case.

It took almost one hour waiting, but in vain. He wanted to leave, but it was so dark down there, and he could not find the stairs.

Suddenly, a big man came and asked him, "What the hell are you doing here?" He explained that he paid a lady for sex, and he told him, "Take your ass out of here; this is a porno studio making films."

He begged him to help him and show where and how to get out; he showed him with his torch, and thank God, he was out in the daylight.

Outside, there was a Cypriot guy speaking Greek, and before reaching too down to the second basement, he saw him passing by him. He told him in Greek, "Shame on you to have me down there and fool me with that girl."

He answered, "Fuck off before they punch you badly." He indeed ran away.

In London, he met one of the three guys that graduated from the Heidelberg University of Hotel Management; his name was Christos, a very good man; he was something like 12 years older than him, and he took him with him to the restaurant to make salads at the salad kitchen buffet.

He had a Greek girlfriend, and he invited him to his apartment (one single room), and that Greek girl brought another Greek girl.

They were close to each other, the two couples in separate but very small bed, but his bed was more a sofa than a bed.

Christos with the one Greek girl and him with the other girl on another narrow bed somehow like a sofa.

He was fighting whole night to convince the unbreakable denial of this girl to make sex; she was refusing, until at 4 o'clock, he could notice, as he was touching her from behind, due to the narrow bed, she was soaking, so after so many hours, he managed to bend her denial, and they made a nice Mediterranean sex, but nothing to compare to the Biarritz black-dressed lady, nor the Nurnberg high-ranking unforgettable lady (Artemis) or even that divorced lady where he was staying in her home.

The owners of that restaurant chain told him that he has a big future with them, and he will step up the ladder.

After staying in London for four–five months, at the end, his friend played a role to convince him that it was enough; they had wandered all Europe so let us go home.

They gained enough experience and good expertise to run a hotel, especially him, but not that much his friend.

They took the train and then the ship to Patras and then the bus, and they reached Athens. Christos had nowhere to stay, so he invited him to his home, and he was heartily welcomed by both his mother and father.

So, now starts the real work in hotels at this time, not aiming for a high salary but the best hotel with the best position. Christos went to the National Tourism Organisation, and he finished there after he moved from hotel to hotel and from small hotel to bigger; he became a manager and always at state-owned hotels, so he had the security of the state employee for life and good pension.

Areus had a unique CV. All the big hotels were fighting over who would take him. It was the Grande Bretagne Hotel, King George Hotel, Hilton, and also Kings Palace Hotel. They all wanted him as assistant to the manager or food and beverage manager. Kings Palace Hotel wanted him as the general manager already at his 25 years of age.

His uncle again told him to choose the most prominent hotel in Greece, and so he did, and that was Grande Bretagne.

He was mainly in charge of the economy of the kitchen, and that was a unique experience, dealing with big chefs and many important cooks and pâtissiers.

There he found a situation of zero economy control, just for one single example, they were selling weekly maybe five portions of caviar, and they were buying two whole tins of caviar with 60 portions inside.

The chefs respected him and, among all, his taste. He had every day to taste all sauces, especially the consommé and the day soups.

One day, the chef called him to taste the consommé. He went to the big casserole and put his nose and smelled. He asked the chef, "Why did you not put salt in?" He was amazed.

"How can you discover by just smelling that salt was not yet in the consommé?"

He said, "Just by smelling, I have the right nose for this? He added that the salt erupts a warmth."

They said, "No way, you just guessed that there was no salt. OK, let us test you again." And they indeed did. Inside five potatoes, they added salt to all except for one. He started to smell one after the other.

So, he said salt was in the first, the second, and the third. There still remain two. With salt in the fourth, so there was one left: the fifth. He smelled deeply the fifth one, and indeed, he did not smell the characteristic warmth that salt gives to the potato or soup or consommé. He said this one has no salt. They looked at one another, and they all remained speechless at how he could find out of five potatoes the one that had no salt and only by his nose. Since then, they always trusted his taste even more.

The hotel, although very famous, had not at all good organisation. Some of the staff were making money by deceiving the management and selling even many and whole dinners for their own pocket in cooperation with the cashier. He had to stop this, and he did.

He let it be known that he will start the new control system next Saturday. They were all shocked—maître d', hotel, waiters, cashiers—but the cooks were not involved.

He cleverly started the checking four days earlier, and what did he find? Eighty-nine portions of the plat du jour left the kitchen and for how many bills were issued? Just 33, so all that money was distributed between pockets of the involved persons.

One day, he was at the hotel as always for his usual long shift as a manager of the kitchen, when his mother called him; she said, "Here in front of me in our house, there is a very beautiful German girl asking for you." He asked her mother to pass over the phone, and he heard the voice of Julianna.

She said, "I'm here in Athens, invited by the Athens parachutists club, and I had your address, so I thought that my short time lover might still be interested to see me again."

He answered right away, "Might? Of course, I want to see you. I will never forget you. How long will you stay?"

She said 10 days. "OK, you stay in my home."

She liked this as she had not made any hotel arrangements. "Stay there, unpack, relax, and I will be the latest in three hours."

He asked his mother to show her to her bed and give her to eat her best specialty and leave her to sleep as she must be tired. She answered, "How can I not be very hospitable to this such beautiful girl?"

He was happy, but at the same time, he had to face her anger and apologise to her as he stood her up in Heidelberg.

Indeed, his mother prepared for her the second bed of his brother's as he was in the sea as a salesman to become captain. His mother called him again and told him that she was an adorable, beautiful creature, and she fell asleep right away without eating anything; she added, "Such a girl, one day I want you to bring me as your wife."

When he returned, she was awake and was talking in the living room with his father and mother. They embraced her as if she were their daughter; he couldn't understand how she magnetised them.

First, she gave him a sweet slap, telling him that he fooled her letting her standing up, waiting for him, but he was already on the way home, but right away, she embraced him, and they kissed with powerful passion and in front of his parents, noticing that their eyes met as this reminded them of their own love story.

His father was shocked with the slap and asked him why. He told him that although they had a date, he never showed up. His father answered, "You did this? Then you deserve the slap."

His father was telling him how intelligent she was and how he, who is difficult in connections and relations, was touched by her, so was also his mother, looking at her as if she were her son's wife.

It was already eight in the evening, and dinner was ready. His mother put a new tablecloth; silver cutlery all were taken out from the drawer for the special guests. They both were so happy to have on that dinner table at last a girl who they approved 100%.

The dinner was long as she was telling stories of her parachutist adventures and how one time she had almost lost her life, and his father was also telling stories of his youth, his mother, and how they met and fell in love.

They laughed a lot, until 11, waiting for his parents to go to sleep; they rushed to go to bed, and in seconds, they were naked. She told him, "Do not dare to do to me what you did that last and only sex we had; you have an unfinished business."

He told her, "Do not worry; this time, sex with unlimited time is fully dedicated to you." He asked her that they do it in silence because the two bedrooms' in-between glass door was not that thick, and they would hear them—not his father, as he could hear almost nothing if he removed the hearing aid he uses, but his mother hears well.

But he knew that even if his mother heard peculiar voices and sounds, she would still feel happy.

That was not possible as that bed had a metal kind of spiral joint to hold the mattress. The desire of sex was such that they both ignored the sound, and they had sex with a duration of almost one hour. Him licking her so beautiful, small pussy; she also licking his penis that ended up to a 69.

When he heard her coming, he was feeling so happy, and after that, he turned her around to make the real fuck from behind, doggy style, and again turned around having her on top and lowering, allowing her breasts to brush his face and get one of her breast in his mouth.

Then changed direction, having her buttocks against his belly, him having her gracefully spotless back as perfect view same wise full eye contact to the penis going back and forth; they did all possible positions; her face brilliantly shined; she was ultra-relaxed, and she obviously was in heaven.

The sex was so wild that they lost balance and slipped off the bed and landed down on the wooden floor; she turned to him laughing and saying, "Well, one time you let me down, but now you fuck me down."

After he had a gorgeous orgasm, he went to the bathroom to wipe off his penis; when he returned, she was just there where they had fallen, still at the very last fading out spasms; he felt so happy to bring her in that dreamy situation.

They slept deeply like babies. When they woke up, his mother was there with a rich breakfast; she kissed Julianna as if she were her daughter.

In fact, both his parents missed the sweetness and charm of a girl, a daughter; they had two boys who were always away, and when they were there, they vanished chasing girls. During breakfast, Julianna told to all that she first time felt how the family ambience is, because her parents had separated when she was six, and her father went to Berlin, and he never returned, and his traces disappeared. Her mother got married again, but she cared more for her new kids and showed almost no interest in her, so she was living with her aunt.

The next day, she had to go to that parachutist club and asked all three to come to see and admire her. His father and mother were not as eager as they were afraid of what they were to see.

Julianna was so clever; she went to his father, embraced him and kissed him. Never any girl had kissed his father, and she begged him, saying, "You are my parents; I want you with me."

She managed to overcome his objections, so she also did the same with his mother. That girl was so sweetly persuasive that no one could deny what she asked for. It was unbelievable for his father to leave his home to go and attend an unknown girl's fall from the sky, who had appeared in their life only two days before; it was impossible to believe and comprehend.

The neighbour had a taxi, so he asked him to make for them a nice fare to go to that parachutist club as that was almost 100 kilometres away from their home. He indeed agreed as he was a very good and friendly neighbour.

So, there they were heading to that club; when they arrived, they all were waiting for her as she had the fame of one of the best parachutists in Europe.

His father refused to watch this; she again kissed him many times, and she said, "Daddy, please." Hearing this word, how was he to deny it? She left them to go for her gear that they had ready for her; his parents were in high anxiety and fear.

She was in a small plane with two other parachutists, so there were three to fall from the sky. She greeted them before entering the plane; his mother became pale.

The plane left, and after making a round, the three parachutists were in air; they, including the neighbour taxi driver, were watching breathlessly. All three fell from the plane, allowing first Juliana to fall; she did not open her parachute yet; she was falling like a gun bullet. His parents closed their eyes, and they thought she was falling to the ground, but then she opened the parachute.

Her parachute was closing down; she made a sign of victory with two fingers. His mother held her mouth with her hands, until at last she landed first and before the other two guys. She professionally gathered her gear, and they went to deliver it to the club's responsible person.

She was running towards them with joy, and what did she do? She did not come to embrace him, but his father and mother; they both were so touched, and his mother had tears in her eyes. This girl achieved to win the love of his parents so incredibly fast.

The days passed. He took her to see all of Athens' monuments; they also went many times to the beaches for swimming. Her incredibly well-shaped 'mignon' body impressed all; he was so happy to see her in a joyful situation.

Most of the time, he asked her to go to the tavern. She said, "No, I like better to eat with the parents." She stopped saying 'your parents' but just said 'parents'.

They had sex that she will never forget. She was telling him all the time that she does not believe that she will have such sex ever again. She added, "I am covered with sex for at least one year."

The days passed, and the time came for her to leave. His mother and father asked her to stay, but she said she had to go to her job. She cannot let them down as she was responsible for the Radio Luxembourg news. She promised to return.

The tears and hugs at the airport were indescribable; she flew and left behind three speechless persons who equally loved her.

After Julianna left, leaving a big emptiness in his heart, he met some nice girls working at the nearby big hotels. They met after lunch at a small café at the central square. He was 24 and a half years old, and, especially from the ladies in charge of the hotel floors, chiefs of the chambermaids, most between 30 and 40 years old, he was for them considered a fresh 'virgin' fruit, not knowing, of course, what huge sex experiences he disposed, having the sexual life of a man of 50 years old.

One of the ladies put him to her radar, like the flying eagle spots a hare, and invited him to her home. She knew that he was a manager, and he knows how to appreciate a good dinner as the rumours of him being a gourmet ran fast.

She told him that her specialty was veal mignon sautéed in white wine, adding coriander seeds, but in his opinion, estragon would match better than coriander. He had and still has a gift when one describes a food he has this food in his mouth already before eating, and he virtually could taste and judge if a dish will be correct or not.

Anyway, she put extra pressure on him to visit her home, and at last he 'bent', and he went to her home. They ate outside on her small balcony. It was a very hot night. That specialty of the veal was not bad at all, and the red wine was carefully selected; the mistake she did was that she sautéed the veal with much of wine, and the wine covered the veal taste. They drank a bottle of red wine. He was sweating, and so was she. The night was proceeding, so he had to take an initiative to go to the main dish, which was her bedroom.

He kindly asked her if he could have a shower as he was dripping due to mainly the fever generated by the heat and also the wine they drank. She got the meaning, and she was also happy that they would do what they were from the beginning in a pursuit to do.

She told him that a big towel was behind the door. This was it. When he came out of the shower wrapped around with the long towel, she was already on bed with an obvious appealing smile and a see-through lingerie that allowed all her body to be seen.

A second lady who wanted nothing else in the world than to lick his anus. He does not know that maybe that operation he had in Denmark made his anus attractive for the ladies; she wanted to go as deep as possible with her tongue while playing with his penis. There was something that he could never imagine that a lady would like to happen and have such a desire for licking his anus.

She was at her sexual peak, such hedonism in a woman was seldom to meet and having her tongue in his anus, she said in a commanding manner, "Now fart."

He said, "What?"

"Yes, now fart." She wanted to feel his fart in her tongue. What a horny and kinky lady she was. What an anomaly this is.

He said, "Fart is not coming on command." He tried, but in vain, he could not. That was the horniest sex peculiarity he ever had to face.

She, making humour, told him that next time you come, the dinner will be beans. They made so many tricks and sex standings that he was amazed that after so many experiences he had there were always novelty tricks to learn.

She did allow after pressure to do this from behind, and although she had an advanced age, it seemed to him that she had not tried this before, or perhaps she pretended that this was new for her. In fact, she was not prepared with Vaseline on the bed side table.

It was hard, so she went to the bathroom and took toothpaste, which helped. That toothpaste was with menthol, which also gave a flavour to the several attempts to go inside, which indeed happened after all. When they were done, he told her the French women never finish the sex without the desert, which is sex from their derriere. He was happy that he taught her something, and he was sure that from that day on she will put this in her menu.

There is a saying, "Old dogs do not like new tricks," but 'mature Ladies do like new tricks'. He always writes the word lady with capital L because indeed they deserve it. She told him that he must not repeat this visit because she has a fiancé, and it is not appropriate already and so early to cheat on him. She added laughing, "When I get married and you still want me, then I might cheat on my husband; it is worthwhile."

He met another girl who was for him to have sex and nothing but sex and they did it in the car, in the forest in many cheap hotels but also, he took her to his home when he knew that his parents would go to the cinema.

He remembered when his parents went to the cinema, he told them when they return and see that light in the front garden on, and means do not come in as he will be inside with a girl. So, this happened they arrived the light was on, his mother told to his father let us walk around the block of the houses to give him time, but again after the first walk around the block, the light was on, his mother again "let us make another time around the block", his father protested but his mother convinced him saying, "What do you want our boy to go to dirty hotels?"

So, they took the third round but the light was still on. His father said "that's it I want to go and enter my home for heaven sake I am tired walking three times around the block the neighbours will think that we are crazy".

So, they entered but it was the time that they also finished and the girl was ready to leave. That affair went not that good as he discovered that she was black mailing him that she is pregnant. That proved to be a lie so he gave an end to this.

She was chasing him all the time and for months but he explained to her that he took his decision and this was the definite end of this relationship.

Back to the hotel the very big owner and president, called him after he heard his optimal results to the kitchen and the restaurant and he told him, "You are with me and only with me you are my eyes" but the same happened also with the General Manager and also the other partner who was with fresh ideas to fight the internal dysfunctionalities, but the system had deep corrupted roots.

The involved fraudulent parties made a group and turned against him especially when there was a big open buffet reception and he dared to enter the restaurant where he discovered that many whisky bottles were disappeared and passed through a side window that was facing the side street where there was another guy receiving the bottles.

Having this bad climate and at the same time having a new much better offer from a hotel and casino as general assistant manager he decided to walk away and brought again his brother to take his place and follow his steps and he also had the chance to enlarge his knowledge of the kitchen of a hotel restaurant.

Now here he is at the hotel casino. That hotel was abandoned for many years and one day the owner of the casino got the licence from the government to establish there the first casino in Greece and at the same time bring back the luxurious status of the hotel.

They went up to the mountain to see in what condition the hotel was. This owner already had a casino in London. He drove up to the mountain with his Rolls Royce, when they arrived at the top and there the hotel was impressively standing.

The doors and windows were broken and in the lobby was a mountain of snow, nothing to remind the luxury hotel that four or five years ago he worked there at Christmas as a stagiaire. The owner trusted his opinion and was always asking him what to do here and what to do there, even when he decided to employ the hotel General manager, he insisted him to be present at the interview. He did not consider this as appropriate but had to obey his boss's demand.

When the candidate manager left, he asked him if he approved him and he gave his consent. That time he had a good friend from old times who spent most of his life in Brazil and was involved in politics.

He married a French or rather a Tunisian girl. They had a nice apartment with full view of the sea. With that friend he was almost every day playing chess.

He wanted to beat him but Areus never succeeded. He started reading books for chess to learn some famous defences, but still no success to beat him. At this point, he had to mention that when he was in Denmark, he took part in a championship and he advanced two rounds but in the third round although he captured the opponent's Queen he finally stupidly lost.

One afternoon, both on the same table were playing chess with an impressive chess he imported from the Far East made of ivory, the bell rang and he knew already from before that they were expecting a married couple of friends.

Indeed, one short guy came, one short girl and a tall girl, so he presumed to his regret that the short guy must be married to the short elegantly beautiful, mignon girl. He said to himself 'lucky him', but to his pleasure that was not so the short guy was married to the tall girl. So, there he had a nice eventuality to try to conquer that extraordinary sweet, a divine mignon creature. Despite his experience to claim a girl, that girl magnetised him and turned him to a shy boy and he could not grab the initiative but to his surprise she did this instead.

They turned into a big group of many friends, mostly couples and decided to go to a dancing club, ordering four taxis and leaving their cars behind so that they could drink more.

The four taxis came, he was there searching to which taxi he will step in and to his delight he saw a hand grabbing him saying, "You come with me and I accept not any NO." That was the sweet, mignon and extraordinarily beautiful girl.

That was to be the end of his, here and there sexual life, and that girl was his destiny.

They met many times and they were in love, she was a brilliant and joyful and humorous girl, she was dressed subtly but with absolute taste, more or less the exact girl who he wanted one day to marry. If he wanted to compare her, she was very close but superior to the parachutist Julianna girl and the mignonette police girl.

They had nice harmony and synchronisation in sex and, of course, respected her without having to exercise all those sex tricks he knew, because that woman seemed to him to become his future wife.

There was a problem, she was engaged with a young doctor and that relationship was taking many years without any actual marriage proposal.

When that doctor heard that she was in love with another guy he furiously came back proposing marriage. Her parent's, very decent people, wanted the doctor as their daughter's husband while they did not know their daughter's new love affair. She was in a very serious dilemma; she loved him, but she was engaged for years, and all of a sudden, the marriage proposal was there.

One day, she called at the luxury hotel, he was working asking for Areus. The telephone operator asked Areus who was the plumber or the electrician?

She called her close girlfriend who knew about their affair saying to her that he is either a plumber or electrician but she doesn't care, she loves him.

Of course, in the hotel he was known not just as Areus but he was known with his surname as being the assistant Manager of the hotel.

Her father asked her, "What is the profession of this new guy who appeared in your life and brought things upside down". She said he is a hotel employee. He was very naïve and telling her, "What? Hotel employee, means standing at the hotel reception passing around condoms to the illegal couples to spend a few hours in the hotel."

He was shocked to hear that definition of his profession, he with three diplomas figuratively seeing himself in a cheap hotel reception offering condoms to the illegal couples.

Anyway, time was passing. He was always with his girl but she was forced to make a decision with whom she will go on and whom she will let down.

The pressure from her family became tougher, also all her friends, saying to her, "Where do you go with the new guy who will not have money even to buy toilet paper".

What a disappointment to hear all those comments and their unbelievable opinion about him.

The decision was rather closer to the doctor than to him. His mother, when she was calling him and she was the one to pick up the phone, told her with warm words, "Marry my son he will make you a princess, he is a very nice and a real gentleman". So, he took the initiative and called that doctor guy and told him, "Look we meet at this café, and we call the girl to come and ask her to choose now and the loser will leave for good. OK?"

"OK," he said. Areus then went to the café but the doctor never appeared, probably afraid of the comparison to her eyes having the two guys side by side and according to their appearance, as he was told by people who knew both, was by far more handsome than the doctor.

Finally, she took the decision to turn the doctor down and they continued their pure love.

The offices of the hotel-Casino were in the very centre of Athens Syntagna square. The hotel manager took the post and he as assistant manager was recruiting first the leading staff such as head waiter, the chef and the leader lady of the etages (floors) etc.

The general hotel manager seemed not to like the fact that he was present at his job interview believing that he might be the snitch of the owner, so he employed a second assistant Manager but the new guy as front manager while he was Food and Beverage Manager. This guy was a very nice person from a well-known Greek family. They became fast friends.

After he finished recruiting the staff, he gave to the General Manager all report and lists.

He started making the kitchens layout (two kitchens one for the hotel and one for the casino restaurant that were both under his command). The General Manager was very much impressed by his deep knowledge he had and he started coming closer to him rather than to his front manager.

After quite some time, the hotel took on the luxurious status. For the casino a new huge place was built at the side of the hotel. So, the hotel with the renovations and a lot of money spent by the owner reached the super luxurious standards as it was, quite some years before under Swiss Management.

At this point, he remembered a small but cute story. When he was 19 years old and at the Greek school for hotels during Christmas, the school director asked who wants to have during Christmas his practice at this hotel, which those days had the top fame.

He decided not to spend Christmas with his family but put his career first.

They were all waiters while the girls were chambermaids. When they gathered to talk about what happened during serving, he told them and they all laughed at him, "When the time comes, I will return to this hotel but as director".

He will never forget he was serving breakfast in the rooms. In one of the suites was the singer and dancer of the nightclub, what a woman, what figure, what long legs. He brought the breakfast to her and she was there almost naked with a complete see-through robe.

He put the breakfast on the table and she touched him from behind. She caressed his head and telling him, "Do not rush, and stay with me."

It was obvious what she wanted from a hot 19-year-old boy, a nice morning fuck from a 'virgin' boy as she believed. He was stupid to deny and told her, "Sorry but my boss will kill me if I delay as we have a full hotel and there are many breakfasts to be served."

She said, "Do not worry, I will call him and convince him." He stupidly again denied, and he regretted that he did that because he could have the sex of his life with a 35-year-old lady, and what a lady, a dancer with long legs and fabulous breasts; what amazing sex she was able to teach to him.

But never say never, at his afternoon shift the telephone rang and there she was, she wanted an afternoon tea. He was the only one on this afternoon shift. Well, what shall I do? Go and see what happens, maybe in the meantime someone else enjoyed her charming body and her lust was settled. He took the tea and walked to her suite, she opened the door and with a wide smile,

"Oh my dear shy boy come in, probably this is a time that you are more relaxed." He nodded and admitted that indeed so it is. She asked her where to put the tea, she said, "Follow me," and walked to the bedroom. There was a side table and on the big bed there were many pillows and some hard plastic rounded rods that to his knowledge were unknown what these serve. She noticed that and asked him to stay there on a small sofa at the edge of the big bed.

She with lustful movements slid very charmingly like a big cat, her gorgeous body to the satin bed sheets. He was stunned to see that under her pink negligee was nothing at all, she lifted that and opened her legs, he looked shy-face what he saw was for him difficult to grasp, such a vagina with not a bit of hair and these big puffy pussy lips were astonishing and glistening with moist on.

She grabbed one of those plastic rods, a kind of fake penis, later he heard that this was called dildo, and gave it to him. He was amazed at what he was up to with that big rod that had the same thickness as the horizontal-bar that he has in his home garden to exercise his body.

She opened her legs wider and with a glance made him understand to insert that rod to her pussy. She had a seductive attitude obliging him to obey. He could not believe it and asked her, "But this is so big and your beautiful vagina is so narrow."

She replied, "Do it and you will see that my vagina can take it easily and that will not be the first time." He took place closer to her body with the rod in his hand, a tempting smell of her fantastic aroma made him almost dizzy as if he were hypnotised. He was just one centimetre away from her pussy even her pussy odour had a strange but delightful scent, the sort and well-rounded edge of the rod approached her pussy entrance lips, her neck fell behind awaiting the rod to touch the lips and go slowly deeper.

And so, this happened, she started moaning and groaning, he was worried maybe he would hurt her, she with her hand touched softly his hand helping to get the rod deeper until that rod almost disappeared in her divine vagina.

She whispered, "My boy, make some smooth strokes in and out," and so he did, the woman was in another imaginary world of sexual enjoyment. She with her hand started caressing his black hair while she had multi-orgasmic spasms.

See asked to remove his hand for that rod and let this stay inside her. He noticed she was squeezing her body to feel this inside her while that squeezing reflected also to her anus that was also participating in the enchantment. He took an initiative this time without asking her and inserted one finger inside her anus, causing her to look at him sweetly, "You naughty, kinky boy, how did you find out that this is what I needed and I was about to ask you?"

That took some time until a second orgasm came but more intensive this time. She got rid of that negligee and put the rod in the drawer of the side table. Her body now was nude from toe to head. "So, what are you waiting for, do not make me feel like a slut, undress yourself and lay next to me unless you are a queer."

What a smart woman to offend him so to wake up his masculinist instincts and him almost tore down his dresses with a hard cock laid himself next to her. She gazed straight to his penis, saying, "You have a very aristocratic penis, it is the ideal style and size I like, I hate monster cocks, so all women do, your cock is the exact size that will please not only girls but also married women after several marital and not only, intercourses and births."

That 'aristocratic penis' is not the first time that he hears, that prostitute who stole his virginity she used the exact same word to characterise his cock, he thought that she then just was complimenting him to make him hot and finish fast so that she takes the next to come customer in that pink room, is it coincidence?, or indeed his penis radiates a gentleness?

She adored it, touched and played with it until her mouth took her turn and the tongue was licking it so nicely that he was almost there to come, she noticed that and she encouraged him to go and do it.

He reacted saying, "But please then remove your mouth or else."

She stopped him. "Why?"

She answered so naturally, "I want to swallow your virgin load go ahead" and so he made her feel so adorably nice and comfortable.

"My boy go to the bathroom as your sweat overpowers my aroma, take a bath and come back we have to continue this time to the real, you know what I mean."

That moment the phone rang, he told her, "That must be my head waiter and he is missing me already for long time."

She answered, "Fuck the headwaiter you are my servant for the next two hours if not longer."

He was afraid that he will lose the job and lose face, but she looked non-negotiable so he went to the shower ignoring the desperate probable calls of his head boss.

He took a hot shower and he dried his body and also took a perfume and sprayed his chest.

He stepped out wrapped with a pink towel, looking somehow like a 'sissy boy' but with the glorious by then, 'Aristocratic' cock in 'battle' position.

She was on the bed, the body covered almost the 60% of that bed, and she made a familiar gesture to drop the towel, his penis was already darting her but also the ceiling.

He lied next to her, she whispered, "I want with your penis to paint my whole body, starting from toe up to my ears."

He asked "Paint?"

"Yes, imagine that you are a famous French painter, and your penis is his brush, so brush me with your tool all over, as I see it is already moist and purple."

That 'painting' was finally not an easy job, because he had to stand up on top of her and drag his penis over all her body, in some amazing body parts was stuck or maybe preferred to extend the 'painting', either in her divine triangle that was formed by her legs where the clit was dominating, or on her navel which novel was also a piece of art, special painting circling her nipples and the in between the two tits smooth 'canyon'. He reached up to her mouth where he stopped for a good while not only on his intention but to a large extent hers also, continuing exploring her eyes and even almost blocked her ears.

Then turned her on her stomach, what an impeccable back, the 'painting' had a lot to wander around. The legs, the thighs and especially the ass that was an ass that many movie and TV stars will envy, the painting particularly on the ass was fussily, for the spotless back he 'painted' in zigzag motion to reach up to the neck.

She was shivering wherever the penis was touching, raising her body, as if an electricity current hit her. She had two or three climaxes only by that 'painting', so what was to happen when he at last will exercise the real thing, the 'aristocratic' penis in her pussy?

For a small-time gap, she fell somehow asleep having so many climaxes that was natural, but she never let his hand go, as if she wanted to tell him please allow me to have a small rest, do not run away I need you.

That woman probably had some sentimental disappointments and she wanted to burst and satisfy her revenge on whoever let her down, with a pure, fresh and kind of awkward young 'stallion'. She in no case wanted his job to win over the pleasure with her.

She never tried to loosen her fist and let her already beloved boy leave her alone. He respected that as she already generously gave him such a pleasure so much to know what a woman needs and what the real 'lust' as word can include.

He stayed there admiring her body, a movie star body that was at his avail. That silence in that bed full of soft feather filled pillows also brought his eyes slowly to close for a heavenly nap.

It was her to wake up first and she bent over him worshiping the calmness of the face of an aristocrat in all senses. She in total silence not to wake him up she went to the bathroom; at that moment he also opened his eyes. She went to the bathroom to make herself even more beautiful for not any mature lover but for him for her beloved boy. What a compliment that was for him. He felt so proud that such a woman who several men masturbate having her as fantasy when she dances at the nightclub, but she chose him.

She came out of the bathroom with new negligee, she hugged him so tight that his bones cracked. She murmured into his ear, "You cannot imagine how you revitalised me after a recent disappointment. I am grateful to you and your altruistic gentleness and natural politeness.

If you want to go, just go, if not I want to live at least two more hours if not the whole night with you because you are not just a boy to offer sex to a lady, but you are the cure of any woman and this due to your elegant sexual approach.

With you I feel like a teenager falling in love for the first time," and added, "Such a man like you, any girl, must dream to get married, so consider me as a girl of your age and let us enjoy our first real lovers' sex."

He was self-conscious and shocked to hear this 'confession' and at the same time felt his obligations towards that incredible woman, to be immense.

He was committed and must comply with her expectations and right away bent and gave her a passionate kiss, his tongue totally exploring her artistic mouth with white shiny teeth.

She responded, as she mentioned before, like an innocent school girl, but the witnessing God of sex was waiting just there 'around the corner' on his turn for the inevitable and most wanted sexual ceremony.

Legs were mixing with each other, arms, hands and tongues were searching each other's body, secret angles, holes, members all were playing their game.

How his penis magically found hot shelter inside her is a big question mark, it just came as a sequence as if their movements were conducted by an orchestra director.

More deep, less deep, harder, less hard, up and down, forth and backwards, sweating, groaning and moaning succeeded the one the other until the moment came and both let their satisfaction free to meet each other's peak of a heavenly pleasure.

It was 'done', they remained side by side with closed eyes allowing the last spasms to enjoy the fulfilment. They did not kiss goodbye, just said good night but that was more painful than an actual goodbye.

Was it a fantasy? Is it supernatural what happened between a boy and a lady? No, it was not, it was real but unfortunately everything happens to come to the end when the orchestra director's baton signals and all instruments pause and their romance had the same fate.

He returned to the bedroom with the other boys-students and girls and they were all worshiping him as they all knew what happened but he was sad because he knew that she was also sad. The next day, asked his head waiter to change post so that he will not be the one to serve her breakfast. But she sent an envelope with just few letters in her handwriting

"I will never forget you."

Back to the hotel-casino inauguration night that was the event of the year. Everybody was obliged to come with black suit and fly. The ambience probably was equal to what they were seeing in movies of the Monte Carlo casino.

Greeks are crazy gamblers and the casino owner; he knew it and he spent huge money for the whole complex but all returned back to him very fast. There were gambling more than 1,000 people, the casino could not take more, but the maniac gamblers were queuing outside waiting in the cold.

People were losing money even ladies of upper class were losing all but with no money left how they could go back to gambling, so they went out to find a taxi driver and sell cheaply their body and get money to continue and maybe get back what they lost but this very seldom happened.

In many cases, again back to the taxi drivers, frankly he envied the taxi drivers and in many cases from the window of the manager's office where he was when the general manager was not there, he could watch the whole fucking process in the taxis. Many such stories but need hundreds of pages to write all those stories.

The casino restaurant that was under his management had incomparable glamour. He was often flaming Crepes Suzettes in front of the most prominent customers taking this in special cases from the head waiter's hands.

The restaurant manager (him) with a black suit and white shirt and cufflinks doing Crepes Suzettes Flambé without allowing any drop of oil to fall on his white sleeves that was a part of the show every night and he enjoyed it that was lesson and a show he learned in the Hotel Du Palais in France from the French Maître d' Hotel.

The director of the hotel started to appreciate his skills and the depth of the knowledge of the restaurant and kitchen secrets. He started to have him always on his dining table and the director many times invited him in the kitchen to cook their own specialties. His specialty was chicken Mithridate.

In the very beginning, as assistant Manager he had a small office with three desks. He wanted to hire two assistants and receptionists as he was still recruiting staff. He ended up with two girls and asked them to use the two other desks in his office to start working together for the plans of the hotel of the reception desk and more and seeing their abilities then only he will decide to employ them.

One maybe 20 years old, the other maybe 28. Both extremely beautiful and both became fast good girlfriends and maybe with lesbian interests especially the 28-year-old was looking at the younger girl as if she were a fruit fell from heaven.

Then they started teasing him and all the time they were more and more sexually provocative. Every morning coming to the office, they both lifted up their skirts showing him their tiny thong panties allowing their slits to be slightly exposed.

"Look Mr assistant Manager, do you like my panties?" Showing panties from the front and behind they turned him crazy and horny he could not work, having his penis below the desk in bone hard growth, almost ready to explode.

How can he resist such temptation, he wanted to keep the seriousness of his managerial position but how? It was impossible they were sitting opposite to him and he could see under their desk they both were caressing their legs reaching up to the pussy and looking at him so that they are sure that he is watching all this activity.

It was a torture for him, many times they were telling him that they will go to the toilet as if they wanted to invite him to follow them, but that was risky what if one catches them there, and he loses his most promising job.

One day, they had to stay longer and the staff buses left. He had his car, so he invited them to take them to their home with his car. They, of course, accepted staring at the other with a meaningful but also joyful smile as if they planned this delay and the loss of the bus departure to happen.

Reaching down from the mountain, there was a small forest then the one, the younger one told him, "Oh Mr assistant Manager I want to pee, can you stop?"

He could, of course, not deny. She stepped out of the car and right there in front of him, she did not go far just there, she took down her panties and oh my God what a perfect arse he loved watching her peeing when finished she took off her almost peed panties and this due to her hurry to go for what she pre-aimed for, and threw the panties away to the forest and remain pantyless and only the fact that she had a free vagina from any cloth obstacle made him extremely horny.

The other that was sitting next to him smiled and without any loss of time she bent and expertly unzipped the fly of his trousers seeing that he was in an immense erection and systematically started a combined job with both lips, mouth and hand. He could not deny and resist how to find the strength to tell her No.

The younger finished her peeing she came from the other side opened the car door at the same time that the other one was doing a great blowjob and started kissing him, she removed her bras and put her soft breasts in his face, so he was having on his

face the one girl's breasts and horny nipples while the other was performing an excellent blowjob.

The younger one tapped the head of the other asking her to allow her to continue the blowjob and so it happened and at the same time with no panties it was easy for her to caress her pussy and come when the time was for her to come.

The elder one on his side, she took her panties and took his hand asking him to play and caress her pussy and her gorgeous clit but she wanted more, she mounted on top of the younger one that was performing the blowjob putting her legs left and right to his knees and brought her pussy right in front of him and shoved him to reach that, so could not lose that moment and he started licking her with the professional way he knew, it did not take long that she came with spasms.

The younger one was continuing the sucking of his penis until he came and what she did she swallowed it all. Such a sex entertainment never happened to him before and probably will not happen again in the future. That was something that he still flashes back in his memory as an unrepeatable 'mission impossible'.

He begged them to stop this and there will be no more this to happen again as he had his regular girl and he feels not so nice cheating on her already from the first weeks.

They did not, they continued provoking him this time taking the panties and showing to him their butts again and again, even the younger one she brought a vibrator and in front of him she was inserting it all in her vagina, he could not stand this and had to run to the toilet and jerk off. He managed to let them go

for higher salary to the casino as groupiers and as they were working the nights, they did not have the same working hours

He was happy but unhappy at the same time that he got 'rid' of them.

As time passed he was always doing a great job and showed his managerial skills and deep knowledge. He lived in the hotel for as many hours as possible there, and he started to bring his beautiful girl and later his fiancé also to sleep there and enjoyed their pure love.

When she was not there with him but downtown, she was calling him 10 and 20 times daily as she was a jealous girl and she knew that he was also in charge of one of the most famous Nightclub in all Athens for the best dancing ballets with French Moulin Rouge ambience.

He was the only one to enter their changing rooms and they were mostly naked. Some of them were smiling at him, teasing him and telling, "Look, Mr Director, how do you like my tits and my ass?"

He being young and handsome was not difficult for them with pleasure and lust to reveal all their graces in front of him. He smiled but he always had to be serious to gain respect.

His fiancé knew all this and that is why she was jealous and was after him all the time.

In fact, she knew that he was a woman hunter and had a unique gift and charisma having all in front of his eyes and could visualise how each woman's body is on her bed or on under the shower and what they hide under the skirt and panties.

He knows he could imagine and guess before she gets undressed if she has a shaved pussy or bush of hair around it.

He does not know how he manages this, but he smells and portrays, has that so-called blind guess and an innate imagination, and in almost all cases he did not fail. He can imagine if a girl or better, a lady will sweat during sex before this happens, he can predict her sex choices and preferences this is a Charisma with big C that was 'given by God for free'.

He remembers one night the owner invited him to have dinner with him at the casino's restaurant. He was fond of him and respected his ideas and suggestions, even if those were not according to what he believed, but that was also for a big and exceptional reason.

One day, he had to contradict him for a specific matter, telling him, "Yes, you are a successful businessman, but this does not mean that you are always right and does not make mistakes and wrong judgements."

No one ever dared to talk to him like that, and showing his determination, he closed the door loudly behind him, leaving the owner's office and a stunned owner at his audacity. They all told him then that next day he would fire him, but what happened was the complete opposite. When he was in his office, he sent someone to ask him to come to his office where the day before he had an argument with him. He was sure that was his last day in the hotel, but no, it wasn't; the owner admitted that he was the one to have a right on that particular case and asked him to solve this matter his way.

He recalled one time dining with him at the casino restaurant; they had also on their table an Italian-American expert in casinos, who knew who was who among all the world gamblers.

In between dinner, the casino director came and said to the owner that there was a guy who kept winning a lot at the roulette. The owner asked him if he was sitting or if he was standing up. He told him he was sitting, so he answered, "Do not worry; at the end, he will lose as he will never go away to lose the privilege of having a chair at the roulette table."

Then the casino manager came again, announcing that at the blackjack table there was one unknown guy, who was never seen before in the casino, who was making a fortune. This alerted him, and then that Italian-American guy asked the manager to show him who that gambler at the blackjack table was.

Indeed, he showed him the blackjack table he was playing at. The expert guy was then totally angry and shouted at the casino manager why he allowed him to enter the casino. He was blacklisted in all the casinos of the world, and so they dragged him out.

One day, the bad news arrived: the Cypriot owner was killed down the mountain in a car crash by a big military vehicle. He never believed that this was a coincidence, but maybe it was a conspiracy, as he was planning to invest a lot of money and make big things in Athens, expanding his businesses to many sectors.

He was always using one of his two Rolls Royce, so why on this day did he use a small Fiat 126 and especially had a girl from the accounting to drive?

Anyway, unfortunately, he was gone; pity, he considered him as if he were his son, always asking him to come to the casino and leave the hotel; you would get four times more money, but nothing could constrain him to change his plans; he was faithful to his hotel career and was always denying and displeasing him.

Now what? His young son came from London. He did not know where to start from. After five days, he was in a real mess, trying to learn things and how to run the casino.

The first shock came; he called his hotel director, telling him that the junta asked him to fire him as he was a socialist and he couldn't stay anymore there and he has to go immediately.

The owner's son asked him to recommend a good hotel manager to take his office; he did not think for a single minute and told him, "The best is already here." The new boss was surprised and asked him who he was. "My assistant director; you will not find any better director than him."

And so, he was announced general director of the hotel, and only at the age of 27 he was having 170 staff under his command, which was not an easy task at all.

From that day, he lost his smile; he was too young to impress his staff and make them all respect him. He had to pretend to be very serious, but that was not needed to win the respect of all as he won them all because of his deep knowledge of hotel management, especially the kitchen controlling system he imposed.

He started very hot and started making crucial changes with continuous department heads meetings; he passed over to them all his enthusiasm, and all went according to the plan.

Until one day, the 'snakes'—there are always snakes in big businesses—the chief accountant, a complete ignorant man who was there to make compliments to the owner and the wife of the owner to ensure his post, discovered a story and told the son of the killed owner that his father had promised for the hotel director's position to another hotel manager of a small hotel in Piraeus.

So, the son, if so it was true, which, in fact, it was not, had to follow his dead father's wish.

That manager indeed came, and he went back to the assistant manager's position. All department heads were very displeased, and naturally, he was too.

He asked for his annual leave, and with his girl and future wife, they went to Peloponnese to a small seaside village where they used to have their vacations.

The brother of the dead owner who supported him and they were cooperating perfectly well. After only five days, he called him, "Come back and take the managerial position again that you deserve." So, after only five days, they fired the other guy.

The handover of the management back to him pleased all the heads of the departments, and now started the running to show how this hotel, which for almost 20 years was always in losses, could find the way to turn this around.

The Swiss management before had tried during the first years with the support of the Karamanlis Prime Minister at those times, but they failed, and others who arrived through the National Tourism Organisation also failed. Now was his turn to try, a young man of 27 years of age but with ambitions and, most of all, knowledge and a restless spirit.

He started changing all in the casino restaurant; he brought the tavern spirit with Greek BBQ in the casino restaurant, taking care that not any smells would reach the casino players. That was well received by all and was very successful; the restaurant was fully booked, winning more and new clientele, who did not need to go down the mountain to enjoy lamb ribs and gyros, as these were there in the casino restaurant.

There were even clients who came only to have lunch or dinner; the lunch was served in the hotel's big restaurant. They all enjoyed the extra special 'plats du jour', mostly indicated by him, and the chef executed it. There were customers in the restaurant who came to enjoy lunch or dinner without even gambling and not even going to the casino at all. He managed to upgrade and gain fame for the restaurant. The BBQ night was only one night per week.

Then he went to Piraeus and bought an old wooden boat with sails and put it in the centre of the casino restaurant, having one day of the week as fish night, and that was another success.

He advertised that the hotel was not only a casino but also the best hotel with three restaurants and a nightclub, which was indeed an architectural miracle; the club of the hotel indeed was similar to the famous French Cabarets.

He chose special ballets and janglers, famous singers and orchestras, and slowly, but steadily, he managed to attract VIP customers and more people to go to the club and spend quite some money, opening expensive champagnes to show off to all clients there, who were all known businessmen and ambassadors.

It became the club for all, a must to go to show themselves off and enjoy an exceptional program and exquisite dishes rich in variety from a carefully organised menu.

In order to obtain economies of scale, he suggested to the Beirut casino, the famous nightclub Casino du Liban, that they hire ballet dancer groups, giving them two jobs one after the other. So, they first go to the Beirut casino nightclub and then directly come to his hotel casino nightclub or vice versa. That was agreed as they both obtained much better contracts.

They invited him to go to their Casino du Liban nightclub, and indeed, he went there with his fiancé. The show was indeed great; there were even horses with dancers on stage and spectacular ballet dancers equal to or better than the Moulin Rouge.

The bad experience was that in those days started the civil war in Lebanon. Beirut was the Paris of the Middle East, and all Arabs from the rich Gulf countries had to have a villa there and spend their money in the casino. But with the civil war, all was completely destroyed.

They faced strange and very dangerous situations, having tanks and military blocks. They were lucky and left in time before it became fierce.

He did not stop there as he was looking for ideas that would not cost him much but have positive and profitable outcomes, so he invited Hungarian, Mexican, and Argentinian groups in cooperation with the embassies but also with the National Tourism Origination of these countries.

They came with awesome ballets and dancers as well as singers and with their cooks and local products, plus their best and unique wines, organising festivals of food and wine, music and dancing, so it was indeed great, as many people came to have the total experience of those countries with food, music, and dancing.

All this was free for him, plus it was big and free advertisement as ambassadors came inviting other ambassadors also to come to enjoy the country's specialties and shows.

The hotel ambience changed from a sleeping lobby to a joyful, glamourous and full-of-life lobby; this also added gambling income as the hotel, restaurant, and nightclub customers were eager to try even for one time to go to the casino and gamble and try their luck.

The time approached to get married and his fiancé to become his wife. It was a full church, his ex-Air Force general uncle was the best man, and they were bound with the holy matrimony.

The newspaper that his wife was working for made a big announcement about 'our girl' marrying the hotel director.

They only enjoyed three days of honeymoon at the Lagonissi Hotel and had to return to continue the honeymoon in his hotel. From the very beginning and before the marriage, he made clear to his wife that he will never cheat on her but if he will, it will only be paid sex without any engagements and obligations.

He organised shows and also model haute couture shows. A famous Mikonos designer of that time was maybe the most famous haute couturier (designer) who organised a special fashion show in his hotel restaurant. It was a big success to bring the elite Athenian ladies to the hotel. The designer 'personally' liked him, and he suggested to him if he wanted to take part in one of his model defiles, which, of course, he denied.

He organised jewellery shows, and the economic indicator chart on the wall of his office was climbing up and up all the time, narrowing the distance from the red losses line, and he managed to miraculously overpass that red line and brought the hotel to profits for the first time after almost 20 years.

Being a restless spirit, he always wanted to have his own company, and indeed, he had his own office just opposite the Greek Parliament building.

He started with delicatessen food imports and whiskeys from Scotland. So, he started importing frozen lobster tails and frozen Scotch smoked salmon that, when defreezed, had not a single difference from the fresh famous taste of the Scottish smoked salmon.

All his imports were right away sold and purchased by the brother of the dead owner as he was the purchasing manager, and he made his profit creating a small capital at first. Even with his whisky, he bought the whole container at a good price for the hotel, which was also good for him.

He never stopped thinking about how to increase the already profitable hotel by sending thousands of letters to attract international conferences and conventions, and indeed, he managed to steal from Hilton the big General Electric Convention for one week, which added fame and revenues to the hotel.

There were also bad and significant matters that created obstacles to his hotel's progress. The casino made a deal with an Italian gambling trip organiser to bring big gamblers from America, the so-called 'Junkets'. So, groups of 30 and 40 arrived almost every week, the New York group, the Boston group, the Chicago group, and so on.

They stayed in the hotel for free. This, of course, was a burden for the hotel's economic results, but it was good for the casino as they were strong gamblers but not necessarily losers due to their casino's experience in Las Vegas.

When he signed the deal with the International Convention of General Electric, all the hotel was fully booked for the participants and their wives. One night, a very furious and angry-looking guy entered his office; he was the Italian-American organiser of the Junket Groups and told him in a rather aggressive manner to cancel the General Electric Group as they wanted the rooms for his Dallas Group. He denied as contracts were signed with strict clauses, and it was impossible to do this; he felt that he had in front of him a Mafia guy who could even harm him. The Mafia knew ways to bring problems to his plans.

He was always and simultaneously taking care of creating business also of his own office. He managed to get the first licence of IKEA for Greece, but it needed big capital to start such a first shop in Greece. He also managed to get the representation and agency in Greece for the famous Dewar's Scotch whisky but here also the lack of capital did not allow him to go ahead, and that brand later became vastly known with incredible sales.

At those times, his brother was a manager at a hotel on a big island. When he came back to Athens after the summer season ended, they met at his Athens office, and they had the idea to open a restaurant together in that famous restaurant and have as partners two cooks whom he knew were good cooks from the other hotels.

Indeed, during winter, the restaurant started to get organised, and in the summer, the restaurant was doing very well, but that summer was a bad summer as the Turkish troops invaded Cyprus, and the season abruptly stopped as tourists were afraid that a war was possible to start with Turkey against Greece, and the tourism season died.

What shall they do? No one could know what would come next year, so they had the idea to bring the restaurant to Athens. This happened, and they found a nice, old building in the northern suburbs of Athens, and there they opened a restaurant. The success was unbelievable; in only two years, that restaurant was the number one in Athens.

Ministers, VIPs, business CEOs, and marketing and sales managers were having business lunches and dinners there; all of them had to pass by this restaurant. Among the many specialties was also fresh fish, plus live grilled lobsters. After two years, they employed the ex-chef of the Grande Bretagne Hotel, and the restaurant was even more upgraded.

Then came a brilliant idea that changed his whole life and future. It was at that time that everybody was talking about the Arab Gulf countries, the petrol countries with the sheikhs and the emirs and the big money that must be exploited by Europeans. So, he contacted all the Arab embassies as well as the managers of the Arabic airline companies and at the same time sent letters to all Arab Gulf countries' Chambers of Commerce (Saudi Arabia, Kuwait, Abu Dhabi, Dubai, Qatar, Bahrain, Sharjah), telling them that he would have two floors of his hotel where Greek exporters would expose their products, and he invited many Arab businessmen to come and stay in the hotel free of charge.

The response was unbelievably great; the airline managers were telling him how this was welcome to all the Arab countries. So, it started, and the whole project was a success as big deals were closed and contracts were signed, and not only that but all these Arab businessmen also spent a lot of money in the casino, maybe much more than what those American Junkets spent, to whom the casino also paid for free first-class air tickets. He sent letters to the government, telling them that this was the first official Greek-Arab business exhibition and convention, and he needed the state to back him to create an even bigger second Greek-Arab convention. What disenchantment they answered was that the government decided to assign the so-called Arabic opening to an ex-ambassador.

Many announcements were made through the press, but absolutely nothing happened, only big salaries and expensive offices but zero results.

They said they would hire a big vessel where there would be booths with Greek exhibitors and would visit all the harbours of the Arabic countries, a big project that never came to realisation, only words and nothing as action.

This brought his enthusiasm down, and for quite a long time, he had not the will and the mood to do anything new to add revenue to the hotel's outstanding economic results.

Then for one whole week, he suffered from a staff strike as the hotel staff was asking to have an increase in their salaries, a huge difference from the casino groupiers. He begged the 'board of directors'—an absolutely ridiculous board of directors.

In fact, after the death of the big man, all collapsed, and an ex-police colonel and other military forces ex-lieutenant general were the heads of the board of directors. Ignorant people that they were, who were there just to enjoy a thick salary. He begged them to do something, even a small salary increase. He had a full hotel but no staff. What he had worked for so hard for years, he saw it getting collapsed.

He was obliged when almost whole veal or beef was coming in the grade-manager department (Butcher's department) to cut in the appropriate pieces, to grill and serve to the hotel clients alone all this done by one single man, cook and waiter.

The poor business-minded, military educated members of the 'board of directors', came one night, and he asked them to come to his office, telling them he cannot do it anymore, that he was exhausted and that clients would leave the hotel without even paying.

They answered stupidly, "Do whatever you can; they care less what happens in the hotel."

Then one suggested to the other with an irritating sarcastic laughter, "Let's go down to the foothills taverns and eat some nice lambchops."

What an answer. So, what shall he do if they do not care despite his will? he cannot continue doing this. The next morning, he went down to the square where all the staff were peacefully protesting, and he announced to them that he was on strike, supporting them.

They all embraced him, and it was funny that even the communist newspaper wrote about him with a big BRAVO, mentioning at last the director of a big company joins and is on strike with his staff.

Two days later, they fired him. The good news came from most of the airline managers. He was officially invited by all the presidents of the Chambers of Commerce of all Gulf countries, with free five-star hotels and free tickets for him and his wife.

He took his wife and organised a big trip, where he met the most important personalities of the economic life of the Arabic countries.

First stop was in Kuwait, where he met the brother of the minister of petroleum. An important man married to a beautiful Egyptian lady of high education. Many prominent Kuwaitis get married to beautiful Egyptian ladies who are well-educated and belong to the elite society so that they also become next to them upgraded.

They agreed to meet again with proposals for tightening the relations between Kuwait and Greek business.

He also met the only local (Kuwaiti) military man who reached the rank of colonel (that was an exceptional honour for a local military man to reach so high in ranking); he was the agent of Lockheed in Kuwait and also the agent of Olympic Airways, as during those times Olympic Airways was flying to Kuwait and Dubai. A sincere friendship was created that lasted for quite some years with business that came later.

There, he was introduced to two important Lebanese and Jordanian importers of fresh fruits, and they asked him to help find the best price for big quantity of Greek oranges that would be the destination for the Iranian military forces. He will come back to this a bit later.

The next stop was Qatar. He met one of the biggest businessmen of Qatar but also with big activities in Abu Dhabi and Dubai. This man was indeed among the top businessmen; he was the one who constructed all the roads that connected

Abu Dhabi with Dubai, Sharjah, and Ras Al Khaimah. He had two international hotels in Doha.

He took him on his private jet to go to Abu Dhabi and showed him around his offices. He and his wife stayed in his villa, which was on the outskirts of Abu Dhabi, the last villa where right after starts the desert. What was amazing was that the main entry doors were always opened during lunch or dinner time. He asked him the question why all the doors were open; he told him that the door must be opened because at any time any day ministers might come for dinner, and they have to find welcoming open doors and ready food in abundance.

So, there was always a huge (maybe 10 metres' diameter) white plastic tablecloth, and on that was any possible food, mountains of foods that one cannot easily imagine. Many times, the two were eating alone, having in front of them all this huge variety of food, and after that, the food was given to the staff, and what was left was thrown in the garbage.

They then flew to Dubai; there, he met the president of the Chamber of Commerce, who, in fact, is the first minister of the state as there was only commerce in the country and oil, of course, so he is the top-ranked minister. He confessed to him that he was the first Greek to sit in that chair of his office and came up with a semi-official suggestion to do the second Greek-Arabic Commercial Exhibition and Convention.

He was delighted with the idea, and he told him that he will heavily support this and invited him to dinner, a dinner equal to that of the Abu Dhabi villa.

At this point, it has to be mentioned that all these Arab Gulf States were those past times, not what we see now. There were just one or two main streets with asphalt, and all the side roads were almost covered with desert and dust so one may imagine what happened when a car, especially those huge limousines, were passing by and the mountain of dust that was produced.

The next to visit was Bahrain; he was invited by one of the richest families, who, among other businesses, had a bank and also the biggest chain of travel agencies in all Gulf States. Here again, they were warmly welcomed and invited to dinner. More than 70 people, all men, were all around, and on top was the big man, the owner, who was cross-eyed and you could never understand who he was talking to.

He was always commanding the waiters to take care of him and his wife; it was a mistake to bring his wife with him as there were 70 men, and they all were staring at her with the black 'hungry' eyes. He was afraid of this situation, and after a while, he pretended that he felt sick and left; he felt those many men would 'eat' his wife with their eyes.

The next day, he went to see them at their offices, and they were very happy for the success of the first event, and they agreed to continue. He also wanted to participate by giving free tickets to Athens for the important businessmen who wanted to visit the second Greek-Arabic Convention and Exhibition.

When he returned, he wrote letters about all these big meetings and his successful initiatives to the offices of the prime minister, to the president of the of the Chamber of Commerce and the Minister of Foreign Affairs, but not even one answered; they were heavily promoting in newspapers the so-called 'Arabic Opening', which, in fact, remained only in papers.

In the meantime, the hotel where he was a manager was substituted by another manager, who did nothing; he even took down from his office the graphics and the charts with the progress and the red line overpassing the losses line in his times.

He was very surprised to get a call from the owner's brother. "Come back and bring the hotel in good numbers and revenues and again organise your successful events."

He said yes, but this time with double the salary as they were, after all, appreciative of the job he had done, how he had upgraded the hotel, and what happened after he left.

He was in steady contact with all those big businessmen from the Arabic countries whom he had met during his long trip there, and later probable good business outcomes would occur.

He always had his office on the fourth floor of an old but special architecture building facing the Parliament in the very centre of Athens.

He was called by those two Jordanian fruit importers, and they told him that they needed a huge quantity of oranges for Iran and he had to hurry up with the best price. There started the telex commutations (in those times there was no fax or any internet).

Negotiations and bargains, agreement for the price, endless telex communications, day and night with all the Peloponnese orange producers. He took with him a friend who was a sea captain, asking him to help with the sea shipments. The delivery days were too tight, and he had to appoint new staff as needed to make substantial quality controls. He was straight and serious in this and, of course, very honest; he could not deceive the buyer as he wanted to build a relationship.

The telexes kept coming and going until they fixed the final price and so he also did with all the orange producers of the Nafplion and Corinth areas. He also engaged with a pre-contract for three Swedish fast and very modern fridge ships. His profit in that business was quite essential, and he was happy not for the profit but that he started the business.

All was settled; the two importers were to come to Greece with the Letter of Credit in hand, and what was needed was just to go to the bank and transfer the L/C to his company.

He welcomed them at the airport with a limo. He took them to the Hilton, and he made special arrangements for the night, including hostess ladies as those Arabs always liked to have ladies when they enjoyed the night life. Then something unexpected happened. One of the two businessmen suffered from stomach problems. He said he was sorry that he couldn't go out because he was sick, so they agreed to come tomorrow at nine o'clock to pick them up to go to the bank.

This unforeseen incident was the first bad luck to come. At about midnight, that guy felt better, and they decided to go to the hotel bar for a drink, and there was the bad luck, a Greek producer of fridge trucks (they had bought from him quite a number of fridge trucks) 'coincidently'; he was also at that bar with some other businessmen.

They started talking and drinking and during those drinks he asked them what the reason was that they were there, they told him that they made a deal for a big shipment of oranges. He was foxy and smelled that there was money there, so he asked them what the agreed price was and indeed they told him the price that was fixed after so many telex exchanges and almost two months of negotiations.

He called an exporter of fruits who was in the northern part of Greece. He just made a counter offer without any hesitation one or two cents less and the truck factory owner gave them his personal guarantee for his suggested 'fruit exporter'.

The next morning, he, in full joy, went to the Hilton to pick them up to go to the bank and transfer, as was agreed, the L/C to his company's name. There he faced a shocking situation as they told him that they would finally transfer the L/C to that other Greek as they had the guarantee of the fridge trucks' producer, whom they had known for many years. So, the business was lost to his big regret as well as the costs that were associated with all these dealings and handlings.

Two years later, when he was entering the Kuwait Sheraton Hotel, and he saw them coming out through the circular hotel door. He, as a polite man, shook hands with them and asked them if all went fine with their fruit business with that other exporter.

They told him that they lost all the money because that dishonest man they sent the oranges to went all around the Saudi Arabian Cape, and what he did was that he sent the ships on this long trip under those hot conditions, not in fridge vessels but just with a ventilator, and when the ships arrived at the Iranian sea port, the oranges were all black, and they had to throw all to the sea. It was a big disaster, and since then, Greece could never again export oranges to Iran.

The next year, he was in Dubai trying to export Greek products as a hotel owner. He noticed that in those old times there were only two to three big hotels, and there were also some ugly small and dirty hotels. That was a brilliant time for him to suggest solutions.

He became known throughout Europe that a European guy had good relations in all Gulf States, and one day, he got a telex that a huge 10-storey-high cruise ship was going to be sent to Singapore for scrap. He got all the ship's plans, and he saw that this was indeed an opportunity to seize. He asked them to give him two weeks and not yet send it to Singapore.

Indeed, they gave him these two weeks. So, he easily fixed an appointment with the help of his relations with the president of the Dubai Chamber of Commerce, whom he had already met before, and asked to meet him again, which he did with pleasure.

This was easy for him as they all liked him as a decent man with a good reputation, so they fixed the appointment. He told to the president of the Chamber of Commerce, "Look, you have in this beautiful Dubai Emirate only a few big hotels and several small ones, and soon many businessmen and also tourists will start coming." Dubai was known for the bazaar where one could buy not only cheap gold and jewellery but also gold bars at a very good price.

"So, with only a few hotels, what will happen when soon many visitors will start coming and have nowhere to stay?"

His suggestion was to bring that huge cruise ship and cement it to the edge of the harbour with capacity of a hotel that can accommodate 2000 people plus also food in the many restaurants for another 2000 people because the local restaurants were also not enough to serve so many tourists and businessmen that were to start coming and quite soon.

That notion made his eyes wide open. He called the president of the Bank of Dubai, and he enthusiastically reported the idea to him. They immediately fixed a meeting at the Bank of Dubai headquarters, and they all were delighted.

It is worthwhile to mention that his profit in that business was more than half a million dollars, which was huge money 50 years ago. They asked him to keep that proposal a secret and allow them to find how to raise the funds for this project.

They met again and again and again, bargaining and again negotiating in the presence of lawyers.

All was settled; he called his wife, telling her that they were very soon to be very rich. Pre-contracts were signed, and after quite some days, at last came the time for the final contract to be signed.

He asked his Abu Dhabi friend to help him with his known lawyers to read the contract carefully and locate probable mistakes or traps and basic factual errors. All was impeccably done with no problems, not any grey clauses.

The final big day was fixed to be at the headquarters of the Bank of Dubai. The hall was full with a joyful atmosphere around, and on all corners, plenty of champagne was served after the signatures' formalities.

All of a sudden, when all was ready for the signatures, a short Arab guy appeared in his long white traditional dress. He was a minor-grade accountant. Nothing of any high-ranking officer.

He took the ship's plan and asked him what the submersion low point of the ship was; he told him who cares about this and how deep this goes. He said it was important because the Dubai harbour in those times was not deep enough to accommodate big cruise ships and that huge cruise ship could not get in.

He was angry and felt so bad that he was about to faint. In conclusion, the project fell apart. One more project collapsed a few minutes before the signatures.

Parallel to being in the Gulf States, he managed to get some orders of used construction equipment from Germany, Greece, and Italy, such as excavators, bulldozers and graders, allowing him to cover all his trips and accommodation expenses.

He never gave up trying to become a millionaire; he remembered one day, approximately at 5 p.m., it was very hot; he was at the villa of his good friend

Abdulrahman; they went to the very top terrace of his villa just to sit there and enjoy the breeze coming from the desert to feel a little cool sitting there with crossed legs squatting. They discussed many different businesses and future plans but also problems.

So, he told him that he faced a huge problem in Doha where the Pan-Arabic Football Tournament was to take place. He owned the only two hotels where he could accommodate a total of maybe 900 people, but there would be thousands coming from all Arabian Nations, and there were not enough hotels and even less restaurants.

A thought came to his mind right away; one of his relatives was the biggest cruise ship owner in Greece, and being winter in Greece, his ships were available. He called and asked him if he could send two to three of his cruise ships to Qatar, and the answer was very positive.

Abdulrahman right away was shocked by his great idea. He asked to get his private jet ready and fly the next morning to Doha and arranged to meet the number one for crucial decisions and, at the same time, the secretary of the emir's office to go to Doha and meet him.

The next day, he was on the private plane flying to Doha.

The meeting was arranged at the general secretary's office, and he remembered he had to walk almost 60 metres from his office door to his desk.

He came straight to the subject and told him, "Abdulrahman said that you have a brilliant solution as an idea." He explained to him how the accommodation problem could be solved by having three cruise ships be at the dock of the harbour and be able to have more than 2500 people to sleep, plus it would come with food supplies to be able to feed another 3000, considering also the lack of restaurants in Doha. The man was shocked; his face turned white, and then he said, "Oh, why did you not come two days ago?"

He said, "Why?"

"Because two days ago, we ordered 3000 tents from Lebanon." So, another big and profitable business crashed, a business that would have let him have a profit of, in rough calculations, 1 million dollars. Always, all business failed just a few minutes before the realisation.

He returned to Greece after a long absence, back to his family and also to the hotel where he was always the director and well paid, leaving during his absence two assistants to run it.

In those times, the country was governed by dictators and the junta. One night, a minister of the junta came to the hotel and specifically to the nightclub to enjoy the nice program with famous Greek singers and the big ballet they had at that time.

Those ignorant members of the board of directors obliged him, as the hotel manager, to go and join the minister's table and enjoy the show together with him. He told them no way, he was not that fond of either that minister nor the junta that he represents. So, the next day, he was fired again for a second time with a well-paid reimbursement amount of money.

So, now what was next to do? He was sitting in his own office in the centre of Athens, thinking about what next business could be done to keep him alive.

One of his school friends was a jeweller—not a big one, but an ambitious guy and quite promising together with his brother.

He then went to his shop and informed him, among others, about his big relations and acquaintances he had in Abu Dhabi, Kuwait, Dubai, and Bahrain. The jeweller had never even heard of these Emirates before, and he had to open a map to show him where these Arab Gulf States were.

He convinced him that he had many friends there and that he could organise an exhibition at the Kuwait Sheraton Hotel with Greek jewellery, something that had never before happened not only for Greek jewellery but also for European jewellery. It was the first ever European jewellery show in Kuwait and especially only the fact that it was Greek made it to a great degree attractive for the local ladies and the elite feminine class. As a hotel manager, he knew how to organise an exhibition and especially take care of the details, as unforeseen details could destroy an event.

The exhibition was to be organised quite soon; he had with him two assistants with vast knowledge of jewellery. They had three big pilot cases full of a big selection of impressive but also expensive jewellery that almost all had something derived from Greek mythology. Impressive necklaces covered with diamonds, rubies, sapphires, emeralds, turquoise, and pink gemstones; many ancient-looking all golden bracelets, earrings, and rings; and many but exquisite jewellery fancy pieces.

The inauguration was a big success; all his local important friends made phone calls, and from mouth to mouth, that exhibition became known among the elite community and many important ladies came, all covered from top to toe in the local black dress but also men of high rank and ministers came to buy gifts for their ladies—wives but also mistresses. The sales went perfectly, beyond any expectation, and although there were two more days, he decided to limit them to one more day as most of the jewellery was sold on the very first day.

So, he started a new venture of selling and promoting expensive Greek jewellery in the Gulf States and even entering palaces with the help of saleswomen that he had with him as no man could enter the palaces.

The rumours went around, and then they got a call that the Kuwait Seicha who wanted, exclusively for her, at her vacation palace, a presentation of the best Greek jewellery.

One of his friends gave him his big jeep with a driver, and he had to travel through the desert for three hours until they reached an oasis, which was just the palace and a Hilton Hotel for the visitors of the palace.

The Seicha, among other very expensive necklaces, earrings, and rings, spotted the one most expensive necklace with top quality diamonds and sapphires with a selling price of 100,000 USD.

Seicha asked his first saleswoman to come back with a discount. The first thing that the Arabs say when you deal with them is the word 'discount'.

He called the jeweller in Athens, and he explained to him the situation and what better price he could give her and how deep the price could go so that he could make the best and most profitable negotiations for him, which was always through the saleswoman. He told him you can go down to 50,000 and still even down to 20,000 (one may understand how big the profits were of such high-priced jewellery pieces).

The next day, he called and told him he was sorry he could not manage to sell as she asked for a lower price. He, in despair, told him 10,000 was still OK.

He then told him with pride that not just 10,000 but what he managed to sell that exclusive necklace was 95,000 dollars, which was 5000 less than the initial price. For a few minutes, he heard nothing from the other side of the line. It took the jeweller quite some minutes to realise what a huge profit he had arranged for him.

This business continued successfully in Abu Dhabi, Dubai, and again Abu Dhabi, Qatar, and back to Dubai and Kuwait, as well as Bahrain. He remembers once in Sheraton of Kuwait he had with him one man and one girl for sales, and there was to be a special event around the swimming pool, so he asked them to go down and amuse themselves while he had to stay in the room to guard the jewellery. It was funny to observe from his balcony that all were drinking coffee, but in fact, what was in the coffee cup was whisky.

He couldn't forget when he was in Abu Dhabi with fresh and new merchandise. The first to come to pick up the best pieces was his friend Abdulrahman. He put all the rings (he was buying only rings) on his hotel bed, and he, with his big hand, started picking up rings as many as could have in a handful without asking for the price. He just asked him to send the bill to the office and they would pay.

Abdulrahman was a tall and handsome man with blue eyes and was of Iranian descent. He needed the rings nicely wrapped in beautiful velvet boxes as this man had to have another girl in his bed every day and needed the rings to give them as a gift.

So, every day, there was a big parade of absolutely beautiful girls, especially airline hostesses, for him to pick one, sometimes even two, to spend his night with; in a few cases, he also asked him to pick one and take her to his bed, and he did not one but many more times enjoy sex with ethereal God's creatures. To his deep regret, Abdulrahman died at the age of 50 from cancer, and he lost a true friend.

He also decided, for the first time, to go to Saudi Arabia. He had a friend there who had an impressive villa, and they were to organise a show/exhibition in his villa. He invited friends, but Areus did not wait for the villa owner to bring buyers, he took the yellow pages and started calling and inviting, and this worked greatly indeed.

Many came, and most of them through his telephone calls and invitations to persons whom the villa owner never met or knew. Among them was a Pakistani worker in dirty clothes; he asked him politely to leave the exhibition, but what he did was take out from his pockets thousands of dollars rolled as a big tennis ball. He bought jewellery and left with a big smile.

He couldn't forget what happened during that show. All of a sudden, they heard ladies' voices and laughter, and a group of 20 ladies came, all dressed in black long dresses covering all except their eyes.

His staff was very busy, so he also had to make the sales. One of the ladies seemed to choose him to serve her, asking him to show the best they had and make a real presentation for her, but that needed time so she stayed there in front of him quite a while. He was presenting her the best pieces they had, but at the same time, he could not take his eyes away from her eyes.

Such beautiful eyes he couldn't recall having ever seen before. He was presenting to her real diamonds, but her brilliant eyes by far exceeded in carats the diamonds he was trying to sell her.

She noticed that his eyes were on her seductive eyes, and he could see through her black veil that covered her mouth and concealed almost all her face—a sweet but shy smile, a smile equally beautiful as her eyes. Then he felt the villa owner kick him hard from behind.

He turned around and asked him, "What the hell, why did you kick me?"

He said, "Down with your bloody eyes; you are not allowed to look at her eyes; she is a princess; you can even end up in prison for this."

Afterwards, he realised that she made it to him through both eyes and smile, a kind of sign to lower his naïve eyes and avoid looking straight at her enchanted eyes.

That jewellery business gave him some money to live on, but not the big money of the previous businesses that he literally lost at the very last minute.

Not to forget that upon arriving at the Jeddah airport, they had to empty all the luggage contents for the customs officers to check inside. They discovered in his luggage a PlayBoy magazine, and right away, they took him to the airport prison; luckily, his Saudi guy arranged that he get released fast.

He mentioned a local colonel to a Kuwaiti friend before. This was a big honour for a local Kuwaiti to reach such a high military ranking as a local Kuwaiti military officer. He called him, asking to pick him up from the airport as he was there with a business to discuss with him. He was always open for new business as the jewellery trip came to an end, so he had to look for new business.

Indeed, he told him that he took a big contract to Khartoum in Sudan, which was to organise and take the management of the biggest convention and conference centre in Africa, which was built as a donation from the Chinese government to the Khartoum government; those days, the man who ruled Sudan was the dictator Nimeiry. Here starts a new escapade in the wild and primitive Sudan.

Tickets were always free from the Sudanese government, and he also stayed in the 'best' hotel of Khartoum—the Sudan Hotel.

So, there he was in the airplane together with a Lebanese guy who was a partner of his Kuwaiti friend who was staying permanently in Khartoum. The convention centre was indeed huge and needed a lot of staff to run it.

Local staff, such as waiters and cooks, were not available at the quality that this centre required, and he had to bring all from Greece. The general situation there was horrible; although he was staying in the best hotel right on the River Nile to take bath in the bathtub, he had to first drown more than 30 cockroaches. In this country, all moved slowly, no councils' decisions were taken fast; even ministry meetings were never to bring any result and finalise the details of the contract that was signed, but there were many open issues and not any advance payment so far according to the signed pre-contract.

He brought In Sudan his head waiter and his chef so that they would start professional lessons and teach the locals how to do the job. Each one was to have the responsibility. But the government officials and ministers were slow with no progress for weeks, but during each meeting, the meetings ended with the famous 'bukra inshallah', meaning tomorrow if Allah allows and just leave it for tomorrow.

The heat was incredible; 47 degrees under shadow; drinking beer under the shadow of a small tree outside the hotel, but that local beer was awful.

The chef told him in order to sleep long and forget the problems that he was facing during the day, he better eat many garlics, and so he did in order to sleep as fast and as long as possible. One night, he was sleeping, but he felt that there was something on his chest. He put his hand on his chest, and with the other hand, he switched the desk lamp on, and what he saw in front of him and inside his flannel was a huge rat the size of a cat.

Without intention, he was holding the rat there with his hand so the rat could not find a way to escape. He found Heracles' force to tear off his flannel, but that was not enough as the rat went down to his belly, and there, he made a hole on the flannel and ran away. He then went down to his colleague, the hotel manager, and told him what happened; he seemed so conformable as if this were a usual matter that happened many times in his hotel.

He found the excuse that there were two problems; one that the hotel was next to the zoo (a real dirty zoo without any safety measures). The second reason was that there was the River Nile only a few metres away from the hotel, a real dirty river.

About that zoo—he had a bad experience. The security measures were non-existent; the crocodiles were in five square metres, which was supposed to be a closed area and just a 40 cm high wall that anyone, even a child, could easily touch the crocodile and lose his hand.

He then went to the lion cage; the heat was such that even that lion was down to a deep sleep; its nostrils were almost out of the poor material cage wires. He put the sharp end of a corn near the lion's nostril, and it woke up with that huge head, looking at him, wanting to tell him, "You son of the bitch, if the wire was not there between us as it is now, you would have been in my mouth."

He liked to visit the monkeys' cage; a dark chapter in his life occurred in a huge cage with many monkeys of many colours and sizes. But what the hell? There was a bloody short, ugly monkey who was approaching him, and what did he do? He simply demonstrated masturbation.

In fact, all there around him were black, and him not being black, he was for the bloody monkey as if he were a Swedish blonde girl. He said no, it was a coincidence, so he went there again the next day, and what did he see?

There were many people, and that bloody monkey with his eyes was looking to find him, and again, he proceeded with his masturbation, so he decided he wouldn't go there anymore and make him feel ridiculous.

There were four days of national holidays, so the dictator gave orders to pick up the four foreign businessmen from the hotel and, with his private plane, fly to south Sudan, the city of Jumba, for a real safari.

He wanted to please them with this gesture because in Jumba, the south of Sudan and the biggest southern city, was the real and virgin safari and not any tourist safari like in Kenya. They woke up early, and the government car took them to the airport. These four persons were a German, a Frenchman and an Italian man.

All roughly of the same age, they were there for different projects and contracts with the government, but they all complained that the final contract was never to come to a final signature as the ministers all the time during meetings said OK but 'Bukra inshallah', the usual 'tomorrow with Allah's blessings'.

When they reached the airport, they found out that the Italian, who was supposed to go directly alone by taxi earlier, was not there.

Areus called the hotel and told him, "*Ma che cacho dove say*?" Where the hell are you? He was sorry he overslept. He actually gave him the advice to eat garlic so that he could sleep long.

He promised to take a taxi and come the fastest. That delay may have saved their life because the plane with the pilot, a Philippine pilot, was waiting, but suddenly, the government issued instructions to close the airport and any communication with Jumba of south Sudan was stopped because there appeared the so-called, in those times, disease of the Green Monkey (later called Ebola).

So, thanks to God, and the Italian, they never took that trip, or else they would have been there and be isolated or even dead by that disease as many had died.

He was bored, so were the head waiter and the chef. They never paid them the first instalment of the bloody contract.

He had that Lebanese friend who gave him some nice times by bringing him around some good food places as he knew where to go after being there for years. He also brought him to find a special place where maybe the best black women were available for money.

He noticed that she took off her dresses and a very black body appeared. He couldn't say that he was crazy about that black body, but he needed a woman after so long and desperately. What she did was for him a first-time experience.

There was a burner, and she stood up naked with her legs wide open so that her pussy gets hot. That was a tradition for pleasing the men, a habit there to make available to the man a hot pussy. Frankly, it was not that pleasant to have his cock almost burned in a deep black hole.

The Sudan adventure ended with no financial income; he totally lost his valuable time and nothing more.

He was back to his own office in Athens, thinking in real depth that he had to find a new job and source of revenue. One day, someone knocked on his door, and a guy who was working at the casino as a groupier came to visit him as he was fired, and he thought that he might be able to find a job for him.

That guy noticed on his office desk that he had three peculiar gadgets. It was one lighter looking like a blow torch and also a lighter again looking like that magical pot of the genie type, but that was a simple and impressive lighter. He also had on that desk a small gadget that when one calls on the phone and he asks him to wait for a minute, just put the receiver on that gadget and that plays music so while waiting he listens to music.

He also had on his desk a thin pilot case but a very thin kind of the so-called James Bond case slim to keep a few documents inside.

All these were gadgets that he had bought somewhere from a bazaar in Abu Dhabi or Kuwait or any of those Arab Gulf States.

That ex-groupier asked him if he could lend him these four items for a few days. He asked, "What for?"

He answered again, "Just lend these to me for a few days," without revealing to him what he needed them for.

"OK, but I want them to be back in six days, OK?" And he agreed.

Indeed, he came back but two weeks later; he was sure that he had lost the three gadgets, but there he was back, asking him to import 200 each of these three items. He told him, "Are you crazy? How can I know who is the producer of those items? I bought them from a bazaar." And he could see and read that all three were made in Japan. He was always able, even without Google in those old times, to find sources, so he went to the Japanese Embassy and asked them to help him find the makers, and indeed, they succeeded.

So, having the makers, he sent telexes; he got the prices; he gave that guy his selling prices, adding 50% and 70% for custom duties, plus his profit, and to his big surprise, the guy got the orders.

He asked him where and to whom he sold these, and he revealed to him that many companies, especially at the end of the year, give gifts to their best customers to thank them for the orders they placed, and so they added a marketing and public relations tool, and this is called advertising gifts.

He thought could this be a new profession for him? So, he added some items such as marble paperweights that he imported from England and some pens and keychains from Italy (it was always easy for him to find sources and the best makers with the help of the languages).

He then himself started going out to visit customers, many of whom he knew from the casino, and they also knew him as a decent and honest man, so they easily agreed to meet to discuss his new venture.

They all placed orders with him, impressed by what he had shown them and also by the trust that was projected by his personality as the best ever hotel manager who passed from that five-star hotel. So, a brilliant and very promising new profession started for him with unpredictable prospectives.

In some circles of those important customers, who all were gamblers, he heard that there was an official from the casino of Monte Carlo looking for a representative in Greece who knows the good and serious Greek gamblers.

There a bell rang for him. He sent a letter saying who he was, and a beautiful letter came from Monaco with all the impressive stamps of Société de Bain de Mer, announcing to him that they will come to visit him.

Indeed, a real gentleman, a Monegasque, came to meet him, and his good French speaking helped a lot. They went out for dinner and told him that they want him to bring every week 5 to 10 important Greek gamblers and he was the one to indicate the roof for each one to be given as credit from the casino.

All these gamblers were to get free air tickets and live for free at the most impressive hotel, maybe in all Europe, the Hotel De Paris, where he had not just a room but a suite. They suggested to pay him not on commission as he did not want to make money from his gambler's losses. No, he denied, and they fixed a Monegasque salary, a quite big salary of the Greek standards.

He started calling the best gamblers that he knew that are decent, polite (guaranteed politeness because many look polite and gentle but when they lose money, they get an unrecognisable different character), and serious, and he told them the whole story.

They were delighted with the invitation. The Monegasque also made a deal with a travel agent to supply the free tickets; the travel bureau that he recommended to him was the same who had issued the air tickets to Sudan. So, he was to issue a free ticket to all his gamblers for the direct trip from Athens to Nice. And this started, and in most of the trips, he also took his wife with him, and they spend a somehow second and best honeymoon. His gamblers were gambling, of course, not in the first hall of the casino when entering the casino but in the private, where the big VIP gamblers enjoyed a luxurious ambience.

An impressive casino ambience like those that they see nowadays in the James Bond films. There was at the end of the private hall a nice restaurant with full view of all roulettes, blackjack, etc. And further inside the private rooms was the baccarat, where three of his best invited gamblers who could sit next or opposite to famous personalities. His gamblers were happy to gamble at such an impressive and warm environment, much more elegant than the Athens casino.

He remembers he had one client, a short guy not of any high education but a real bon viveur, the only one who indeed knew very well what and how to eat.

He had his own gambling club in Athens. He was famous because while the first lady singer in Greece was singing at the dancing and singing clubs, he threw real pearls at her feet and not break ceramic plates as other did.

That gambler was gambling only red and black, but with a big money chip of 5000 French Francs. He asked him why do you play only with big chips of 5000 Francs; he said because when he wins, he gets one more big chip (plaque) of 5000 so he cannot give tip to 'poor les employees'' because, as he said, all gamblers that use smaller chips when from time to time, they win, they always give tips for the groupiers, and this at the very end is a lot of money during a whole gambling night.

Life in Monte Carlo was nice. They were arriving there on Friday and departing on Monday, and he went back to his office and back to his advertising gifts business, which began to increase slowly but steadily, step by step. He slightly increased his range with some more keychains, and he was running selling advertising gifts to the top and important companies, and mostly, the presidents of the companies were welcoming him as he was always a very serious man and his approach was trustful, always gently dressed in expensive suits that inspired confidence.

Capital was necessary for making his imports of the coming orders. Here, he came back to his friend Abdulrahman; before dying, he was the one to call for money help and financing, and he did with great pleasure, and so with his money, he started the advertising gifts business.

With his gamblers staying at Hotel de Paris, there was a funny story.

The Hotel de Paris has impressive bathrobes with the coat of arms (emblem) of the Principaute de Monaco, which has value for collectors and is ideal as a memory and souvenir.

One morning quite early, all his Greek gamblers gathered down in the lobby with their luggage to wait for the bus to take them all to Nice airport.

From the impressive staircases, they saw a man coming down with two big dogs, so as a joke, he told them that these dogs were specially trained to smell from the luggage of the customers the hotel's bathrobes. In a minute, they all felt embarrassed as obviously they all had taken one such nice bathrobe as a souvenir.

One other noteworthy observation was that in the centre of the lobby there was the statue of a metal horse. One could easily see that although the whole body was black, the knee of the horse was gold. All the gamblers that stayed in the hotel before going to the casino rubbed that knee that was supposed to bring luck.

Back to Monte Carlo, staying at the exquisite Hotel de Paris, he remembers one day his wife and him were late to wake up, as he always stayed late at the casino to make sure that his gamblers were to feel that he was there to back them in case they wanted something and have him to support them in case they were losing.

His wife and he decided to go shopping before leaving for Nice to have a fast lunch, a fast one at the famous restaurant called Salle Empire of the hotel.

But how fast can you have lunch in such a restaurant as the whole process takes a long, real culinary, long-taking bon viveur meal? How can you dare to order in such a restaurant just a fillet steak? The maître d'hôtel will stare at you as if you were a peasant or an American tourist who used to eat hamburgers.

You have to start with the hors d'oeuvres, then go to the entrees, continue with the main course, then cheese and dessert. All this process takes two hours so no fast lunch or dinner existed in such a luxury five-star hotel restaurant.

One time, instead of returning with a direct flight from Nice to Athens, he decided with his wife to fly back via Geneva. As an ex-hotel manager of a five-star hotel and Heidelberg manager's school graduate, he was given a free stay invitation by the manager of the impressive hotel Du Rhone in Geneva. He took the yellow pages and tried to discover if near the hotel was any company dealing with advertising gifts, and indeed, there was right around the corner of Rue Du Rhone.

He called telling them who he was and presented himself as an advertising gift company in Greece. They were very polite, inviting him to come at any time to their company and showroom. Indeed, he popped up, and what did he see? A huge showroom with thousands of samples. He was crazy to see what a huge variety they had, having in mind that in his showroom were just five–six items. The manager was a very welcoming person, and talking about the business, he came up with a suggestion that changed his life completely.

He told him that they have a group of companies, a club maybe, for advertising gifts agents or dealers and promotional gifts dealers all over the world, and they have one selected member in each country. At that particular period, they did not have any Greek member because they kicked the former Greek member out, who only appeared to the meetings the first day and then 'vanished' with his girlfriend, and each time he was seen with another escort girl, probably picked up through newspapers ads.

He did not contribute to the group, so they stopped him. He asked him if he was interested in this. He said, of course, with a big yes. He asked what will be the next step; he said the president of the group will visit him in Athens to see who he is and see his offices and showroom.

When he returned to Greece, he had to organise his office; his office, in the meantime, was not in that expensive area opposite to the Parliament but was just a single room on the southern part of Athens, so what the hell showroom he would show to him? He was worried that the president seeing his small room office and a tiny showroom would never accept him as their exclusive Greek member.

Thank God, he got a telephone call from that kind Swiss guy whom he had met in Geneva, telling him that the president, who was a very strict and severe Dutch man, cannot come so they invited him as observer, which was to take place in France next to Switzerland, on a nice, low mountain with fantastic view and peaceful surroundings. They met at the Lausanne airport, where the bus would take them to that small but nice hotel where the meeting was to take place. There was also a new member from Spain invited to join the group. He was a German who lived for years in Barcelona with a very beautiful wife, and he was also to be interviewed to become the Spanish member.

At the Swiss French borders, the officer was amazed to see that there were 35 people in that bus all with different passports of different countries. This never happened to him, and he went to his chief to ask what to do; the chief, of course, told him to let the bus pass.

They reached the hotel where he was alone without his wife as it was clear that this was a business meeting and no wife was necessary, after all paying for two tickets would have a cost.

Now here, they were in the meeting room. First, the Spanish member was interviewed in the presence of 35 other country members. He indeed had a big company, so it was easy for him to be welcomed and accepted to the group. The procedure was for him to answer all the questions from the committee of the group; he had to tell a story about his company and the perspectives, then after that he was asked to leave the meeting room.

They all then spoke to each other about the Spanish man and quickly decided to welcome him as the Spanish member. They called him back into the meeting room; they applauded and told he was welcomed as the member for Spain.

Then came his turn; his legs were trembling. What the hell shall he tell them? The Dutch president, without a smile on his lips, started the interview.

"How many salesmen do you have?" What to say? It was just him, so he started counting with his fingers—one, two, three.

"Yes, I have three salesmen."

"What is the turnover?" His turnover was maybe 10,000 US dollars, so he told them 300,000 dollars in an unsteady voice; for their standards, that was too low or rather peanuts.

"How many years have you been in business?" He said, including the current year he ran this business for two and a half years; in reality, it only was just six months.

He noticed in the room some ironic smiles. They talked slowly between themselves as if he were in front of the judges of the Supreme Court. They asked him to leave the meeting room for them to make their decision. It was for him a waiting time that seemed to be one year. It was quite longer staying out of the room compared with the previous guy, the Spaniard.

After 30 minutes, he started to feel uncomfortable, believing that they would deny him and he had to pack and return. Then the door opened; they called him in, and what a relief he felt when he heard them applauding. They welcomed him, and with congratulations, they announced him as the Greek member of the group. Later, when he became almost the leader of the group, they confessed that they knew that he was nothing but a small starter, but they saw a fire, a hidden volcano in him.

He swallowed from their many years of experience all their knowledge of this business, their new ideas, new nice items, and new suppliers, mainly from Hong Kong.

The previous Greek member who was expelled from the group was by far the number one in this business in Greece; he had made a fortune, so it was a big distance to walk until he could reach him and overpass him as number one in the field, but with kind of a polemic strategy, this merely took him just one year to fundamentally strike out all market competitors and enjoy the loneliness of the peak.

Attacking the market like a hurricane, all competitors found themselves in front of gritty realism. They felt that here arrived a bulldozer, and suddenly, they had to find ways to somehow limit his uncontrolled advance, gaining one after the other the biggest customers.

They planned how to compete with him, maybe by a kind of coalition, but this failed. His company had a crazy advancing boost with no brakes to stop him. They wanted to create any possible damage with strikes under the belt to harm his company's reputation.

One of them even sent an anonymous letter to the customs authorities that he was smuggling expensive lighters, watches, and pens. In those times, these three items had to pay almost 300% customs fees. One day, eight policemen arrived at his showroom and started searching everywhere to see where he kept the smuggled goods. They even searched in the building's boiler room.

They, of course, found nothing. He told them was it at all possible to even close the roads to the neighbourhood with just an anonymous phone call and create such a mess for nothing.

If he was to be a terrorist, the police measures would be less severe. They indeed felt uncomfortable, so they apologised and left.

Always being a restless mind and always looking for a new source of income, he came up with a brilliant idea.

During the election days and him being a supporter of the New Dimokratia, the conservative party, he gathered some very impressive novelty items and gadgets that were never before seen at the pre-election days, where hundreds of thousands of the party's supporters came to hear the speaker leader of the one to be elected as prime minister.

He visited the offices of the New Dimokratia Party, and he showed them the ideas. They were all delighted. He asked them if he could have exclusive rights to use the party's logo on all those items (mugs, ballpens, decals, keychains, flags, whistles, caps, t-shirts, towels, and many other but new items) and he would pay the party a commission.

They agreed, as no one had ever made them such a proposal.

So, he had a team of 20 staff and 6 big benches where they demonstrated the promotional party's gadgets.

They were following the leader to elect Mr Mitsotakis, the father of the current brilliant prime minister, and they did a great job for the party even through those novelty gadgets, gaining new supporters and voters for the party.

They followed him to all his open public speeches in all of Greece, to maybe more than 20 cities and big islands like Crete and Rhodes. He remembers the morning after they were back to the office with all the plastic bags full of money; he went to the bank to deposit the money with thousands of coins and small banknotes.

The bank was so happy to see that he was growing so fast. His company quickly became one of the bigger customers of the bank, supporting him in all his imports with credits for new capital.

He managed to present to all the competitors' customers fresh and impressive ideas, better prices and that, until then number one, collapsed and retired, and he was resigning from the market. All this operation was parallel to the Friday to

Monday trips to Monte Carlo, and although he was working from Monday to Friday and for endless hours, he had the chance to relax the weekend at Monte Carlo, plus gaining his very good French salary.

Then what a weird thing happened. The Athens hotel casino, seeing that he was stealing from them good gamblers and taking them to Monte Carlo, made him a new one more extra attractive suggestion to return for a third time back as the hotel director, hoping that he would stop the Monte Carlo gamblers or junkets trips.

He told them he would think, and if he decided, this time he would demand three times his old salary because, in the meantime, he also created another business and had limited time to manage the director's job at their hotel. He put a condition that would go there anytime; he wanted any day he wanted and maybe not even whole weeks. They accepted everything. He had to appoint two new assistant managers to run under his command.

In those days, the junta had fallen and democracy had at last returned to Greece.

He had second thoughts: should he continue doing this Monte Carlo job or stop it because what if the state officials find out that Greek money was going out of the country and they start searching, and, of course, who would be the one to pay for this?

Him—the small guy and not the big businessmen that were with him on the trips to Monte Carlo.

So, he resigned, and he accepted the director's post at the Athens hotel and casino with the agreement of his limited presence. So, he was more dedicated to run his company successfully, and he increased his staff to six more.

At this point, and always with the restless spirit he possessed, he was able to create another side business during his time in Monte Carlo.

Going often to Cannes and Nice, he noticed that the French people were crazy for fish and especially lobster, but they were paying 10 times more for live lobster than frozen. He then started searching and found out that the best lobster in the Mediterranean Seas was around the island of Lemnos and the small island of Agios Efstratios.

So, he took the plane, went to those islands, and talked with fishermen and learned all about lobsters. He explained to the fishermen what the project would be and how they could manage to keep the lobster alive flying by air to Nice.

They told him that this could be done if you tied and wrapped tightly the lobster so that they would not do any movements and lose power. So they did; they tied and wrapped them with a burlap cloth wet with sea water so the lobster could still take breaths and swallow life and force from the wet with seawater burlap kind of cloth.

The lobsters at those times were the best in all Europe, so he had a perfect product with a good buying price and, of course, a very best-selling price. He managed to take three lobsters tied up as he described before and flew as usual on Friday to Nice.

He went straight to the biggest fish importer in Nice, and he showed him, after unfolding from the wet cloth, the lobster, which, when unwrapped started moving wildly as if it were just fished out from the sea water. The importer went crazy; they agreed on the price, and the business started.

The last of the three lobsters, he gave as a gift to the Monegasque gentleman (he later became the president of the world Backgammon Association) who had offered him that casino job. He appreciated this gift more than if he had given him a diamond.

So much they loved the live lobsters. The lobster business kept going, but the lobsters became seldom, less and less, and the fishermen were fishing lobster babies less than a kilo, which was prohibited (a lobster to become 1 kilo takes 7 years).

So, this business faded away.

Another bad action was that one fisherman on that small island of Agios Efstratios constructed a kind of big pool and put many lobsters in there to keep them alive. When the lobsters are fished and get out of the sea and then return back to the sea water, their flesh becomes stronger and gets heavier and obviously more expensive.

The problem with that fisherman was that he put many male lobsters that had stronger flesh, but he also put few females, and one day, when he woke up, he found a pool with all male lobsters empty of flesh and dead. The reason was that the male lobsters were killing each other to get the female lobsters as a winning trophy for sex.

So, after he stopped the Monte Carlo venture, someone else took it over who was a travel agent, so in order to sell many air tickets, he was sending to Monte Carlo many supposed-to-be good gamblers without checking if they were real and serious gamblers and also quality gamblers and if they were honest people, so the problems started, and the casino management stopped this.

When he was in charge, there was never any incident at all with all gamblers as they were paying their cheques on time, and never any trouble had occurred.

Now having no Monte Carlo and having limited presence in his hotel management, he started very seriously to grow his advertising gifts company, and that was doing tremendously well.

In the meantime, he became maybe the best member of the group, bringing over the best ideas and winning one award after the other for the best presentation.

When the time came for his presentation of the best 10 ideas/items during the meetings, they turned serious, saying, "Now starts the good business with Areus' presentation."

They were travelling five–six times per year mainly to Hong Kong.

This advertising gift business as sourcing started in Hong Kong as the main source of suppliers, then this moved to Taiwan and later ended for good in China.

He had visited China more than 60 times. All China makers at the Canton fair knew him; they liked him because he respected them as equals while other Europeans and Americans were arrogant and did not deal with them on the basis of equality.

He remembers one morning, he was always the first to visit the shows; one China supplier was having his typical Chinese breakfast that looked like a soup with different ingredients inside. He then took his chopsticks, and from the same chopsticks the guy was eating, he also ate from his breakfast bowl.

He appreciated this a lot because all European or American importers passing by were holding their nose due the unpleasant smell. So, he won one more supplier and, most of all, his best prices, and he was the first to know the new items.

He moved from that small room and rented a big space in the same building, where his home was also on the last floor. There he had a big space for his showroom to grow and be the same size as all the rest of the showrooms of all his European colleagues. The space was so big that his first daughter could use her bicycle to cycle around.

He bought printing machines from Switzerland in the small city of Schaffhausen, where he visited to see those machines in operation, and with a friend who lived permanently in Milan, he went from Italy by road to

Switzerland. Trying to go to the machines factory at Schaffhausen, they took the wrong path on the mountains with deep snow. The car was slipping like a skateboard, and for a moment, they reached a frozen cliff ready to fall and leave all their bones there.

That old Mercedes he found afterwards had flat tyres; he never changed the tyres for years, and the car was slipping on the snow like a boat. They saw death with wide, open eyes, but luckily, they avoided it at the last minute. So, with those Swiss machines as prototypes and with his own engineer improving two Chinese imported machines to be almost similar to the Swiss one and also similar to a hot stamping machine, he imported from Germany, and they also copied.

The business was going fantastic, so he had to resign from the hotel management as there was no time for that anymore.

Not too much later, after him leaving the hotel management, things for the hotel stopped making any progress at all; sales declined month by month vertically down; the restaurants lost the glam that had been under his guidance and supervision. Staff had to be fired, and finally the whole enterprise, including the casino, changed hands and the new owners completely closed the hotel as well as all restaurants.

He was very often visiting the showroom of his colleagues in Europe to see how they had organised their business. Among them, he visited his Belgium colleague, who always at his presentations was showing items that he did for the famous, during those times, brand Kent cigarettes and Lucky Strike cigarettes for Middle East countries of the company Brown and Williamson. During dinner, he made the error to tell him that he was sad as the Brown and Williamson Middle East offices would move from Brussels to Athens.

That information was equal to a gold vein. He searched and found their offices and paid a visit to the lady in charge for purchasing promotional gifts. That was for him the biggest ever business in the field of advertising gifts. He presented the latest ideas he had to show to gain her interest and impressions. They were delighted with his novelty ideas and prices and also very happy that they found an equal or even better supplier than the one they had in Brussels.

That time when he entered, Brown and Williamson was in the middle of the year, and there was not much to do for the Greek market as the main advertising gifts 'season' started after August, so he put all his efforts, and with his biggest delight, they started placing huge orders that he managed through his partner agent office in Hong Kong to always send on time directly to the Middle East countries (Saudi Arabia, Kuwait, and all Emirates).

One day, at a meeting of the group of 35, he was approached by his Austrian colleague, telling him that he was agent in Austria (he was always the FIFA exclusive supplier of giveaway gifts for all football events) of a Luxembourg Agency for football events and whatever was related to football, such as buying and selling football players, etc. and are looking for an agent in Greece.

He contacted them, and they were happy to have him as their manager in Greece with a basic salary, plus commission from the arrangement done by him in Greece.

So, he started this secondary business by contacting the major football teams and telling them that with the backup of the well-known Luxembourg Company, they were able to do whatever they wished for. The phone calls started coming from the presidents of the biggest football teams, asking him mainly, before the starting of the National Championship season, to find good teams, preferably British, to arrange for friendly pre-season matches.

So, this started, and they probably were asking British Premier League teams.

He remembers, among others, when he brought a good coach to a football team of Patras and also organised several matches.

The biggest success of all was having the German team Hamburg, the Champion of Germany, that year with the famous British player Kevin Keegan. He fixed a match with the winner of that year's league cup. That team's stadium was 100 metres away from his office. The fame for that match was so big that the stadium of the league cup winner could accommodate 10,000 fans, but as the demand was so big, they had to move to the Athens central stadium that could accommodate the double.

One more time, the luck turned back to him because the Hamburg team before arriving to Athens had three other matches, and in each match, they were losing one or two players because of injury, and in the end in Austria, when playing with Vienna, they had just 11 players, so the Athens match, to the regret of all, was cancelled.

He continued that, but this demanded him to travel a lot to all of Greece, and the time was short for him, and his advertising gift business required his presence. He regretfully decided to stop this football manager business. Now he saw that this was a mistake as this business became a booming business and he was the right person for this, speaking five languages and taking the exclusive rights from players and trying to get rich contracts for them.

The BW Kent business was growing so fast that he started creating a substantial capital. The need to buy a house and not rent anymore became a necessity. He was always thinking big; he did not want to just rent an apartment, but as the company was growing so fast, he needed a big space and a combination of home and business to be in the same building so he could work many hours without being away from the family.

That time, having so many ideas and gadgets that he discovered during his numerous visits to the Far East (mainly China), he decided to open a shop with gadgets, which was the first gadget shop in Greece. The success was big so he decided to step into the franchise business, the first of such type of business. In fact, he was always the pioneer of ideas and new ventures.

In only one year, there were 12 such gadget stores in Greece. Being very known and successful, the chain kept growing. The first serious issue appeared when in order to obtain good prices in China, he had to import whole containers, and the 12 shops could not absorb and dispense all of the quantities, so the warehouse started to get filled up, and the capital was remaining in idle status; the first clouds of danger and warnings appeared.

One day, he went to a southern suburb, maybe the best suburb of Athens, to find a shop for a new gadget store. He went to a real estate agent, and just in order to impress him, he asked him if there was any big plot available for buying.

He told him, "Yes, just now they informed me about such a plot, which I have not seen yet, so let us go together to see it." They indeed went there and very near to the centre, and it was still a peaceful place; that piece of earth was one acre big and was a real paradise with all kinds of trees and a small house at the end of the right corner.

He asked him the price, and as it was January, and in January he always had cash money due to the fact that December and Christmas are the best months for advertising gifts, he had quite a good cash. Hearing the price, he said right away, "I will buy this now."

Here again, his famous bad luck returned as after they agreed the price, only two days later, there was a devaluation of the Greek Drachma, so the owner asked for more money, so he had to pay more, and he did as he wanted that plot desperately.

Right away, he started the building. He hired an architect who was very young with nice, fresh ideas, and they started in express fastness to construct the building.

They went 14 metres down as he needed to have three basements for the printing machinery but also to make the, first in Greece, private indoor tennis court.

Why a tennis court? Here is another story. His wife and his elder daughter were vacationing for years in the same place in Peloponnese, where he made friends with a young engineer who had his own hotel and also two tennis courts.

Another one was the manager of an airline company, and he possessed a nice villa (later he also built a tennis court in his home), and there was a banker who had a nice house right on the sea. They were playing tennis, and he was watching at that time, maybe 35 years old; he had never before touched a tennis racket.

In the next group meeting, he, as the secretary of the group, suggested organising, during the next meeting, five months later, in Salzburg, a tennis tournament. They all accepted; most of them were already good players. Two of them had a tennis court in their garden.

He was fat, 90 kilos, so he started early in the morning daily lessons of tennis, and in two months he went down to 75 kilos. The days approached for the tennis tournament in Salzburg. He drove his car with his family and stopped for four days in Bologna, Italy, at a tennis academy for a few more lessons.

He arrived in Salzburg, and the tennis tournament started before the actual business meeting. They were playing, and the winner of each set was the one who first reached the 11 games. First game was with an English friend. He was 30 years old, and he won with difficulty 11-10. Next came an Austrian guy, who unfortunately beat him 11-7, so one win and one loss.

He was watching the other courts and noticed the other players, especially the German, the Spaniard, and the Swiss guy were playing fantastic tennis.

He said, "Well, this is it; you will not progress further." He remembers those days watching tennis on TV; he heard the so-called top spin; his teacher taught him flat, and he followed through. So, although he never knew how to play that top spin, he said, "Well, you are a loser, so try it anyway." What a surprise that it worked!

He played using topspin, a rather primitive topspin that he improvised at the spot, but he was still successful, followed by shouting loudly, exclaiming a wild shriek that made the opponent get scared of his loud and rather wild screaming.

So, he beat the Swiss, he beat the Spaniard and reached the final against a German lady, the wife of the German member, who was by far the best and was playing with a charm and real tennis, not any amateur like him. He then using his primitive top spin and loud yelling, he beat her also, winning the tournament.

Tennis came into his life, and he was getting better and better, beating also all those guys at the vacation resort place, who were his mentors.

Unfortunately, due to mistakes done by the socialist government of those times by asking the offshore companies to pay local income taxes, the Brown and Williamson Middle East offices moved to Cyprus, so he lost an exceptionally big customer.

Many famous offshore companies that had their Middle East offices in Athens moved to other countries, and a big revenue was lost for Greece. He had money in America, which he had earned from Kent cigarettes, and that was indeed quite an amount. The bank manager in charge of Italy and Greece was coming all the time to visit him, wondering why he kept the money without any interest and not allow them to make for him a stocks portfolio for Wall Street.

He denied; he was conservative and wanted that money to stay untouched for the family's future. But after hard pressure, they managed to convince him to buy shares, and he was owner of shares of American Express and Saudi Petroleum. It was 1974, and a few days after they bought shares for him, the luck again turned against him. The US stock exchange crash of 1974 came, and he lost half or more of the value of his shares.

Before that catastrophe, when the money in America was still available, an idea came from his friend to step into ship ownership.

There was a big icebreaker ship under sale. The expert friend of cruise ships told him that this could be turned easily to a nice cruise ship.

For a moment, he was ready to buy that, but he had the pressure of his wife to buy a house or build their own house. So, the dilemma was to buy the icebreaker ship or forget about it and start the building.

He decided on the second, and he regretted because that ship was sold in only one week for double the price.

In the meantime, the building was in process, and he had money shortage to finish it as it finally reached to be almost 3000 square metres, a most impressive building of six floors above earth and three basements, including the tennis court.

Inevitably, he had to ask the bank in America with collateral for those remaining shares to give him a loan and send him cash money to use for the completion of the building. He had to pay back the loan they gave him, but he could not, and they liquidated the stocks that would now have a value of 30 million dollars.

The building caused him to suffer a lot with money shortage, and he was very close to derailing the company's growth and ending up to catastrophically inevitable bankruptcy.

He lost money by having all the loans with the banks in Japanese Yen, and that was sinking, and he also lost a huge amount of money.

He reached three times the brink of bankruptcy, but always, the ideas that he had saved him again and again.

First, he introduced to Greece the promotional gifts as until then it was just advertising gifts or, better say, Christmas gifts, so he started persuading international companies to take the first step to that promotional tool by adding to (as example) a whisky bottle a lighter as a free gift, and during those times, each whisky brand was selling 1 million bottles, so the promotional gift business brought him back to healthy company, and he was again climbing up in income and high profits.

He then approached the weekly magazines and convinced them to add to the ladies' magazines a handbag. He remembers during his salesmen meetings telling them that if he manages to convince one of the many magazines to do this, then all would be obliged to follow, and so it happened; he maybe could be in the Guinness Book, selling 3 million ladies' bags in a year.

In the years 1997 and 1998, the company was strong and very well known as a healthy company with the restless spirit of the owner. One expert in the stock exchange told him why don't you apply to become a public company. He thought this was a joke, but it was not.

One bank approached him asking to buy 10% of his company, offering big money. They made accounting checks (due diligence) and found that this, as they called it 'a blooming flower company'; they were pushing him day and night to sell them the 10%, but he did not as he did not need the money in those times.

That bank was always buying shares of companies that were close to IPO (Initial Public Offer). That was his mistake because he did not know that if a company increases the capital, it cannot go public but only after two years, so he lost the 1999 big party, but he still applied.

Those times were the big booming of the stock exchange. They told him that when listing the shares on the stock exchange at the IPO, he could easily raise funds of up to 8 million euros. But his listing to the stock exchange was delaying, and others who applied later than him, having political connections, went public faster than his company.

At last, in late 2002, he went public with shares available for purchase by the general public and the IPO raised 4.5 million euros, opening new opportunities. The value of the company was 55 million euros. His company was the first European company in the field of advertising and promotional gifts to go public.

All European and US magazines of this type of business were triumphantly talking about this, and he got many invitations to hold speeches among them; he also got award in Brussels for the one among the fastest growing European companies.

He was visiting all the fairs all over the world: Italy, Germany, France, Hong Kong, China, Taiwan, Japan, Indonesia, Malaysia, also America, but America with less interest, etc.

During the hundreds of visits to the Milan Fair (Macef and Chibi), he remembered a funny matter; his wife spoke no Italian, and so he had to accompany her with her shopping. They were at the famous Rinascente department store, next to their hotel, Duomo Hotel. They were on the ladies' underwear floor. His wife chose panties and bras, and she went to a changing room. He was tired from walking too much at the fair and found a nearby sofa to rest his feet.

Suddenly, he watched that the curtain of one of the changing rooms was half or little opened, and he saw a lady was undressing; he got hot with sexual excitation; he was watching to see more of the body behind the curtains, when suddenly, the curtain opened and a voice came, "Areus, you like these panties?" What a disillusionment! She was his own wife.

He always chose to stay with his wife mostly at the most luxurious hotel, Grand Hotel et de Milan, which had opened in 1863 at the famous Via Manzoni, and he remembered also that one time he booked the hotel room where the famous Maestro Giuseppe Verdi used to stay.

He also remembered that they also stayed at the Carlton Hotel in Nice, where he also booked the room that Jayne Mansfield stayed, and that was more than enough to raise his sexual desire.

Also, in Dallas, they gave him the room that Clinton stayed in some months before.

There was a show in Las Vegas for electronics, so he had to visit that exhibition too. He was amazed by Las Vegas, with the huge casinos and hotels, but all in a big level of exaggeration. Trying to copy Paris Tour Eiffel, Acropolis, and London Bridge, they, of course, impressed, but that was indeed 'too much'. Nevertheless, any man has one time in his life to visit Las Vegas, the Disneyland for adults.

Parallel to the electronics show was also a famous exhibition related to porno, which was also interesting to visit where porno movies and videos were filmed; naked girls were promoting sex toys and more for the female sexual pleasurable stimulation and many other toys and inflatable girls, etc.

His hotel was huge in order to walk to the reception, dragging the luggage and walking through hundreds of slot machines. The room was not anything special, and there was no mini fridge so as to oblige the customers to go down and drink and unavoidably to gamble.

Even in the toilets, there were gambling games and automatic condom machines. The hotel had maybe 15 different restaurants of all choices; one could believe that he was outside seeing the stars, but it was not so; it was a huge plastic dome with lighted stars. He walked around and entered all the casinos, all within walking distance, some connected with a small kind of train.

Inside were thousands of fanatic gamblers, half-naked girls offering drinks, above on a huge balcony a ballet of maybe 50 dancers in the centre of a big cage, where there was a lion. What a show all for the gambler's pleasure! He had a nice dinner at a supposedly Paris restaurant that was nothing to compare with any French cuisine. He then went to the room looking at the yellow pages where he could order a girl to come.

Indeed, there were many for 200 dollars; he said, OK, 200 dollars for a fuck is OK. He called, and in 20 minutes, there she was, knocking on the door. A tall, well-shaped woman. She said, "Money first." He gave her 200 dollars. "OK," she said, "let us talk." He thought what a nice prostitute that she first wants conversation; this is seldom.

He said, "OK, but let us go straight to the bed as I have not much time and have to sleep."

"Bed," she said.

"Yes, bed, where else on the floor we fuck?"

"Fuck?" she said. "What fuck?"

"But this is why I paid you 200 USD to fuck."

"No 200 dollars is to talk and another 200 for a fuck."

He was crazy and angry; she said, "OK, calm down, show me your dick. Oh, I see you are ready and hard, so I would give you a great masturbation for your 200 dollars."

What could he do? He said, "OK go ahead."

During masturbation, she wanted him to finish fast, so she started saying, "Oh, what a horny cock; what a great penis you have got to make women happy." That was very professional, and he came faster as usual. She cleaned her hand and left. Leaving, she told him, "Keep the penis hard, and you would always get ladies to come after you." What a 'philosopher' she was.

Those long walks on all those fairs and him always being the first to come and last to go, created problems with his feet. He had horrible pain in the soles of his feet.

It was the so-called Morton syndrome. That became impossible anymore to walk, so he had to undertake an operation. He also did with his right hand from too much typing, hand shaking at the fairs, and, of course, tennis playing. So, he had the so-called collateral damages.

What made the company especially famous but also easy to compete with all to come inquiries was the software that he created himself called Pandora, created with his instructions by his software team he had in his own company. That was not only a data bank but also an incredible system that made it so easy to get ideas, old but also the very newest novelty items with price comparisons.

He created in house (he had software experts under his command) a software under his guidance and instructions that could help salesmen and him as he was also dealing directly with the managers of the purchasing department and marketing managers of the big customer who wanted to talk directly to him as the boss with the famous name. The software had many thousands of items and ideas with both cost and selling prices.

The Pandora software had the enhanced ability to fill up details such as the activity of the customer (products), what was the wanted quantity, what the price range was, what they did before and what their competitors did already so as to avoid duplications, seasonality and more to add details.

The idea was that with one click, after filing up the customer's details as mentioned before, all the ideas that matched exactly the customer's given details were there on the monitor all ideas/items to meet all that the customer wanted.

He remembers that many companies' managers were calling him and giving him those simple details, and he said, "Just stay online, and you will get the ideas in your mail in a few seconds."

They could not believe that until the mail arrived, and they were amazed how fast they got the ideas that matched their inquiry.

Pandora won many awards, and many colleagues wanted to buy it, and indeed, he sold it even in Chile. It was widely acclaimed throughout the specific business fields, and so much advertised on all local new technology magazines that even the current prime minister of Greece was reading about this software, and him also being a fan of new technologies came to his office twice to see with his own eyes the functionality and the thereafter abilities of 'Pandora'.

A letter came inviting his company to take part in an international contest for promotional gifts given to doctors for promoting new medicines from a huge pharmaceutical company among the three most known in the world.

They carefully selected only 10 promotional gift suppliers from all over the world; among them was also his. That pharmaceutical company's headquarters were in the heart of Paris in a very modern building. He booked at the George V Hotel, as it was always his wish to stay in that hotel as a customer and not as a practicant at the kitchen many years ago.

Indeed, so it happened, that hotel was famous for the best croissants in the world, and indeed, so were these. He ate seven as indeed they were a breakfast marvel. After that unforgettable breakfast, he went to the contest meeting.

At the entrance, he showed his name card and passport (the security measures were very strict) and was allowed to enter and was guided to the room where another nine guys were waiting. Four of them he knew from the different conventions and fairs.

Each was called inside to present his ideas and how he works and what system he possesses and convince them that he can be among the three that are to be finally selected to cover all Europe.

Europe was divided in three parts, cantons let us say. The first 'canton' was France-Spain-Portugal-Italy-Greece, the second was all the Scandinavian countries, plus Holland and Belgium, and the last, the third and maybe the most significant, according to the volume of sales, was Germany-Austria–Swiss and some important eastern countries.

He was sixth in the row to make his presentation, and he had nothing else but to show photos (as at those times there were no laptops yet) and results of the searches, plus the well-presented functionality of the unique platform 'Pandora'.

All in that room were impressed. All 10 passed the first test, and the four were excluded, and there still remained six to compete.

They again were called inside one by one to make the last and final more particularly specialised contest, and that was for a specific drug that refers to pathologists and what is the appropriate promotional gift within the given target price. They had to suggest six ideas in the last 10 minutes.

It was quite easy for him as his specialty was pharmaceutical companies. But all the rest were also as the invitation came from the sister companies in all countries with the question 'who is your best local supplier for promoting gifts?'.

He was the fastest to suggest six ideas and left the room. All six nominees concluded their presentation, and now they had to wait one hour for the decision. George V Hotel was nearby, and instead of waiting there, he went to his room, took off his shoes, and rested.

After one hour, he returned; the lady in charge came announcing that these three of them (she gave names) were not to be in the final list and among them was not him. So, he knew that he was among the three selected ones, the winners.

All three, one Dutch, one British and himself, the Greek, were in front of the committee. To his big surprise and gratification, he was the one for the number three territory/canton that included Germany, the major country for such promotional pharmaceutical gifts. They thanked them and informed all three that they would get a letter with all details and contact names.

It was a great success, and he went back home with a big achievement in his luggage. Two weeks passed, and the much-expected letter arrived, and to his surprise, outrage, and anger, he read that the German company refused to accept as their exclusive supplier for their doctors' gifts a Greek company.

That was a typical racist action. He wrote a letter to both headquarters and that German director saying that this was an outrageous, unfair action that Europe does not deserve.

He had to forget that with bitterness as things were and look ahead.

Life was not easy being public. The shareholders were calling him to push for bigger sales, bigger profit announcements for quarter and semester results; this pressure pushed him to make mistakes. He put his personal attention more to the share and less to the business.

He left the business to be run by his managers, but they all proved to be insufficient in the managerial running of the business and followed the methods he was inventing to keep the company growing. He had to do something as he already had almost 60% of the market, but this was already the roof; at the same time, competitors started stealing small pieces of his market share.

He started the first online shop in Greece for novelties and gadgets, and it started progressing very well. Again, his collaborators could not continue what he was building, and that was also driven to an abrupt cease of continuation.

He, following the suggestions of one of his managers, ran out of cash by buying many upgraded printing machines that, in fact, were not needed. So, no capital to support his imports, salesmen were coming in having in hand big orders, but as no company gave a deposit, he had to finance the imports, and with no cash, the orders were cancelled.

A competitor, who in fact was a nothing, won a lottery, and all of a sudden, they found his small company with a lot of cash. He 'bought'—this is the right word—his best staff, the three best salesmen, by giving them not only big salaries but also cash upfront as a gift for moving to his company.

He even tempted them with high salaries, as did his two purchasing managers, who taught them the business and passed them all the suppliers he had in China.

So, he had to react and react fast. He put as collateral his building and got a loan of 2.5 million euros.

He had a friend who was living in Sofia, Bulgaria. He said, "Let's go to Bulgaria to see what the situation there is." His eyes opened widely, and he could see there was a future in real estate.

He used those 2.5 million and opened his Bulgarian company, starting to buy plot by plot, piece by piece.

The 2,500,000 euros he invested in this country was huge money, and he was maybe the biggest investor of those times to invest in Bulgaria. He was invited by the prime minister. They stretched the red carpet for him. He was there from one side of a huge wooden communistic type of table, and on the other side was almost the whole ministry council.

He bought piece by piece of 560 acres from 560 Bulgarians, one by one bringing them to the notary office to sign the contract; some even came with Kalashnikov on the table.

He had to bring small owners or co-owners from Cuba and Canada, owners who had a small piece of earth and had to pay all the trip expenses to come and sign the contracts.

He finally was the only owner, the sole owner of the biggest estate in Bulgaria, and that was in front of the Sofia airport. His Bulgarian company went public at the Bulgaria stock exchange.

Simultaneously, in Sofia, he acquired a good emerging telecommunications company and managed to run well and also went public at the Sofia stock exchange.

After reaching quite good capitalisation, he sold that communications company to another public company, obtaining a good profit.

With that money, his Greek public company acquired a close-to-bankruptcy company in the computer and software field, which he managed to bring to stable feet and later contributed a lot to improve his award-winning and internationally known Pandora software, revolutionising the incorporate search engine, focusing exclusively on achieving growth in the field of advertising and promotional gifts.

Banks were pushing him to sell that huge Sofia plot. He did not want to sell as he noticed that the real estate business was growing fast in Bulgaria. The banks made an estimation that this had a value of 4.5 million. He told them, "You must be crazy. I will never sell it at such a low price."

So, the offers started coming: 5 million from Spain, 6 million from America, 7 million from a Greek ship owner and finally 8 million from a Jewish American company.

He pointed out to the banks that it was a 'crime' and a big mistake to sell even at 8 million euros. They objected and told him that this was the deal of the year buying the plot at 2.5 million euros and selling at 8 million euros and only in one year.

He said, yes, this is small money for this plot. But they put the knife to his throat, and he had to sell it, and despite their assurances that the money would be split between banks and his company as working capital, they did not keep their word and agreement and took the biggest part of the money, leaving the company back in Greece with peanuts working capital.

The agreement that was made with the banks was 'betrayed'. The Jewish American buyer sold that plot only six months later for 50 million dollars to an American fund. When the banks heard that, they asked for their apologies for not listening to him, but it was too late as they ruined him.

While in Bulgaria, he had contacts with officials in the city of Ruse. Ruse is the northern city of Bulgaria, right on the River Danube and at the borders with Romania. Ruse is also known for the most beautiful women of Bulgaria.

The officials offered him a big plot inside an already big abandoned factory. A brilliant idea came to him.

The main items for the promotional gifts business were the bags, all types of bags, such as sports bags, backpacks, travel bags, waist bags, cosmetic bags, rucksacks, etc.

Bags represent the 70% of all the promotional gifts inquiries. All these bags are all imported from China, but the shipping time to reach a container from China to Hamburg is more than 30 days and nowadays even 45 days, and this is a huge problem, and many orders were never placed.

Bulgaria has cheaper labour costs than China and is so close to central European countries.

Through Danube, the ship reaches Frankfurt in only one to two days. So, why not produce all those bags in Ruse that would be cheaper and, at the same time, just one to two days away from Germany. He mentions Germany often because Germany is the biggest market for promotional products.

He called his major Chinese maker to come to Greece and then together flew to Bulgaria to stay two days in a factory that was producing clothes and dresses as well as swimming suits, so he checked the capacity of the Bulgarian workers in comparison with the Chinese workers.

He stayed there one day, and the outcome was that the Bulgarian workers, mainly women, reached 90% of the working ability of the equivalent Chinese women workers.

So, this seemed to be very positive and encouraging. The next day, they flew to Ruse to inspect that factory, and he was impressed by the good condition that this was and how big that was.

Funny was the night at the hotel. He ordered two girls, and two big women came, nice with big tits. When the small Chinese guy saw these big women with the big tits, he looked at him as if he wanted to tell him 'how can I manage such big woman with my rather small penis?'.

He took him inside the bedroom, and he told him, "Well, this is a fantastic chance for you to be in bed and fuck such a big woman; you will remember forever and narrate to your friends in China."

He agreed and answered, "OK, I will try my best."

When the girls left, he told him that he could not imagine there existed such big women; he was telling him that he put his head between her tits, and his head disappeared in there; he said his penis was inside doing the job, and suddenly, she turned around and told him, "At last, when you will put in your penis inside?"

He answered, "I have been inside you for a long time, and I will come in two seconds." That was so funny.

So, back to the factory, it all seemed to be a good idea that could bring huge money. Greek banks that were installed in Bulgaria showed interest in this project.

The Chinese guy expressed a big interest to be a partner in this, and he said that he could send many machineries, such as stitching and sewing from China that he had as surplus in his factory but also get more from neighbouring factories.

They sat down to discuss details, but there was always a 'but'. Where will they get the materials and the numerous material colours? The accessories, the zippers, the zipper pullers, the buttons, the threads, etc. had to be imported again by China.

So, the brilliant project collapsed with a big noise.

A sad incident carved his existence, bringing his life almost to the end. During those negotiations for the selling of his plot, one Saturday, that Greek friend, who had helped him a lot to buy that plot from hundreds of Bulgarians, came to his office with a Greek businessman who was also public to the Greek stock exchange.

He then went down to open the black iron gate of the building and bring them to his office, which was on the fifth floor, where he had a full view of the sea and even Aegina Island.

That very moment, he felt that something was going wrong with his chest. They went up to his office and started the negotiations to sell the plot. During those bargains and dealings, he felt a big pain in his chest, and he told them, "Gentlemen, there is a problem, and we must stop right now." His friend walked that businessman to the exit and returned to him.

In the meantime, Areus went down to the third floor, where his bed was, and before lying on the bed, he took two aspirin pills. His friend came back. It was Saturday; his wife was out. His friend called her, and she was at the hairdresser's, hearing the bad news, she stopped and rushed back to the house.

He told his friend, "This is not anything to worry as I had the same but slightly less yesterday, and after I took two pills, it went back to normal." Here is a lesson, the heart always gives a first warning.

Luckily for him, that friend read in a newspaper just a day before coming with that businessman to his office what the symptoms of a heart attack were.

Before his friend came, him lying on his bed, he stared up to a big Byzantine-originated icon of art showing Christ. That was the only piece he took from his father's home when he died; his father had that on the wall above his bed.

So, looking at Christ, although he couldn't say that he was a fanatic Christian, he spoke to him. "Eh, you guy, why you abandon me?"

His friend came and told him, "This is a heart attack, and you have to go to the hospital."

He answered to him, "No, this is not so, and soon I will be OK." But the 'blessed' friend, without asking him, ordered the ambulance.

His wife and his daughter arrived; his younger daughter was abroad and was informed what happened, and she rushed to return. The ambulance car arrived, and heading to the hospital, the car was stopped as there was a big demonstration in front of the American Embassy, and the hospital was right there.

The driver made many efforts and manoeuvres to drive through all these people, and they lost more the 20 minutes. They, at last, reached the hospital, and they checked his heart first down at the primary emergency section, and immediately, they gave order to bring him up to the ultra-emergency last floor.

The guy who was driving him up could not find an available lift, and he was running like hell, while he never believed that he was about to die, he told him, "Look, calm down. I will not die from heart attack, but you will kill me in a hospital traffic accident." And he laughed, him not being aware that his life was few minutes before the end.

They reached the last floor where the emergency big room was, and luckily for him, some young doctors and an older one with big experience, they all went to him, activating all the needed injections for a thrombolysis.

The pain on the chest became unbearable but giving him all needed medicine and injections, and thank God that pain started to slow down.

They later told him that two major arteries were blocked almost to at 90%. He stayed there during the emergency for two nights, and then they brought him down to his room. He stayed there one more night, and next day, they were to proceed to more examinations. He could not stay there secretly, and without any approval of the doctors, he put on his coat, took a taxi and went back home.

It was not only that he wanted to return home but to stay longer in the hospital. His office staff would suspect that something was going wrong and the rumours might start spreading around, and that could reach newspapers so his stock value at the stock exchange would fall down dramatically with big offers and less demands.

After two weeks, he then went to the appropriate cardiology hospital where the president was a friend of his from the military service, and they put two stents in his arteries. Since then, never ever had his heart to annoy him.

He gave an oath that after 10 years, he walks that distance but on foot from his home to that first hospital opposite to the American Embassy.

They say that when you have a heart attack in the first 10 years, you might get it again, and this time, it will be fatal. Indeed, he went by foot all this distance, passing also by the cemetery where his parents were buried and put one rose on their tomb.
So, he fulfilled his oath by walking 25 kilometres.

It is worthwhile to mention here that the religious icon coming from the Byzantine ages originated from his ancestors. That was above the bed of his father and then after he died was also opposite to his bed.

One day, before his father died, that icon fell down with a loud crash noise. This happened again in his bedroom one day before the heart attack, with a big crashing sound that he and his wife believed was the TV that exploded.

Was it a coincidence, or was it a sign that Christ was warning him?

While in Sofia, so many times, he had a taxi driver; his name was Zlaten, to whom, before flying to Sofia, he was ordering a girl in his hotel, and so he knew that at night at 10 a girl would knock on his door.

Ninety percent of them were very beautiful as Zlaten knew well that he paid more to get the best girl he had in his selection. The best girl and despite the big demand from many especially Greek businessmen who were visiting Sofia and needed a girl. In those times it was not so easy to find such beautiful girls and in decent hotel rooms in Greece.

Then 10–20 years later started the 'wave' of Russian, Ukrainian and Romanian girls to arrive so Bulgarian girls were not that anymore in demand.

Zlaten one night send him a nice girl with an incredibly formidably shaped body, a body that, he can say, could easily be compared with all those film stars and most female famous singers.

That girl, Gerda was her name, was not a prostitute; she was married, but her husband was not at all a gentleman; on the contrary, he was a nasty bastard who abused her outrageously; he was the miserable evil person in their own home. He did not have any permanent job, so not enough money in the family; she also had a daughter with him.

He came almost every night home drunk, and she had no sex for months, so she, as a young and beautiful girl, was missing and desiring a good sex. So, she told to Zlaten that she would do this for money, as the money was heavily needed, but she does not want any old and fat men, so he chose for her mature men but with good 'record' and behaviour, large in tips and good-looking.

He kept a record of who of his clients are giving good tip, who are gentle and not violent, who are not asking for anomalies and never creates any problems for his girls.

So, Gerda came one night, starting to undress herself so attractively and slowly that he could not spend any minute waiting for his penis to rise up.

Seeing this, she was happy that she did not have to make extra efforts, which is usually needed to have the man who she was about to have sex to bring him to an erection. She was completely nude, turned around to go to the shower, showing him her wonderful arse.

She came out of the shower and came right next to him, touching his dick, expressing adoration for the perfect erection with an awesome smile.

He was a professional and expert pussy licker; he asked her to just open her legs, and she distinguished his intentions. She did this with pleasure, flashing her pussy, and there he was licking her pussy with his 'master' tongue.

It seemed to him that she, as a 'prostitute', no one ever licked her pussy, or maybe she did not allow this to happen.

She was crazy; she was up in the air with lust and sexual explosion; derived from the lack of sex for weeks or months, she grabbed his head and dragged down to her pussy at the same time nuzzled her pussy towards his tongue, and so she came with spasms and shattering moans and overwhelming pleasure, while his chin was wet from the vagina juices.

She right away went down and started licking his penis; this was very seldom those girls did; they always ask for condom to do this, but she was in such a sexual excitation that she wanted to please him for what he just offered to her to reach such a great climax.

A charming intercourse followed. He use the word charming as it was not any violent or aggressive sex but smooth and synchronised, having two sex partners in a perfect coordination. Reaching almost to the climax, he stopped and wanted to lick her asshole, but she was ready to come for a second time and exclaimed to him, "No, please return to my ready pussy," and indeed after few seconds, she came one more time, showing him with a sign of appreciation the pleasure she had, and at the same time, the 'approval' for him to lick her perfect from point of view of morphology anus, and he also with loud groans as her hand expertly and between her legs gave him a professional handjob.

It was good that no one passed by the floor corridor, because hearing those groans, he would think that there was a murderer in that room.

Furthermore, that girl when they were performing the so-called 'scissors or pretzel' position and both partners' legs the one goes in the other legs, so having easy access to his anus, she had a fetish and that was to put a finger in his anus. In the beginning, he took her hand away from there; she again did it, and then he let her do it, as it seemed to him that was a nice extra to her overall sex 'additives'.

He asked her why that; she told him that this makes her even more horny, proving that he was not the only fucker on that fucking bed, and as she said, many men in the beginning react peculiarly, but then they showed some fondness for it, and the next time, they even asked for this.

These girls, if you do not offer them good sex, they never come to climax, or they pretend that they come, and many in order to make you believe that you are a good performer, they scream loudly, pretending that they enjoyed, so the man accelerates believing that he is the best sex performer in town.

She left and kissed him on the mouth as real lovers as she indeed was offering him frank sexual moments and not considering him as a client. He ordered her to come again and again, and many times, he paid her double to stay longer, so they had repeated sex performances.

Having her phone number, usually these girls were not allowed to give their phone number or they would lose their job, but she gave him because she trusted him.

So, before leaving Athens for Sofia, he was calling her, and she was so happy that she would meet him and have that special sex he was offering to her, which was for her an incredibly required and longing sex having not any at all with that punk as husband.

Two times, which is very seldom, she allowed to make sex with him without condom as she was to meet him after not any sex for 10 days with anyone and him first that night and not any other for again another 10 days, as she slowly was removing her disposal from that paid sex hotel visits as she found a day office job.

Always, after their usual good sex and him paying her very well, she would return home, thanking him for the quality sex moments he offered to her apart from the good money. One time, he even could not pull out in time and had all his load to rest in her vagina, and if that brought later on any baby, he would never know.

His Athens business was somehow fading, but before he was to get in bankruptcy, he made a last attempt to have the market finance him, and he opened the first big store of houseware novelty items. The first store they went to found him buying from local importers, so they, in fact, financed him.

In one year, there were 12 such big stores until IKEA came to Athens, and, more or less, a 40% of what he was selling at their chain of stores, they were also selling and IKEA much cheaper at and additionally by distributing 1 million huge IKEA catalogues and making big advertising on TV; it was a fierce and uneven competition. Inevitably, it went bankrupt as a result of wanton spending on excessive advertising and sending millions of leaflets, and finally it happened.

The company finally went into liquidation, and this was the end of a brilliant and long, with many ups and downs, adventure.

He was the most stupid public company owner in the history as he sold, when the company was high up with 55 million euros of value, only 8% of the shares, and even that money he put back into the company, trying to save it.

The wise was that his wife before any problems at all appeared with the company sold shares of a value of €500,000.

The money, he advised her to send to his very best and very honest Chinese supplier and invest in his business. His business was based on his recommendation to all group's members, and he became almost the exclusive supplier of the group, making good money. That invested money turned on a later date the board life saver.

Given his economic situation, suddenly appeared, as if he came from the sky, a Greek guy who knew that he was an acclaimed guru in the specific business after the recommendation of the bank manageress who respected his abilities. He told him what if they start a collaboration. He said, "Look, there is plenty of cash money, let us start again but under my existing company."

So Areus, a 65-year-old guy, started visiting the big companies again. They all knew who he was and what deep knowledge he had in the promotional field. The orders, although that was a one-man business, started coming one after the other, bringing revenues and good profits, so he started feeling himself again able to stand on his feet.

At that stage, he got a letter from a once-upon-a-time employee, a Chinese young man whom he had employed two years ago, to his company to have a Chinese guy to talk to his Chinese suppliers.

He told him that he has a small company dealing with what he taught him, advertising and promotional gifts, but he did almost nothing but small, non-significant orders that allowed him not to survive and keep his family in any good status.

The idea came to his mind to start a business with him as a partner. He had no capital but placed orders to him from Greece before stopping cooperation with that Greek kind, 'saviour' fellow; he passed him quite some orders with 5% commissions, and gradually, they created a small capital.

That Chinese young man, he even had no 15 dollars to register the website that Areus created, because that must be under the name of the Chinese guy. A Chinese website registered to a Greek guy sounds no good to the eyes of European buyers.

So, it started; Areus did all the Chinese guy had nothing to do, just follow the orders.

He started sending flyers, under his Chinese name, and he used the name of Liu (his fake Chinese name), to thousands of mainly German and European companies. Those flyers with ideas and photos on the buyers' monitor and with just a single glance one could see the new ideas, was a 'revolutionary' idea. Interesting inquiries were coming in bulk.

He did all this, despite the fact that he was not in China but 7000 kilometres far away; he was one to find the Chinese makers for each item; he to negotiate the buying prices with both Chinese makers, and he also to offer the selling prices to the German buyers.

Of course, he could not present himself as Greek so he always used the name Liu, so the German buyer knew that they were dealing with a Chinese guy and the whole idea worked fine. The business started to grow amazingly fast.

Back in Greece, the banks put all the buildings in public auction floor by floor. Here comes his wife's clever idea to send the 500,000 euros to China to his good honest friend, and he opened under his name, a Hong Kong company, depositing her money.

So, as Hong Kong company, plus lending money from friends and relatives and additional bank loan under the name of the younger daughter and collateral the only flat that was with not any burdens, they started taking part in the public auction, getting back floor by floor, basement by basement, and so this was indeed a marvel to have now the building back that has, due after the increase of the recent real estate market, a value of 4 million euros.

The year was 2005, and the business in China was booming until that partner guy started to think that as he by then has the capital, ideas passed through his mind that he can do the business without Areus as a partner. In those times, they got a huge order of 10 million dollars, one of the biggest ever in their field, for a big worldwide promotion of a famous petroleum company.

Areus made big negotiations and bargains with several Chinese makers as that order was so big that not a single maker could take over and had to place the order to several makers, and at the same time, he also made the big deal with the customer.

That order with the humblest calculations was allowing a profit of 600,000 dollars. The time was passing, and the deliveries started. The Chinese partner started telling him that he had to pay more money here and more money there with different reasons and unjustified excuses.

He could see what he had in his mind, and at the very end, that bloody Chinese crook partner announced that the final profit went down to just 50,000 dollars. He was crazy, and he stopped the partnership as he became a big cheater, and the guy who had not 15 dollars in his pocket to register the website in his name, suddenly, he was very rich.

Rich enough to pay and have two children as at that time in China, one was allowed to have one only child except if one had money and could pay and have one more. He was telling him lies that he wants to go to his home city and open a restaurant, but that all was nothing but lies.

That guy wanted him to leave the cooperation and leave him his German customers and a big database with a good Chinese suppliers list that was created for years and only by Areus himself.

Suddenly, he was without a partner in China. He tried another and another, and they were all cheaters. Coincidentally, he read at Alibaba that there was a German guy living in Shanghai doing business in promotion or rather in stationery. He contacted him, and they agreed to cooperate, explaining to him that he was the pioneer and absolute guru in the promotional gifts sector.

He was operating under a Chinese company owned by a Chinese lady, and as a foreigner, he was not allowed to be the owner of a Chinese company. Before even starting, he got an email from the lady owner of the company that this German guy left the company, but she was willing to cooperate with him.

She had no idea at all what advertising gifts, giveaways and promotional gifts were, so he told her no need for her to know, he would do all; she only had to do quality control after he gets the orders. She was a real lady; honest ladies are very seldom to be found in China.

Now he had to change his name from Liu to a feminine pseudonym name of Victoria, so for the Germans he was Mrs Victoria, a Chinese saleswoman. He did that as he felt compelled to hide his true identity as the Germans would not feel comfortable dealing with China but through a Greek guy.

In those times, the big business in promotion was the beer companies in Germany. There was huge competition among the breweries.

Too many brands and they all were looking for the best gift idea to sell to wholesalers a full crate of beers adding an attractive gift, either this was a bag or a pocket knife or a pocket tool or picnic blanket, or beach items, depending on the season.

Him being an expert to suggest ideas, the orders started coming in volumes and fast; that lady partner could not believe that he was bringing so many orders so fast and with very good profit percentage.

Victoria helped even the German company to extend their range of business to other sectors and opened their eyes to go for new business and not only promotional gifts, and they were grateful to Victoria.

The old cheater came back to him, telling that he was not doing well and humbly begged him to go back with him, even offering him an upfront big amount, but he was engraved in his memory as a cheater so that guy later lost all.

Well, what is his current situation? Despite his age of 69, he still works like hell (Victoria), waking up at 4 o'clock in the morning to be at the same time with the Chinese makers and suppliers and also the Shanghai office and stay late until 8 o'clock to be online with the Germans' working hours.

Still playing tennis, taking part in tournaments, beating, even nullifying the age superiority of the opponent players of 30 and 35 years old. He swam almost daily 1 or even 1½ miles but very strong athletic swimming, and climbing mountains that took four and five hours had an ideal physical body standard.

Back to the liquidation of his company, at the age of 65, he was completely broke. He did not have money to pay even the electricity, and they even cut it; he was living in the dark.

Here, it is must to clarify that the bankruptcy and the liquidation came at the same time, so he found the way to skip the bankruptcy and go to liquidation so that all his staff get all their money, even reimbursement money for all the years they were with him, so all the staff left happy and with a lot of money. In fact, the company left a big property of high value, so all staff got well paid.

A bankruptcy or liquidation is always followed by many headaches and problems.

Many suppliers sued him, and they had the whole right to do so. Lawyers for such lawsuits cost huge money.

At the courts, he lived in disgusting situations, many perjuries, many fake witnesses that could bring false convictions, which meant more money to make appeals, many false sentences, which brought prison sentences but with suspension and could get paid off.

Court of law cases with the state owing taxes.

A disturbing case of a corrupted tax controller, who came to make accounting control and because he was not bribed, he created huge false and fake problems as revenge. That reached 1 million euros as penalty, an outrageous action of that disgraceful tax controller who got no money but get money for what as the accounting of the company was impeccable. This fake report followed Areus later in his life. Areus appealed to the special committee to resolve tax differences. The committee justified him, but the tax bureau ignored them, and the penalty remained.

In all cases, there was not in any court proved any fraud or deceit.

But that fraud penalty of that nefarious tax controller changed his life seriously.

The lawyer advised him to stay in his home and not circulate too much as if they caught him, then he would be in trouble. In fact, it was correct that if three years passed, the penalty would become much less.

He anyway did not go out as all his business was operated from his office with his computer and his three monitors in a nice environment, overlooking the sea and the Aegina Island, so there was no need to go out.

So, it happened, but one day, his daughter was away for vacations on an island, and he had to take care of the small black French bulldog. His food was finished, so he had to go buy food for him. The old black jeep ran out of battery, and in that jeep, he had all his credentials (ID and driving licence) so he had to take his daughter's even much older (30 years old) jeep, and he went to buy food for the dog.

To his bad luck, two days ago police found in that area a jeep with hidden drugs. So, they stopped all jeeps. They searched his jeep; they, of course, found nothing, and then they asked him for his ID or driving licence. To his stupid bad luck, he had left those in the other jeep, so he had nothing to show them.

They said, no problem, give us your name, and they will find your identity. Searching on their mobile phone data, there they found that there was one pending warrant due to that fake tax controller's penalty.

So, they asked him to follow them to the nearby police station. He started trembling, knowing that the coming developments would be bad.

The officer went up to the office and to the files, and they found that one single pending warrant took him down to the police cell jail.

Here, starts his Odyssey.

He was always proudly, rather stupidly, saying to his friends that in his life he experienced everything except jail, and here he was to fill up this gap.

That police small jail was 1 metre × 2 metres. Him being claustrophobic, he was feeling horribly; he wanted to break his head on the bars. He was there for seven hours, thank God, that police station was almost next to his house so his wife and daughters brought him a sandwich and some water; they also brought him enough money in case it was needed. He stayed these seven hours looking down, avoiding by all means to see that he was in such a narrow cage (police prison), or else the claustrophobia could bring him into an uncontrolled situation.

Everybody in the police station respected him face wise and viewpoint; he looked gentle, and they all asked him to have patience; in fact, he hated that word as it was also repeated by his wife and daughter. Late in the afternoon, they came to tell him that they moved him to the nicest suburb of Athens, where the police have cells/jail with showers and beds, etc.

So, he felt better, and indeed, a police car drove him there; he was supposed to be lucky to be transferred there, but for how long, no one yet knew.

His lawyer was informed and started the process to free him from there. In fact, he was telling the lawyer all the time to merge the two tax convictions and pay and avoid any prison. Although he was paid for this, he did not do it, and this would take quite some weeks to be done.

They arrived at the police station; indeed, it was nice outside, and inside the officers cordially welcomed him as they knew that he neither was a drug dealer nor a criminal, but he was here for owing taxes to the state.

So, he told them as a joke, "Where is my suite?" They said two basements down, so here they brought him down in an almost complete dark 'jail' with a faded light, like a candle.

The door bars opened, and here he was. The place was terribly dirty, the smell of cigarettes unbearable. He looks down, and he saw thousands of thrown cigarettes on the ground forming a mountain of used cigarettes. The rooms were three; the beds were stone beds with dirty mattresses, all in there stinking.

He was angry; he had to shout so loud that they would hear him to come after many shouts and attempts to be heard. After all, they came, and he told them, "What the hell is this? Are you proud of this? Animals will stay here? Bring me a broom and shovel, and I will clean the place." Just the room that he will stay and sleep. At the same time, he called his home to bring sheets and blankets as well as water and a sandwich, but in fact, he had no appetite at all. They also brought him a book and newspaper to pass his time, but how to read, there was almost no light.

They brought a broom and shovel, and they showed kind of willingness to help him with the cleaning.

So, his room got rid of the mountain of the smoked cigarettes.

Family came and brought what he wanted. They did not allow them to see him but only between bars, they passed the sheets. They were crying, seeing where he was in that dungeon.

He then went to see the next room, and there he saw leftovers of food on the floor and tens of cockroaches patrolling around that food. God knows how long the dirty food was there.

So, he went to the bathroom, and the so-called showers were both used as a shitting place. Shits all over. He tried to wash his hands, and what he saw, the water fell on his shoes; there was not any pipe to channel the water to any sewer.

He was crazy; he took photos to send to the ministry and the city hall where that shameful 'hole' was. So, then he checked the other room, and what did he see there? Half-naked, black kind of 'man'. Later, he heard that he claimed that he was Iranian, but he looked kind of Indonesian or Pakistani.

He was angry at him because he cleaned the place from the mountain, smoked cigarettes as he was searching one by one and with a lighter, tried to smoke just whatever smoke was left and threw away and to the next and to the next and so on.

He was in a situation to cry. They described that he would be in paradise, but that it is worse than hell. For sure, all those that described that place as paradise were never down there to see the reality, so he does not blame them.

He laid on the bed, and there he saw that black, dirty, half-naked kind of 'anthropoid' look at him with hate; he threatened him and showed him his genitals. He stood up looked at him very angrily, and with an extremely loud voice he shouted at him, "Get the fuck out of here." He got scared; he saw a rather old man, and he did not believe that he would react in such a wild and dynamic way.

A loud voice was heard, and then two policemen came down. He told them, "Either you take him out of here or lock me in a cell so that he cannot come to me. Having a lighter, he is always an active danger."

They did not know what to do; what they only knew was that at midnight it was expected that they would come to get him and take to jail. So, inevitably to protect him, they took him up to the police balcony with a nice view, and he felt like a human being. Indeed, they came and took that son of the bitch, and he was back to his 'suite' alone.

He slept as he was so tired after he sprayed the place, and this, they allowed him to use it one time and took it back. They always took the laces of the shoes, probably for two reasons: not to hang yourself or to not asphyxiate other prisoner or maybe also without laces in case you escape, you cannot run.

The days were passing, and he was always in that dump hole down there. Sometimes in the day, they took him up to stay at the balcony so as to see the daylight as down there no daylight was to be seen. He was protesting to the lawyer, but he was calming him, saying and promising tomorrow and again tomorrow and so on.

Unfortunately, instead of the big jail in Athens, they sent him to the jail of Larissa (300 kilometres away from Athens). This he got to know later.

The fifth day arrived, and he was always down there; many came overnight all these days, mostly drug users or burglars. He removed all the mattresses from his room so that they could go to sleep in the other two rooms. One was a Greek guy who told him that they would take him to a jail in the south, and he had not a single euro in his pocket; he gave him 100 euros, and he thanked him a lot.

The fifth night, at 4 o'clock, they woke him up; they said to get dressed to go to the centre of where all prisoners were to be sent to their final jail. With difficulty, he called his daughter, asking her to go to that hole and get all his stuff as he was on the way to a jail that he did not know which one it would be.

Later, the daughter that came to pick all his stuff from that 'hole' and told him when he was back, that she could not believe how it was possible for him to live and sleep in that filthy basement shit hole.

They arrived at the in-between kind of jail room, one more time in a small room with most of them to be Albanians and Pakistanis and only one Greek young man. Among them was also a small 100% looking like an anthropoid or better monkey, never seen before, uglier creature. That small Pakistani was coming next to him wherever he was; he moved, but he followed to come closer to him, most probably, they are so skilful and able to steal from pockets money.

After waiting there for three endless hours, a huge bus came that was the prisoners' jail bus. What a bus! That was a bus with small cages of 1 metre by 1 metre with two metallic benches that were supposed to take four prisoners inside.

So, there was him and that sympathetic young man, and two Pakistanis slipped in. He loudly protested to the guards, "You have plenty of space at the last part of the bus, so move them out. I cannot breathe. I suffer from claustrophobia." So, they moved them away to the back of the bus.

That huge bus with maybe 20 prisoners was moving very slowly as that was the peak traffic time in Athens and had to pass by many prisons to pick up prisoners to move them to other jails to other cities all to the northern part and many to the big Larissa jail.

He felt so bad, so narrow in that cage prison, the young man was always anxious to see the Larissa jail; he was telling him that he was many times in jail but never in Larissa.

He asked him, "Why? You are a good-looking man; you look also well-educated, why jails all the time?" He said to survive the only easy way was to move drugs around as a drug mule.

They also passed by the women's jails, and there, six girls came, all of them probably from Thailand and two of them looking very nice. These girls were also locked in small cages. They suffered by the rest of the Pakistanis in there, teasing them about their cunts and assholes, all dirty words; leader of those all was that monkey-looking creature; they all spoke quite good Greek, meaning they were illegally in Greece for some years.

The prisoners, after three hours' drive, protested and asked the guards and drivers to stop somewhere to pee. They denied, but it started to be dangerous, a kind of small riot in the bus, so they decided to stop, and one by one, they went down to a small toilet to pee. He remembered when the girls went down to pee, those guys were telling them so many dirty words like, "Darling, I want to come and clean up your cunt or your asshole." Those girls indeed suffered.

After long, they arrived at the Larissa jail; most of them had many things with them, mattresses, blankets, sheet, towels, everything; he was the only not to have not anything, and this was because of lack of experience, believing that, as he saw in films, that jail supports all prisoners with clean sheets, pillow, towels, blankets, etc.

So, he only had just a plastic bag wherein he had a toilet paper, a box of tissue papers, some baby's kind soft wet tissues, his earbuds and his mobile phone with charger; that was all.

They were making the queue, and they told them that all would be taken from them, including the mobile phone. He was searching in that bag with his mobile phone to call family and tell them where he was, but the mobile phone was nowhere to be found.

He turned that bag upside down; his mobile phone was nowhere, until they entered the first inspection rooms. He thought maybe the mobile phone they kept at first in between to move building for the final jail; he could not get any other explanation, or it was stolen by the guards themselves.

There, he had again another two hours of waiting; he called a guard saying, "Look, I am an old man and need to go to the toilet."

He said not allowed; he was about to cry. The guard saw this; he said wait; he asked a superior, and they indeed gave the OK, and he was accompanied to the toilet.

They called him in the director's office to ask him if he arranged with his lawyer for a short stay in jail; he said yes so it is. He told them that he had a heart attack and he takes pills. They asked him if he knew which pills; he said not because this was what his wife prepares, and she gets ready for him to swallow.

So, he had to call his home and ask for the pills and also tell them that he was at Larissa jail, and at the same time, he asked them to call and push that bloody lawyer to get him out of jail.

He was the only one who had certificates for all three vaccines, so the director was asked where they should send him as he had all vaccines. He said he would be out soon so send him to the big quarantine room. They took him there after they took all except the toilet paper and a towel. Thank God, he had with him the wet tissues and his earbuds and also; he had pills for two days.

They went there, and he saw a big room where more than 50 prisoners were there of different races, colours and countries. When they saw him, they called him, 'Uncle', and they politely rushed to get a mattress for his 'bed' next to another Greek guy who was also old, but although he was 20 years younger than him, he was looking 20 years older, and that was why they gave him the name of 'granddaddy'.

So, here he was; they all had sheets and blankets; he had nothing on. He found one empty bed and took two blankets and put his towel under that, kind of 'pillow', so as not to touch that dirty mattress and blankets that formed a kind of pillow.

At least here there was daylight, but they were not allowed to have an exit outside for walking to the prison yard. Before coming, he had to deliver his money, and they gave him red and yellow chips for the money that he exchanged so that he could buy a coffee or a glass of water and also bought two telephone cards as there was one card telephone in that room.

After only two hours, he was called; he hoped that it was the time that the lawyer fixed everything, and he was to go. He asked, "Shall I take my bag with me?" They said no.

They took him to the director's office; they asked him to sit, and there was a sofa. The second in command officer asked him if that teared off box of tissues was his. He said, "Yes, and they took it from me." Then he asked him if he had a mobile phone. He said, "Yes, and I lost it when I came before entering the door. I was searching like a madman to find the mobile phone to call my family to tell them where I am, but the mobile phone was nowhere to be found in that plastic bag."

Then he said with a strange look, they found it, but it was well hidden in the tissue box. He said, "Oh thank God, I did not lose it as this is precious for me with all my bank details and the e-banking and hundreds of useful phone numbers." He noticed that this guy, but not the director, was not convinced with his story. He went mad and angry and he told him, "Do you dare to think that I had this hidden in there, in that almost destroyed tissue box that became so teared off, after I was desperately looking for my mobile phone and probably this slipped between the tissue folds?"

Then he told him, "When I saw that the tissue box was from the very beginning a destroyed box and was taken from me, I did not react at all; if I had, as you say carefully hidden the mobile phone, would I not find an excuse to say, but where is my mobile phone? Oh, there it is between the tissue folds in that box so that I would not lose it if that box was to be thrown to the trash?"

They did not want to show that they were mistaken and at the end agreed that the whole was absolutely irrelevant and took him back to the quarantine room.

In that room, there were all foreigners, mainly Albanians and Pakistanis but also some from the Balkans (Serbians, Bulgarian, Skopians, and from Kosovo, etc.). Only him and that neighbour old guy and another who looked to play the role of the leader (the capo) and finally the young man who he was in that bus together, these were the only Greeks among 50. The Greek young man took the first bed at the entrance, and he was so organised he even had a television.

Then suddenly, a nearby guy with four others asked him, "Eh, Uncle, what do you believe that Skopia is Macedonia?"

He answered, "Look, I am Greek, and I will never call that country Macedonia; Skopia yes; Slavomacedonia maybe, but simply Macedonia, no." Seemed they looked angry at him.

He thought that this was a mistake. Who tells him that during the night they come and beat him? This is a routine action for them.

He was worried and concerned; he went to that young man who travelled together (Nikos was his name), and he assured him that if anyone dared to touch him, he would handle this so also told that to the Greek who had the viewpoint and attitude of being the 'capo' in that jail room.

The days were passing, and he was always on the phone, talking to his family and lawyer's assistants, who were running for his matter; they were assuring him that it was a question of one or maximum two more days and to be patient.

He said, "I do not want to hear that bloody word again, 'patient'. I am in jail. What patience can I show?"

That guy's neighbour had a difficulty with his ugly teeth, and his voice was so bad that he could not understand what he was saying, and at the same time, he was also having 40% less hearing ability from one ear; the conversation was a torture.

During the day, he was walking around to exercise, and then there was an Albanian who wanted to walk with him. He asked him why he was there; he said that he wanted to rob a house, but the owner was in, and there was a fight with the owner, and he shot him, but fortunately, he did not die; such good boys were there in that room. There were also two Africans, one from Sudan, and he remembered the adventure he had in Khartoum.

There were also three Arabs; he did not find out from which country, probably Iraq or Syria. They were praying to Allah three times per day. He was admiring their religion's dedication and how that prayer was so important for them. They had three rugs, and they put them down and prayed. They were just in front of his 'bed'. There, in front of him, they were shouting silently, "Allahu Akbar," bending down the head to reach the floor, and up again, they were holding their face and praying.

There was the leader, a very strong man with big muscles. He looked like a wrestler. He was in front, and he gave the command, and he was the one to pray in the Arabic language. One day, he was in real danger; they were there just in front of his bed, just half a metre away from his feet, and he was watching them, but then he wanted to fart, but he had to hold, imagining what would have happened if he farted while they were bending there; they would have killed him for sure for offending their religion. He prayed to God to help him to hold it, and with great difficulty, he managed to hold it and ran to the toilet.

His wife was very worried and concerned as he had left with nothing, not any jacket, not any second underwear, shirts and a pullover but also toothpaste and toothbrush. She was calling the jail, begging to give him something. One afternoon, he heard his name, and someone loudly said, "Here, clothes for you."

He said, "No need; tomorrow, I will be out."

He said, "Take and do whatever you want with them." He took, and then 10 of the guys rushed to him, please give me this, give me that. The guy next to him was the first to get; he had nothing; he gave to him socks and a pullover, and he was happy.

The next day, indeed, he was called, and this time, they told him take whatever you have, you leave the jail. They all came to say goodbye to him, 'giving fives'.

He then went to that young man, Nikos, and told him, "Promise, when you get out, you will never again do that drug dealer job." He also told them all, holding a small speech, telling them, "Love this country that give space to live and stay away from drugs, robberies and killings because you will come and go to prisons all the time."

Frankly, he was not sure if they disliked the idea of being in the prison as they had their free roof and food; they were playing a kind of chess game, and the time was passing for them pleasantly.

They took him to the office. They gave him his mobile phone and his small recorder that he asked for when he was in that previous police dark hole, wanting to tell his life story, which he is now writing.

He got his money and ran to get a taxi as the train was to arrive in five minutes. He told the driver, "Run as fast as you can, and I will give you double the fare." He managed through side roads to arrive at the same minute as the train; he went to buy a ticket; they told him it was now closed, and he can buy it in the train with a penalty, so he rushed and got into the first class.

He was a freeman again.

In the coupe of the train, there was just one man: a Jewish Belgian fellow. He told him that he was just released from the jail; he seemed afraid and worried; he told him not to worry, and that it was for taxation reasons.

He was soon with his family, and the first thing he did was to weigh himself. He had lost 7 kilos in 10 days. He went for a hot bath, being 11 days without a shower and a good dinner. That was a new experience, but after all, it was an experience that was missing from his quiver.

It has been 15 years since he last met his old times' good friends from the promotional gifts group. They had email contact, and one day, one of the members (they all retired from business except him; he was still working but with pleasure) suggested that they hold a meeting of the veterans 'Old Tiggers', so the meeting was called.

It was decided the meeting to take place either in Barcelona or in Milan. They asked Areus, and he said, "Sorry, guys, I want to see you by all means but having problems with the tax bureau, I do not dare to go to the ministry to extend the validation of my passport."

They then, with one voice, said, "We go to Athens as meeting without Areus is no meeting."

So, they all came, most with their wives. It was George from England, Marcel from Switzerland. Heino from Germany, Fritz from Austria, Saro from Rome, Timo from Finland, and Sedat from Turkey (the first four unfortunately by now are no more). They spent two exceptional days together at a nice seaside hotel with a lot of seafood from a nearby restaurant, where they all laughed so much, remembering so many funny moments during those many meetings all over the world. Many funny things had happened in the Dallas meeting. Areus was the one to orchestra the joy with his joke-telling. He remembered, in Dallas, when he arrived at the reception, he saw in the lobby, there were maybe 200 or more girls; he thought, *God, is this the paradise? Let me sleep the night, and tomorrow I will move in.* But the next morning, the lobby was empty. He asked the receptionist where all those girls were; he answered it was the L'Oréal meeting, and the meeting ended, and they were all gone. He also remembered they hired a car to go around to see more of Dallas on a Sunday.

The English good friend, George, bought a newspaper to read the news, so after reading, he made a ball out of that newspaper like a basketball, and from a distance, he threw that into a big trash bin. When that ball-shaped newspaper fell in that bin, a black man jumped out and shouted, "Eh, what the hell are you doing, man?"

Probably, he lived in there or was searching for valuables. On the way, they saw a hut, and on the top label, there was written 'Chamber of Commerce of Dallas'. What a laughter. They ended at a restaurant, and when the bill time came, the Belgium guy, another George (he also passed away), gave his credit card and his passport. The waitress looked strangely at the passport, saying, "What is this? This is nothing. I want your driving licence."

Seeing that they were many from different countries, she asked all where they came from? She also asked Areus, and he said Athens, Greece. "Oh. Athens. I know there is a nearby village called Athens, but what is Greece? There's no such village around here." So, much was to be remembered.

Back to the Old Tigers meeting, they took a tour to Acropolis and Plaka (the picturesque old city of Athens), where they had a great lunch and a last night for a drink and food, always at a seaside tavern with music; they all were in full mood.

He also recalled that while he was still in the group and also very active when he had developed the famous 'Pandora' software, four of the committee members came to visit his office to see that software.

They were crazy for the meatballs that they all ate for lunch at a nearby tavern, and in the night, he took them to a kind of strip tease nightclub, which was called at that time 'Diamonds and Pearls', and although they were rather conservative guys, they were crazy having extremely beautiful dancers to dance for each one and many times between each other's legs. They never forget that night and mention it for many years and also at the Old Tigers reunion.

At around the age of 68, he never showed any infidelity to his wife, with exception of the paid sex; after all, he was very frank. He promised to her on the very first day of their marriage, he would never have any affair but maybe pay for sex when he is away on business trips.

But after the 70s or even 75s, one feels maybe morally free from the pre-marriage statements of loyalty and fidelity as at that age, the wife, if she has the same age as her husband, seems not willing for any sex encounter.

So the sex shelter can be found with gorgeous Russian girls, but paying quite a lot having clean and good quality sex in five-star hotels.

There were many such experiences with Russian, Ukrainian, Romanian, Bulgarian and some Czech girls; girls who upgrade the sex to a science; girls who, yes, were paid, but he would rather prefer to call them Ladies with a capital L.

With good sex experience, there was nothing more satisfactory having those professional girls to bring them to climax.

It would sound to the ears of the readers kind of 'graphic' or rather an unreal belief that a man of 70 or 75 or even 80 years old is a sexually retired man; this is a total mistake that debunks that myth.

Age doesn't matter as the urges remain. A man feels and conducts his sexual life not according to what his ID mentions as age, but to what degree his libido can reach. So, never devalue the sexual ability of any man at whatever his age is.

The golden rule is, 'Whatever you abandon, it will abandon you.' So this is applicable to a man who at whatever age he reaches wrongly believes that this is 'enough'.

No, there is never enough. They must never allow the sexual desire to sleep; keep it always awake and keep busy with whatever means and you reserve surprise to your sexual partners. If a sexual partner is not temporarily available, then masturbation is a healthy solution.

Areus never abandoned physical training and fitness coaching even if there was not a gym nearby; he always travelled with his equipment, such as a metal bar to fix at the door and do pull-up exercises at least five and also at least every day 50 push-ups. His muscles, as funny as it might be heard for the age of 69, on his abdomen were to be seen, surprising women and girls, believing that this cannot be true.

The libido can last and exceed the age of 80, provided there is always a good breakfast where banana is a must and with all possible nut's species, and in the salad always have avocado and eat two small-sized cucumbers daily with the skin.

Always where he was, he selected where shellfish is served, such as mussels, oysters, sea urchin and many seeds: pumpkin seeds, pine cones, sunflower seeds, but also buckthorn and quite some more that he always carried with him in small tin boxes. When in Greece, he had such foods at least three days per week.

In later ages, when he could afford, he always had wild Lachs Caviars that ejected the libido to unbelievable heights. So, no wonder why a 60-year-old man can please and fully satisfy with considerable sex duration and, above all, altruism, all the sexual desires of mature and less mature ladies.

Retaining body in perpetual fitness and with the diet, this is not at all difficult to be attained; it is a must to respond to all the demands either mental or physical.

The ancient Greeks said, "Healthy mind in a healthy body." The archetype pilot is to have a well-trained body that hides the age from the eyes of women and keep both libido and stamina at highest level with the appropriate sustenance and exercise wherever he is and under whatever circumstances.

His mother-in-law was trying to put in order old photographs of both her daughter (his wife) and also his photos. Among these, she found a small notebook, which she gave to him. There he found, and evoked memories, the phone numbers of many old times friends but also girls that passed by his life and all left only beautiful memoirs and emotional tracks.

With amazement, he found with big and pleasant surprise the phone numbers of his dearest Anabella, but also Johanna.

So, at the age of 50, he took the challenge to call Anabella. The telephone was ringing, and unbelievably, she was on the line. He told her that he was Areus the Greek, and for a moment, there was no response, and this took only a few seconds. Anabella, with big surprise, expressed her disappointment telling him, "It took long and many efforts to convince my father to accept you, and you what? Simply disappeared."

She was angry, but he could feel that she was also his old times Anabella and that she loved him passionately.

He apologised, telling her that life brings changes and also his career forced him not to follow his heart but his career's future.

He asked her about her life. She calmed down and told him that she never abandoned him from her heart and the nice times they had together. She told him that her father died and her mother, although old enough at the age of 70, married again and this time with another very wealthy businessman.

He asked her if she was married; she told him that she did not because the guys she had as boyfriends during all those years were below her expectations, and also, she always compared him with them all and that could not free her from removing him from her heart and memory.

He told her that he was married and had two daughters and one son. He cannot say that she was very joyful to hear this, but being polite, she congratulated him. They talked maybe more than one hour, remembering the moments they lived together, and for quite some time, although quite some thousands of kilometres away, they were still so close as if they were sitting on her sofa, holding their hands and kissing each other.

She gave him her address, asking him to send photos of him at that age when they were together and also photos as he was now in his 50s. She blamed herself that she did not take photos those times, but she did not believe that they would ever be separated. She started crying, and he could also not avoid doing the same, and with this scene, both crying, they terminated that phone call. He heard her lips sending him a kiss. He tried to do the same, but he could not succeed.

At the age of 67, he started having company in China selling to the German market, that was always the leading market, and this he still does at the age of almost 68, at the same time being a sportsmans, taking part in tennis tournaments and swimming almost every day, nonstop 1½ mile and climbing mountains as he already mentioned before holding the golden rule 'never abandon; never give up; it is never enough'.

Talking about swimming, he discovered a spot at the sea only three minutes' drive from his home, where no one dared to go there, as to reach the sea, you have to go down through many rocks and huge, sharp, big stones that are dangerous, and the same dangers you face when you are down and have to get in the water.

He being faithful to the 'vivere pericolsamente', both in life and in business always took risks. There, he enjoyed the paradise, loneliness, and many times, he was completely naked as no one approached there.

One day, a beautiful lady managed, after many tries to come down, and she went for a swim; he told her to watch the stones carefully and where to step on so that she would not slip and break legs and arms; he also advised her never to do this again wearing sayonara slippers but use only sport shoes or she might end up with a broken head. When she was in the sea swimming, he turned around and changed his wet swim pant with a dried one, inevitably allowing or better not knowing that she could see his naked buttocks.

She then quickly swam back and picked up all her belongings and rushed away; maybe she thought that he might be a satyr. He laughed a lot; he gave her so many advices, and she had dirty thoughts passing her head.

Another day, coming down from a distance, before reaching his special spot to climb down, he saw on the highest rock there was a young man with a very well-shaped, not athletic with soft and smooth muscles, but slim, soft-shaped body, standing on the highest stone, and what he did? He was masturbating; maybe that unique solitude there inspired him to jerk off. He ignored him, and he went to his spot only five metres away from him and did his usual hard swim exercise. Few days later, he came again, this time closer to the five metres with a small string swimsuit, looking more like a sissy boy. He looked at him rather angrily, and he obliged him to move away.

He called Johanna, the East Germany fugitive girl. That phone number was not valid but belonged to her old apartment owner, and she gave him her new phone number, advising him that she was now married, as if she recognised who he was.

She was so happy to hear from him, and that was easier as she got married and happy with two sons, both of whom have their own families and her husband passed away after a long fight with cancer. She also told him that only good memories stayed deep engraved in her heart from their relationship and was happy to hear that he was also married and happy.

She reminded him of their several love nests in the different Manheim hotels and also the 'first step' she took at the hill small forest so they moved from many smothering kisses to real sex.

They laughed and wished each other the best of family life. The end was in German; she told him, which came from her heart, "*Areus ich liebe dich*."

One day, someone knocked on the door, and his wife opened the door. There were three men speaking German and English, so she knew that they wanted him. He then went to the door, and there he saw the two German boys, not boys anymore but old men. They were at his home to help him improve his German, and they invited him back to Germany for Christmas holidays, and him, the 'son of the bitch' had sex with their mother, which, of course, they never knew.

He embraced them, and they introduced to him their younger brother, who although they both were blond, he had dark or rather black hair. He asked them how they found his home; well, those times through the internet it was not difficult. He invited them inside his home for a drink and later for dinner. The one became a dentist, and the other, a businessman importing timber. The younger brother was with no profession; he was more or less the black sheep of the family; his only job was to run after new girls and as he heard also his son was the same type of girls' hunter.

It was nice to remember moments they had together in both Athens and Stuttgart and laughing when they tried to teach him skating on ice, but it was impossible for him falling all the time.

They had a nice dinner time, and before leaving, he asked them to give him their home telephone so when he is in Frankfurt, where he goes often for the Frankfurt Fair, maybe he could pop up at Stuttgart to see them.

When they left, he made deep thoughts about how come the younger brother had black hair. All those memories walked, figuratively, in front of his mind. He remembered that when he was making love to their mother, he several times ended up inside her; she never objected to that. Could this boy be his son? No, cannot be, but why not, and he had to find out.

He picked up the phone and called that phone number, and there was the mother, already an old woman of more than 95. He told her who he was, and she immediately hung up the phone.

He was shocked how come she hung up the phone; maybe she did not understand who he was, and he tried again. It took quite some rings until she picked up the receiver. He told her again who he was and that all three brothers, her sons, were here a few minutes ago, and he was glad to meet their younger brother.

He asked her, he had to, how come he had black hair. She, for a moment, was silent, then she told him, with a broken voice, that one of her husband's ancestors had black hair, and he, the husband, had not blond but brown hair.

She wanted to change the subject, asking him if he was married and had children. He came back insisting about her husband's family roots with black hair. She politely asked him to shift away from the conversation as this was a family matter that does not concern any other non-family members. The word 'concern' was not that steady and stable. She wanted to cease the conversation, and he could not keep her on the phone any longer.

He thanked her for giving him so much experience in sex; she also admitted that she also loved that she was the one to take his virginity, and they said goodbye, and that was it.

Since that time, he always had that question mark, the cloud of self-doubt and the unstable assurance of the mother about the hair colour of her son, and the family's roots explanations were to him not so convincing. Could he be his son? Shall he let this go, or…? He better forget and avoid to create problems.

He now, at his 68 plus, is an ambitious 68 plus years old 'startuper'.

He managed to sell the building with a good amount of money, and so he secured for their whole life time, his wife, his two daughters and his son, who turned out to be a musician. So, they could buy new houses and still have enough money to live a comfortable life or rent houses; it was up to them.

He is almost 69, but they all say that he looks 55, and frankly, sexually, he feels as young as if he were in his 50s. Still, he has continuous erections and from time to time needs to masturbate to calm the 'junior' down.

Those times, after COVID, it was not the best thing to do to take a risk for sex with those fabulous girls coming mainly from Russia, because he does not feel sex without kissing and also licking their smooth pussies, but this due to Covid was very contagious and dangerous.

He was still playing tennis with opponents who were even half his age, and they all could not believe that he was nearing 75 years of age. He was competent, involving strategy to his play, adding some of his specialty shots and according to where he could locate the opponent's weaknesses.

During breaks, they go to the bench to rest for a while; he tells them, "Stand up, man; you are so young; why do you need to rest?"

As already previously mentioned, he swims for eight months every day at that isolated, risky, rocky spot that he discovered.

So, although he was so near his home, he felt as if he were in the very last isolated island of Greece, below the island of Crete.

There is no need for him to wear a swimsuit as no one approaches. He swims in crawl long distances almost 1½ mile (2400 kilometres) nonstop.

He remembers, one day, he was swimming past a 10-metre rock where at the edge there were two fishermen fishing; he then felt a stone to pass no more than 10 cm away from his head; that stupid criminal fisherman threw a big stone from that height to make him stop his swimming from there, as he was frightening the fishes.

If that rock had hit him, he was to be killed right there and drowned. He always swims with specially made sea glasses and snorkel, so those long distances he enjoys and admires the sea bottom with fishes of all types, many octopus and even turtles, not to forget, the ancient Greek broken amphora from old shipwrecks.

Always with a very advanced laptop, he can travel and still not stop his business. He can neither abandon his excellent lady partner in China nor leave his German good customer. If he goes, they both would be in severe trouble, as both depend exclusively on him.

Having all family well financially settled, he asked for their permission to go for a small trip to Germany and Denmark to meet old friends.

The permission was given, and, of course, whom he visits first? Of course, Anabella. He arrived in Munich, and he called her telling her that he was there. Her joy was indescribable.

She rushed to pick him from the airport in a big jeep, good to go to the mountains for skiing despite her 68 years of age. She looked at him; he looked at her; the fire was still there. Despite her few wrinkles and his well-shaved bald head, they both looked much younger for their ages. No innocent kisses on the cheek but on the mouth right away and an intimate embracement.

She was perfectly well-preserved, and same as him, she was hiding her age; one easily could say that she was 60.

On the road to her home, she asked him how long he intended to stay, and he answered, as long as she cannot stand him anymore. They laughed, and she seemed to be happy about this. This time, she was living at her father's big and extra comfortable home as her mother moved to the house of her new husband.

He was still carrying almost untouched all those dresses and suits that she bought for him almost 50 years ago. He kept those suits in perfect condition as those were evoking memories that must be preserved. He explained to her the reason that he must work for a few hours wherever they are, and although he did not need to, he had to work, telling her that by not having anything to do is also a real threat to health as Alzheimer is always lurking, waiting well-hidden at the corner.

She had hung all his dresses in the closets; this time, he had many suits and short dresses as well, so she could see that this time there was no need to do any shopping for him.

She gave him a robe de chambre of her father to feel comfortable. They sat near the heat of a fireplace, and they started recounting about their lives.

He told her all about the job in Denmark, about the business in Middle East, about him to become director of a big hotel and also managing to get his company to the stock exchange, about his wife, his son and daughters (here he noticed clouding in her glance) and that he had a heart attack and quite some more events.

She also told him that she had been unhappy all those years, and she blamed herself why although she loved him so much, she did not allow him to ejaculate inside her, and maybe now she could have had a son or a daughter from him.

She told him that her life was skiing and again skiing and no other interest. She had some relations with men, but they all disenchanted her; either they wanted her money or another one that she thought could go on well proved to be gay. She blamed him as she was always comparing him with those that passed by her life, and the outturn was always negative.

Drinking quite a lot of the 12-year-old whisky with peanuts and more salted biscuits, they became a little dizzy, so being dizzy, the words come out easier and with no control. He told her his story at the age of 18, when he was invited to the home of his two young, same to his age German boys, in Stuttgart.

He told her that he came in sexual contact with their mother when she was around 45–50, believing that she stole his virginity and she allowed many times to finish inside her to enjoy it all.

Believing that probably she was already on menopause so there was no possibility to become pregnant. He also told her about the two brothers who after so many years came to Athens to see him, and there was with them their younger brother who surprisingly had black hair, same as his hair.

Shadows of doubts came to mind, and he called that lady mother; she was by then almost 96 and, in no case, wanted to admit that this boy was his son. That 95-year-old German lady told him that the dark-haired son of hers also has a son of about 19 years old, so he is her grandson.

He had to go to Stuttgart and find out by all means if indeed he has a son with her. Anabella surprised him by telling him that if he is your son then she wanted his young son as her heir or better adopt the 19-year-old boy; she had a fortune and not any heir. She would prefer to adopt that grandson because she wanted, as she said, "Something that is yours."

The boys told him that time while in Athens that after their father died, their financial situation was worsening and their mother was very unhappy. She even complained that her black-haired grandson was not interested in studying, and he was all the time after girls, and she did not know what to do and what would become out of him.

Anabella opened her eyes and was surprisingly very happy to hear this and repeated telling him that she always wanted to have something that belonged to him, so she said again that she could, if indeed it is his grandson, adopt him to at last have an heir of her big fortune.

He was shocked to hear this. So, they both agreed that she would drive him to Stuttgart to find the truth, and if he is indeed his son, invite him to a dinner so that they would meet both son and grandson.

The night they slept on the warm bed, one close to the other; she was astonished to see that he had the old times' good erection, and they tried to do it, and they did it quite affectionately in total darkness as an old couple—better do whatever in dark, imagining the older times when the couple was young. She was happy. Oh God, how happy that woman was!

They spent two more days in Munich, having nice lunches and dinners; this time with him paying, and next day, she said, "Let us drive to Stuttgart and find the truth."

Indeed, after a nice drive and stopping for some lunch, they reached Stuttgart. They stayed at the best hotel in town, and the next day, he knocked on the door of the lady who was many decades before for four days his sex mentor.

She opened the door, and she could not immediately recognise him, so he had to tell her who he was, and with great pleasure, she invited him in.

Her sons were both married and live in their own apartments. Only the black-haired grandson, Evan, stayed with her as his father was not that successful in his business, and therefore, only she could afford to have the grandson with her and maybe the last years of her life. She was not happy with his conduct as he was always not there, overnighting with different girls, which reminded him of himself.

They discussed all those years he told her about his life and about his beloved Anabella. The discussion came around Alexander, her black-haired son; she was reluctant to talk about this. She gave him the name of Alexander although no one in the family had that name but that more or less reminded of Greece, but in any case, there are many Germans with this name.

After long, she indeed reconfirmed that there was in the family a black-haired ancestor, and definitely, she could not verify that he was the outcome of their sex, because sex she also did in the next few days with her not blond but dark brown-haired husband when he returned from a business meeting in Hamburg. Then a few months after her menopause came, he would never be sure that he was his son although deep inside him he believed he is, but there is not any convincing evidence.

He kissed her goodbye and left with deep doubts about this that would always torture him but have to let it go as this might also create other problems with his own family and his daughters and his son. Nowadays, there is DNA, but how can he ask someone to make a paternity test and why. He better leave this as it is and forget about it.

Anabella was very unhappy about the outcome, and he begged her to remove this from her mind and return to Munich.

He stayed in Munich two weeks, and again for the fourth time came their tearful goodbyes, promising that on his way back he would visit her again.

He flew to Heidelberg to visit his hotel school and tell them how well he did as a director.

The school directors made a special presentation for him in front of an audience of 300 students, telling them that he was there 50 years ago, and he became director of a big luxury hotel, and they all applauded him.

It was planned to have an influential speech, and indeed, he did so; he described to them what a manager has to do, what stages must follow to become a good director, as those students were all destined one day to become hotel directors.

They were amazed how many countries he visited, what more schools he graduated to finish as a director, obtaining deep knowledge and discovering all secrets of their profession. That speech he held was a seminar.

He explained to them where the dangers for a hotel director are hidden.

He emphasised that the kitchen is the department that usually negatively affects the financial figures of a hotel enterprise, unless it is well organised and with constant supervision.

Trust the chef but not limitlessly. The chef wants to make his show and get the credits of a nice dish and menu. You have to control what the kitchen has as leftovers. With a clever presentation, you can turn to a delicatessen dish and make money from whatever was left behind, and usually, the chefs destined these to staff's lunch. Making money from 'wastages' is the director's achievement to rein in costs, which is a must and reflects the profitable balance sheet of the enterprise.

The menu must not always be in the hands of the chef as he is not aware anytime what clients the hotel has, what nationalities, if there are groups (imagine having a group of Jews and he suggests porch as plat du jour), so the director is the one who knows what is his clientele in the hotel, and he has to combine what is at the Garde Manger-butcher, 'which has to be consumed in time before it is too late'.

The city hotels that are near fairs and exhibition halls are the hotels (example Frankfurt hotels) that are the most profitable, but the country, beach or mountain hotels are also profitable, provided breakfast and lunch or dinners are served wisely. It is beautiful to make impressive buffets, and yes, it must be done but with cleverness.

More decoration like ice animals and sweet statues that impress, as example, and less expensive delicatessen like prosciutto and smoked salmon or smoked reindeer and expensive cheeses.

Impress the customers at your buffet and add a lot of green, fruits and pommes frites and spend as little as possible for costly food. The more the clients see, the more they fill up their plates, and the result is that 30% goes to the trash bin.

Put behind the soups or the piping hot consommé your best 'salesman' cook. If the client starts with a soup, they then have less space for much more.

Whatever remains at the buffet must be well preserved and make a menu that would have cold food (ham, salamis and cheeses, etc.) so these leftovers on the buffet would bring money. Chase and run after conventions, conferences and company meetings that brings money as you offer bed breakfast and a lunch or dinner, where cleverly you channelise your by-products and inventory hangovers. A fillet Stroganoff is an idea as main course because you make a beautiful dish with small pieces either from the fillet or the sirloin, adding pappardelle or rice and that is a money-making dish.

"You as directors must be able, and this is the main tool you will get here at this very institution, to control the accounting. If you can't, you might find yourself having a full house, and at the end of the day, the accounting shows a different picture either by mistake or why not also not by mistake."

He remembered a chief accountant of a huge hotel who was a regular client at casinos that his salary could not justify the heavy gambling.

"Well, this is a rare example, but better be sure than find yourself in uncomfortable situations. Manage to make the chief accountant believe that you are able to control him, and read numbers and balance sheets and you will do it suddenly without warning."

They applauded him many times, and in some moments, he even had tears in his eyes, bringing back the times he was there as a student applauding other successful directors like him being there.

The school's directors and teachers praised him for addressing such a lecture; they congratulated him saying that this 1½ hours' speech no one before kept the audience in such an interesting modus. They invited him next year to hold such a speech again for the new students.

It was a very moving moment, and he remembered that all those three Greek friends of his that also graduated were no longer alive. It was very depressing to walk all those streets where he knew almost everyone and now he was a total foreigner to all.

He called Johanna, the pleasure was again difficult to describe. He told her that he was there. She asked him where he was staying; he told her that he left his luggage at the airport safe lockers to go to the hotel school as an invited VIP graduate student to hold a speech and that he plans to stay in a hotel. She denied and told him, "No way, you stay with me; I am alone and there is plenty of space and three bedrooms that you can sleep in."

He fetched his luggage, took a taxi and went to her place. She kissed him warmly, and he was, after Anabella, at another ex-girlfriend's home. Johanna was not as well preserved as Anabella. She was 82 with an athletic body, a quite wrinkled face, but she was still a nice old woman. They sat in her cozy living room and remembered so many moments 55 years ago.

She confessed that those times she pretended the she might be pregnant due to her period delay just to see his reactions, then she regretted for this and told him that there was not any delay, so it had been a false alarm. The night came, and he went to the bedroom where one of her sons slept few years ago before getting married.

For the morning, she made a nice breakfast and went out to walk on streets, where he was many times with his friends. He stayed for two days, and he kissed her goodbye and flew to Copenhagen.

He then went to the asylum hospital, and to his surprise, it was closed with a label saying that due to inconvenience, the asylum was moved to other more modern installations.

His mind was always on Mathilde, the badminton girl, but how to find her? The stupid thing was that he did not leave his trolley luggage at the airport and he was carrying that like a stupid tourist. He then went to a hairdresser, and luckily, it was still open.

He told them whom he was looking for, and they gave him her address. He then went there by foot as it was near, knocked on the door, and there was a beautiful girl of about 35 years old. He told her that he was looking for Mathilde; he was an old friend.

She smiled. "Are you Areus, the Greek, Mother's crazy lover?"

He said, "Yes, that probably is me." She told him she was expecting him to be an old man, but he looked so young. She asked him to come in and make coffee for him.

She told him that her mother was kind of coach or councillor to the badminton team and she was on a tour for three or four days. So, he said, "Then I better leave."

"No, stay. I make coffee for you, and then you leave."

Indeed, he stepped in and was waiting for her to make the coffee. She came with the coffee and sat opposite to him. He noticed she had excellently shaped legs.

She told him the story of her life and also told him that her mother, despite being married to a handsome man, who passed away two years ago, was always telling to her girlfriends about her Greek lover and the many ways she enjoyed sex with him and his tricks and 'appetisers'.

Bells started to ring in his mind. He felt embarrassed that a 35-year-old blue-eyed girl made him feel like a young boy.

He explained to her that sex variety is his secret weapon, and they laughed again and again. Time was passing, and he said it would be better to move to catch the flight although he was planning to stay in Denmark for two to three days.

So, she said, "You stay three days so my mother will come back that third day; she certainly would love to see you. She will be angry at me for letting you go; she will be very happy to see you."

"OK, is there any hotel nearby?"

"Why don't you like this house?"

He said, "Sure, but is it appropriate?"

"Do not mention it; you will have your own bedroom."

So, he started unpacking for the third time, and the time came to have dinner.

In Denmark, dinner was always romantic with candles and never lights on. She prepared some Danish specialties and prepared the dinner table. He asked her to go to his bedroom to change his shirt as he had that on for one whole day. He also asked her where the bathroom was as he needed a shower, walking with that wheel luggage he had sweat all over. She showed it to him with a smile.

When he returned to the dinner table after he changed his clothes to be more comfortable, she was dressed so impressively and looked great as a real woman who was aiming for something more than a dinner.

He knew with his long experience what that something was, and he inside him was not negative to whatever that something could turn out to be. She opened a bottle of wine, and they sat opposite each other; he noticed how she was licking the wine glass; her tongue was so provocative as if she wanted to tell him she knows how to lick also 'other' than the lips of a glass.

She persistently came back to the same subject of the several ways that he made sex to her mother and laughed with her full heart. Well, he said since then he enriched his sex menu with extraordinary varieties.

She was laughing so beautifully, kind of inviting to tell her all the menu's suggestions. It was clear what she wanted and in full awareness, and he was also turned on with her beautiful body and her open laughter and slightly, but ideally, opened legs that imagination was not needed as it was there to be seen.

They went back to the sofa, always laughing and licking the edge of the wine glass that turned him on; he adored such lips. He took the initiative of telling her that her tongue is the tongue of a woman who knows how to use it.

She laughed and asked him with a slightly half-closed or, rather to say, horny eyes what he meant, but the answer was obvious to her. Karla, which was her name, stood up and came to him; she took his hand, this reminded him of the 50-year-old lady; she had done the same to him when he was 18; now this was the very contrary; the 35-year-old girl takes him, the 69-year-old man, by the hand to lead him to the bedroom.

He felt extremely nice but at the same time guilty towards her mother, Mathilde.

A stream of consciousness passed all the way through being in front of such an unpredictable situation making love to the daughter of his beloved, old times girl, whom he was so close to get married. Although oddly compliant to Karla, he took the advantage of the enchantment of the situation.

They are now in the bedroom, and one can smell the other's desiring body, seeking for hedonistic activity; he avails that ability to know what the next steps would be.

She gets undressed, reminding him of films where the star allows piece by piece to fall on the ground, revealing the charm. God gave charms with playfulness to that woman; she had not anything under her dress, just untie and tug the knot from the top shoulder part of the dress and the whole thing fell down, and there was a breathtaking, full of lust, impeccable body.

She suddenly became aggressive, claiming, in a loud but, at the same time, mighty voice, "Take me, do with my body whatever you want; I am your slave; I always wanted you after the descriptions of my mother and masturbated for you many times; here I am your sex toy; take it, exploit every centimetre of it."

He was shocked that never ever any woman wanted him so hard, so infinitely and especially at his age of 69. Every word she was expressing so furiously was another message to his penis to obey and comply.

He started getting him undressed and reached to his slip; she took that out; she first watched his athletic body (he shaved the hair from his chest and also all hairs around his penis so as to look younger and bigger) and was amazed to see that this was not the body of a 69-year-old man. She caressed and licked his sunburned chest from the swimming and the sunbathing, and then seeing the erected penis, she showed admiration.

She knew it; she knew it; she knew that it would be true what her mother was telling her about his always express erection, and she hated her because she lived it many times. She took a hold of his penis and caressed it softly, not squeezed it, but kissed him excitedly without removing her hand from his penis.

He adores ladies to caress the penis, not masturbating but with the tips of their fingers try to deplore any single millimetre of it before the unavoidable soft blowjob.

She laid down on the bed and arched her body like a cat on a stretch and again there she was. "This body is yours; please do more to what you did to my mother; promise to me that you will do more."

Well, that was the moment that he found himself in front of a commitment. He, as a sex connoisseur, had to please her extraordinarily and started softly with his 'famous' sexual hors d'oeuvres. He went down to her little pussy, which was well waxed without a single hair, indulging himself to explore it; he always liked that rather than the bush of hairs.

The heavenly done vagina looked as if it were a baby's skin, slightly pinkish, and that is what his favourite pussy is; that angelic pussy turned him on, and he activated right away his extra efficient tongue; he was endowed with that gift to know when his tricks are to be engaged. She, only with the first touch, started small but sweet spasms; she probably knew that when she approached the culmination of her orgasm, she shouted loudly, and she took the pillow and bit the edge of the pillow, so to allow her watching what he was so nicely doing down there to her humid vagina.

The tongue was working with exceptional skill and mastery; she was approaching more and more to the climax, and she took both her hands, caressed and held tight, or rather hardly, his head. The moment she erupted, that woman had firepower, she shouted, but the pillow softened her groans and moans that escaped from her. She had six or seven spasms until a deep relief showed a calmness on her entire face. He kissed her on the mouth with a tongues' tango.

She told him in his ear, "This you also did to my mother, and thank you for this, but I want more, more that my mother did not enjoy."

He had to ask her, and he did. "How is it at all possible that your mother narrated to you in all details all our sex contacts, such as positions and all tongue tricks?"

She answered, "I obliged her to do this as she obliged me not to marry that nice Tunisian boy who I was in love with, and, of course, after all she described to me, I had to rush to the bedroom to enjoy a nice masturbation having you as a fantasy."

Next, he exercised the normal traditional intercourse, but in a harmonised way, he led her to follow his in and out motions, and after a short while, she managed to follow his commanding but rhythmical movements. She slightly raised her hips with her face down; he grabbed her hips and whole pelvis; she raised further to meet each thrust and obtain further deepness in the penetration.

That was a perfect seminar kind of sex performance; a second climax followed; this time milder but with longer duration; he could not hold anymore the hard-on was such her vagina was so squeezing that he hardly managed to get the penis out of that fabulous little pussy; he suspected that something of his seed might have been planted deep in that sweet vagina.

Actually, from the very beginning when he asked for it, she denied any condom to be applied to his penis, saying that he also always wanted to feel the soft vagina walls without any plastic in between; condom kills a big part of both partners' pleasure. They now are next to each other, enjoying the last spasms.

He whispered into her ear that there was much more to teach her, but let us do this tomorrow. She answered back, "Yes, and yes, I want all." She kept repeating that she wanted more from what he gave to her mother. "I have reason for this."

She told him then that she wanted somehow to take revenge on her because she denied her relationship with a Tunisian cute boy she was in love with when she was 20, and it was a big controversy between mother and daughter.

Since then, no one could fit to her desires, just sex substitute via masturbation and more often and better with the use of different shaped dildos and vibrators. Now he understood why so much she wanted him to act and much better to her than what he did to her mother.

He was so tired from the trip that he did not even went to the bathroom for a pee or even brush his teeth and fell asleep right there, completely naked.

He felt that she covered his body with a sheet and light blanket, but before doing this, she gave a passionate sucking kiss with her delightful lips to his buttocks.

Not to forget that during breaks, he was always working on his laptop without abandoning his business at all.

The next morning, he woke up in the best mood but also had an appetite. Karla prepared an impressive buffet style breakfast that one can only see in big hotels. This means that she woke up much earlier to prepare all this and all in sizable abundance.

The heat was high up, so one could even walk around the home naked. What he saw made him very horny. Karla had just an apron on, and he could see her gorgeous breasts to move without any difficulty that was for a normally an ideal good morning.

He sat on the table but could not stay there as she turned with plenty of charm to the sink and he saw her from the back; she had on a kind of cotton material culottes that emphasised her voluptuous figure, as if she knew that he gets crazy when he sees girls or women with cotton towel style shorts wrapping around the ass and part of the thighs and cotton towel soft shirts to embrace the girls' braless breasts.

He approached her from behind; he took his already in full erection penis and moved her culottes on the side; he pushed her to bend more to the sink so as to adapt herself according to conditions and project her ass, but that culottes was not a string so it was little difficult; she then with a skilful left and right charming fond feeling feminine movements of her ass, managed that the culottes falls down by itself and got rid of that last obstacle, a full and prime view of her pussy and her cute vagina ready to accommodate his penis in an erotic delight.

The mirror above the sink gave full view of the shortly to come sexual rich visual feast; he just had to slip his cock with an extraordinary hard penis and as deep as possible in her hot and super wet pussy; no pain, no objection at all, the pussy welcomed him, and the tango started. What a perfect match they made.

After a small while, he lifted her up, as if she were an inflatable doll, pushed away all what was on that table and gently let her lay on the table with legs high up and his torso almost touching her tits.

Having his penis at same height to her vagina, she clasped him tightly, and their harmonised cooperation effected so that both to come exactly the same moment, him being careless and impossible to drag the penis out so the full load of his sperm nested inside her.

He asked her to rush to the bathrooms to wipe herself off to avoid complications, and indeed, she did but strangely not in such a hurry. She returned, and they sat down to enjoy with incredible appetite the rich buffet in front of both of them.

Karla kept him in the house as if he were her sex captive; she explained to him that it was better to leave before her mother comes, and she does not want the neighbours see him coming and going, so better stay the two more days inside and then leave, so his mother would never know that he was here. He agreed and stayed two more days with her inside her home and most of the time inside the hot juices of her impatient pussy.

They had sex two times per day—the sex the way she wanted. 'She wants all'; that was her desire, so he gave her all, disposing the art of 'listening' his partner's desires, and when he says all, he means all, including backside penetration that she had never before experienced. He taught her all the secrets and tricks of sex, and she was grateful, and she said, "Like my mother, I will also never forget your optimal performances."

Very funny; he came to meet his since 55 years beloved girlfriend, who for her shed tears leaving Denmark, and now what did he do, the big son of a bitch? He had wild sex with her daughter, but better say the truth. It was not him to aim for this, but the magnificent daughter of hers; Karla was the one to drag him to a kind of sex orgy.

They had numerous goodbye kisses, and he was on his way to the airport; he gave her his phone number, but correct or wrong? He chose without knowing why he gave her the wrong number.

Arriving at the airport, he changed his mind. He wanted to visit the new place where that asylum hospital moved to new installations. He had the address, and in a taxi, he went there. Indeed, what he saw was not easy to describe; such modern installations were unbelievable. It was difficult to explain to the door guards who he was as his Danish was coming back but rather slowly, until they called the management.

He explained to the assistant director, who spoke perfect English, who he was and seemed to know his story and his brother's story. They asked the guard to allow him to enter, and a 60-year-old secretary arrived to accompany him to the management offices. There, he met a warm welcome reception.

The director introduced him to all the doctors who also knew about those achievements; unfortunately, both boys, Ules, had passed away.

They asked him if he could give to the whole nurses and men carers (in Danish, *Plejer* means the male nurse who takes care of the patients) a kind of lecture about his experiences of those times 55 years ago.

He told them that he left his luggage at the airport, so they offered him a luxury stay in their VIP guestrooms as that lecture was to be for the next day. So, many memories and many moments were unlocked. He lived there, and one picture after another, the one memory after the other were running in his mind like the LED indicator of the stock market.

The next day, he was taken to a huge hall, and there were maybe 200 doctors and nurses.

He was shocked by the big audience and also by the beauty of those nurses. They applauded him, and the director told them who he was.

So, he was describing all of the story with both Ules, him with his Ule achieving for the first time in his life to speak even one single word and that was a success; he had to tell them how and with patience and affection that could be accomplished.

Then also his brother's Ule, who managed with only a few commanding signs to calm down and tame the wild Ule with complete obedience and discipline, to whom the nurse had forgotten to give his pill in time.

Those, of course, descriptions took quite a long time. When he finished, they all stood up and applauded for almost two minutes. He was happy about that, and the director told him that he could stay at his VIP apartment as long as he wanted.

It seemed to him a good idea to wander around the so much modernised clinic and visit all the departments and meet all the head nurses of each department.

Nearby, just outside the main gate, a few metres away, there was a tennis club with four courts, indoor and six outside. He was so envious, but he had neither shoes nor a sports uniform or even a racket. But he went there.

He saw how they were playing, and he asked the owner who is the older one of the club, and the answer was that the older one is 68 years old. Areus told them who he is and where he lives and asked them to call the director of the clinic to verify who he is. Indeed, the second co-owner, who was in that standing meeting, left to call.

After he returned, he said something into the ear of the club owner. So, a crazy idea came to his mind that very moment and he suggested playing a match with that 68-year-old player.

He told them that he was not prepared for playing as he had nothing with him, not even tennis shoes. They were surprised with this suggestion, and they found it funny, but at the same time, interesting. They seemed to like the idea after they called that guy; he was not there that time, and probably, he also accepted the challenge. So, the subject came about his uniform, shoes and racket.

They told him that there was a shop in the club. "You only buy shoes, and we will give you the rest." He did so, and they arranged for the racket and uniform, and right away, he announced to those who were playing that next day at 11, a veteran match would take place between a Greek player and their club's eldest club player member.

He then went back to the director's office and told him that this would happen and that he needs fans and avid supporters. This sounded to his ears more as a joke, but he agreed that they would back him with their presence.

The next day, after a slight breakfast, he did not want to fill up his belly, he walked around the block and arrived at the indoor tennis hall (rain was expected, so it must be indoor), and he faced with enormous surprise almost 50 people who were members of the club but also quite some doctors and nurses, and surprisingly also some kind of dancing cheerleaders from the hospital.

The ambience was celebratory as if it were a tennis festival. He felt very bad to make such a suggestion, and what if after 30 days of non-playing tennis, he would be humiliated by that opponent who was more than 10 years younger than him? He tried to give courage to himself, but was that enough?

They gave him a racket and the full sports uniform, which they later gave him as the club's gift.

It fit him well, and he looked in that tennis sport uniform not a 69-year-old man but much younger, having also shaved his head and be skinhead that gave to him extra glam and hide years of age. There was a problem; he told them that the older player that he was to play with, must neither be a professional nor an ex-coach, but that the 65-year-old guy was an ex-coach. So, how can it be possible for him to beat that professional guy who spends all his time holding rackets and with almost 10 years of notable age difference?

They started the warm-up; he noticed the opponent was playing really well, but he noticed he had a weak point. His running was not fast; he was slow, so he had to make such a strategy plan to hit him there to slow his running as that was his Achilles heel.

The play was to begin after the nurse cheerleaders danced, and they, indeed, danced charmingly as if they were NBA cheerleaders.

The game started with that guy; Alex was his name, same height as him, a snobby blond man with blue eyes and showed excessive attitude of superiority.

Alex won easily the first two games, the second with a break as his serve was not that hard for him to return.

Having not touched a tennis racket for maybe 30 days, he was not that comfortable, and also the racket they gave him was not his racket that he was accustomed to play well.

So, he decided to exercise new strategy so stopped the hard drives, and he moved to top spin but high balls that threw the opponent far to the back wall, so when he was returning, it was easy to activate his favourite, his specialty drop-shot so one first ball far away and high and the next to come drop shot very close to the net.

Like this, he managed to win many points, but at the same time made the opponent extremely tired by running from the very end and six to seven metres behind the baseline to the net to reach the drop shot. He could see that the tiredness and the obvious fatigue would bring him soon to an advantageous situation. The only thing he had to do was to win his games and also make two breaks to the opponent's games.

He started to win the wide audience and sympathisers. They were admiring his guts and his clever shots, both drop shots and skilled sliced shots with intensity that the opponent had to bend very low down to return, but almost all ended up on the net. He won, to his surprise but also with immense satisfaction, the first set. The opponent needed to go to the toilet for a toilet break, so he had the chance to open his laptop and rushed to send mails and offers to keep his major job running.

They all turned crazy; that was never done between the breaks of the single game, the one to run to the bathroom and wipe his sweat from his face and change underwear, while the other was working on his laptop that was never ever done in any tennis court in the world.

Alex returned, and the second set started; following the clever strategy he won the first two games and lost the third, but then he saw that Alex was ready to fall down being extremely tired, so Alex came close to the net, he gave his hand and very gently congratulated him and resigned for the rest of the set. He had a glorious victory.

Alex was a very gentle and rational person, and he revealed to him that his great-grandfather was Greek and maybe the first Greek to come in Denmark, and despite what it was believed, those times, he was a tall guy with blond hair and blue eyes, so he inherited the same characteristics and features.

They all applauded; he was the unexpected winner, especially his hospitable audience who were happy as he honoured the name of the hospital. After he took a shower, they walked him, triumphantly, back to his VIP apartment. The whole hospital knew what happened, and they welcomed him as if he were a Roman gladiator or a Greek Heracles.

He was tired, and even though he had showered at the tennis club, he had to take one more shower. Going through the corridor, heading to his apartment, he watched the lady in charge of the five VIP apartments, watching him not only as a fan or admirer but also with a different look that after his long experience he knew what that look was meant to be.

He, being in sport shoes and with a nice blue-green sports uniform, could hide at least 20 years of his age. With his shaved bald hair, looking like Bruce Willis or rather like Yul Brunner. In fact, a well-shaved head without white hair hides many years, and having a forehead with no wrinkles at all was cutting even more years from his real age. There is also a saying that bald men have higher libido and stamina; ladies are aware of this saying.

He entered his apartment, got rid of the sports tennis uniform and went to the shower. While hot water was running all over his body, he heard the door get unlocked. Well, he knew from his hotel experience, that she, as chambermaid or chief chambermaid, possesses a *passepartou* like in the hotels, a key that opens all doors and is used by the chambermaids.

She pretended that she wanted to prepare a fresh bed, and there he was again in front of the same story as 55 years ago to be repeated. He pretended that he did not hear that she was in the room and came out of the shower naked; he tried to cover his penis area, and she also pretended that she did not know that he was there. But that was impossible as entering the apartment, she could hear the water running in the shower, and also, she watched him entering the apartment.

He pretended that he was tired, and he begged her if she could give him a massage on his back and thighs as after that hard tennis match, and being almost 30 days with no exercise, he felt pain on his back, neck, hands as well as legs and thighs.

She said, "I am not professional for this, but, of course, I will try."

Here, his fame as the winner of the tennis match worked.

Well, fame as the man who had such achievements 55 years ago and was invited to hold a speech, fame that he beat in tennis a good player and after all these also the sight of his always erected penis that betrays his horny status. He laid down on the bed on his stomach, and she started giving him a massage. She took off her outer dresses as she had to mount on the bed and mount on his body to perform the massaging well. She was doing so well that he was almost about to fall asleep.

When she finished from behind, giving special attention to massage his buttocks and inevitably her hands had to touch and maybe even fumble his testicles from behind and also made a soft, highly skilful massage to his asshole area, avoiding to bring in awkward situations his masculinity.

He was in such a hard painful erection due to his body pressure that he had to slightly lift his ass up and displace his hard penis between and under his legs that made obvious almost the whole to be seen although he was on his stomach.

She had the full view; he could not see her reaction. She, knowing that uncomfortable situation, asked him to turn around with the excuse that playing tennis what is most to be massaged were the thighs.

He told her with shyness, "Sorry, I can't do this." She asked with a naïve 'why', although she certainly knew. How to explain in words, his penis was already a flagpole.

She smiled and said, "I have no eyes, only hands."

So, he turned around, and it was difficult for her to describe how a man of this age has such a hardness on his dick. She started the massage, but he could feel that she was in a desiring situation; her breaths became short, whooshing and piercing his ears. She massaged his thighs; he was supposed to have tired thighs, and slowly, she went upper and upper until her hands were holding his penis. She looked at him as if she wanted to tell him, "Shall I play with this?"

His eyes were, of course, giving the approval, adding the thumb signal of 'well done', so also did his penis be able to signal by a side move. She felt that motion in her hand increasing her already terrific lust.

She took off her shirt and bras and two adorable breasts were facing his sex organ, lowering those to touch his penis, and she massaged it with her breasts that reminded him of Philippines and Thai girls, specialists for this.

He begged himself not to finish, succeeding this by turning his mind to other matters such as fetching his luggage from the airport so that he fools his penis desire to come, as she did this so nicely, so softly, so gently that the breasts were caressing his penis like a bird's feathers.

She stopped that and started masturbating also in a soft way; he stopped showing that he wanted more; she got the message; she bent and started sucking it. After a while, he stopped that also and made a recognisable sign that he and she are ready for the final stage.

With not a least of objection, she removed her slip, and there she was on top of him, having a face full of joy and amusement; she was after all fucking the superstar of that day.

That mysterious woman had a kink, was kind of the seldom women that when they reach a certain point before orgasm they turn wild using loud dirty words that could even scandalise a whore. So she suddenly changed to a lewd woman, shouting to him but in Danish, "Fuck me. Fuck me hard, you horny son of the bitch fucker; fuck my wet pussy. I am your slut, fuck it all. I want with my pussy to punish your hard bloody penis to not dare to fuck any other than me, you hear? And do not dare to come, you bloody Greek fucker, until I come."

He had to comply with her commands. She bit one of his nipples, and her nails sunk and scratched his back furiously as if she wanted to mark him, like the cowboys do to the cows, burning on their buttocks the symbol so that the ownership is undisputed. She made it distinguishable that this man belonged to her. My God, that was for him something new; how one beautiful calm face can turn into a wild nympho, turning him into her servant.

At the same time, with her wild dirty words being there on top, they heard the door to open again with that special key of the chambermaids, and her assistant, a foxy girl of 22, was in front of not only a porno show but a spectacular porno attraction with words that she never heard before coming out of the mouth of Emma.

Her face shimmered, her body shook; she strangely stayed there for two to three minutes like a marble statue, watching and not intending to leave, wishing to hear more dirty words and see Emma 'horse riding'; she bashfully apologised and closed the door behind her.

Emma, already on top of him, never stopped the loud dirty fucking words; even when her assistant entered and kept watching, it seemed to him that she controlled her well, and she would never talk.

He then had second thoughts; maybe that he might expect a new round of another nice and maybe easy to come fuck, but with that much younger mignon girl.

Her sexual energy culminated, and she came, and despite her rough, wild double-faced performance, her climax was silent but adorable and immediately managed when she felt that he was also to come to pull off and masturbate until he had his load in the palm of her hand. She rushed to wash and also brought two paper tissues to wash him also.

She changed from wilderness to calmness and did that with affection, not to harm the by then soft penis as the erection was totally subsided; she would need this in good form again and again the next to come days. At least, that was her intention.

He was so tired from the tennis play, he could not unlock any of his exclusive extras and tricks that he promised her to do only with description and signs that can be postponed for later days. She kissed him and said rather plaintively, "Please keep our secret well preserved and stay away from that small bitch, OK?"

The next day, he had to visit the director's office, and there, to his surprise, he had a proposal to stay in the asylum and teach the nurses and carers how the job could best be done and offered to him a big amount of money with upfront good amount of cash, which he, of course, did not need, but always, extra new money is welcomed. He was at the threshold of a new era in teaching this time and not nursing.

He told him OK he accepts the proposal or rather the challenge. Then in the afternoon, the tennis manager came to him, and he told him that he played excellently with an admirable prototype strategy, and he also offered a job to instruct not the young boys and girls but mature guys and ladies to show them what tennis strategy means. Another good money job was proposed to him that he could combine both and, of course, always his laptop to reciprocate to his China/Germany high-demanding business attendance.

He called his wife, son and daughters, and he explained to them what was going on there in Denmark, and they all told him, "Enjoy your stay there; you managed after so much hard work and for so many years to make us have plenty of money to live a comfortable life, so enjoy your life too and return back when you feel that the time has come."

The management arranged to send a driver to collect his luggage, so all was settled.

The next morning, with the white long dress of a doctor, he was visiting the first department. He was supposed to visit all and for one week each department to see how the section was working and make his weekly reports.

Needless to say, how many beautiful girls he met, but he had to keep his serious status and avoid new relations. After all, there was one waiting volunteer, the 38-year-old Emma and that 22-year-old fabulous creature; he could foresee that she also would soon want to enjoy sex.

Both were right there in his own room so no space and need for new sex encounters. He was sure that after what she saw when entering 'by mistake', the 22-year-old beauty brought home a nice masturbation work.

In the afternoon, he went to his other job, the tennis lessons to older men who wanted to see how an old man can use specific skills and strategy to beat much younger players.

At the same time, he put on the table a suggestion: why not organise a tournament there at this club for the veteran players of each tennis club from all over Denmark over the age of 65? That made them open their eyes wide and grab the idea that would make their club famous and gain many new members.

A tournament that never was done before and that idea came from him—the Greek smart fellow. Of course, his laptop was working at full speed whenever he found even five minutes of free time so as to not neglect his permanent and fruitful job.

The whole thing was running well. Some of the visits to the different hospital divisions were accompanied by male carers (*plejer* in Danish), so they could see how he sees the matters and what questions he puts to the head of the departments so they can understand how he operates. The first section was the half-mentally ill patients, the department where he was also as *plejer* 50 years ago.

He made the report that this department was working well, but a little more care was still needed, especially to those who believed that they were not insane, and they should not be there and are equally sensitive with all of the rest normal healthy persons.

The next department was the hard one, the one that his brother was working in, and he had to enter the room where 20, at least 19–21 years old, young but strong patients needed very special treatment, and always the pills must be given in time or else there was dangerous trouble. He asked them to enter that room alone; they all advised him not to do it as it is very risky as they do not know him.

He said, "Do not worry, and just leave this to me to handle my own way." They stayed outside, looking what he would do (reminds him of when in the movies when in the police department they are questioning a criminal the others are looking through a mirror what is going on inside and if need be, rush inside).

He was in, and he locked himself inside with the almost wild and untamed incredibly strong boys. He looked at them with an iced glance; they looked at him curiously thinking, *And who the hell is this bald guy?*

He lifted up both his hands and the one pointer finger of both hands showing one by one with a very angry and severe or better angry glance. In a minute, it came to his memory when he, as a rugged outdoor-type of man, was climbing up on a mountain, reaching high up after four hours of hiking and climbing the so-called 'mountain hikers trail'.

After a gruelling climb to the top of the mountain, there was a high up inclination, and at the top of that trail, he saw two big, probably wild, black dogs sitting. He pretended that he ignored their existence, and he kept climbing up, approaching them. They saw what was going on and decided to stand up on their feet, staring at him quite angrily and fiercely, thinking how he dared, and their teeth were showing to him that they were ready to attack.

He kept going up until he reached seven metres away from them; he then lifted up his hands with the finger pointing to them and with a cry or, better, a screaming that was to be heard in the whole mountain; he terrified them, and they curiously ran away, each one in a different direction. He was told by professional hikers that it was a very dangerous and stupid thing to do. Hiking alone on a mountain even the hardest are reluctant to essay.

Here, it must be clarified that he does not consider these boys as dogs, in no case; they were human beings and as such must be treated; he loves them a lot and wants to add a small stone to their better living.

So, being in that room more or less, he did the same but no scream, just an unnatural roar for a man, not a lion's roar, but kind of similar and more destined and directed to one after the other, approaching just half a metre away from them.

He then sat down and, with his finger always pointing on them, commanded them, always with that severe glance, to obey and do the same. And what a miracle; they slowly, one after the other, sat with crossed legs, facing him with always a question mark on their face but also a submission. Inside the 'cage' because that was kind of a well-done room-cage, a cage of good meaning, not a prisoner's cage; it wasn't any such.

Outside, he saw more than 40 nurses and men doctors and carers watching what he was doing in there, them being afraid that from moment to moment the boys would behave in a hostile manner towards him. Just one kick is enough to break his head. They stayed there; they were around him, which was not clever as he also had guys behind him.

He stretched his hand softly, changing to friendly his glance and softly touched the cheek of all of them, one after the other, seeing that their scared face turned, not completely, but slightly to a rather welcomed with soft and, at the same time, shy smile. He stood up, and this time again, with a severe gesture, he asked them to stand up and walk around and play as if he were not at all there between them.

That was it; he gained their confidence but mainly their obedience and discipline as well. One of them addressed to him, also pointing with his finger at him, calling him, "Pouli." He was shocked as that name was also given 50 years ago to his brother by another boy in the same room. Probably, this meant for both something; this was an issue that must be investigated by the psychologist of the hospital.

He unlocked the door and went out; all were staring at him as if he were a phantom. They could not believe that he left the boys there in a peaceful situation and in rather joyful conduct with no crazy sounds and high pitch of the voices, but they were 'tamed' ordinary young men.

They even looked at him when he was out with affection, not with fear. He gave to all a lesson that these young men might be under certain circumstances hostile, but they are also willing to cooperate, provided you obtain the upper hand and keep it with prudence. The potent rumours spread throughout from section to section and reached the management team; it was the subject of the day and maybe the days to come.

At the tennis club, he had quite some newcomers aged between 60 and 70, who heard about the new strategic tennis of an old Greek player and they came to see and possibly pay the fee to become members. It seemed to him that with only a first match he obtained fanatic sympathisers. That was his goal, and the goal of the owner that something new would bring additional players and accordingly also income to the club.

He was happy that they were very glad as new members came, and he was working in pleasant tempo, but at the same time in an enjoyable tennis job as that was also, after all, his beloved sport and hobby.

At the same time, the agreement with all club tennis in Denmark for the 'Old Tigers Tournament, OTT', he gave that name to the tournament, same as the old group's name some years ago. They all preferred that they have the games to take place at one club and avoid the overaged men to travel so many times from club to club from city to city, not to forget the islands because Denmark has islands among them, also Greenland not as an island but as a 'colony'.

He took the initiative of sending them the video of the first match that he had there with that gentle 65-year-old ex-coach, Alex, who showed them exercising this nice sport strategically differently to the usual. So, he succeeded in the tennis old men's tournament to take place there in 'his' tennis club. That was a big success as first many players would come followed by their families and would also give life to this luxury suburb of Copenhagen with sufficient hotels available.

He had to stop giving lessons of 'smart tennis', as he was calling it, as he needed himself to have intensive and rigorous training. His only complaint was that the tennis racket they gave to him was not the one that met his demands and was rather inefficient for his style of play, so he again went to the special shop, and they paid for a nice racket that was a copy of his racket he left behind in Athens.

All was running perfectly well. The tennis club had indoor four courts so there would be games simultaneously, and the tennis tournament would take place after 12 days. It was unknown how many would register and each one had to pay the participation fee of 200 euros. If the weather was to help, then they have six open-aired courts, which would be more convenient.

The money prizes for the finalist would be 2000 euros, and the winner 5000 euros. The revenue was to come not only from the participation fees but also from the advertisements.

The local newspaper, the local radio showed vital interest, but then the local TV station also mentioned that they would cover this event. That was bad for him because it might be a possibility that Karla would watch the games and see that he was still in Denmark and did not fly back to Greece as he had told her. Well, no other way than to take the risk.

Famous brands related to Tenuis as advertisers showed interest in covering the walls of the club inside and outside, and that was very good income for the club. The hospital also supported by offering an ambulance car and medical staff, just in case as they well know that old men would play singles and not double, and singles for this age is quite weary and needs intensive stamina.

They were all grateful to him, and they asked him to stop for a while what he was doing at the hospital and concentrate on his training. They also looked forward, and why not have him as the winner to represent the clinic.

His laptop was always on fire as too many inquiries came from their German customers and he needed many Chinese suppliers to submit competitive offers.

He had to concentrate on his training, and they provided him with a good coach from a central Copenhagen club. He was training daily for more than three hours; they all were impressed by his stamina and the fast improvement of certain shots. He had to take special diet to lose some weight and with extra exercises to strengthen his wrist, which was quite stiff; his wrist was always his advantage.

All were concentrated on him, hoping him to win the tournament so as to turn the unknown until then tennis club wide known in Denmark. That club had four indoor courts and six outside for the summer, but the weather was not always clear, and rain was always a threat.

Back at the asylum, he was enjoying repeated formidable sex with Emma, the 38-year-old head of the two chambermaids' team at the VIP guestrooms. She wanted to have the exclusiveness of his preference, allowing the 22-year-old girl, who was witness to their first ferocious sex action when she opened the door and stood there speechless for a few minutes, observing the whole sex process having both her hands in her mouth but then gaping at what she was seeing.

Emma changed her shifts and always be there with her sometime, allowing not to have the chance to enter his room while she is absent.

He was doing all possible to get the chance to bring that girl to his bed, but that Emma was smart and foxy; she managed to organise the younger one's (Pia was her name) shifts to be such that were combined with his absence either in his working hours at the hospital or during his tennis engagements.

The tennis training was going well. He even had a doctor to follow his health as he told them that he had had a heart attack 20 years ago. These 12 days that he had in front of him were improving his tennis potential, adding some new drives and volleys to his favourite drop shots. After all the training, they used a big bathtub full of ice cubes so as to have his muscles relaxed.

At the club, he was treated as if he were Roger Federer. They wanted him to win by all means.

The hospital supported him by giving him long days off and even put ads on the announcement boards with him there holding a racket as the club needed spectators to bring to the club added value from the entry fees.

At the clinic, all considered him as the hero not only for the upcoming important event of the tennis tournament but also for the performance that he demonstrated in that so-called 'cage' with the untamed, strong boys who, with him, became peaceful sheep.

The combination of both activities tired him out, so he asked the hospital management to extend 10 days off so that he could concentrate on the tennis tournament. They agreed without cutting his bonus. So, he was in a full training program.

One day, he felt a small pain in his elbow, and he decided it was better to stop for the day and allow his elbow to relax. He returned to his apartment, where Pia, the 22-year-old chambermaid, was already in his apartment, cleaning and preparing the bed and bathroom for him, believing that he would come in the afternoon. He entered, and there she was bent on the bed to fix it for him.

He watched her ass, well-shaped and magically attractive. Seeing him at the door, she was surprised that he came so early. He asked her to continue to do what she was doing and ignore his presence, but he had to change the sports uniform, and he did it without considering that she was there, seeing that she was also looking clever without stopping the bed fixing. He took it all off and went to the shower.

She said, "Oh, sir, I am sorry I did not put yet towels in the bathrobe and in the shower; shall I bring them?" He said yes, no problem, so there she was with the towels in her hand in front of him, completely naked. She felt a little embarrassed putting her hand on her mouth, telling him that it was the first time that she saw a naked man with dark skin and black hair on chest, as in the meantime after the shaving black hair started to grow and to be seen.

Her eyes concentrated on his penis that was as always in erected situation. She asked him innocently, "You in the south, you have always have a hard penis; how can you hide this under the trousers?"

He said, "No, darling, this penis is so hard after you appear with your charming face and your gorgeous body that is hidden behind that dress."

She asked him, "Can I touch it?" How could he prohibit her to do this as this was also his desire, and so she touched, and she squeezed to see how hard it was. This amazed him, and he could not resist asking her why she looks at the penis as if she had not seen a penis before. She confessed to him that she never had sex with anybody and she is a virgin while having tears in her eyes for being at that age and still being a virgin.

He embraced her, wetting her apron with his wet body. "Why do you have tears? This is normal for every girl. Other girls lose their virginity at the age of 15, but many even after 25, so it is not too late." This intrigued him as it was always his individual complaint that he was with so many girls, but he never took the virginity of a girl.

He asked her when Emma was to come for her shift; she told him in the afternoon, so there were five hours for her to come.

He asked her, "Are you ready and willing to lose your virginity?" He explained to her that he has a lot of experience and that he would avoid causing any pain to her. She turned red-faced and was, for quite a few minutes, silent, thinking and hesitating to give her consent.

But for her was also the time to decide. It sounded strange to her how it was possible to lose her virginity with no pain. "Do not worry," he said while she was still holding his penis as if she were holding a golden bar.

He took the towels that she still had in her one hand, and he was still with wet body. He took her by his hand and led her to the bed. She told him better lock the door from the inside just in case, and she did so.

He sat on the bed, naked, and he started to unbutton her shirt, and there her gorgeous tits were in front of his eyes, almost on the same level, as he was sitting, while she was standing covered by a small bra; she continued having a blushing face and maybe also quivering.

He removed the bras gently, and he gave a kiss to both tits and sucked slightly her nipples that were erected either were so always from her nature or from getting hot by thinking what was going to follow.

He started to gently nibble her nipples, and she enjoyed that in the fullest. She seemed to accept this with remarkable pleasure; he then unzipped from the side her skirt, and the skirt was down, and there he saw a body that was indeed virgin and untouched, so smooth, soft like a baby, tiny panties, kind of seamless, thin, skimpy belt, was difficulty hiding her puffy pussy and on her ass backside cutting in two her bums.

He asked her, "Now you remove your slip slowly and charmingly like you see in the strippers' films."

She tried to do this as gently as possible and gradually revealed her miniature kind of puffy vagina. To his immense pleasure, he noticed that there was not a single hair on her spotless sweet pussy.

He asked her to lay down on the bed, and he started licking her pussy and sucking her clit, adding extra sensations; her flesh was cringing, the angelic body was clenched, but at the same time, in a high breathy stimulated condition, she seemed to be at the peak of her ecstasy. She felt nice with a glowing face that showed signs of calmness, and in seconds, she came with absolute silent virgin kind of spasms, believing that this was what an orgasm was all about.

She turned to him asking him, "Now am I not a virgin anymore?" He explained to her that this did not happen yet; he noticed a shadow on her face, believing that coming with a climax with his tongue gently in her vagina meant at the same time that she is not a virgin anymore. He asked to change roles and lick his penis; she did not know how to do so, and she took the whole penis in her mouth.

He said, "No, lick first the top part smoothly, move your tongue around it, then take some of it inside your mouth." And she did this very efficiently, creating for him a divine feeling only with the idea that a virgin tongue is doing this to him.

He then told her what 69 means, and he did this in practice; she was down to his penis, licking, now she knew how, him licking her angelic pinkish vagina, a few minutes, and she came again.

He then told her that now is the time. "Your vagina is wet, let us do it patiently and with love and affection."

He turned her on the side and lifted her one leg so the ultra-tiny and maiden vagina can be accessible for as much as possible for a professional penetration.

The head of the vigorous penis was hovering in the very entrance of that marvellous vagina for a second; she pulled herself; he brought her back to the primal position so the foreskin of his penis allowed the head to try one more time and half of the penis head lands softly but firm in her vagina.

He stayed there so that the vagina takes the appropriate shape to accept millimetre by millimetre the rest of the penis.

He drove himself firmer and firmer, deeper and deeper into her, and there he could feel that there was a small obstacle and with a small effort the hymen, that membranous tissue, broke rather easily; he heard a slight, sweet, painful sign, but that was it, the rest of the penis inserted slowly deep in her, and the beloved well known to him movements started; he could hear slight moans from her angelic mouth; he was performing the in and out moving always with care and love but always in controlled tempo, then he felt that she also took part by thrusting up and down her thighs. Well, then that was it, she became a woman; he 'plundered' her virginity with her absolute consent.

No longer than four minutes, she came again, but this time it was a longer orgasm and with pleasure holding his penis inside her squeezing it as if she wanted her vagina to hug and kiss his cock. He had difficulty dragging it out, feeling that he was ready to ejaculate.

She turned around, and he saw a calm and relaxed face, and her flesh looked glittered and fresher; he told her to get it in her hand and act a handjob so that she can see how the penis when is about to come turns to look.

She took it with her tiny hand; he with his fist squeezed her fist around the dick, both fists were moving sweetly up and down to show her the proper way; she opened her eyes widely noticing and seemed to be worried, having not seen this from so close and because the head of the penis became well swelled, very moistened, bit reddish, starting to stiffen until he ejaculated in her hand; she was surprised how this comes out of the penis.

He kissed her, took her by the hand together to the shower, and they both had a hot shower. Back to bed, they saw a red spot. He told her, "That is from your tiny hymen, a small spot of blood, so you must find the way to throw away that sheet before anyone, especially Emma, finds this." She dressed fast, kissed him and ran to bring a new clean sheet.

So, his dream to 'loot' the virginity of a girl came true; somehow the same way a German 50-year-old lady had done the almost same to him, at least so she believed.

He told her, "Next time, I will teach you much more, plus I will also take your other virginity."

She looked at him curiously, saying, "What? Is there a second virginity?"

He said, "Yes, there is, and I will explain to you next time."

So, all went so well, having two jobs, plus his major one on the laptop and having two girls to relieve him when necessary. The one well experienced, the other virgin until he took her innocent virginity.

The training restarted; he heard from the club owner that the participation reached 25, but there were almost nine days to go. Those 25 were between 60 and 68, but there were two also at 70 and 71 (60 was the minimum age for the veteran participants). It is a fact that playing at this age single is not easy and requires athletic skills, lungs as well as strong feet, so many avoid exposing themselves to such health risks, and if they love, tennis they go for doubles, which is less tiring.

He got an unexpected phone call from a friend 58 years ago at the hotel school. He was the only Danish guy at the Heidelberg School. He got his telephone number from the management of the Heidelberg Institution, where he had held that speech.

He, of course, could not imagine that he was in Denmark.

He thought he was in Greece, and as he and his family were planning to visit Greece for their vacations, he wanted his advice where to go and what to visit.

He told him that he was there and very near to him. He was totally surprised. He told him a little of his story and invited him to go to the small mountain country hotel he owned. He was running with his wife and daughter to a small hotel with a nice restaurant.

They fixed the day, and he came with his wife to pick him up. He looked at him and was amazed how younger he was looking in comparison to him. On the road, he told him a few of his adventures, but to tell him all his long story, he needed so much time as if he were to drive from Copenhagen to Madrid. Both he and wife were impressed.

They arrived at his country hotel. A nice 40-room hotel with a nice restaurant, and that restaurant was 'supposed' to not only serve the hotel customers but also people who were living nearby and other visitors.

They gave him a room to rest a little and invited him for dinner in their restaurant. All his family lived there.

Indeed, at 7 o'clock, he went down after he had a shower. They were already there for dinner. He told him about his vast experience he got, especially to control the kitchens whoever the chef was and that he also had once the best restaurant in Athens.

He asked him to give him the menu to study it with the eyes of an expert. He made some observations on the menu, but he also wanted to visit the kitchen. So, his friend took him to the kitchen. He just needed a few minutes to locate some or, better, many dysfunctionalities. But it was not the time to tell anything yet to his friend.

They enjoyed their dinner and drank nice white wine at first with the Norwegian smoked salmon and then red with a 'rather' well-done sirloin steak, although he had asked for medium rare.

His friend confessed to him that he worked in many hotels but mainly at the receptions as a head receptionist and later as a manager, but he had never any good experience for the kitchen. Areus told him that this was the weak point of all hotel managers, while on the contrary, that was his expertise.

Daughter and son seemed to him that they were not that interested in running the hotel forever. Both at the age of 50–55, not married. His schoolmate also felt quite old; he looked old to keep running the hotel, and he was in a stage of uncertainty about what to do.

He told him that this hotel was ideal for him to run the way he knows, but has to return home to his family in Greece. He then came to him, saying, "Look, you look much younger than me and much stronger; I suggest you to rent the hotel with a very low yearly fee."

He did not want to disappoint him by denying and told him, "Let me think about it." Inside him, he was ready to take this challenge as he liked both the small hotel but mainly the restaurant, which was big and accommodated maybe even 100 customers.

He thought maybe, as far as they sold in Greece their building and live in rent, why not bring his whole family here and run this small beautiful hotel in such a nice small village. But this required the consent of his wife, son, and two daughters.

They finished the dinner with Danish cheeses but, of course, nothing to compare with the French cheeses and his favourite Swiss Gruyere. The Danish are proud of their blue cheese, which apparently is not bad at all but is not a dessert cheese as they presented it. He would like to stay overnight, mainly to see what the kitchen offered as breakfast. Arne (that was his name) gave him a nice room, and indeed, he slept there.

The breakfast was good, but having only 15 customers was too big, and the wastage was far too costly. He mentioned this to his friend and what has to be done was to advertise to the village and the nearby villages that a great breakfast would be served every Saturday and Sunday, so maybe attract people to come for the well-to-become-famous breakfast.

He opened his eyes and said, "Oh God, why did I not think of it?" He explained to him that there were many things that can be done to turn the restaurant into a favourite place to come from even central Copenhagen for lunch or dinner.

They drove him back, and he promised to come to watch him play at the tennis 'Old Tigers Tournament'.

So, now where does he stand? He had a two-month contract at the hospital, and he also had a job at the tennis club with unlimited duration, and suddenly appeared a new challenge, without forgetting his China-Germany business that he runs from wherever he is and through his specially upgraded fast laptop to accommodate all his immense data bank.

Nevertheless, his sexual activity was ideally clear, having two mistresses available when he needed a relief and the burden of his daily hard training.

At this point, he has to say that among those ladies that he had in his tennis teaching group at the club, there are two or three married, good-looking ladies, who do not look at him as coach but also differently; that glimpse is easy for him to recognise. But he does not want to create any scandal in the club.

One time, when he was upset with especially those ladies who did not follow his instructions, furiously, he entered the locker rooms without knowing that are next to the ladies' showers, and there were all of them naked, him in a shocked situation, but he ignored what he saw and shouted to them, "Why you do not follow what I teach you?"

They laughed and smiled and tried to even better demonstrate for his eyes their charms and attractiveness. One of them told him, "Look, Mr Areus, I fell down; look at my buttocks, I had to rest as I have bruises."

She turned around to show him the bruises and her whole great arse but without any bruises; she provoked him so much that he was about to grab her and make her know that he can also be a good fucker for her by side to a tennis teacher. Although he got crazy at what he saw, he had to stay serious and, to his regret, leave the locker room.

That coincident, an unintentional entrance to the locker/showers, opened a window, but he better forget about it and close it.

He had a day of relaxation from his tennis training, and he decided to go to the special department of the hospital where there were boys with a certain syndrome, who sit in a wheelchair all day, and they move their head and shoulders up and down unstoppably. He asked the head of the department to bring all nurses and carers to see what he was up to demonstrate.

He approached one boy in a wheelchair, and he sat opposite him, the one facing the other. He looked at him curiously, and probably, the patient thought, *What the hell he wants by sitting opposite me?*

He started doing the same movement like he was doing, up and down continuously. Areus created a competition to him and tried to do this faster than the boy but cleverly allowed the boy to win this, and the cute guy smiled loudly and joyfully showing that he won with the accelerated movements.

Areus pretended that he was sad that he could not follow his fastness. So, competition was going well, allowing him to win all the time. Then, suddenly, after moving up and down, Areus decided to stand his body up on the wheelchair and stand still.

The boy looked at him, always moving up and down, as if he wanted to tell him 'what, you resign?'. He then started again up and down many times, but again, he stayed up, always sitting on the wheelchair for a minute and back to the down and up motions.

Like this, he provoked the boy to do what he does or else he was the winner. He kept doing his program faster and faster but from time to time up and again staying still; the boy showed signs of a loser and accepted defeat. He tried many and uncountable tries and for hours. In the meantime, he had an audience of about 20 people.

All this up and down started to create a pain in his back, and this it was not good to damage his back having a tournament in front of him. But he had to succeed.

He followed his program, and he did the same thing, always one minute up and back to the routine.

He suddenly noticed that the boy wanted to try to beat him even for that up staying for one minute. He made extra hard efforts; he managed maybe 10 centimetres to stay a little up and still, showing to him as if he were to say, "You bastard, I will beat you again."

The audience started to talk among themselves, seeing a slight progress that they had never seen before with that guy since he was born. With a triumph in his eyes, he kept after many ups and downs to stay upright, sitting on his wheelchair, following strictly his program.

Then a miracle happened. The boy stopped the ups and downs. and with a smile of a conqueror, he stayed straight up and stayed there for half a minute. Big applause from all who were watching this.

He felt again that he beat him, and with that peculiar smile, he wanted to show to him that he was the winner again. He kept doing his ups and down, and same as him, after maybe 20 or 30 ups and downs, he managed to stay still and straight for almost one minute. Areus had a defeated face; he stood up and went with his head bent down, showing him that the boy is the winner and he left defeated and humiliated while the boy was smiling for his success and his incredible achievement.

He heard that since then, he managed to stand up with his head and shoulders straight up, which facilitated the nurses to feed him.

He again was the centre of all talks, and they all respected him a lot; some nurses even showed to him that they were ready to offer to him their body for him to play with his ups and downs and his standing up, but this time not with his body but with his penis. He wrote this down on his mind, locating the most beautiful one of them when the time comes as an excellent substitute to wild Emma.

The tennis tournament was approaching, and his training was proceeding perfectly. One night, he took Alex, that guy whom he beat at their very first battle to have a beer. He was a very pleasant-type of man, single as he never married although being very attractive and very rich.

He was telling him that he loves mountaineering and hiking and, in general, dangerous sports. He told him that he often goes to Greenland and he has a good friend there, a fisherman, a kind of Viking. Areus also told him that his dream was to go to Greenland. "Well, let us go after the tournament. It is summer, the best time to go to the southern city of Greenland called Nuuk, where also my fisherman friend is."

Areus told him, "Well, sounds nice, but I cannot as I have a deal with both the hospital and the tennis club."

He abruptly told him, "Fuck both, and let us enjoy there in Greenland." He seemed to like him, and it would be good for him to be there with someone else and not alone in that so-called 'Viking' village. He described also about the northern iced part where he also almost came face-to-face with a white bear.

He warned him that if they go, they would stay on top of the only bar of the place and better not show interest to the barwoman; she is the owner of the place, because if you do so and she also happens to like you, she would drag you up the wooden stairs to her room where she would tear you off with a wild sex, a genuine Vikings sex.

She is big with big tits and big thighs and a vagina that grabs like a plier, especially when she is coming; she would squeeze your penis so hard that you might lose it inside her depth. Do not dare to ask 'how much'; she would throw you from the staircases down. It happened with one Norwegian guy who believed that she did this for money.

All this description despite the wild and primitive sex from the barwoman intrigued him, and he gave him the promise that when the tournament ends, they would go, and he would resign from both jobs, except, of course, his laptop, hoping that up there in the northern part of the European continent, there is still a fast internet connection.

The day of the tournament arrived; he refrained from any sex activity before that even for four days, and this despite the hard objection of Emma.

Before entering the court, they went to the owner's office, and he told them that first if he would win, which he believes he would not, he would donate the prize of the 5000 euros to the club, and that also after the tournament, he would resign. They were very unhappy about this; they actually knew what was the reason for him changing his mind.

So, there were 40 'Old Tigers' there; they even had labels engraved with the Old Tiger's logo, so each one had the label iron glued on their shirts.

There were more than 350 spectators, among them was his friend, the hotel owner and his family and many beautiful nurses, among them was that one that he especially liked and seemed that this was mutual.

The Old Tigers made a parade in front of the spectators. It was funny seeing 40 old men make a parade like gladiators in the Roman arena. The cheerleaders made a great performance. The local TV was there as well as the radio.

The rules were 'knock out', which means once you lose, you are out, and the games are up to 11, the first who reaches the 11 games is the winner and no tie breaks.

The tournament started.

He was playing with a guy from Odense. He was 64 or even below, looking strong. The game started; that guy was playing very offensively, and Areus was struggling to return his balls. The Odense guy easily was in the lead for three games, causing his fans to be disappointed.

There was a conflict inside him: what shots to activate against him as it was said he is among the best player of the tournament. Sliced shots or flat forehand? Drop shots or lobs? Anyway, there was nothing to lose and to implement what he was meant to be, the guru of the drop shots.

Drop shot is a spectacular shot but very risky; the chances are less than 50%. But he was expert on that shot, given that, he started to climb up with winning games until they were 3-3, but the Odense guy stroke back and advanced 5-3 and 7-3. He was in bad shape seeing that he cannot beat that Odense guy as he right away understood his strategy, and he could not allow him to activate his specialty shots.

So, he moved to sliced shots so to just pass over the net, and that created to that opponent many problems as his big shot was the drive (forehand), but having a ball too low, he could not go so down to uplift and return the ball, and that ended to the net.

So, this was it, 7-5, 7-7. The Odense guy again 9-7. Then he changed, seeing that he cannot confront his sliced shots, so he advanced to take the ball as volley before the ball touched the ground that succeeded to equalise 9-9.

That worked, but at the same time seeing that he was advancing, he added lobs to his game, and these were winner shots combined with drop shots. The opponent had to run back far and with a precise drop shot; it was Areus the winner at 11-10.

Big applause, they were all happy that the 69 plus years old foreigner was the winner over a 16 years younger man. The club owner told him that as he was able to beat him, the rest of the players would be less good, but this was subject to be seen later, as with tennis, you never know; a bad player can have a good day and become unbeatable. They had between games a three-hour rest and went to his apartment to have a small nap.

Arriving there, Emma was almost at his door. He told her, "Rush for a best massage, but do not dare to ask for more; am I clear?"

She, in fact, did her best, making him very relaxed, but at the same time asked him to allow her to hold his penis and also a peculiar wish to have his finger in her anus, and at the same time with a vibrator, she succeeded in multiple orgasms. Well, that was OK; he did not have any intercourse to weaken his strength and stamina.

He asked her to wake him up in one hour as he needed a one-hour nap.

Indeed, he got that helpful nap; she woke him up with kisses, wishing him new victory. He got ready and went back to the courts. The next player was from a famous Copenhagen club. He beat another player in the previous game with an easy 11-5.

His age was 70 but seemed to him to be one of those players who aim to break the nerves of the opponent. He was justified; this was the type of player who just returns balls and does not try to make any winner.

He tried hard to activate his usual method, but that guy was running like hell returning all the balls. But for how long? He cannot do this forever. They reach 4-4, and the first signs of tiredness were obvious for both.

So, he had to keep on before the fatigue breaks him down. It was an amazingly good game for him for his serves, which usually is not his strong weapon, but it worked fine, and at the end, he smashed him with 11-4.

So, now he was among the 10 that were to advance. The 'spectators' were applauding him as he was the oldest in that tournament, and he was still alive in the last 10. Surprisingly, his 65-year-old friend, Alex, with whom he had plans to go to Greenland, was also advancing to be with the last 10.

He took a nice shower at the club's bathrooms and changed shorts and shirt and returned to watch the last two players still playing hard. He was to play with the winner of that couple.

Both were 60 years old and in a good physical situation; he thought seeing the quality of their play that well, either one or the other as the winner, would be the end of his tennis tournament adventurous trip.

He then went to the bar, and there he met among many nurses and doctors also the 'one', the 'special one', the girl he liked the most and seemed to have a mutual attraction. She congratulated him, telling him that she was there, hoping that he would come to the bar. They had a quite long discussion; she told him her story. Although only 29, she had already had two bad marriages with all the negative behavioural characteristics.

Both were indifferent to any close connection; they were more interested for friendships with male friends than with her. He asked her if they were gay; she denied, but they considered sex as a marital obligation to try to make her pregnant just for a child rather than please her but also themselves with a good sex.

He could see where she was aiming at, and there, he had to grab the chance with his vast knowledge of what to do. He told her that sex is the main requirement for a relationship. Good quality sex with variety brings the couple closer.

He emphasised the 'variety'; she seemed not to understand what variety means in sex. He then went straight to the point; he bent to her ear and asked her, "Have these guys ever given you the pleasure of anal sex in combination with masturbation?"

She looked at him as if he came from planet Mars. She said, "You mean from behind?"

"Yes, this is what I mean."

"But how can it be done at the same time?"

"Well," he said, "yes, this is my specialty, but anyway forget it and try to find a guy who will love you and, most of all, give you good quality sex with multiple orgasms; sex unites the couple; with no variety and quality sex, you will have another disappointment."

He kissed her cheek and looked like he was aloof and left her staying there with a face full of dizziness and certainly soaked panties, hearing the multiple orgasms that she never experienced. He turned a little to see her, and he observed she was still holding her mouth with her hand, but then she was gaping as if she heard something curious but, at the same time, funny. He winked his at her to make her understand what he meant and let her fantasise the scene as he described.

He then went back to his apartment to get a nice sleep as tomorrow was the second day before the last day of the final. Emma was still there although her shift was over. He felt his legs and thighs very heavy. He asked her to bring a lot of ice cubes. He filled up the bathtub, and naked, he jumped in.

Emma came and found him in the bathtub; he asked her to throw all ice cubes in. She said, "No, you will freeze."

He said, "This is what I exactly need," and so she emptied the bin with the ice cubes and relaxed for a few minutes and straight went to bed for a good sleep.

Next, he had to face a good player who was the eldest of all; he was 72, so quite close to his age.

It wasn't easy but also not that tough. He beat him, with an 11-8. At the next court, there was no game; he asked what happened, and he heard that the one opponent did not show up, so probably tired, he left the tournament. So, he had to wait until after the semi-finals was to be played and decided better go to his apartment for a rest.

After a good nap, he returned for the semi-final with a 60-year-old player in good shape and, unfortunately, left-handed. This always brings him in confusion and not only him but all right-handed players.

They started, and that guy was a hurricane; he tried hard but no way until he advanced to 5-0. Then he saw him collapse. The doctors said he fainted, but the doctors could bring him back, but they did not allow him to continue, so due to his opponent's abstain due to health reason, he was the lucky one to play tomorrow in the finals.

He then went to the bar for a quick beer after a quick shower, and there, she was waiting for him. She approached, and with a broken voice she told him, "I am ready to try it."

He said, "Try what?"

"Try what you proposed to me yesterday."

Well, now what to do? Emma at the apartment was his bodyguard, allowing no one to get close to him. He told her, "Wait and see what tomorrow's final result will be, and either I lose or win, we will still celebrate this at your home with champagne, OK?"

She said OK with a big smile and probably also with wet panties.

After a good night's sleep, he was ready to play the final with an opponent, whose, as he was told, weapon was his lethal serve. If he manages to have good returns, then he might have slight chances to win.

On Sunday, the last day, a lot of people came to enjoy the fiesta as this is what it was—a big celebration.

A feast for the village they never had before in any such event and so many visitors, and that was all due to their hero, Areus.

On the board of results, his name was mentioned as 'Areus, the Spartan King'.

He thought, *Well, but I must win, so the party, the extraordinary and unique local event will have a happy ending.*

The two finalists were presented as if it were Roger Federer against Rafael Nadal, and the game started. Indeed, his serve was a killer serve that you see at ATP professional games. But that was all this guy had to show, his only 'exterminator' serve and nothing else.

He was easy to make unforced errors, all he had to do was just block his serves and return into his court, and that's it. Easy to say, but very difficult to do.

The opponent won the first three games, his left-hand shots were confusing him, but he had to think well before he decides how and where he must send the yellow ball.

He noticed that his two-handed backhand was very weak and slow, and he difficulty could not return, so that guy was moving all the way with footwork to reach his forehand, leaving big, empty space from the other side. That big gap he was leaving on the other side, he had to exploit, and so he did.

The left-handed guy won two more games to a 5-0. Now he knows him well and how he has to face him. His serve was not as good as the first five games, so he was returning almost all balls and forced him to his weak backhand, and that was the strategy.

Tennis is a spiritual chess game; all depends on strategy and finding the weak point of the opponent, and now he knows all his problems; hitting him at his backhand, he moved all around to return with forehand and then was with a nice drop shot on the other side no way to catch, and so he managed to get the first game. So, 5-1, there he heard the people trying to give courage to him, 5-2, and 5-5.

The opponent's good serve returned, so he then went ahead with three games 8-5, him back to his strategy 8-8, and that guy again 10-8; he was only one game to win the tournament and the 5000 euros that he in no case wanted his club would have to give to his opponent.

Areus asked the referee for a toilet break; after all, they were old guys, so peeing is needed from time to time. In the bathroom, he was alone; he did pee, and then he looked at himself in the mirror, begging or rather commanding himself to do everything not to disappoint all the people that were there for him.

He took deep breaths; he hit his chest, and he shouted to himself in front of the mirror, "You are a Greek, so fight like a Spartan!" He entered the court not as the old guy but as a Spartan, with his teeth well tight. It was his turn to serve, and surprisingly, his old times' good serve was back; he paid extra and stronger attention to his sliced serves that sent the opponent almost to the neighbouring court, and this was done and finished that game with 0 from the opponent so now 10-9.

The opponent's serve as always was good, but this time, he returned all his serves not with forehand as he used to do by blocking a strong serve with forehand because the ball picks up the speed and strength of the serve and goes far away out of his baseline; on the contrary, blocking the hard serve with backhand and sliced the ball just passes the other side, and there, this specific opponent had problem to run and return, so he beat his serve and achieved the break, and here they are 10-10.

The opponent asked for his turn for a toilet break. People were cheering him; he was almost deaf; he wanted to hear nothing. He did not sit down on the bench, but he was going like a tiger in a cage, left and right and again right and left with no rest, just waiting for the guy to return; with his eye, he showed at the corner that beautiful girl, so he said to himself, This is your trophy, fight for it.

The opponent returned with fresh shorts and shirt, looking fresh and determined to win.

It was his turn to serve, hoping again the slice serve would do the job. But that guy knew that he again goes for sliced serve, and he was there to return. Then he remembered his first tennis coach that tennis is also psychology, so try to break the nerves of the opponent.

So, he did what Djokovic does and bounced the ball more than 10 times, and he could see that the opponent was getting nervous at the same time looking at the referee, but he ignored him and did another two bounces and then a kick serve.

The kick serve was the solution as the ball bounced high up and it was not easy to return, and that worked, 15-0. Second serve he was expecting a sliced serve and left all his left side empty, and there he hit a flat serve and an ace 30-0. Now he was in confusion seeing him that he abandoned the sliced serve, so he was waiting for him at the corner but not that far from the corner so then was again his sliced serve; the ball reached the next court; he ran but no way and 40-0.

They all stood up, applauding continuously, but that did not disrupt his self-concentration, so he starting bouncing the ball, 8, 9, 10, 11, 12 times, breaking the nerves of the opponent, following Djokovic's nerve-wracking method, and having the momentum and with obvious self-confidence, he decided not to go for a flat serve or for sliced serve but the shot of the famous and unique Kyrgios (he is also half-Greek) that refers to the underarm serve, where the ball goes slowly and slowly reaches the net passes above and falls with a side spin on opponent's court, and the ball dies down in the terrain. That last point was executed faultlessly and absolutely cleverly as the championship point.

He was the winner; underarm serve is rare to see on courts, but that was easy for him because he was a good drop shot player. People started chanting his name and running to the court took him high up. "Winner is Areus, the Greek Spartan!" Congratulations came from all sides, also from the players that took part in the tournament.

The club owner officially gave him the trophy, a check of 5000 euros. With his eye, he tried to detect among so many people where that girl was, and he found her with an inviting smile.

Then all at the bar for drinks, he first went for a shower and back to the bar; they drank also with his good friend Alex, with whom he was to go the next few days to Greenland. He was also happy that he was the winner. Arne, his hotel old friend, was also there to congratulate and remind him to take that decision.

He promised that he would do it soon. Alex reminded him that he made all arrangements and they would leave on Thursday, which means in four days.

After some beers and glorious speeches for the winner, he had to search for his 'trophy date'. She was there, waiting for him at the exit gate; she was tremendously hot after the juicy subject of the anus sex, for which, as he described, was a fanatic mentor.

Her car was just outside, and they were driving to her home. He sat next to her, adoring how beautiful she was; her hair framed her pretty face; her body was gorgeous. In a few minutes that body would be at his entire disposal and activate his sex variations and activate his abilities gathered from all those past years with several girls and ladies of all ages and sex peculiarities.

Her name was Lorna, and she was waiting for him to exercise among many other positions on her, the so-called anal sex, which she never before enjoyed and not even imagined how that could work.

Her home was a beautiful and cosy apartment with candles already on and red French wine with surprisingly French and Swiss yellow cheese on the table. That girl spent a lot of money for what was on that table.

He told her that he was still sweating from the hard tennis game, and that he needed another shower. She showed him where the shower was; she also gave him fresh towels.

He enjoyed a hot relaxing shower. He looked down at his friend (his penis) and asked him if he was ready. The answer was yes with a rising up and down small movement, which confirmed the right away availability together with anxiety.

In the meantime, Lorna put on something more comfortable that allowed her magnificent body to show more vivid with a visible panty line across her bottom, a body of a supermodel, an angel face with inimitable hazel eyes. Ideal characteristics that thousands of men never had or would have the chance to enjoy, an ultimate pleasure was in front of his eyes.

She was such a nice and full of joy girl, always with a smile on her mouth; she also had a lot of humour. They spoke better in English; he preferred English as his Danish was coming but too slowly back. They drank the good French wine;

she specially selected this for him, knowing that he is a bon viveur a connoisseur. He came closer to her, and he took her hand and led it to touch his rampant penis that was already in the usual hard and in 'battle-ready situation'.

She somehow felt embarrassed, and she showed a sign that she was not yet ready and took back her hand. He kissed her on the cheek, and she answered back and kissed him on the lips. He got the message that this girl wanted things in slow tempo, gradually, step by step, and he had to respect that as the whole night was theirs.

The second kiss instantly became intense and dominant; this was an even more real lovers' kiss, where lips and tongues met in a full of passionate Brazilian samba. They took a break to drink their wine; the cheese was also carefully selected. They moved to the sofa; he laid down on the full length of the sofa, having his head on her lap.

She caressed his head, and she unbuttoned the first buttons of his shirt and started to caress the black, already quite grown hair on his chest and was now quite obvious after shaving a few weeks ago. Very rare for a man his age to have black hair on his chest.

She kissed his chest with her tongue licking his chest with a tongue as soft as the brush of a painter. It is amazing how these Danish girls get crazy with the black hair of the chest. He sat next to her, and this, time he unbuttoned her shirt; to his pleasure, there was no bra under the shirt.

Two incredible, this is the accurate word, breasts appeared in front of him, caressing these in an awe. He relaxed his head in the in between the two tits 'river', having his cheeks to caress the two magnificent tits, admiring the tenderness and delicate softness of both and looked for the sweet taste of her nipples, the wonderful, not red rather pinkish, also perfectly shaped erect nipples but at the same time having a certain inverted structure. Mother Nature sometimes is extravagantly generous to some girls, and she was one of them.

It took not that long to find themselves naked in her bed; she told him that she had in this bed a very bad experience, chronicling her first guy who wanted to take her virginity was very violent, pushing his penis in her with such a force to break the intact hymen, creating to her a big pain, and then after he did that, he pulled out his penis and masturbated, dressed and left, and he was supposed to be a boy at her age that was in love with her.

And what did he do? He announced to all friends his deflowered the most beautiful girl in the whole area, leaving behind a psychological trauma, similar to what happened to his Anabella.

He told her that violence for him is an unknown word; he is an altruist; he cares more to bring full joy and pleasure to his sex partner than himself.

This said, they started caressing each other, and well, what happened in almost two hours is difficult to be described in words. He would need 20 pages to enumerate, and in French, *explique* all details of the countless sex interchanges and positions but with excess of love and tenderness.

Lorna proved to be easy to learn almost all Kamasutra positions and still utilise that unique situation, looking for even more. She was in such a merry mood together with a remarkable lust and in such a situation that he did not dare to tell her that this was all he had to teach her. He even had to improvise for new sex settings to satisfy the angel.

She was constantly repeating, "Take me, do more to me, this is why I am here for." So he said to himself, *Man make her feel as a real princess, activate all sex skills and unlock all your abilities, if necessary invent new; turn yourself to her sexual therapist; the weapon is there to obey to your commands.* Although they were for two hours utilising all possible positions, the one that she liked most was the 'scissors or pretzel' position as his penis reached the ultimate depth of her.

But the actual 'discovery' for her, and that was the flashpoint of their sex date, was no other than the anal that he had whispered into her ear when they were at that bar, and it had rang loud bells in her ears but, at the same time, 'annoyed' also her pussy feeling that is losing the game versus the anus, till then they did not perform that.

He whispered into her ear, "Is it now the time for the promised anal?" She just had to say yes by bending her head, accepting the challenge.

It seemed that she was prepared, went to the bathroom and brought Vaseline jar, but before applying the Vaseline, he laid her down to fully expose her ass; her anus entrance was tight; he licked her there; he loves the aroma of the asshole; his tongue helped to lubricate enough her butthole, and then Vaseline made all easier, so that love night ended with the optimal manner, the sexual apotheosis.

He cannot say how many times she came all these two hours; it was uncountable, but he kept himself, not to finish wishing nothing else but to give to her more and more orgasms; each orgasm she had it was for him an alleviation, as if he also had his climax. He, after two hours, permitted himself for a comforting orgasm in her anus as that would not have any unwanted consequences.

They both went to the shower being the one so close to the other as one body and indeed metaphorically only one person was under the shower.

The sleep was immediate after all these two and more hours, they woke up at 11 o'clock next morning.

She prepared a fast breakfast as he had to be back to resign from both hospital and the tennis club. He told her that he would leave for Greenland for one or maybe more weeks, and he would probably return to her.

She drove him to the hospital, and he rushed to his apartment, where he faced a freaked Emma; he invented a good excuse that they drank beers with Alex and as it was late and impossible for him to drive, they walked to his three-bedroom house that was close to the bar, and they slept there. It was the first time that he told her about Greenland, and she was about to cry in tears. He told her that he would be back, and this calmed her.

He changed his dress as he was still smelling the Lorna's body sweat aroma; he ran to the tennis club, returning the 5000 euros cheque as he had promised. They were vertical; they did not accept that; there was no other way than to tear the cheque in pieces.

They thanked him a lot, and they told him that they would never forget what he did for them. They would plan one of the summer courts to name it Areus, the Greek. He wished them that one day they would become the biggest tennis club in Copenhagen and he would also keep them well preserved in his memory.

Right away, he then went to the management office of the clinic.

He told them that he resigned due to obligations at home. There, he faced only sad faces; they asked, "Why are you so welcome with us?" He answered he knows, but he had plans to go to Greenland and then back to Greece. It was a life's dream that now would become true. The accountant came, and they gave him a good amount of money.

He asked them to keep the apartment for three more nights until he leaves for good; they had not any single objection. They all stood up and thanked him for all that was done by him and wished him good luck.

Alex asked him to meet and take him to the shop where he could buy warm garments. Yes, it was summer and in the south of Greenland, it was not that cold, but if they decide to go to the north, then he would need heavy coats and trousers, hats, gloves, socks and many more necessary accessories. He also asked him for his passport to arrange for the visa.

He was in an enthusiastic situation that he would at last go to Greenland, and especially there was a good friend of Alex who knows all the people, so he would not be a foreigner between foreigners.

Alex was a rich man; his father left him a fortune as he had shares at Wall Street since 1972, and those shares brought a lot of profits from dividends. So, Alex had shares and a big amount of cash at the banks, and he was always telling him that he is eager to do business, but he is not that capable to choose what business to do.

Emma and Pia were sad; he asked Emma to keep some of his clothing as he would need the trolley luggage to put in different garments for Greenland. She said she would keep them in her house intentionally so that he would be obliged to pass when he returns from her home and as her husband works at the Swedish city of Malmo, and he comes one or two times the year and more or less they were in a separation process, so the house is only for her and always a warm bed ready for him.

He bought all the necessities, and two days later, they were to fly to the only international airport of Greenland, Kangerlussuaq Airport.

He wanted to call Karla, but for a reason that he did not know, he did not call her.

That night, he stayed there in his apartment, and smart Pia managed to stay hidden in the locker room so that when Emma leaves for her home, she comes to his room.

They had a nice sex, and she also lost her virginity from the backdoor. She was so happy that it was him who took her virginity from both tiny 'caves'. She slept there the night as she had the next day morning shift, and they enjoyed a very relaxing sleep, having their bodies tightly embraced.

Alex came with his car to fetch him from the Clinique, and there, what he faced was unforgettable. Managers, doctors and more than 50 nurses, among them Lorna, Emma, and Pia, were all there to say goodbye and wish him good luck.

Alex turned crazy seeing this and asked him, "Who the hell are you to have so many fanatics to cherish you with tears to say goodbye to you?" He told him he simply is the Greek who is always ready to please and fascinate anybody.

On the way, he got the phone call from his friend, Arne, the hotel owner, who was insisting to take the decision and take over his hotel for one year to make it run well. He asked for not any rent money and whatever income is his, just deliver the hotel to him back with new clientele and fame. He was with family to move to his brother who lives in Spain. He promised to take the decision fast.

He talked to Alex about this and told him that it is a challenge to turn a hotel, especially the restaurant that is rather declining, to a successful business, but now Greenland is the target. They were to fly with Air Greenland; all the rest, where to stay, where to eat, where to drink, he left all to Alex's fisherman friend. He did not mention where to fuck as that is a big question mark; there in such a small community is not the best thing to fuck the wife of a 'Viking'.

Alex told him that the flight usually takes a bit less than five hours, and from that international airport, they fly to Nuuk, the biggest city in the south of Greenland, a 'mysterious' place for adventure. They arrived at the Copenhagen airport, and he left the car at a special parking lot for a long period stay, but one relative was to pick it up from there.

Air Greenland was there. Alex arranged that day as it was the only day that an airbus was flying and not the usual turbo aircrafts, but the turbo aircraft is to fly from the international airport to Nuuk.

They had to pass very strict virus checks, and they were on board. Alex told him that if he would not sleep, then it was nice to enjoy the flight view through the window, but, of course, there was nothing but sea, even Iceland, which is on the way, the plane was not flying over due to the fear of the volcano eruptions.

He told him that last night he had a beautiful girl in his bed, and so he said he would rather sleep during the flight.

The airbus took off, and they were on the way to Greenland. A southern Mediterranean guy would become a Viking in a few weeks. The flight was good with some turbulence, but he slept like a baby. When he woke up, it was the meal time. Beautiful Danish girls were serving a nice meal that he especially liked, the sandwiches called smørrebrod, which one has to eat by all means in Scandinavia.

Blue cheese, of course, and a white wine that was not the best he ever drank but, in any case, matched the sandwiches. They, after exactly four hours and 50 minutes, landed at the Kangerlussuaq Airport. They did not at all get out from that airport but through closed corridors, and they went straight to the flight gate to Nuuk.

Alex informed him that the flight was about one hour.

They needed to wait two hours there at the airport and drink a coffee, and the time passed fast, and there, they were on that turbo aircraft, heading to Nuuk. Alex arranged that his friend, the fisherman, the one with the biggest ship to fish at the fjords, would pick them up from the Nuuk airport.

It was a nice view outside the window, and then in almost 55 minutes, at the small Nuuk airport, which is usually covered with snow, but as they were in June, the temperature should be around 10 degrees Celsius, so the runway was clear.

Alex knew some important words in the Greenlandic language, but where they stay, where they would eat and drink, all speak not perfect but understandable English and Danish.

Tuppi was the name of their friend. The fisherman was there to pick them up in a Skoda car. He was a nice, big fellow and very friendly; he spoke little Danish and little English; it was difficult for him to communicate, mixing words from the two languages so that they could, more or less, understand each other.

They arrived at the centre of the small city, and they went straight to their hotel and not to that bar with the Viking barwoman, who was for unknown reasons closed those days. He was amazed how nice hotels there were around, even with a spa and, of course, bars and nice restaurants.

All seemed to be so nice and calm, not many tourists running around to destroy the calmness of the place. Alex made arrangements for the night with Tuppi, and they went to their rooms to have a small nap.

It was about early night as time but daylight; he asked where is the northern light (Aurora Borealis), Alex told him that it was not to be seen in summer due to the sun that is bright at midnight; that you can enjoy and admire after middle of August.

They relaxed for a small while, and Tuppi was there again to go for dinner.

He told him that he wanted to eat a seal or whale, and he said in a rather funny way, "What you eat here is mine to arrange, and you will not regret it." He said OK, he is in his hands, but as a hotel manager and restaurant owner, he wanted to eat everything, not only fish but also meat and even birds if there was such hunting; he wanted to taste all as this had been his job for many years.

"Oh," Tuppi said, "then you put me at ease. Alex is easier, but be sure that what he orders for you will please you very much."

He made them walk a little around to see the Arctic Sea, and the shops and how the locals were dressed. More or less, European, but there were also some women having pullovers with beads. Most were carrying coats and trousers made of animal skin, and he thought that it would be nice to find a shop to buy for him too.

After a nice promenade, Tuppi brought them to the restaurant where they were to eat. It was a nice place with nothing to remind, of course, of those Vikings taverns that are seen in different Vikings films. The restaurant was not big, but there were so many ornaments on the wall of the bar, and there were also barrels in the centre of the restaurant. The chairs were comfortable but not any luxury type of chairs with ordinary dark-coloured wooden tables. Tuppi did not ask what they wanted; he took the initiative and ordered.

Right away, there was ale on the table, and that was the one that is famous from Nuuk, called Codhaab Bryghus. The taste was good and close to good German beers or, better, close to Carlsberg and Tuborg of Denmark. The first dish arrived. It was the hors d'oeuvre, a humpback whale with mustard and onions together with hot white bread rolls.

It matched well with the beer, although he, lover of good wine, would rather prefer to have a white wine. The first dish was excellent and new for him, but the second to come was what he needed, and it was reindeer tenderloin with celery root, excellent taste and excellent the way it was presented; the chef gave to that a master's excellent dish for awarding.

The ale mugs were fast emptied, and new came very instantly. The next dish was what he mainly wanted: smoked whale that paradoxically was black that was from those huge humpback whales' meat, superb, and for him was the sensational dish that he wanted from the Greenlandic kitchen; it was served again with some kind of roots and potato puree, and he, must say, believing that this was all, he was already not only with a full belly but also complete with culinary perception.

But unexpectedly, still there was a new dish that was cod, kind of smoked but not exactly smoked. He wondered why this came almost last and not after the hors d'oeuvre, that was also perfect but what a pity no white wine to go with. The menu ended with a cream cheese ice cream with yogurt.

The money they paid was quite a lot compared to Danish or, in general, European restaurant prices, but, of course, what they ate there was unique and was worthwhile. Alex and he shared the cost of the meal of Tuppi.

Then the night life ends always at bar, where to his pleasant surprise he saw at the bar quite some foreign girls; he tried to hear the language, and that was

German. At this point, he got the info; he does not know why he brought this issue right there while looking at the girls, that prostitution in Greenland is illegal in contrast to Denmark and although Greenland belongs to Denmark.

It was not the time after such a long trip to hit on the German girls at the bar. Tuppi seemed like if he might not like this as he has a good name in Nuuk, and his friends must also behave accordingly. Anyway, good ale was there and German beer.

The bar was full, and they had to stand as there was no stool available. The problem was that he felt that one of the German girls was hitting on him, so what shall he do to pretend that he is a gay? As Tuppi did not approve that they end up bringing girls in the hotel that he booked for them under his name. He turned his back to her, being sure that she would think what a prick; she hits on him, and he turns his back to her. This was also something new for him, never did such a thing ever happened before, as he always grabs any such chance.

Tuppi, after they drank quite some beers, suggested that they go to the hotel and have a deep sleep as tomorrow, at 7 o'clock, he would be at the hotel to fetch them and go with his boat to the fjords and also deep waters fishing. They agreed as that was indeed something new that every man would dream to live it.

At the door, going away, he threw an eye to the German girl, making her understand, by lifting his shoulders, that he wanted, but he couldn't tonight.

Back at the hotel, the first few hours at Nuuk were very interesting; the food was excellent, but as he said to Tuppi, tomorrow if they again eat fish such as whale, seal or shrimp and more fish specialties, he must have white wine, even if that is very costly.

The sleep was immediate and deep after such a tiring trip and also after a heavy meal and many beers. He woke up at 3 o'clock because he forgot to fix the alarm clock that was available on the bedside table.

He woke up at 6 o'clock, dressed fast, shaved both beard and head, and they went down where a nice breakfast buffet was expected. Many impressive new foods for him, among others shrimps, smoked salmon and smoked slices of the heart of the reindeer and many nice small fish products.

Alex was late, but he came the very last minute before Tuppi was to arrive; he ate fast. When Tuppi arrived, they invited him also to have some reindeer, but he denied as his wife did arrange for his early morning meal.

They reached the harbour, and Tuppi's ship was the biggest one from the many that were ready to sail and also seemed to have a very strong hull.

The sea was calm, and this guaranteed a pleasant fishing trip in the Arctic waters. Tuppi was their trip skipper; he said that they would have three hours at a fjords safari, and if they are lucky, they can experience trout or cod or even, with even more luck, redfish, but catching a fish on the hook with no lure is pure luck. He added, "If where you throw your hook a trout is hangry and bites, you find yourself proud for what you fished."

They were all lucky the Greenlandic seas and fishes were very friendly to their hooks. The whole was a magnificent experience that no one must not miss if he believes that he is or wants to become an adventurer.

They returned being so happy that they experienced the tour to the Greenlandic fjords. They went back to the hotel for a hot shower and lay for 30 minutes in bed, where from his mind passed all those that his eyes saw at these fjords and how he was privileged at this age to be able to 'explore' the maybe most northern part of Europe.

But now, his belly started pottering being quite empty. He got dressed and went out for dinner. Tuppi wanted to please him, and the dinner had smoked reindeer and kind of carpaccio, and the main course was a real surprise with wild musk oxen meat with red wine imported from France; that dinner was a culinary delicious apotheosis.

Who could tell him a few days ago that in two days he would taste what he dreamt to eat, humpback whale, Arctic cod, smoked reindeer and musk oxen? Alex was also enthusiastic because he insisted on good and different meals. Together with him, he would also become a 'bon viveur' and a good degustateur. But there are many more to try, such as seals and also maybe chase birds. He wanted to know if there were birds they hunted there, hoping not eagles as they are a protected species; seagulls are also protected; he was curious if there were any. It seemed there were not any.

So, the next day's meal must be seal meat as seal hunting is allowed in these Arctic seas, plus whatever other plans Tuppi has for them.

Tuppi has a family, so they allowed him to go home, telling them tomorrow to sleep as long as you can. He would pass by their hotel at 10 o'clock to take them to the famous Nuuk Brewery to see all the ale production process. That was indeed a good idea to enlarge his restaurateur's experience.

They then went for drinks at the same bar, as last night hoping that the German girl who was last night there would also be there tonight.

They entered, but at the bar were only men, so it seemed that he lost the open invitation he had the night before; such a chance appears once, and you have not to let it go.

Anyway, they ordered beer, but this time Dutch beer; to his left and right, he was hearing different languages, such as English, Danish, German, Swedish and a local language that was quite peculiar, but he thought what peculiar would it be for them if they hear the Greek language; they would say the same, "What a peculiar, funny language."

They drank two beers each, and to his happy surprise, he saw the three German girls entering. There was no stool available at the bar, so they took a table. But there were many young men, and they also looked at them while entering with the glance of men who are long without sex.

He, as a smart guy on such occasions, wanted to gain and attract the attention and the preference from the girls. He asked the barman to bring three beers and three snaps to their table, and so he did. The barman showed them who the 'donor' was; he lifted up his glass of beer, and they did the same with a 'Zum wohl' Scol I Scandinavia countries.

Behind their table, there were two men who noticed his gesture to the girls. They were battling at a Bras de Ferre contest, and they seemed slightly drunk. The one celebrating his victory against the other with a big and wild scream that made all turn to see what happened.

He turned himself to him and said, "Eh, you Blacky." He turned to see who was there behind him, but there was no one. He answered in a hostile and freaky manner (like Robert De Niro in the film, *Taxi Driver*), "You talking to me?" He repeated, "Are you talking to me?"

Alex was holding him not to continue this dialogue. The guy shouted, "Do you see any other spaghetti man in this bar?" He, a hot-tempered guy, tried to rush forward against him, and the situation was close to a bad escalation. Alex stopped him. That guy was in an uncontrolled situation.

The barman intervened and tried to calm down their nerves. The guy then said, "If you want to claim our girls, then come and fight with me in a Bras de Ferre, and if you win, I go, but if I win, you take your ass out of this bar." Saying this, he giggled as if he were already the winner and looked at the girls as if he were the Viking of the night.

The girls were also frightened, looking at him in a very angry way as he was talking as 'our' girls as if he possessed them while they never knew him.

So, he had a challenge he cannot deny as he would be humiliated and lose the girls while the first step was already done. The guy was strong one could easily see, but Areus possessed the technique; he won such competitions with stronger guys than him. His secret was his strong wrist and this was due to the sliced tennis, which creates a strong wrist.

He had in his building his own indoor tennis court, so every day, he was training, and every day, a fast ball throwing machine sent quick and strong balls to him, and he had to return, so his wrist was extra and unusually strong, while the other guy had strong arms and muscles.

He took the challenge and on his turn, said, "If I win, you take your filthy ass out of here and never bother the girls, OK?"

The German guy said, "Yes, and you have 1% chance to win."

Areus wanted to make him feel ridiculous, telling to the German, "I suggest that you go to the toilet and shit in there because during the fight and with the pressure you will take a dump in your trousers."

They all laughed while at the same time he noticed that at the bar there was a betting situation.

The barman asked him to delay as the betting was on fire. They all bet for the German except Alex, who put a lot of money on him and alone against all the rest. Areus told him, "You should not do this; the guy is strong, and there are very limited chances for me to win."

Alex reminded him of the tennis fight, "They all bet for him, but at the end, you won, so I trust your sneaky strategy."

In the meantime, Tuppi also came as the rumours ran fast, and he heard that a Greek was fighting, so he rushed to come to save him from troubles.

He made a sign to the girls that, well, he would do his best, but he would be sorry if he loses; they showed him the two fingers of the victory. Meanwhile, the fight news went around fast, and many came in the bar (that was done cleverly by the barman; he sent someone around inviting more to come) to see, and the betting was up to quite big amounts; it reminded the hard fights that they see in films with the legend Bruce Lee. The bar was crowded. That German guy was looking as if he had already won and sent smiles and kisses to the girls.

Tuppi arrived and approached Alex; he asked what the hell was going on, what the hell he was up to?

Alex asked him, "Do you have money with you?"

He answered, "Yes, I just sold the day's good catch." So he asked him to trust his advice and 'put all the money on Areus'.

"Are you sure?"

"Yes, I tell you to do it before they close the betting time."

"You know what my wife will do to me if I return home with empty pockets?"

Alex told him, "You will need more than two pockets to put the money that you will win tonight; trust me, that Greek son of the bitch hides strength and strategy in whatever he does."

The barman announced that betting was over and turned to Areus and told him, "Go, and I hope you lose as I bet for the German."

He smiled at him as if he wanted to tell him that he made the wrong decision.

The girls again were in favour of him, applauding him when he stepped down from his stool to go to that fighting table.

The one hand met the other, his much smaller than the German's. The barman gave the command to 'Go kick-start'. Areus was staring at him with a satanic smile that worked as a driller but also as distraction; he was not looking at the two hands but into his eyes; the German tried to avoid his diabolic glance and concentrate on the actual fight.

He indeed put incredible force; he was about to bend, but he spoke to himself, "Hold, and again hold." He could not believe that he still was holding, and the other guy added more strength that was unbearable, and his hand bent but still not that much; he with remarkable resilience was still holding. He noticed that the German started to get tired, as his strength had less dynamic.

So, he thought now is the time to activate the smart trick of his wrist and add his positive mindset to overcome the pressure.

He squeezed his wrist towards him, bringing the German's wrist in kind of defecting position; he heard an 'Aaaahhh' from the people, some thinking that they might lose their money so also the barman who bet all his night's earnings for the German, while with a glimpse he saw slight smiles from Alex and Tuppi; the latter was sweating, having in his mind the face of his wife if he returned empty-handed. More people came, and the place was crowded. The one was pushing the other to have a better view of, at a first sight, an uneven duel.

He kept his wrist in that situation, not trying to bring it back to a vertical position and not also trying to bend him. The German tried to grasp with his other hand the corner of the table, but that is not allowed, and they all told him that he would get a penalty and lose right away. He removed that hand from the table. He started to have a red face either for being angry at him and in the anguish of the defeat or for himself being unable to get rid from the wrist squeezing that was exercised on him but also from that demoniac eyes of his opponent.

Areus always didn't look at the two hands but smiled devilishly, and at the same time, his eyes deeply penetrated the eyes of the German; this turned him crazy, always trying to avoid his diabolic eyes. This is what is called phycology (Greek word); his phycology started to break him down, but he did hold and made another, maybe the last enhanced, attempt to finish the fight, having all people around them to encourage him to put an end to this torture of all feeling that they would lose their money.

When he noticed that he gave all that he had, he started slowly and gradually to change the status, centimetre by centimetre turning the hands around him, being in defence, he now is on attack, his glance to him always piercing the guy's eyes and his mind like a screwdriver.

No more strength left in him, he simply put an extra strength, and he was down with a suffering scream. He did not congratulate but took his friend and left the bar in deep humiliation. There was applause from the people but also sorrow from those who bet all their money on the German.

Alex and Tuppi were cheering; they won a lot of money, especially Tuppi, who told him later that the money he won was for six days' of fish catch.

He was praying all the time, what would he say to his wife if he returned home without money? His wife, according to his descriptions, was a strong woman kind of a Viking (like a Norse) woman. He congratulated Areus and ran home with the big money trophy.

He had an unfinished job; he took Alex by the hand, and they went with a triumphal smile to the table of the girls. They congratulated him, one even kissed him on his cheek, and they were so sorry that they had no money to bet on him.

They told him their story. They were all school friends from the age of 19 although they looked 25. Their dream since they were at school was to come to Greenland, but their parents were not giving the consent, so they gathered as much as possible from their pocket money. But that was not that much and was enough just for flying to Nuuk, plus some extra money for a sandwich and a beer.

It seemed to him to be from a good family from Hamburg. He asked them in which hotel they were staying; they looked at each other and answered, "What hotel? We are sleeping in a tent in a sheep farm. We are dirty, with no showers for many days."

How they took this trip with little money, he could not understand.

They did not count that everything in Nuuk was very expensive, even a simple sandwich?

He looked at Alex, and he understood well what that look was to be meant.

So, he told them that they live in a nearby hotel so they can come and take a shower.

They jumped up to the air and kissed him, all three; Alex feeling somewhat neglected.

They paid the bill. The barman was very sad that he bet on the other guy, but he congratulated him telling him that he was smart as he understood the trick he did with his wrist.

They walked to the hotel; the receptionist seeing three girls with them, seemed to prohibit the girls from coming up. He passed a 100 euro banknote, and he closed his eyes to what he saw.

He suggested to Alex to pick up one of the three girls and he takes the other two. When entering the room, they were dancing and kissing each other.

He asked them to go to the bathroom and hide, so that he would ask the chambermaid to bring more towels, bathrobes and slippers. He had to hide the already existing towels and called in an angry way to say that there were no towels in the room and no bathrobes. A chambermaid brought right away new towels and two bathrobes as he explained to her that he was expecting his wife with the early flight.

He picked up from her hand towels and bathrobes; she apologised that she forgot to put bathrobes and towels. He asked the girls to come out, and he was not surprised at all that they were already naked and gave them the bathrobes and the towels, and they both rushed to the shower. They looked so naked that they did not care at all, and that was a good sign and had to prepare for it for four days.

In the shower, they were singing, chatting, laughing and splashing each other. He had to go to them, telling them to slow down their singing, and with a shocking surprise, he witnessed a hard lesbian situation, kissing each other on the mouth and each other's hand masturbating the other.

Perfect, desirable young figures, they looked at him asking him to join.

He said, "Finish your shower, and then we see what we all three on the big relaxing bed can do."

They were bathing for 30 minutes; he, on bed, was also naked with a penis pointing up to the ceiling chandelier. He was in such a horny situation that he could not wait. He started to masturbate, but in the middle of that, they came out of the shower with the white soft bathrobe; they picked up his hand from his penis and one after the other started to lick his erected penis.

They did this with enormous joy as they probably did not have any real sex apart from the lesbian trio in their tent.

He pleaded them to take a break because he had the horribly bad smell from their mouth, the mouth of someone who has not eaten for two to three days. He ordered room service, smoked salmon and ham sandwiches and a champagne, but not the most expensive one.

They went to the bathroom to use the hair dryer to dry up their hair and also took his shaving machine to also shave the hair of their pussy, leaving only a little triangle above the pussy. They used all his aftershave perfume to spray their pussy. He asked them to stay there until the waiter comes and leaves.

The room service knocked on the door; he left the tray; when they heard that the door was closed, they rushed like wild animals to the food. He was so happy to see them eat and enjoy the champagne.

After many days, they felt really clean and with a full belly. It was again so inexplicable to him all three being from wealthy families how they took that trip leaving the comfort of their homes to come to Greenland with just pocket money.

Anyway, after eating all, but really all even licking their own fingers, they jumped up to the big bed, taking off the bathrobes. He asked them to wait. He had to go to the bathroom to pee. When he returned, he saw they were jumping up on the bed with a joy; that pleased him a lot.

They jumped on the bed, all three naked, and the orgy started. They were so happy that he had such a hard dick; they could not wait for the preliminaries as he told them before going for peeing.

They jumped one after the other on his penis while at the same time kissing each other passionately. They came one after the other with tiny and less tiny moans. He told them, "Let us take a break and have a sip of champagne."

He called Alex's room and asked him what was going on there. He told him that he was so happy that three Viagra pills were forgotten in his toiletry bag. He was so jealous of him, narrating him many stories, and at that age, he never needed Viagra.

So, back to his orgy, he said to the girls that he wanted to fuck their two anuses. The one looked to the other and said, "What shall we do?" Glances between them were to be seen; they gave him the impression that they did not do this before.

The one asked him, "But is this painful? Or?"

He said, "Not that painful but extremely pleasurable if you manage to moisten your anus with any kind of cream." He asked them to go to the bathroom and look at the hotel amenities. A small toiletry bag must be there, shaving foam or maybe a liquid soap. They came both, the one holding the liquid soap and the other the shaving foam.

He stood up at the edge of the bed and asked them to turn around and come to the edge of the bed showing him the whole view of their asses, exposing the asspussy nicely to him.

He started using them both liquid soap and foam the one after the other and same time fingering them and try to enter to their tight anus one finger and then another, when pulling out were glistering with shaving cream, two fingers started to be able to get inside, so the two beautiful assholes were ready; he noticed they were looking the one to the other rather with pleasure awaiting with anxiety the penis to start getting inside; he asked them to get their hand under their legs and start a sweet caress of their pussy so to abstract them from what he was to do from behind and from a possible slight pain.

Doing that, it was for him metaphorically as it is said in basketball 'a free throw shot or a piece of cake'; the penis was easily inside after a rather simple pre-preparation; they were masturbating with lust and passion; the libido was high up from them, same from his side.

He penetrated the one until he heard that she came and then to the next and hearing and feeling that she was very 'randy' and also about to come; there came to him that anomaly that happened to him once before, so he asked her to fart; she asked him, "Are you sure?"

He said, "Yes, can you do this."

The other one looked at her, asking her to press herself to do this, thinking that this would give him extra pleasure. She squeezed herself and that gave extra pleasure to his cock, and then he felt that she was sweetly farting right on his penis already deep inside her.

He could not hold any longer; he let his load finish in that tight and narrow gallery of lust. He fell on the bed, worn-out as all this happened while him standing up at the edge of the bed during all the anus penetration process. He fell with sound on the bed; they came to him and they both kissed him as they were delighted after what happened.

All three fell asleep naked, having their bodies tight, as the bed was big but not for three. The one girl was covering his half ass with her thigh while the other allowed her big right boob to be squeezed on his chest side.

What a scene even Michelangelo would adore this, yearning to depict this on his canvas. They woke up all around 9 o'clock, all hungry like a herd of wolves.

He called Alex; he woke him up. He said, "All OK?"

He said, "More than OK." He asked him to call Tuppi to tell him that they would not need him today, so they could spend time at the hotel spa and gym and relax all day with their three angels.

He told him, "We go down for breakfast if you feel like coming and join us."

The buffet was astonishingly rich and all the delicacies were there. Smoked Norwegian salmon, smoked reindeer, carpaccio also from reindeer, eggs prepared on the spot, all kinds of cereals and marmalades and many more. His two girls were eating as if they never ate before. He enjoyed looking at them with an enormous appetite.

He announced to them that they would spend the day at the relaxing spa, with massage and fitness.

They got crazy, but they did not have any outfits. All they had were at the tent. He asked them to go to the tent to fetch the rest of the dresses, and while they are at the spa, he would ask the chambermaid to arrange an express laundry for all their dresses, underwear and whatever, so the night they go out to a nice restaurant.

They rapidly did so and returned rather fast. In the meantime, he arranged that the chambermaid, giving her 50 euros a tip, to bring three fresh bathrobes and three pairs of slippers and if she also could get from the spa one swimsuit for him and Alex and three bikinis or even better, tangas for the girls, adding another 50 euros. She did all possible to bring all that he asked for.

He called Alex that he arranged for all of them. He understood, and he expressed his admiration for his organisational thinking, allowing not any details to escape from his mind.

He asked him if he called Tuppi; he said that he was more than happy as he had so much money that he need not to go out for fishing for six days and that he would enjoy with his wife nice romantic dinner in nice restaurant at last after uncountable years.

All went as planned; he adores to foresee that nothing would be missing and never find himself unprepared.

The girls returned with plenty of bad-smelling dresses. He called the chambermaid with another 50 euros and asked her for an express laundry and ironing.

So, all five of them went to the spa with their bathrobes and swimming suits. The girls had nice bikinis that added extra compliment to their perfect bodies.

They spent many hours there; they had a professional massager to treat their bodies with care to relax all muscles. The girls were in heaven with all these unexpected treatments after sleeping in a tent on sheep blankets. They were now in a luxury spa, enjoying the whole of it. They were boozing with cocktails at the spa bar, and they were all in a most happy atmosphere, difficult to hide.

He asked Alex to talk to him in the changing rooms about how he enjoyed that girl. He wanted to kiss him for the joy he gave to him. He asked him, "How do you feel strong? Is your heart fine?" He did not want to have any heart attack from the too much sex and Viagra pills.

"Shall we change partners? You feel like handling two girls and I take your girl?"

He seemed to be sceptical about this, so he said, "OK, we swap my girl, with one of yours from yesterday." So they did a swap, and both liked the idea.

He asked him, "You did not take all three Viagra yesterday?" He laughed.

"No, one, and luckily, I have two more."

The arrangement was done; they only have to announce this to the girls. Not to forget that during the time they were at the spa, he booked for all three the hairdresser at 5 o'clock.

At about 12, they had a very small quick snack as lunch in the spa and ended at 3 o'clock in the afternoon in their rooms for a nice nap.

Amazingly, they saw all their dresses were hanging in the closet in polybags, well cleaned and ironed, and they felt like princesses. He explained the swap with Alex, and they had no objection although the one that was to go with Alex, she preferred him, but the deal was done.

At 5 o'clock, all three rushed to the hairdresser, so he had one more hour to sleep this time alone in his big bed.

At about 6 o'clock, they came, and they indeed looked like film stars, unbelievable how a girl adding the essential comforts and caring can have such a metamorphosis.

He asked the concierge to book the best restaurant in town for six at 7 o'clock; he asked for six and not five so they have more space as he desires a very rich dinner.

At 7 o'clock, they were all down in the lobby and almost starving. Alex said, "The dinner is on me. I made a big amount of money betting on the outsider, the day before."

He called the maître d' hotel and told him that he was also once maître d' hotel and hotel manager as well as restaurant owner, so he said to him, "I will leave it all to you to make the best menu with plenty of variety."

He asked him if he had white and red wine, and he said yes. He asked if he had white wine Riesling but from the German side of the Moselle River; he also nodded yes, for the red wine he lived it up to him.

So, he told him they want to start with fish appetisers, shrimps, whale, smoked cod, proceed to seal and then change the white wine to red and have wild musk oxen with mushrooms and whatever is used here in Nuuk as side vegetables.

The maître laughed, telling him that he had asked him to do the menu for them and 'leave all up to you'.

"But you did all already," he said.

"OK, forgive me, but still follow my menu."

The dinner was as planned perfect, and they all dined so nicely; the girls dressed in clean outfits did not look like girls but like captivating ladies, as that was what they, in fact, were. Alex paid, and before leaving, he put in the maître d'hôtel's pocket one additional 50 euros.

So, let us go for a few drinks to the bar from yesterday where he was already famous. Entering there, many pointed at him, silently telling to the one next to him, "He is that Greek Hercules guy."

The barman was so happy to see him, telling him that he went to his hotel to find him. He asked, "What for?"

He said, "You made my bar famous to all nearby villages. They all talk about the Greek who won against the big German guy."

He turned to Alex saying, "Oh no—not again, the same story like the tennis club."

He asked, "What did you want me for?"

"Just defend your title."

"What title? I haven't got any title."

"Of course, you have, and tomorrow at eight, it is organised for you to fight with a local, big, strong fisherman."

"Why did you organise this without asking me?"

"This is now too late; it is done and settled. If you do not come, it will mean that you are afraid; you are a pussy."

He was angry and upset he wanted to leave the bar but Alex and the girls calmed him down.

This is just a fight and it doesn't matter whether you win or lose so he cooled down and they kept on drinking and brought the merry mood to the very highest.

The girls were shining. Frequent customers could see a metamorphosis both to their image but also to their amusing mood.

The conversation turned around what happened to his room yesterday with the liquid soap and the shaving foam and there was plenty of laughter. The laughter and the temperament were up to the finest level and the third girl who was with Alex, kind of grumpy, complained to Alex

"Why did you not act this method on my derriere and I did not live that experience?"

He calmed her telling her to be patient and she would have this chance tonight.

It was a very big enjoyment to see these girls in such a happy condition.

Tuppi came with a big smile, he said that was the first time that he needed not to wake up very early for fishing and he spent a lot of time with his wife and kids. The calmness on his face was more than obvious.

He wished them happy continuation for the night and he went back to the hug of his also happy wife.

They all decided to leave for the hotel and managed the swap with Alex and a new sexual happening is to start. Alex's girl was inpatient to live the experience of the liquid foam and the shaving foam that was so well described by her other two friends.

They changed to more comfortable and they were all three in the bed and he gave to the new girl the performance she was anxious to live.

They had a nice night and slept in a good mood.

He could not have easy sleep as he was thinking what he had to do tomorrow with the giant as they described that he was.

First time after a long time he had to take a cut in half sleeping pill so that he can sleep. The two girls slept both having one of their feet on his penis area that made him feel the king of the night and from time to time he felt the heaven in their emotional cuddling them changing positions and sides.

The girls woke up early, they let him sleep longer and they went down for breakfast where Alex and their third girl were all in a great mood. After half an hour he was also down with them.

Alex told him that Tuppi was to come in one hour to take them to the famous Nuuk Brewery and see all working procedures to all stages.

That visit was important for him as he was never in a brewery, he was in Scotland many years ago at a whisky distillery, also in Germany in a big wine cellar testing wines, so for him this is a new experience.

Indeed, Tuppi came in an excellent mood. He looked as if he were a completely new person and looked more like an accountant than a fisherman.

Tonight would be their last night in Nuuk so they had to swallow as much pleasure as possible.

The brewery guided tour was more than interesting.

All workers were smiling, pointing at him knowing that he was the Greek gladiator of the brass the ferre duel, who would fight with their local hero.

He noticed the girls showed signs of sadness as the time was closing to the farewell as tomorrow Alex and him were to leave.

They were supposed to stay three more days and go back to that filthy tent, how they would feel living for three days in a luxury hotel with all comforts, plenty of nice lunches and dinners, having quality full of variety sex and then again back to that sheep barn.

Anyway, now he had ahead of him that duel that he did not want at all but they already organised this without asking him and not only organised but they also advertised it.

He had to do this and not act like chicken shit, hide and run but whatever it is to happen let it happen, he won one duel and he would lose another, so what?

They went back to the hotel and passed by the spa for one more massage to have the muscles loosened a little.

A nice swim in the spa swimming pool, all of them in an excited mood.

They had a very nice European lunch this time and went back to the rooms for a nap.

But that was a very long nap, probably the massage and the swim brought the body to a leisurely calmness and they slept until six.

He shaved while the nice girls were caressing him all the time. They did not dare to ask for sex as he had to use all his whatever strength to bring down the arm of this ferocious Goliath whom they all called him, "Giant."

Time came and they went to the bar. It was crowded, to his surprise he had fans although he was supposed to have a head-to-head or rather arm to arm fight with the famous strong and wide-bodied local fisherman.

Time was passing he was supposed to come at 8 it was already 8.15 and he did not show up, Areus was hoping that he would not come. He thought what an absurd thing to do fight that huge man what chance he had? Simply nil.

But the wish of him not him to show was not accomplished, the door opened and he as a dreadful wrestler made an impressive entry. Oh God, a rugged and terrifying hairy man who looks like a big mammoth, fearless plus kind of barbaric, after all he was a real Viking.

He looked intimidating but his manners actually were quite friendly, he gently approached and shook hands. But what hand that was a shovel not a hand. His name was Túpe. Areus was seized with a sudden impulse to run away but that would mean an immense humiliation and offend his opponent.

He stood up to the bar and made an announcement. He would fight with Túpe but confessed that this a duel between David and Goliath but he had no stone to throw to Túpe, they all laughed and they all came with plenty of money in their pockets to bet for Túpe.

They held a meeting about what should be do. This guy had a huge right arm but he noticed that his left one was rather weak or rather atrophic, he thought, *What a nature's mistake*. He also noticed that he was hiding his left arm.

So, he speculated that there is a small chance, so he played it smartly. "OK," he said, again standing up on the bar. "I accept the challenge, but I had an accident this morning with my right hand, and this is a serious incompetence to use this hand." He hid his thumb behind the other four fingers; it showed that indeed he had a problem. "So, let us go for the duel with the left hands."

He remembered once in Biarritz that he had such a Bras de Ferre duel with a huge Austrian colleague he was left-handed so he asked him to fight with left hands.

He then remembered that his left hand was extremely strong and also had an equally robust wrist, the same as the right wrist, so he felt that he might have had a slight chance.

Túpe did not like it because he knew his weakness but how could he deny showing ridiculousness, he thought, *What left or right? I am so strong that I win 100%.* And he agreed.

So, the bets started, more and more came into the bar to bet and they all were cheering Túpe seeing the big body difference and knowing the fame of the colossal man.

He turned to Alex and he asked him to follow him to the toilet. He asked him to bet as much as he could on him and he gave him all the money he had in his pocket and asked him to give it to the girls so they also bet on him. He also asked Tuppi to come but he wasn't there but he later appeared wishing not to lose this.

The barman strangely could read his eyes and he bet on him and not on the giant fisherman despite his wife's instructions. She also gave him all her money to bet for Túpe as well as her mother's money. He took a big risk, but everybody else was on Túpe's side. So, he just had as it seemed Alex, the girls and the barman whose name was Sáka. Not to forget that also Tuppi changed his bet from Túpe and bet all the money he won two nights before on him despite his wife's different instructions.

They kept betting the money that was gathered was a big amount. Time came when Sáka rang the bell so betting was over. Túpe took his sit and the chair almost collapsed from his weight and he, the little guy although he is almost 1.80 and 82 kilos of weight, was opposite to him. Túpe forgot the deal and put the right hand on the table, he showed him the left hand and he said sorry (he was a nice fellow despite his fierce look).

The hands were on the table. Sáka, acting as referee, held the two hands steady and said a word in the Viking language that probably was meant to be a 'GO'.

Túpe wanted to finish it in a second and put all his force but Areus held and squeezed his wrist on his side, that was always his trick, in official such contests this is not allowed, but no one knew this in Nuuk except that smart Saka, the barman.

Túpe started to feel uncomfortable and from a smiling face turned to a seriously worried face. He did the same strategy as to the German two nights before. He was looking angrily and aggressively to his eyes, managing to have the eyes opened with not a single click. He, as master of mind games, played more with the eyes than with the hands, which was like a wizardry look that started to turn Túpe's mind to a nightmare. Icons passed through his mind how he would go out having a defeat from a 'dwarf' comparatively to the two bodies, volume and sizes.

The bar suddenly fell to a 'tomb' silence, they were rubbing their eyes seeing that the Goliath was still not able to bend his cheeky arm. Túpe started to sweat while he was irritatingly cool, this gave him extra pressure in conjunction with his satanic glance that penetrated and pierced deep Túpe's eyes.

Túpe gathered all possible strength that was still available and made the last attempt but he faced again a wall at that point, he felt that he surrendered, there was no need to exercise any extra annihilating strength, he bent him slowly and respectfully.

Túpe was a real gentleman; he stood up and congratulated him.

The only laughing guys in that room were Alex, the girls, Tuppi and Sáka. Outside was Sáka's wife, when she heard that Túpe lost she almost fainted she lost all her money and her mother's money. Sáka was told that his wife outside was shedding tears, he then went out and whispered into her ears that he did not follow her instructions and that he bet against Túpe.

She gave him a hard slap on the cheek for disobeying and right away a kiss for doing this. They won a big amount of money.

Inside people were still there trying to realise what and how it happened. He stood up on the bar and shouted in silence. He had to protect and restore Túpe's name. "Listen up, Túpe is the strongest man who I have ever met and telling them, although that was a big lie of course, that I was once champion for Bras de Ferre but only with the left hand, so obviously Túpe could not compete with a champion."

He continued. "But if I was to have a duel with him with the right hand, he was so strong that he could smash my hand in one single second. So, you must all be proud for having in Nuuk such a strong man who can easily become a world champion."

They all applauded. Right there came an idea to his mind that would make them very happy.

He announced, "I will talk to the International Association of Bras De Ferre to organise here in Nuuk a world championship of Bras de Ferre with Túpe as the unbeatable Viking. This will make Nuuk known worldwide as many visitors will visit the town."

They all forgot the money they lost and were cheering in full mood as having that World Tournament in Nuuk they would benefit a lot having so many visitors to come and make Nuuk a famous destination town.

This indeed was the element to make the Nuuk citizens to forget the shock of having their Goliath to lose.

Back at his table the girls started to count their wins, he stopped them and told them that they would do this at the bar of the hotel. It is not nice to provoke all of them who lost their money.

They drank two beers more and went back to the hotel in plenty of joy.

They went for a last drink at the hotel bar, then he asked the girls to count their money and finally they were close to 12,000 euros, exactly €11.900. He asked his capital back, and he told them, "Keep the earnings, and so the rest of the days that you stay in Nuuk, you will live like tycoons."

The joy of the three girls was indescribable thinking that they would not sleep any more in that dirty tent but like princesses, that they in fact deserve such a luxuriousness.

The team remained the same as last night so they had to celebrate the wins of the girls with the appropriate party.

It was indeed a sex party, the girls being now free from any money worries they decided to give him a top sex performance. That was so unbelievable with what real love they did what they did to him each one taking her turn and him thinking how blessed he was at this age to have two angels but also at this age he was still proud to rely on a penis that never failed and let him down.

They had an excellent two hours sex and fell asleep.

The next morning after breakfast they had to have a tearful farewell. The girls decide to book a suite in the same hotel so they could stay all three together and enjoy the gift he gave them.

Putti, of course, but what a surprise Sáka and Túpe were there for the goodbye.

Too many tears from the girls and Tuppi drove them to the airport.

Alex was nervous and said that he feels that this trip must not end by having only Nuuk to visit in Greenland but they have to go north to the real snow and maybe he will have the chance to see bears. He said OK but he does not have any heavy coat and trousers and all necessary gear for such an altitude. He said,

"I made a lot of money from you. I will buy for you at the airport of Kangerlussuaq all needed fittings."

So, it was decided for him to reach the northern part of Europe.

Indeed, at the Kangerlussuaq there was a shop specialised for the north Arctic gear.

He bought all the must and they were ready to fly from Kangerlussuaq Airport to Qaanaaq at a fly time of about 1½ hours. Alex being there several times he made the necessary arrangements that they would be picked up and also book the best accommodation there.

Alex told him that they are lucky to be there in summer and enjoy the midnight sun shining because the nine winter months is a total darkness.

He also told him that the guy who would pick them up, his name is Pavia, is a specialist for reindeer hunting and the best in bow hunting for caribou (reindeer).

Alex also told him that he ordered the lunch and dinner because as there are no restaurants or bars in Qaanaaq food is served only in the hotel where they would stay.

So, all is settled when they arrive, they would also know the program that their friend Pavia had arranged for them. One thing is for sure that there would be no any girls or women there to enjoy the same as they were lucky to do in Nuuk. Well maybe a sexual break is from time to time necessary if not a must.

The turbos Air Greenland plane landed at the most northern city on the planet that according to what Alex told him this city should have been the Santa Claus starting trip and not Rovaniemi of Finland. The locals are not happy because only Qaanaaq has the features to gain that Santa Claus fairy tale.

Pavia, a nice always smiling guy but with hard and deep face characteristics, was there to welcome them with his car.

The first sight of Qaanaaq was impressive, small houses in all different colours.

The temperature is four degrees Celsius. He drove them at their seafront hotel a very cute hotel not, of course, as luxurious as the hotel of the capital of Greenland Nuuk, but very cosy, the hotel had only three single rooms but with all the necessaries, like internet access among others, as that was for him more than essential for his laptop, as he never stopped working wherever he was.

The dining room was with big benches that could sit 8 and even 10 people. Pavia told them that they are lucky as the last four days was raining all day long and night as in fact there is no night in July in Qaanaaq, and it seems that the three days that they would stay no rain would ruin their adventure because he planned reindeer hunting.

Food as Pavia told them, is in their hotel, they serve European food but mainly what is served is fish and seal meat as well as reindeer meat, but whatever the choice is must be ordered one day before.

They settled down to their rooms, he ran to open the window and he saw a magnificent and breathtaking view.

They rested for one hour and then went down to the dining room for the lunch that was already ordered from Pavia.

Well what else to start with than sea meat with good German beer. He revealed to both Alex and Pavia that to have a nap after lunch was always a must habit for all his life, and maybe this is the secret of looking 20 years younger to what he was and also active in all 'activities' as if he were 55.

Pavia revealed the whole three days program given that there is 24 hours daylight. So, first after their nap they go for sightseeing and locate reindeer and musk oxen but not hunting as this requires professional guide outfitter.

Tomorrow a helicopter is ordered to bring them to the very northern part where dogsledding was ordered.

The next day, there is a magnificent boat tour to reach as close as possible to the North Pole.

All is well planned and he was delighted to see what their eyes are going to see.

So, after the nap he took them to the wild where reindeer and muskox can be hunted.

He asked them to follow exactly his instructions and not take any initiatives as both the ground and rocks are menacing to slide and fall and break a leg or a head.

The scenery was spectacular, the wilderness and the remote environment impressive.

He was jealous of those that are able to go high up in the mountains and hunt reindeers but for the ages of both him and Alex it is rather very risky.

One can see at very far distances the iced mountains and the glaciers and many sea eagles.

He thanked God for allowing him to live all this and near to his possibly last life decade.

They 'hiked' through Arctic hills and valleys with views of the Greenland ice cap, quite a lot and became tired and Pavia drove them back, but what they left behind was a dream that not many or better say only few in their life had or would experience.

They spent one hour in their rooms rest and charge their batteries and down to the dining room where Pavia was there waiting for them.

He asked him that he wanted no fish but start and finish with meat and by all means a good red wine whatever it might cost. He managed for all what he asked him and started with smoked reindeer, he loves this much more than any or any other smoked meat or fish, but he also likes as starter oxen carpaccio, is delicious, the wine was a Bordeaux not one of the best but it was red wine and that is what was wanted and the good is that they had second bottle, because there is nothing worse than start with a certain red wine and when this is emptied they tell you, "Sorry, we do not have this same anymore."

The main course was a surprise, that beside the oxen musk meat was also hare, yes hare that he asked for it when they were in Nuuk. They cooked the hare their own way adding artic herbs and was a dish for many Pirelli stars.

They drank three bottles of wine, were three plus two other Swedish guys quite younger than Alex and him, who joined as to their long table and there was plenty of mood.

Those Swedish guys were professional bow hunters and they came every year in the same month and they told them so many stories and also the risks they lived. They were so good to describe all that as if they virtually were almost there in person. They were also to fly north the next day.

It was time to sleep as the next day they had an early flight with the helicopter to go to the northern part of Europe and most of all enjoyed the dogsledding.

It was impossible for him to sleep as the curtains were thin and the light came in the room, luckily, he had those sleeping pills and he slept late but enough.

When they woke up, he got two phone calls, one from his Danish friend colleague Arne asking him if he made any decision for running his hotel, but his answer was not yet although that idea was always running through his mind because that was indeed a challenge.

The second phone call was from the Nuuk German girls that were at the spa living the best moments of their life thanking him a thousand times telling him that such men like him became very rare or better say, disappeared.

Well today is a big day. Pavia drove them to the airport where the helicopter was waiting. The Two Swedish guys were also on that helicopter with their big bows. He had a kind of certain fear as this was to be the first in his life to fly by helicopter.

The flight despite his worries was perfect and they landed to the more northerly landing place maybe of the world.

Their tour guide welcomed them and he with his car drove them there the dog sledding tour was to take place.

10 gorgeous dogs Alaskan sled dog racers and huskies were waiting for them, the sled could take two of them plus the driver who was a tiny man and Alex (he is also very light weight) and him both were not more the 135 kilos the driver must be a lightweight guy so they do not exceed the 200 kilos that 10 dogs can carry. Pavia stayed behind; he had done this tour before.

A tour from the last Greenlandic city of Qaanaaq the driver is also a hunter and what he hunts is walrus, muskox and polar bears. They travel and breathe the for sure cleanest air in all the world.

They asked their driver that they only want a tour and not any hunting. They only wish to admire the scenery and if they see from a distance wildlife is still fine, so they made it clear that they are not adventurers but admirers of the legendary Thule district.

He could understand as he saw that they are not any Indiana Jones of the Arctic but two elder guys who want to enjoy the snow and have this unique dog sledding.

But nature is never predicted. While the dogs were running in a peaceful atmosphere, suddenly the driver looked worried and pulled the dog's bridles, obliging the dogs to abruptly stop.

He raised his head up allowing his nose to smell, but smell what? This was unknown to them but not to the driver. They saw the driver was uneasy or better frightened.

He tried to get from his back this bow, but then they all heard thunderous animal feet beating behind a small hill and a huge muskox appeared in full speed aiming at them. The driver could not reach his bow, the muskox was very near to them, and they understood that this was their end and closed their eyes. Suddenly a heavy loud bang and silence.

They opened their eyes, believing that they were dead. They see the huge muskox just half a metre away from them lying dead with an arrow on its heart side. The two Swedish bow hunters were their saviours.

Areus made his Christian Orthodox cross so also Alex and they thanked their Messiahs. The driver was almost still unconscious, he also expressed his gratitude.

It took two hours of total silence and returned back to join Pavia to whom he narrated what happened. Helicopter brought them safely back to Qaanaaq. They all were hungry so after fast changing they went down to the dining room, always silent as if they were just spiritually there and not in reality.

They ordered from the previous day a variety of fish, so it was shrimp, salmon, seal, trout, cod and narwhal meat. All were in the middle of the table in two big oval metal plates so one could taste all.

White wine was ordered from the previous day and so they managed costly wine but this is a must with the fish. They drank as many bottles as they could take just to forget that monster animal attack. It was more than an enjoyable dinner as they realised that they were there enjoying that rich dinner just by coincidence and their big luck due to those blessed Swedish bow hunters.

A good sleep was needed as tomorrow was a big day for the boat trip towards the North Pole without, of course, reaching the North Pole.

The dizziness from the wine allowed them to sleep without the help of sleeping pills.

The waking up was easy, feeling fresh and ready for a boat trip to the North Pole.

He had not to forget to call Emma in Copenhagen to tell her that the day after tomorrow he would be in Copenhagen so she would have to come to her home to get his luggage, she told him, "You can stay at my home as long as you wish." And that was good because he needs time to think what will be the next, stay in Copenhagen and run his friend's hotel, or go back home to Greece and see his family. All was in a state of uncertainty.

A good breakfast and a hot coffee and all three were at the small harbour where the boat was waiting.

They sailed past Siorapaluk, the most northern settlement, the view of the many glaciers is absolutely unique. In small distance they could see walrus and also seals taking their sun bath on the ice edges.

Far away, there are the Canadian mountains. On the land they could see huts of muskox hunters, maybe the two Swedish salvagers were also there. There is a glacial lake where one can walk but the danger can always be there. Some did dare to walk on that lake and according to what they saw, they spotted not in a long-distanced muskox in threatening appearance.

The whole trip was an unrepeatable experience, one feels there 40 years younger with so fresh air to penetrate the lungs. Both him and Alex thanked Pavia for the well planned three days Qaanaaq 'exploration'.

At the hotel dining room, a nice rich dinner was waiting for them again on two big plates. No fish this time but mixed meat and red wine.

They drank quite a lot and went to bed as early as tomorrow they had the flight back to the Kangerlussuaq Airport.

After morning breakfast, Pavia drove them to the airport, they thanked him and left the picturesque Qaanaaq with the small colourful houses. They flew to Kangerlussuaq Airport and from there to Copenhagen.

At Copenhagen, Alex's friend with his car came to pick them up. Areus gave him the address of Emma's home to drive him there.

Emma was already outside her home waiting for him, she gave him a sign that there would be no hug as she did not want to give cause to the neighbours for gossiping. He said goodbye to Alex, and they agreed tomorrow and agreed to meet at the tennis club.

He took his luggage and entered Emma's home.

There far away from the eyes of any one she hugged and kissed him with passion. Her blue eyes seemed to reflect something she knew which he did not, that remained to be revealed.

He told her, "I am very tired, allow me to take a shower, and then I need a good sleep."

She had all perfectly ready for him, bathrobe, hot towels, slippers all he had to do was get undressed and under the hot water.

She opened the luggage and put it all in a closet.

While relaxing in the shower he noticed from a small opening of the shower curtains that Emma was fidgeting around and in two minutes there she was naked in the shower with him. He told her, "Emma, I am tired, leave this for later after a good sleep."

She pretended not to hear that, she seized his penis and started masturbating him and herself at the same time.

The down junior, his dick, was already up in the air. She knew well that he gets hard in seconds.

She turned to the wall, bent a little and there was her ass in full view, she grabbed his penis from behind and under her legs and inserted it into the wet and beautiful welcoming pussy, she did all to get his exhaustion to disappear. He again complained to her, "I am tired, Emma; can we not do it later?"

She answered with a frowned face, better say she whipped him with dirty threats this time, "Shut up and fuck."

All this conversation was taking place while she was moving her ass against his penis in and out in a rampant way. He said, "Emma, for heaven's sake, why you talk so harshly to me? I never heard you use the word fuck but only when you are at the very peak of your sex ecstasy, which can be justified."

She then revealed him the reason of her anger, and all this while the fucking was in progress.

"You fucked all the hospital and not only me as you were assuring me."

He asked pretending surprise, "Whom did I fuck?"

"You first fucked that small bitch I had as assistant, and she recounted in all details, how and where you fucked her, showing proudness about her achievement that she lost her virginity from all her bloody holes, and she told that to one of the nurses who was working in the big department where many young nurses work, and they all bet who will be the next one to fuck you."

"So, Lorna managed, and she won the bet."

"I must punish you for that. So fuck me with all your force."

What could he say? Nothing. He just attacked in the same manner.

"So, OK, then stop talking and fuck and ejaculate fast as I cannot hold anymore, and I will ejaculate inside you."

That warning triggered her accelerations with skills of a mature woman's movements and she came with an immense relief, she took his penis out and he released his sperm under the hot falling water on their bodies.

He said nothing she also said nothing again about all what she revealed to him and calmed herself in the shower and during the fucking process.

He fell down on bed like a dead corpse, she kissed one of his buttocks, covered him with a sheet and a thin blanket and let him sleep.

So, the encounter with Emma was turbulent hoping she forgets all his sex achievements with the nurses. He was a little unhappy with Lorna because the result of their love affair was not as pure as he thought but the product of a bet.

The next morning, he woke up and looked for his underwear. She had cleaned and ironed everything. Emma prepared breakfast but she left to go to her work before he woke up and left a message with menace, "Do not dare to look for the two bitches I will kick you out of my home, as long as you stay in Copenhagen you fuck me and only me do not give me more bitterness."

This woman's obsession was him not to cheat on her under whatever circumstances, he thought how desperate for sex she is, probably too long abstaining from sex with her husband and now that she found the good fuck, wanted to get the most out of it.

Anyway, he had to behave from now on so the few more days he stays there he would be her exclusive fornicator.

He then went to the tennis club where they agreed to meet with Alex. He was so glad to see many more courts full of players as it was before.

The weather was good because the last time that he was there rain was expected so the tournament had to take place in the indoor facilities.

The owner's told him how much they missed him and invited him for lunch at the nearby best restaurant together with Alex. It was Sunday and the restaurant was crowded as that day families use to come for lunch to enjoy the nice Sunday on the terrace.

The owner Janus was his name, ordered whatever best was on the menu. He was narrating his 'achievements' in Bras de Ferre in Nuuk and that he gave them the promise and has the obligation to organise there a world Bras de Ferre tournament and this is a difficult promise to keep but he would do all to manage for this.

The Bras de Ferre Association is in Quebec so maybe he had to go there to persuade them by showing pictures of the 'Goliath' Viking of Greenland.

He also told them that they were too close to be smashed and killed after they got an attack from a huge wild muskox.

Another challenge is to take over that hotel from his friend and co-student and he does not know what to do.

He called him almost every day and he wanted to help him as he sees that the hotel is fine, the restaurant is big and nice but him as manager, he showed signs of fatigue and lack of ideas how to promote his hotel.

But at the same time he had mails from his China office that his partner is tired running the office, incomprehensible because he does almost all, even from that distance, so maybe he had to go there to re-organise his office.

While he was telling them the problems, the door of the restaurant opened and he saw Lorna always wearing attractive attire, with her whole family. As he said before, that restaurant was the favourite of all the nearby families for Sunday lunch.

Her eyes could not miss him as he was the only darker skinned guy in there, for a moment she blushed and avoided looking at him, so did he also having in mind the 'threatening' words of Emma.

They continued their lunch and had plenty of fun. Both volunteered that if he decides to take over that hotel, maybe they could help with the one or the other way.

Leaving the restaurant, he wanted to throw a not very sweet glimpse to Lorna but how could he do this as he had such a nice night with her showing to him endless affection and not any sign that what she did was just to boast to the other nurses that she managed first to bring him to her bed.

He sent her a meaningful blink and left.

He wanted to visit the hospital managers but how after all this gossiping in the hospital nurses' circles that he fucked quite a number of them, he better abstain from that idea as he was not sure what he would face.

The next day, he asked his friend Alex to take him to that friend's hotel. He also wanted to hear his opinion. They fixed a meeting with his co-student and there they arrived, heartily welcomed by his friend, his wife and his lovely daughter.

He wanted to see all rooms one by one and see how well they were maintained and how clean and how well decorated. All was nice, just little dust to his finger when he searched for dust on the top upper part of the closet and indicated to the chambermaid who was with them, that she must not look to clean only what is to be seen at first sight, but also what is not to be seen.

He also noticed that the TV was not in the right place so one to watch TV had to get up and sit on the small sofa and not be able to watch TV from the bed.

He asked if they had also several cable TV programs, they told him no they have only the Danish official stations.

He said that is a mistake. You must also have at least two cable TVs, as many couples that come to this nice hotel for the weekend either are married couples or non-married, and want to watch also porno to reinforce their sex pleasure and wilful desire.

His friend's wife, his daughter (40 years old) and the chambermaid were a little shocked to hear this but they seemed to agree. He explained that illegal couples would keep coming if they know that they have the pleasure to watch little porno that would help especially the man to keep on for a second round, laughter was heard in that hotel room.

He asked his friend that what is important for him is the kitchen. But the time passed as they arrived there in the afternoon so he suggested that they both stay there for the night. He looked if Alex had an objection, he did not.

OK he said as they have a lot to see and discuss, he suggested they go to their rooms, have a small rest and come down for dinner at 7.30.

No one opposed this and so they did. His room was maybe the best they had, they wanted to make him feel very comfortable.

He called Emma telling her that he would stay there for one or even maybe two nights. She warned him again, "Do not even think to fuck any chambermaid there, I will check you when you return, I know well if you made sex the night before I know very well your abilities and how far you can go, I will smell you form toe to head."

He answered with a trembling voice as she terrorised him, "OK don't worry I keep my strength for you." After resting 30 minutes, he called the chambermaid and asked if there were any pyjamas for him and his friend and also a shaving razor and foam, toothbrush and toothpaste set. She said no there is no such kit, he said this is not good at all and he would talk about this to his friend Arne.

She told him that she would run to her home and get two pyjamas from her husband so this at least is solved and there is a nearby kiosk and maybe they have not a kit but separate the two necessities he asked her for. He told her whatever she buys he would pay for. Well, he noticed, she had a nice body but also seemed to be in good sex satisfaction from her husband, he had these abilities to recognise this.

They both went down to the restaurant and he noticed that in that restaurant there were only another two tables with customers and that disappointed him a lot. There must be a reason for this.

His friend did all to show that his kitchen was working fine and asked him if he wanted anything in particular. He told him, "Let me see and study the menu well."

He observed a big variety of appetiser dishes and more main courses and many deserts which made no sense. He knows that the sweets desserts have lower material cost but could have high prices but that is not the best menu strategy. He also saw that there was only blue cheese, but blue cheese and a white goat cheese both are not after-meal cheeses.

One wanted to continue with his meal with a nice yellow cheese that was not there, so customers would refrain from ordering more wine bottles and pay a higher bill.

If yellow good cheese is on the menu they order and most probably ask for more wine to join the cheese, but also leave the restaurant with a nice, delightful and slightly dizzy mind that offers pleasure after a complete dinner and why not for this couple to decide to stay the night in the hotel to avoid police alcohol controls.

He also checked the wine menu and there he saw Danish wines and not any white German or French and Italian red wines, another big mistake. Anyway, with all these observations he would have the time to discuss and write his report.

He ordered the usual, that Scandinavians are proud of, the smoked Norwegian salmon, which is by far inferior to the real Scottish smoked salmon, but there was not any other smoked fish such as smoked trout and smoked eel that are great appetisers but also smoked appetisers fish from their colony Greenland.

The white wine to accompany the fish appetisers was kind for little sweet and not dry to match the fish tastes.

He ordered a fillet steak and made clear he wanted medium rare, he wanted to see what they would bring to him.

There was plenty of joy on the table but to his regret there were no more customers to come. His friend reminded him of many funny incidents in Heidelberg with their schoolmates and also, he laughed seeing that beautiful mother ex-owner of his room that was close to the school, asking one by one if they knew where he stays having an obvious and capricious desire but also sadness in her face.

They even made a small joke about "The Greek likes mature ladies while there are so many young girls, schoolmates." So, then he realised why the girls of that school, although they seemed to throw erotic glances at him and maybe hit on him, suddenly stopped as they probably felt offended that he preferred to go with the mature woman and obviously more experienced in sex woman and not with them with the absolute fresh young bodies.

There was much laughter after all he was there with him at the same school for more than a year so there were many incidents to be recalled.

Even the photo they all took when they graduated to give as a gift to their major lady professor which was all to have a photo with boxing gloves. Most of them took funny photos looking like comedians but the lady professor told to all of them that the photo that the Greek took was a real boxer with a scowling glance like the heavyweight boxer Rocky Marciano.

The dinner was proceeding and the fillet steak arrived he cut in the middle to see how was grilled as he asked medium rare, but what they did was well done, this means they had no idea what medium rare means. He showed it to his friend and told him that medium-rare needs three–four minutes from each side but they grilled it for more than 10 minutes and the result was not a juicy steak but a well-done steak.

He asked him if his cook was Danish. He told him that Danish cooks are asking for high salaries so he had a Pakistani Chef. Well, he told him, "Friend with a Pakistani chef you will never get your restaurant full but empty as it is tonight and this is regretful because your restaurant is nice and in a nice location and those cooks must definitely go."

It needs hard work and many changes to bring this hotel in such a first-class ranking to have even customers from Copenhagen to enjoy lunch or dinner in this restaurant. His wife and daughter lowered their faces as they understood that those two were forcing him not to spend more and upgrade their hotel and rather sell it as they were not in the needed mood to run it.

They agreed after having a coffee that tomorrow they would talk again but he asked him that they do this between them and without the presence of any other, he understood that although he was there for a few hours, he located what was going on and where the many accumulated problems derived from.

During that dinner and all were still eating he got a telephone call from Tuppi in Nuuk.

He reminded him that he gave to all the promise to organise the world Bras de Ferre tournament in Nuuk and he must not disappoint a whole town. They all dream of that tournament that will make Nuuk known worldwide. He felt bad because he gave hopes and dreams to a whole community and he realised that with that announcement and his promise he cannot escape.

He told him that even Túpe the so-called Goliath was under hard training and all the city was preparing him to win and give him the so-called winner's psychology.

He asked Tuppi to get impressive photos of Túpe to show his huge arms and muscles and also photos dressed as a Viking so that he will excite the Bras de Ferre Association president and send to Alex with whom he will be in contact wherever he will be.

He also wanted him to text his mobile phone his phone number and address as well as Sáka's phone and address so that if the association decides they could send letters and know with whom they will talk. So, it was clear to him that he must motivate the connections he has to find the way to approach and tempt that association.

He was telling on that table to his friend about this and they all laughed with his accomplishment's exact same situation also to the tennis club tournament where they were present.

His friend also told him that he had two telephone numbers of two co-students of Heidelberg and he was telling them about him and had fun, they both retired from business.

Arne was one of the top 10 students, he was always very serious and not after girls and adventures, he aimed as he told him on that table to finish first but he finished eighth. On the contrary, he told them he wanted to get his diploma but at the same time run after girls and why not experienced mature women who had plenty of sex experience to give to a young man. Invaluable experiences that will be needed for his next sex endeavours as a sex mentor.

He noticed mentioning this that his wife looked as a woman who she did not have enough of sex in her marriage but the sex was right to get pregnant and have kids, so to say an unsatisfied woman, but now is too late for her.

He and Alex asked for snaps so that they fell right away to sleep because, as he made clear to his friend, they need many things to talk about and early in the morning.

In their rooms, they found what was asked, pyjamas well ironed and kind of a kit for the amenities. He had a good sleep, shaved and down for breakfast because this is for him a main issue, the well-organised breakfast.

Well, it was what he was expecting, an imaginative ordinary breakfast of a mediocre hotel. Of course, he understands that you cannot spend for a rich buffet having only six rooms occupied.

So, they held a meeting with his friend, and he explained to him about his nickname Arne. He said why Arne, because was a Viking name of a guy with a hook-nose and he also had a small hook-nose only his family called him so.

OK so they started explaining to him the problems in the rooms of having no any kit of simple amenities cheap with the hotel name on, so they could get that as souvenir instead of taking a towel, not any big kits to have all inside, but simple and cheap with the name of the hotel on.

Must have or at least if not in all rooms at least to those rooms that you reserve for couples or newly married, a mini bar with miniature whiskies, gins, Vodkas and small champagne for two, the German Piccolo Sekt for example is fine.

About TV, there is no need to have to all rooms but for sure to those that are meant for the couples at least one cable TV where one could see among others athletic events and porno. A man always wants to follow his team and spend a few hours in the room while a woman might seem to be shy but she adores watching porn and excites the man companion to go for the second round.

Sometimes they stop to the porno channel as if it were by coincidence but they intended to stop at this channel.

For you this is good as they will also consume some drinks from the mini bar and whatever they drink from the mini bar you charge high because at that moment that they need a drink they do not care and check what the price is.

Of course, the chambermaid must always substitute what they consumed so that you know what to charge when leaving. He described him that the only hotel that he lived and he was in hundreds of hotels all over the world, the only hotels that they did not have a mini bar was in La Vegas because their aim was to oblige the customers to go down to have the drink and at the same time gamble and not stay in the room and watch TV.

He told him to keep the chamber maid she was good and friendly and hope she is also confident in what she sees or what the couples leave behind.

They then entered the kitchen; the kitchen was very good from the point of view of equipment but he saw two Pakistanis and one dirty rather ugly woman probably to assist the so-called 'chef' and also had the task of dishes cleaning and maybe also making the salads.

The chef was also in appearance, he could say awfully unpleasant, but one could see and it was more than obvious that what they were doing was a boring task, so how could you expect from such a chef a kitchen to attract customers?

They must go right away and get young chefs who just finished cooking school. They demand no high salaries but at the same time they are ambitious and eager to show to the owner that they have a big variety to suggest both as plats du jour and as new sauces and tastes.

The waiter and the girl *comis de rang* (assistant waiter) was, as she told him when he asked the previous night, was from the hotel school and he could see this right away because she had a touristic conscience because this is what they first of all learn in the hotel schools.

He told Arne to ask her who were the best cooking students in that school, ask to give you three–four names and call them for an interview, maybe even when he was still there.

The waiter was not bad but the smile was not often to be seen from his mouth. A smile is a must for a waiter to show that he is hospitable and with the smile he could also win more tips.

More or less, this was about the staff.

About how to increase the number of customers and after the must to hire new cooks and maybe also a new waiter, so he starts the transformation of the hotel from the roots.

Prepare the new menu adding more appetisers, he gave him the range, adding also appetisers that you could get from the nearby countries like Finland, Norway and Greenland, the latter not nearby but after all belongs to Denmark, get delicatessen variety of prosciutto, salamis, smoked reindeer etc.

For main course add some specialties not the ordinary grilled food, grilled dishes these are suggested by a cook who does not know what else to cook and he is ignorant and not a professional cook who wanted to offer and gain good comments, even if he just graduated from the hotel school.

Ask the cook to make plat du jour (the dish of the day) that will start maybe to get the restaurant famous for both families and couples in the neighbourhood and not only and make this known by simple ads in local newspapers or local TV and radio.

Let us say for example that every Tuesday there is plat du jour filet mignon with blue cheese sauce with Sous de Bruxelles and baked potato in oven wrapped in aluminium foil, this is just an example, on Thursday, you offer the chef's specialty he will tell you what else and what he best could do and that you supply only and every Thursday.

This is important for the restaurant to have customers at the so-called 'dead' days such a Monday up to Thursday by offering special dishes that they will spread this around from mouth to mouth and with reasonable prices so that a housewife will see that is cheaper for the family to eat there than cook in her kitchen with all what this includes.

The goal is to attract the housewives and have a relaxed lunch or dinner and avoid the kitchen's boring and hard job for them, but not only that, eating outside means more joy more family getting together, more mood for the housewife to get well-dressed and re-attract the bored husband to have a glass of wine and bring him to mood and also bring with him job for her bed.

If you have customers these 'dead' days then you will bring your restaurant to a positive balance sheet. Give added value to the Saturday and Sunday buffet breakfast, ask your chef to use his imagination not only as food but also with decorative elements.

Enrich your wine list with three–four at least German white wines from Rhine and Moselle and add quite some French Bordeaux and Bourgogne wines and maybe one or two Italian. Chianti is good and not expensive.

Cheese must have a good French and Swiss (Gruyere) variety of yellow cheeses and maybe some Italian like gorgonzola.

Choose the cook to have also knowledge of patisserie to make nice sweet desserts. The deserts are money bringers if you combine with a desert drink or even a clever maître D'hôtel could suggest a champagne even a cheaper German Sekt still brings money to the restaurant and not only money to the business but the guests leave the restaurant in a good happy temper. This is the major goal to have guests leaving in a happy mood.

Some may even ask to stay in the hotel for the night or a few hours. Who cares what in that room will take place. If the lady needs sex from her companion, make it easy for them to stay overnight or almost overnight in your rooms for a few hours, the money they leave counts for the enterprise. So, in that room they need both champagne and sexual amusement so give them what they want.

Arne was a little shocked that all these they maybe were against his principles and his wife's principles but what are principles, they are in the room adult couple they know what they ask and what they want provided they pay and preferably not for a few hours but full overnight rate.

He told him you must avoid by all means to get the fame of the illegal nest for illegal couples but this could happen only after they enjoyed their dinner in the restaurant and drink too much and they are afraid to drive. If a couple comes and asks for a one or two-hour rate, you kick them out as the hotel is in a nice and peaceful familiar environment and you must not lose those families from your lunches and dinners not only on Saturdays and Sundays but also during the slack days.

You can tell them that you rent the rooms for a whole night, if they want to leave in two hours, then this is their problem as they paid full rate, but as soon as they reach there, they are already hot and they will not care if they have to pay full overnight rate.

The additional advice was to make every Saturday and Sunday and advertise on local news and radio for the impressive biggest breakfast in the wider society area. Is necessary to achieve that mouth to mouth and widely spread and get known especially among housewives, that they could relax from the burden of the home breakfast and convince all family members to experience your restaurants' famous breakfast either Saturday or Sunday.

So, them be there, you have them in your hands you could do to them whatever you want so grab the occasion and show them the tonight's menu for dinner not for lunch as they had so much for breakfast that they cannot have any lunch anymore.

Serious income is also, as long as you have a big restaurant, to organise one or two nights preferably on Thursdays' special menu with live music band and a singer, music bands is easy to find and are not that expensive.

So, that night will be advertised in all Copenhagen websites and with a fixed menu that more or less you deliver the meat parts that are considered scrap by making a special delicatessen dinner (a Stroganoff or fillet super mignonettes as example) adding to these a nice impressive French title that you invent yourself or the student cook to the dish and you will obtain unbelievable profits.

Arne was hearing all these as if what he was telling him was a mountain to climb over with bare feet but it wasn't. He confessed to him that what he told him to do are great ideas but he had not the guts to do neither him nor his daughter or son who is anyway indifferent.

He told him to let him and Alex walk around and see the quality of the families one could see even from the outside of their homes, their level of amusement they desire all these a professional eye could see and only from their windows even if the curtains are closed.

After they wandered around, they went straight to their rooms for a nice and peaceful sleep.

Emma called again, warning him that she will smell him and she will know if he had any fuck or not. It reminded him of the police dogs who smell to locate drugs in luggage or hidden under cars.

The next morning, he had again to recapitulate his observations. Arne seemed to him not able to follow any of his instructions; he seemed weak and with no patience to manage his hotel. He begged him to take it over and he was willing but first he wanted to return home being away for many weeks and also care about the desperate appeal from his partner in China that things there do not work perfectly well.

In any case, he gave hope to Arne that he would consider his suggestion. They left him and returned Emma and Alex to his home.

Emma was waiting for him to be able to detect any woman's aroma on his body, he told her that he was tired and let all her plans for tonight be postponed for tomorrow.

Indeed, she showed to be calm and agreed to what he asked. She was sure that there was not any monkey business done the previous two nights.

So, after a quick dinner he went straight to bed, but after two hours of sleep he felt that he was not alone in the bed and two breasts were touching him and not just any breast but two hard horny nipples. The two hours of sleep revitalised his libido. The two nipples behind his back were not easy to ignore. She put her leg, embracing all his ass and felt a wet pussy touching his buttock.

He turned and smiled at her and asked her if she smelled any signs of orgies and they both laughed.

She also smiled and said, "Of course, I did, and I found that you were untouched so now execute your task on your host."

He said then, "So you mean, I have to pay for hosting me in your bed?"

She answered, "Of course, nothing is gratis."

"OK, then, how do you want me to proceed, or to make it more clear, how you want me to fuck you?"

"Orthodox sex, having you on top and using me as another dildo, bending towards my chest skin to skin, leaving no space between bodies, playing and aligning your nipples to my nipples, rubbing nipple to nipple, doggy sex, side sex, scissors sex, me standing at the edge of the bed allowing the vaginal walls tighter and increase the intensity? Anus fuck, what? You name it, and me as your slave will obey."

She answered, "Why the one or the other? I want it all." And so, this happened he gave her all as always. When all was given and over, he told her that tomorrow he had to leave for Greece back after many months away from family.

Her face darkened with embarrassment. She did not know that tomorrow he would leave. It was sudden for her that she was in deep melancholia and ready to cry.

She went to the living room and started smoking. She came back begging him to stay one or two days more, he gave her rather false info that he will return as he promised to his friend to take over his hotel. This calmed her a little but still she was suspicious that maybe this is a lie. He assured her that in two weeks he will be back and with that promise they went for a deep sleep.

The next morning, Alex came to pick him up for the airport. He tightly embraced Emma as he knew that he will never see her again and kissed her goodbye giving her hope that he will be back soon.

At the airport, he embraced Alex, and he apologised for beating him at the tennis; they both laughed. "Goodbye, dear friend, you were the one to persuade me to visit Greenland so a dream became true."

A relaxed sleep in the plane was needed as Emma exhausted all his libido reserves.

Wife, son and two daughters were at the airport together with their beloved black French bulldog. Only his three boys' cats were not there. They kissed each other and he was back home after a long time and many adventures.

He did not tell them from the very first day of his return that he needs to fly to China as there are problems there to be solved and this could be done only by him.

Family was happy to have him back again, they had a nice family dinner in their usual happy ambience.

He told them about the adventures in Greenland and the Bras de Ferre win over the Goliath, about the win of the tennis veterans' tournament that was organised by him, about the impressive successes he had at the hospital.

He also told them the proposition he had to take over the hotel of his co-student of Heidelberg. But he did not tell them anything about the wild animal's attack.

He was tired and had to enjoy the sleep in his own bed that he missed a lot.

The next day, they had dinner with their friends in their usual fish restaurant and they all were fascinated about his achievement on the long trip to the north. They all said to him never again leave for so long as we miss your hilarious jokes. He was a great jokes teller.

The next day was a bad day as he had to announce to his family that he must go to China.

He arranged the visa, booked a plane and the next day he was on board of Singapore airlines. The trip up to Shanghai was quite long and weary on the plane from Athens to Singapore in the business class, he met an old friend already from the first school years whom he had not met for more than 60 years.

He was a successful importer of electricity related items such as bulbs, cables etc. The guy was much afraid of the turbulences and each time the plane had such he was always crossing himself and was praying to God for his life. It was funny how scared he was although he was a frequent passenger.

At the Shanghai airport, his partner Sophia picked him up and brought him straight to his hotel, a nice and luxurious hotel. On the way she gave him a report of the problems they have due to the negligence of some of their staff and somehow the loss of enthusiasm for their job.

She will come next morning to pick him up at nine. He was in his room and first he had to order a girl for a relaxing massage that he heavily needed.

He talked to the lady who was the responsible person at the Gym and Spa and he asked her that he gives good tip so send him the most beautiful girl. She agreed.

Indeed, in five minutes, the girl knocked at his door and he found an *optasia* in front of him. He cannot remember all these 45 years that he travelled to China, a tall girl with quite big tits, very seldom for a Chinese girl.

He asked her name and told him her name is Angel and indeed she was an angel.

He started undressing, she turned around so that she would not see him completely naked. He laid on the bed and the angel started the massage first to his shoulders, his back her soft hands then touching him with a unique skill to give to him the best of relaxation.

She went down to his buttocks and her fingers slightly touched his testicles, he heard saying 'sorry', and she then went down to his legs and feet and started from the shoulders again, he was almost asleep. After she finished with his back side, she asked him to turn around to massage his thighs. He turned around and there his pole was up. She tried to cover her eyes but not for long she had to continue her job.

She, after she later confessed to him, could not expect from a rather old man such a hard dick. She made massage all over and then she had, could not avoid, and concentrate around his penis and at last she got grab of his dick, she looked at him to get his approval to masturbate him, she got his OK and she started to do this beautifully, she did this so nicely that he was feeling great, then without asking her to do this she took it in her mouth for a divine blowjob, she unbuttoned her shirt and the two tits fell upon his penis doing a massage with her tits (the so-called body massage that the Thai girls are expert for this) but also with her tits she rubbed all his body.

She put his penis between her soft beautiful tits and she did not stop there, the total sex was on the way. She got rid of her soft towel type tight trousers that allowed her thighs to look great and her tights were pulled off throwing them across that room and there were not any panties at all, and all this without him asking her to do this.

She put a condom on his penis not with her hand but with her mouth, he never saw this before. She mounted him with such a charming way and with a sweet smile on her lips using her hand softly guided his penis inside her total depth and started a horse soft riding of a princess in her castle's gardens.

She was on top of him drawing him inside her but also pressed him out doing this repeatedly, the smile always fell on him and her eyes always looking at his eyes to see that he was very satisfied and indeed he was.

He kept himself not to ejaculate, and he asked her to turn around her in her fours in front of him, seeing such a marvel, such an unusual Chinese girl's ass, so smooth pussy lips and also an ideally shaped asshole.

He penetrated her from behind adding his thumb into her rectum but very delicately and charmingly she removed his hand from there so he could not insist, he respects women and to what they seem not to want.

Maybe this is his secret that ladies and girls want repeated sex with him as he regards and esteems his sex partners to all their prohibited claims but also obey to their in some cases, demand for peculiarities or 'abnormalities'.

He was tired and he could not hold anymore and she helped him also by hearing her coming in an angelic way, so happy that she came he allowed his down there guy (junior he often calls him) to empty his load with no any hesitation as there was the condom to safeguard.

They stayed in bed side by side, always embracing him. Surprisingly, she spoke quite good English. She told him that she is 19 years old and she lives alone. Father and mother live up north, where only farmers are there still to cultivate the land.

She wanted to study physiotherapist but money is needed for her home rent and her studies, so she came to this hotel only as masseuse, but the spa chief lady obliges her to offer sex to the good customers only, but she has the option when she sees who is in that room to deny, and for him it was a big yes.

He was very touched by her story. He gave her 100 euros apart from what the spa will charge on his bill. She for a moment felt uncomfortable and hesitated to take the banknote as if she wanted to show him that she enjoyed it. He insisted on taking it.

Before leaving she wrote on a paper serviette her telephone number telling him that this is not allowed but exceptionally, she did this for him asking him with her finger on her lip that this is their secret.

He was so happy and felt exceptionally privileged and lucky to get the very first night in China such a relaxed massage and had such divine sex with maybe the cutest Chinese girl he ever met.

His partner came to the breakfast room so they discussed a little before meeting about all the staff and the necessity to give them a lecture on how they have to keep on if they want to keep their job.

Nice hotel, well prepared breakfast and night before a girl who was sent from heaven, all great as a start in China. Few minutes' drive there their seven member staff were waiting for him and pretended to look joyful for him to come but he knew that inside them they were to hear hard remarks and scolding after what the lady partner probably told him.

But to their surprise, they did not face such a conduct from him. On the contrary, he embraced them all with his words saying, "How lucky we are to have you as collaborators, and together, we will build a common good future with mutual benefits."

They, but also his partner, looked astonished, they were told that he is a very severe type of man with a harsh and offensive attitude in case he gets angry. But they saw in front of them a cordial guy with a smile and kindness.

He possessed the experience on how to handle such situations, rough and harsh words to sound as punishment to the ears, words and especially penalised words do not have the best results, while warm and generous treatment addressed direct to their professional conscience, brings marvellous outcomes.

Surprisingly one could see there was a happy and content mood on the air in that room. He explained to them that only with good, synchronised and high-performing team work, they will advance.

"Profits for the company assure your job and possible bonuses when the time comes". He explained that the times are bad, that there is recession all over the world, especially the situation in Germany is not the best at all. In Germany are their customers, the energy crisis touched them more than any other country and many bankruptcies are expected, so they have to work harder to maintain their customers and help them to surpass the crisis.

So, now more than ever the team's hard work is more than necessary, he could use the word obligatory but he did not.

They seemed to apprehend the situation and promised that they are determined to work with devotion and follow all orders very carefully.

The atmosphere was excellent. There was a deep influence of his 'speech' to them, he asked his partner to take them out one of these next evenings for a dinner to bring them closer to the partners. Fear and threats bring the worst results but touching their conscience is the best consultant.

His partner told him that he was a magician to bring them in such a cooperative spirit; she was happy that he came as she was losing control and discipline. He promised that he stays as long as he could to follow the business on the spot, rather than from the distance.

He told her while being there that he had to come up with ideas how to improve the business and gain more orders, despite the hard times, and why not think also of an additional business.

He assured her that despite his age he wanted and had the guts to create new businesses. She told him that he was a phenomenon, as in China, men after 65, they retire, but he was still looking for new business.

After having lunch, they sat down to see their financial situation and what could be done to improve their cash flow status. For a reason, he wanted to finish that meeting, and that reason was not any other than the temptation to call Angel and see how she will welcome his phone call.

He reached his hotel, and the first thing to do was to call Angel. She answered right away and gave him the impression that she was expecting his phone call as she was so sweet on the phone. She told him that this was her day off, and she was relaxing at home.

He asked her if she had dinner and she said no, not yet, so he asked her to give her home address and asked her to get dressed to pick her up. She was more than happy for this, but she told him to take a taxi not from outside the hotel but any other from the road so the driver will not see to what address he will bring him. She will wait outside, airing for him on the street, so she will take him to her small apartment as the building was huge with many apartments.

She will then get dressed and walk not far away to a nice restaurant that she arranged to book a table.

He answered OK, he will be there in 30–40 minutes. He shaved well; he washed again and again to have a pleasant breath, put some perfume on him and dressed well as a real gentleman.

He looked himself in the mirror and addressed to himself, "You bastard, how you always manage to get the best girl in town? What the hell of a magical filter you have to make girls and ladies to adore you?"

He took a taxi from the street, not ordered as he did not want to give the address where he was to go, just protecting Angel to be revealed that she accepts customers at her apartment.

The taxi driver drove him there. She was waiting outside so that he would not miss the apartment as there were many flats in that big building, and the taxi drove away.

She welcomed him and took him up to the 12th floor to her apartment. The apartment was cute but had all that was needed. Even a nice balcony where one could have a nice view of Shanghai.

She was dressed casually and asked him, after she checked how he was dressed, for 20 minutes to go to her bedroom and change into a better dress.

He was waiting there, so he had the time to call his family and tell them that he arrived safely, and he managed to bring the office in a good order and functionality.

Right after, who was on the phone? It was Alex. He asked him, "Where are you?" He answered that he was in Shanghai, waiting for an angelic creature to get dressed to go out for dinner.

He was angry. "Why didn't you tell me? I was never in China."

He made a joke to him. "I do not want you because you will steal all available girls."

His answer was, "How can I steal a girl from the oldest Casanova in this world?"

He asked him if he would like to come and he might need him as he may come up with some new business ideas.

He agreed that next week he would inform him when he will be there.

The bedroom door opened, and a divine vision was there; he could not hide his admiration, feeling that he was 'too small, too inferior' in front of that beauty he was to accompany to the restaurant.

She was so happy to see his sparkling glance. She confessed to him that she bought this dress a year ago, but she never had the right occasion to wear it.

He was flattered that this beauty would wear it the first time for him, and he wondered how come such a beautiful girl did not find the man who will make her feel like a princess because this is what she is.

So, well dressed, even if the restaurant was so close, he could not allow her to walk. She dressed like a real diva, and he, a gentleman next to her, walked the streets like an ordinary Chinese woman, he will never allow this, simply because she was far away from any ordinary Chinese girl.

So, he whistled for a taxi to take them there even if that was just a few metres away; the taxi driver was amazed; he gave him more than three times the taxi fare.

The taxi driver also looked at her with his mouth open, admiring that beauty as if she were a TV star and at the same time envied the guy that was accompanying her.

Angel was also impressed by having him take a taxi for just a few metres; he told her that he would not be a gentleman to have a princess to go on foot to the restaurant.

The entrance to the restaurant made big admiration impact to all that they were seeing a so well-dressed couple and him to look like her father; he does not say grandfather because as he said many times, his general appearance hides many years and not any woman or girl could guess his age.

The 'maître' ran to get for them the best table in a rather private corner , away from jealous eyes and not to the table that he reserved primarily for them. He took the initiative to order and asked the maître, if there was wine.

Angel pushed him with her elbow, muttering to his ear that wine here was very expensive. He appreciated her unusual concern, and he smiled and ordered white wine as most of what was there to eat was closer to fish than meat.

She was surprised how elegantly she could eat as if she were a European lady; she asked him to allow her to drink tea instead of wine, and he said, "No, I insist that you also have a glass of wine."

She confided to him with a smile that this was the first time in her life to drink wine and that she was always jealous seeing TV stars with wine glass in their hands.

Angel had something new to experience. Talking about her life again, she despite that she was obliged many times to go to the rooms not only for massage, when entering the room and see who was there, many times she denied, returning back.

There were not more than four men that she had sex, but with these men she did not feel anything at all, and she did not have any orgasm. What it was, just a sex under obligation and money.

She admitted that when she entered his room and saw him tired as he was, she was determined to do only massage and nothing else, thinking that to bring this man's penis hard enough, she would have to spend long time, and this because she told him that two out of these four men although were 35 years old, their penis was never hard enough, and they blamed her that they could not have a hard-on.

So, when she saw him turned around and saw his penis so hard; she was glad that she had not to struggle to get it hard, and on the way, she realised that she wanted to make sex and with him with plenty of pleasure as he looked so tender to her, and so it was done, and she enjoyed it all the way.

He asked her then if these four men had sex with her certainly she was not virgin; she said no, and he asked her who took her virginity; she hesitated to give an answer and looked at him as if she were ashamed about that. He told her no need to feel ashamed what is done is done.

Well then, she described how this happened. In that small village where she was living, one day when her parents were away to go to work at the farm, when she was 12 years old, her uncle came to her home.

She, having no experience as there was no TV in their home, she had no idea what sex was all about. So, her uncle asked her very friendlily to take off her dresses. He wanted to admire how she became so big, almost like a woman. All was so innocent; she took off her dresses, and with the smile of an innocent girl, she showed him her body being proud that she was getting almost as big as her mother.

He came close and caressed her; well, he was her uncle, the brother of her father, and she could not find any reason not to allow him to touch her. He was caressing her also between her legs, and she opened her legs exposing her treasure always with that innocent smile, and he touched her also under her legs, where she had few hairs, and this tickled her; she smiled from the tickling, still feeling that her uncle was innocently playing with her.

Discovering that she was indeed innocent and knew nothing about sex and the human body to her surprise, he also took off his trousers to show her, as he said, the difference between a man's and a woman's body.

Indeed, it was a mystery for her what was that thing in front of him under his belly that she didn't have. He took his hand and asked her to touch it, and she did it, and it slowly became bigger and harder and harder; she was laughing as she saw that suddenly grow so much bigger; was it a miracle, she thought.

He held her up and brought inside the home and at the bed while he locked the door behind him, and then he became violent. He made her stand at the edge of the bed and lean down so that he had her ass all in front of him, and there he felt that in her hole where she uses for peeing, but something was in there. She protested and said, "Uncle, what are you doing there? I feel pain."

He answered, "Shut up and stay there and do not move," and then with a big push he entered with that hard thing in her. The pain was unbearable, and she was crying. He shut her mouth with his dirty hand as he just came from the farm and moved many times harder. She was crying and trying to shout, but her mouth was blocked with his hand.

She then noticed that a scream went from his mouth, and that 'thing' became softer and pulled it out hanging between his legs on top of two balls making an ugly scene.

He asked her to go to the toilet and wash herself down there, and he showed her where to wash as there was blood. She was angry at him, and then he told her that if she tell to anyone what happened, he will kill her. That was a hard intimidation.

Unfortunately, he was spying when his parents went away, and he kept doing this until her age of 15, and then the first time, she felt what was to be called orgasm. Knowing by then that this was not a toy anymore; she became angry and threatened him that if he comes again to do this, she would tell everyone in the village.

Since then, she was always afraid to have any such sex again with anyone, although many boys wanted her and kissed her but she never allowed them to do what her uncle did to her.

Coming back to the spa and her visit to the rooms. He was very surprised as she also told him that there was a woman of 40 years who persuaded her to have sex with her. She heard on TV about lesbian love, but she did not know how exactly this worked.

That woman was a real lesbian, and she made it to be easy licking each other's pussies and also took from her bedside drawer a vibrator (she learnt later the name of this device), and she put this all inside her pussy, and that was so nice that she came with real pleasured climax.

That woman stayed four nights in the hotel, and she ordered always her to come, and they did this so nicely and with mutual affection one time a dildo, as she called that, the on edge was in her vagina, and the other on the lady's vagina, she confessed to him that she liked and enjoyed this.

She also told him that with the three men that she had sex, she felt absolutely nothing. He actually was a little drunk, and he confessed to her that once when he was 22, he fucked a French boy of the same age that was closer to a girl than a boy as he was chasing him for many weeks to persuade him to fuck him. He was always denying sending him away. But this happened in the showers despite his will, but that boy was so smart that he managed, and he confessed to her that his anus was maybe much better than many girls' assholes he ever penetrated.

She turned red hearing this anus fuck and held her mouth closed with her hand as if she wanted not to hear details, believing that if she was to try this will have the same pain as when she lost her virginity from that bad, ugly uncle.

They had a nice dinner and a lot of fun and joy, and all those were there showed jealousy seeing how she looked to be in love with that older but well-preserved man.

He ordered a taxi and drove her home; he asked the taxi to wait, and he accompanied her up to her room. There at the door, they kissed with passion; she then asked him with a complaining manner, "Why do you want to leave and not stay here the night?" He liked the idea, and he said OK; he rushed down to pay the taxi driver and returned to his Angel.

They were naked on the bed; she turned to the other side and his penis was well rested in her soft buttock, but then he noticed that she fell asleep; she was dizzy from the wine; accidentally, he forced her to feel the pleasure of the wine, and she drank two glasses, and there she was sleeping like an angel.

He covered her nicely shaped, naked body and slipped out of the bed, dressed and returned to the hotel. He was so horny, he wanted to order another girl, but that would not be so appropriate, and he wanted with nothing in the world to lose Angel, so he turned to the guy down there under his belly. "You bastard, stop asking for a pussy and sleep."

So, he fell into a deep but pleasant sleep.

The next day, he went to the office to see that everything was getting better from the point of view of the working atmosphere. The staff was working with mood, so was his partner; this was obvious to his eyes.

He asked his partner to look at their financial records to see where they stand and if they have surplus cash flow. The reason he asked for this was because he had something in his mind that he had for years and he never could manage and realise it.

He remembered quite some years ago, he had two Chinese guys as visitors. He took them to a nearby well-known tavern area where there are many taverns known for their specialty, which is lamb on the spit and lambchops. He ordered, and wishing to please them, he kept ordering. He drove them to their hotel and asked them if they liked the food there; to his big surprise, they said frankly, "No, we do not like lamb." He was disappointed, so tomorrow he told them he would take them to the old Athens city called Plaka. There were many restaurants, so let us see if that food satisfies a Chinese guy's *uraniscus* (Greek word for the roof of the mouth). So, when they were there; they liked the ambience and the many small restaurants and the benches that were in the centre of that small square where one could sit and eat and drink beer or Greek ouzo.

So, he ordered the so-called Greek souvlaki and the also so-called Greek gyros, pork meat roasted on the spit. They ate that, and they asked for more. They turned crazy with that meat and taste. So, his idea, since maybe 20 years, was to open in China a chain of taverns where one could eat souvlaki, which was the popular Greek fast food, consisting of small pieces of meat and vegetables, tomatoes grilled on a skewer and wrapped with a pita bread and, of course, the famous Greek salad with the Greek feta cheese. It was usually eaten straight off the skewer while still hot and big gyros spices with pork meat turning all around the fire and get well roasted.

Usually, this was served with the Greek 'Choriatiki' salad, made with pieces of tomatoes, cucumbers, onion, feta cheese, and olives and dressed with salt, Greek oregano, and olive oil.

Common additions include green pepper slices and add to the table to make the meal perfect and rich, adding pommes frites (fried potatoes).

There was no need for more variety of food; the people were more than complete for lunch or dinner, and one needs nothing more.

The advantage of such a tavern/restaurant is that one could enjoy a rich meal and pay less money. The idea seemed great and was in his mind for many years, but he never found the appropriate time and money to do it as he was very busy with his other businesses.

So, although almost in his 69, he still had the guts to start a new business that could widely be spread to all neighbourhoods of Shanghai and later on a franchise basis to entire China and Hong Kong. It may sound very optimistic and needed on the way to establish a big organisation, but he was always of the rule 'Think Big'.

He described to his partner what that idea was; they checked the cash flow and saw that there was enough money to start the first tavern, where mostly people also could call for delivery at home. Cash flow was enough, but better get a partner to add to the starting capital so that they will not dry the cash flow of the main business with no cash flow cannot run and finance the orders. The idea intrigued or, better say, fascinated his partner and decided to do it, so he was at the run to find the investor.

He then came to the idea of what that investor might be, so he informed her that one good friend will come from Denmark and could be useful for all projects as he possesses a big amount of money and is aiming for a good business, trusting him 100%.

The meeting was over, and they decided to go for this new potential project. He then went straight to the hotel and called Angel. She was waiting for this phone call. He told her never again accept any sexual process from that spa leader, and if she has no objections then resign; he told her that he has money to take care of her, and he also has new projects that she could be helpful for public relations as occupation. She was happy that she could at last deny the sexual part of that job and limit that for the time only for massage and that only at the spa and not in rooms.

She told him that after her shift, she would wait for him at her home. He told her that tomorrow he was expecting a friend from Europe, and he asked her if she has any girlfriend so that he can also feel the warmth of the hug of a beautiful girl.

She told him, yes, she has, and she was doing the same job in the spa of another hotel; she was also her same age. He said that this was perfect. His friend is polite and tender like him so she will also feel very comfortable with his Danish friend. The Greek gyros tavern will be named 'Spartan', which was easy to be pronounced by Chinese and at the same time refers and reminds the glorious ancient Greece. Chinese people love Greece and especially the Greek islands. They have to make a first marketing research and see what similar taverns were in the city, which of course, was so big and crowded that it could take many such taverns.

Now the important thing was to run around to locate the place that they rent and where the first Spartan tavern would get underway.

Must be a place with equally big space inside and garden or better a type of yard outside and not necessarily be in the centre where the rent prices are very high, but preferably where many big buildings with many people to live and no need to be there where the rich people live as they were not their target group.

For this running, he also engaged Angel and maybe her girlfriend, who was meant to be the girlfriend of Alex, provided, of course, they find the right chemistry like him and Angel.

Alex is a handsome man and has quite a lot of money. He for sure could add capital and be a partner in the Spartan project. He was expected to arrive tomorrow, and he had to pick him up from the airport, and he maybe need to ask Angel to take a day off to be with him.

Alex could also help to run the already existing office, adding surveillance and kind of supervision. Alex looks for adventure, has no family and obligations; he feels bored in Copenhagen and he is strong enough at his 60s to become like him in his 69, a business startuper as it is right to say 'it is never too late'.

Never too late for business and never too late to make sex and provide good sex to women that nowadays they miss a good and quality altruistic sex.

Indeed, Angel took a day off, and they were to fetch Alex from the airport. Alex was with his luggage; when he saw Angel, he opened his eyes, telling him in Danish, "You son of a bitch, what a goddess she is!" He told him also in Danish, wait maybe her girlfriend might be equally beautiful. Angel hearing that odd Danish language could not hide her laughter.

They took a taxi, and they were at the hotel and let Alex get installed and let him sleep as the trip from Copenhagen to Shanghai takes many hours.

In the taxi to the hotel, he told him that he had greetings from Greenland; Tuppi and Saka telling him that they made big arrangements taking as granted that this tournament would indeed take place in Nuuk. But he so far had done nothing, as there was no free time; he gave them a fake promise that they took that as very serious, and this started to become a headache for him.

His only goal that time after he defeated the giant, was to restore the fame of Tupe, and now he was in front of an obligation that he does not know how to handle.

Anyway, after four hours, he knocked on his door to wake him up to go for dinner, and Angel was to bring her girlfriend for Alex, so that he would not feel alone.

Angel told him when they left Alex at his room that Alex looks fine, and she hopes that her girlfriend will like him.

They took a taxi and went to Angel's place. Alex always trusted his taste; after all, he had those German girls in Nuuk that offered him freshness and revitalised his bored life.

They went up to the 12th floor, and there was the girlfriend, a beautiful short girl whilst Alex was not short guy but the same height like Areus. He, with a known sign and blink of his eye, showed that he liked her a lot. He turned to him saying, "Smuk." Which means beautiful.

Luckily, she also spoke good English as they both attended rapid English lessons as they were to go to the university to study physiotherapy, speaking one language added value to their diploma.

So, they were this night casually dressed so they walked to that same restaurant where they were a few days ago. The dinner was very amusing with too many spicy jokes. Areus, in fact, is the guru of hilarious jokes.

Alex was so glad, and he wanted wine on table; this time, Angel drank this more cautiously but not Melissa. That was Alex's girl's name. She drank more than two glasses, very unusual for a Chinese girl.

Melissa drank wine for the first time, and she liked it a lot. Wine always brings a good mood and in some particular cases brings the girl easier to the bed, but this was not fair play.

She was doing the same job like Angel in another hotel and also in case of good customers she was visiting the rooms for private massage with whatever that might turn out to become. But she was a cute and humorous girl, seldom for a Chinese girl; in any case, she cannot reach the beauty of his girl, Angel.

The dinner ended when they went to Angel's place; he was to stay there, and Alex went one floor up where Melissa's apartment was.

The next day, he told him that he slept there, but Melissa fell asleep right away (same as Angel did at their first dinner) after the wine she drank, so he could not tell him more about possible sex encounters.

He left Melisa's flat before she woke up, and he went to his hotel for a better sleep as Melissa's bed was rather narrow.

They left the hotel after having a heavy breakfast to go to his office, where they were to meet his partner Sophia and introduce to her Alex, the new partner of the Spartan taverns project. His partner Sophia arranged to make a marketing and find out that such restaurants exist in Shanghai but Turkish kebab, which is not the same thing at all.

So, now they needed at least two months to bring the first necessary materials from Greece. When these arrived, then they could produce in China for the possible next tavern to come. They also had to fly all food ready gyros and all food ingredients from Greece, and after they search local factories, they would need to produce in China.

At that point, they had to pause in his mind this project as the meeting was fixed with all staff of the office to tell them how he works from so far away and how from that distance, he was the one to find makers with the best prices in China while they were just there.

So, as they knew already, what he managed to do and with total success, he created five fake companies, with false addresses and no telephone number, just email address companies. So, he had German, Dutch, British, French, Spanish and Australian companies' email addresses.

So, to the Chinese makers and suppliers, they see a Johann Gunter, a Jaroen Noutheyn, a George Smith, a lady Michelle Leclerc, a Jose Morales and a Bob Badenlorger. This trick worked fine to double check if a maker or a supplier was deceiving with different prices to different inquirers for the same or almost same quantity given to the German or the Dutch importer as example. With this system, they get the best prices.

He gave to his partner his treasure, which was the biggest data bank in the world with almost one million items and hundreds of thousands of Chinese makers.

That was a good base, but at the same time, they have to send for each inquired item at least 20 to 30 mails to have a good comparison, but at the same time, with a smart eye check from the website the supplier's profile if he was serious to be trusted or not. An experienced eye could do this and distinguish the serious supplier from the possible cheater.

So they use his six email addresses and not their Chinese email address, as almost all Chinese makers and suppliers prefer to deal with the foreigner than with local trader or any sourcing company.

He told them that he has all the tools to obtain the best prices in the market with his data bank in combination with Alibaba and Asian Sources.

Clever bargain is always needed and then only after you have the best price and you have examined who that maker is, then and only then you submit offer to their German customers, adding the company's profit percentage, and also that profit rate is not stable and standard; it is at the salesman's judgement what percentage of profit to add up; this, of course, requires a smart eye as a small word in the German's mail can hide and reveal what they are ready to hear as price.

He explained to them that his database was well locked with a security system that cannot move from their server. Alex, who was present at this, let us call it 'lecture', was impressed how he smartly he had done all these.

So, now he passed all his knowledge and working system so they can do it by themselves, but at the same time for the big projects and not the ones notify him with a bcc to his mail so that he can check what they do wherever he is and, in some cases, intervene and act before a damage is done by wrong buying or selling price.

He asked them with close collaboration they obtain smooth functionality and increase the score of achieving substantial orders and thereafter as result vaster accessibility to the German and other markets.

The last advice was never to show procrastination but right away focus on the inquiry that just appeared in your monitor, or else that inquiry will remain in the monitor and will have a dissatisfied customer for non-dealing with that.

Be always eager to delve into the inquiry's details and small letters that can hide a big number of secret topics, and by digging this out, you know that the customer is ready and willing to pay as target price, and by that, you obtain a good profit for the company that pays your salaries and bonuses.

What is must to obtain optimum results is that you are perfectionists and in no case superficial; this is a major success rule. They all were amazed and promised to work from now on his way and not as a usual Chinese salesmen or saleswomen does, just and only and after they get the first offer, they simply add 5% and send to the customer, so simply, they in no way get orders.

He needed after that four-hour 'lesson' to relax, so he went to the hotel while Alex wanted to walk and see a little of Shanghai as it was his first time in Shanghai.

Reaching the hotel, the first thing for him was to order Angel to come as she was on duty and relax with a massage from a lover and not a professional. And his angel came with a big smile and big cuddle.

He asked her for a massage and the warmth of her sweet body. She gave him all with an open heart and in abundance. Good sex was finally inevitably on the menu. After both were side by side, exhausted from the total sex, she whispered into his ear, "What about that anus sex you talked to me about last time?"

He told her it was not the time yet; that must be appropriately celebrated so they have to do it another time and most probably in their own luxury apartment with champagne and soft music.

She for the first time heard, 'Our own apartment'. She asked, "You mean my apartment?"

"Of course, not the new luxury apartment that I asked the real estate agent to find and come up with suggestions and in the same building as Alex and Melissa's apartment."

He also told her about the 'Spartan' project that when this will start, she has to quit this spa; she no longer needed to work there anymore.

But he made also clear that until this happens, she has to definitely ask the spa manager that she will not visit in rooms anymore, and she will only make massage in the spa and massage and only clean massage, with no extras.

"If she denies, then quit right away, and I will support you financially."

She promised to do that and left. He needed a good nap as he had to go again for the meeting with his partners, Sophia and Alex. After he woke up, he called Alex, and he came to his room. He was so enthusiastic that after so many years of doing nothing, now he will have the chance to run a business as his partner and a business with so big perspectives and possibility for expansion.

He told him that he talked to Melissa, and according to the impression he got, she likes him. He confirmed this to him as Angel also told him about, so he was happy as that Chinese girl with her smile and spicy humour opened to him a new page to his rather boring and lonely until then life.

They went to the office to meet Sophia, and while they talked about the project, he had to make many phone calls to Greece and re-employ one of the guys he had in his previous company who knew that Spartan project already from those times; he already started before to investigate what machinery was needed and where the food ingredients were to be found and in the due time fly in fridge, small containers of the needed supplies by air that could last at least two–three weeks in the Spartan's fridges and deep freezers.

The machinery could be shipped by sea, including in the container also typical chairs and tables that remind traditional Greek restaurants and also well packed in that 40 feet big container were at least three pallets of white wine and three pallets of red wine.

He would instruct him when the time comes what brands and from which Greece's areas he would purchase the wine. He asked for his bank account to send him the first three salaries and enough money to move around.

The three partners fixed their partnership and each one's shares. It was agreed to go to Hong Kong and open an account there with Areus having 51% and Sophia with Alex the 49%, whereas Alex will finance 70% for the heeded cash as capital; there was not any single objection to that shares' split. He would do all, and he was the leader of this, and both trusted him.

He gave them a promise that they would have such success and make such a much promising and optimistic endeavour with not easy to imagine turnovers and profits that one day, maybe after three years, would go public to the Hong Kong or Shanghai stock exchange and then deliver the business to selected well-educated CEOs.

The ambiance in that room was triumphant.

So, now things started to be on track. His Greek guy searched for what was needed in Greece, and they had to start the running to find the right place for the first 'Spartan' tavern. It must be in an area where middle-class Chinese live and not any expensive area.

They decided to give this job to three different real estate agents and pick up the best spot they would suggest. They must also give the instructions to two advertising agents who, after they profoundly read Greek mythology and culture, come with brilliant ideas for the decoration but also the promotional campaign that would be launched, but always adapted to the Chinese mentality.

Chinese people like to follow American and European ways of living, and this included also eating, they would embrace this new concept for them. He always wanted to keep his mind busy with new ideas that were plenty and crowded within his brains.

Tonight, it was a dinner where he and Alex would introduce their girls to Sophia.

He was not sure that was a good idea as she was divorced with a daughter, and her daughter was older than their girls.

Anyway, it was fixed and could not be changed. His partner made the booking at her favourite restaurant, and they were there with two young girls. At first, she was shocked, but then she realised that first was the business and then if they were happy, so let it be.

During the dinner, she could see that particularly Angel showed affection for him. Sophia, his partner for many years, looked also happy seeing this affection.

So, the first shock was over. The dinner went fine. A lot of joy; Alex was the happiest man on earth, first having a beautiful girl next to him, looking at him as if he were a film star, and then him at last would have something to do with his money.

They left Sophia at her house, and they went to Angel's apartment for a last drink. He then proposed to them to quit their jobs and start looking for two nice apartments, furnished and luxurious, where they all stay in two separate apartments but in same building.

Then they have to go back to their studies as physiotherapists to get their diploma, and they, Alex and him, would help them to open their own spa, fitness and gym at the best spot in that area. They both were enormously happy to hear this.

So, that night, they left them alone, and they went to their hotel so that they both sit down and make the plans.

That week was great; his office started to work according to his instructions and according to his partner; they were all delighted that he came and gave them new enthusiasm as that was almost non-existent before.

Then the Spartan project was also on the way, waiting for the suggestions from the advertising and designing companies, and parallel, they assigned real estate agents to look for five different best places according to instructions given, to find the best location for the first Spartan tavern.

He always had in mind because he was also calling him all the time for a solution for his friend Arne and his hotel. He was telling him that he indeed got his precious advices, but he feels too old and has not the guts to follow. His wife and daughter were pushing him to sell the hotel, but selling the hotel when it was down with only few customers in both hotel and restaurant would be sold for small money, while bring this to good condition by winning fame would add value.

He had an idea and called a relative, who had convinced his son to follow his hotel career and his steps, and so he did. Areus had sent him to Rome to study the kitchen organisation and economy; he sent him to the kitchen of Grand Hotel in Nurnberg and also at the kitchen of Hotel du Palais in Biarritz and also to send him to two other five stars hotels to work at the restaurant, so he had full knowledge of all major hotel departments.

He told him he was in France; he told him that the hotel in Copenhagen would have the position of manager, and he would have all under his control and full responsible management, in other words, a Carta Bianca. He was crazy with idea and his enthusiasm; this reminded himself of his age, and his name was Nicolas.

He called Arne and told him about this young man. He explained to Arne that this young man was the ideal solution; he was honest, he guaranteed for this, as he knows him since he was a boy. He was very well educated from good family; he spoke German, English and French as well as Italian, and he would learn Danish in two months, same as he did.

He told him that when he comes, leave everything to him and give free hand to operate his way and take the family and go to his Mallorca summer house. Arne answered, "If you guarantee for this young man, I will do it." He called Nicolas and gave the phone number of Arne to continue and inform him that all was going well. So, he felt that he found the ideal solution, and he was happy that one headache went away.

Before Alex left Denmark, he told him that Saka asked him to get his address in China as those three German girls wanted to send him a letter. Indeed, they called him from his China office and said that there was an envelope for him.

He had to go to the office anyway to check that all goes according to plan and get that envelope. He opened the envelope, and there inside was a mobile phone, with a message saying, "There is a video but watch it when you are in your bed." Signed, 'Your sex slaves.' He thought, *What the hell they sent to me?*

He rushed to his hotel and laid on his bed as they asked him, and opening the mobile phone, there was a new message:

"Take your clothes off, stay in bed nude."

So, he touched the video button, and he saw the three girls in the spa in big joy, in the massage room, in the pool and then, a new message was there saying,

"Hold your penis and start masturbating."

And in that video were all three in the bed, all naked doing a superb lesbian love. The one licking the others nicely opened pussy, the one inserting two fingers in the other's asshole, the one pushing far deep a vibrator to other's pussy; they were sure that he enjoys and could not avoid to masturbate.

Then the one flashed to him her pussy, saying in a voice message, "You were tightly in here." And the other two turned around and with the fingers pointed to their anus and again the message, 'You were in here'.

And there was laughter ha ha ha…

"You took our anus virginity, but we enjoyed this, ha ha ha."

Needless to say, he had a gorgeous masturbation seeing this pure porno show. "Here are our phone numbers; when you are in Hamburg, call us, and we will be glad to continue what we all left behind in Nuuk." The end of the message was,

"You are a great man, a top masculine phenomenon, keep on, darling…"

That was maybe the best masturbation ever.

He thought, *Shall I show it to Alex? Or not?* He decided to show it to him because his girl was kind of shy, and she did not give him adequate sex pleasure yet. When he met him in the afternoon, he asked him to get in bed with his girl, and they only watch this video so that she gets really horny, and he takes advantage of this. He was happy that this video could make her hot as he was rather timid.

So, he did; he asked her to come to the hotel and started the kisses, and he then told him that being both in bed, he showed the video; she opened her eyes seeing what these three girls were doing, and without knowing why, with an ecstatic look, she grabbed his penis, and when the video was over, they did it with extreme lust an orgy; they had a wonderfully shared sex satisfaction.

He told him the next day, "Well, you are a real magician. How were you so sure that she would get so horny and have wild sex to me when she kind of denied it before?"

He answered, "Now the beginning is done, and she is all yours, so friend Alex, explore her young body and all secrets that it hides, and be sure there are many new things to discover in her nice body, just deploy your cock as 'excavator'."

The next day was a bad or maybe a good day. He got a phone call from a Danish phone number, and who was there? It was Karla. She was angry with him because he gave her the wrong number, and she had to go to the hospital, where they also did not have his phone number. They sent him to the nearby tennis club, and lastly, she had to go to Arne, who gave her his telephone number.

She told him, "Areus, I am pregnant."

He congratulated her saying, "At last, you find the right guy to marry. Is he that Tunisian guy?"

She answered, "You did not understand. You are the father."

He said, "What?"

"Yes, you are the father because since you were there for the whole one year, I never had any sex, and also after you left, I also did not have any sex with any man."

He was shocked he did not know what to say. He asked her if her mother knows about him being there. She answered, "Yes, she knows; she was shocked for a moment. I told her that I had multiple sex with you the same way as you did to her many years ago." And that she did this to avenge her for preventing her from marrying that nice Tunisian boy.

Mother Mathilde, for whom he went to Denmark to meet, but she was not there, and he had sex with her daughter, or better say, she was the one to have sex with him, now carries his baby.

Mathilde showed not any anger; she overcame the first shock and then seemed happy that her daughter at last was pregnant, and they have an heir to take over one day the big factory that her father left to her and that constantly brings good income to them.

She was also happy that he was the father, as she was hoping one day, those old days, that she could marry him and get from him a baby; now her daughter will have the baby instead, so it is still welcome.

Karla told him that she did not call him to support her financially because they have plenty of money, but it was her obligation to tell him that he was one more time father.

He asked if she knew if it was a boy or girl, she told him that by the end of next month, the doctors told her that they would know.

He became kind of sulky but still made efforts to show that he was enthusiastic and happy.

He told her to call him when she knows the gender of the baby. She told him that both mother and daughter love him and sent him kisses and a warm goodbye.

He tried to recall the moments and remembered indeed that sometimes he did not manage to pull out in time, but also sometimes she even did not allow him to pull out.

After that phone call, he was in deep consideration about that, and if it would have an impact on his life. He was thinking that if he lives another 15 years, he will be 94 and that boy or girl will be 14.

He was thinking of this and how he could tell his wife and notably to his son and daughters that they have a new brother or sister and how his wife would face this situation.

He tried to remove this from his clouded mind for a while and concentrate on what he was doing there in China.

Right now, Angel and Melissa have resigned from their jobs, and they went to enrol again for the physiotherapists' lessons to get their diplomas; at the same time, they were looking for two nice furnished apartments.

One of his headaches was also that Nuuk Bras de Ferre tournament that he promised and a whole community lived for; what a mistake it was to give them hope with a fake announcement.

He had a good Monegasque friend who was the ex-president of the Backgammon Association and with connections worldwide in all sports and relevant associations.

He called him and explained to him the whole story about the Giant-Goliath-Viking guy, and asked if he knew the president of the Bras de Ferre Association in Quebec, Canada. He told him that the whole sounds very attractive, and he will try to get connections and will call him.

Monegasque was surprised to hear that at this age he was still so active moving from Germany to Denmark and Greenland and then to China.

So now in a way, he has all the plus or minus under control and waited for the outcomes.

Arne called him to tell him that tomorrow Nicolas would be there, and he would call him again when he meets him and gets his first impressions.

At the same time, Melissa and Angel were looking for their apartments. So, the Think Tank was heavily loaded with quite some projects. While his Greek fellow was purchasing all needed machinery and equipment for the Spartan tavern project.

While waiting for the real estate bureau to suggest to them where the first tavern was to open. While waiting from the designer's office the suggestions for the layout of the tavern as well as the decoration.

Alex suggested to start a little tennis training as they were quite back from any kind of exercise, apart from sex if it could be considered as exercise, so they asked the girls to tell them where nearby tennis clubs were.

There was a nice tennis club not far at all, and they went there to see and make the necessaries to become members. The club was not bad at all; they were cordially welcomed, as they did not have many foreigners as members. They fixed the membership formalities, and they booked a court for training the next day.

He could not take away his mind from the news to come from Karla for the gender of the baby that turned his life upside down for good or for bad it was still to be seen.

Arne called, and with great pleasure, he told him that he was delighted with Nicolas; he said this was the man, a nice modest character with such professionalism, that he could transform his hotel to a profitable one.

He asked him to keep his wife and daughter away from him so that they will not interfere with his job and to let him take initiatives. He was a brilliant young man with deep knowledge of the profession, but he needed time to bring the changes that were by all means much needed.

He would also talk to him to pass over to him his ideas to upgrade the hotel. He told him that he was better to take whole family and leave for Mallorca to his vacation house and let Nicolas feel that he was the boss, and with the accountability that he possesses, he would deliver to you after one year or so, a very profitable hotel. He agreed and thanked him for being a valuable help.

The good news came also from his Monegasque friend. He indeed found the channels and connections, and he talked to the Bras de Ferre president of this association and the idea of the Goliath Viking intrigued them a lot.

They planned to have an association meeting to study this Nuuk/Greenland tournament suggestion, and after they get enough information to where this would take place and if Nuuk possesses enough accommodation to host all those that would come there, they then make decisions.

He told him, if possible, to get him also in touch with his contact at that Bras de Ferre Association so that he would ask his people in Nuuk to send photos and also all info about accommodation and all the rest needed info.

He felt happy that his promise would prove after all not to be fake but realisable. The next day, with Alex, they were to see the apartments that their girls chose and see if these are according to the standards that they need.

Angel was always muttering to his ear that she wanted him to do what he did to those girls in Greenland and watched that orgies video many rimes. She felt that he hides extra pleasure from her but he was always answering 'in due time' and 'this would happen in their own apartment's big comfortable bed'.

His guy in Greece sent him the bill for what all they need for machinery and supplies, and he was accelerating the procedures. He would organise a meeting with Sophia and Alex to get their OK and send the money so that these would be shipped in the next month.

Days were passing; Alex and he were training in tennis and almost every day was inspecting the office to see that all his instructions were followed, but he never stopped his job with his laptop and the contact with the German customers because the prices for the big orders and offers were always for him to submit.

As he was always telling them, it was not easy to make an offer; he had the ability to 'smell' what price he could give, what space he had for good or less good profit according to what he gets by reading carefully the mails of the customers. One innocent word in those emails hides many things that he, as a salesman, or better say as saleswoman, as he was for them Mrs Victoria, could 'hook' out the picture of what price the customer needs to get the order. So, if he gets the pictures and 'smell' that customer has good space, why not exploit taking the advantage?

He never mentioned that from the very beginning that he told them that him, 'Victoria', wanted only contact by mail so that he could cc and bcc to his assistants, and he dislikes all contacts such as telephone or Skype, or WhatsApp as these contact ways with the pressure of the instant decision allow not much of thinking, and many mistakes could be done. So, mail and only mail contact. Customers comprehended this with no objection.

Sales technique especially via mail is not so easy. Chinese they have not that ability; they have a maker's price they add the profit percentage and this is, but no, this is not it; there are cases that allow 3% profit, but also occasions that allow 30% profit, so why lose the 30% when this you feel, or better say detect, that is feasible not to go for just 3% or 5% but 30%?

This priceless experience helped him overcome many problems the past 16 years, where he was financially down to the very bottom of the barrel, needing a lot of money to pay lawyers, plus offer a comfortable life to the family. If he did not have the ability to distinguish what price to give to obtain big profits, how could he have money to face all those expenses and payments?

Alex's dream was once to go to Japan. He loves sushi while Areus loves live grilled lobster. So, they decided to let the girls look for the apartment, and they flew for a weekend to Tokyo.

They arrived in Tokyo. He hasn't been there for maybe 50 years.

They had nice rooms in the best hotel, and they booked the best sushi restaurant where they were also grilling live lobster in front of the customers.

The sushi was great. They were so happy to eat the real sushi the same way as the Chinese enjoy in China their specialty, the real Peking duck.

What made him feel uncomfortable was to see just in front of him the poor lobster who was still alive to put on the hot grill and die there, was a rather unpleasant scene.

Needless to say, that the flesh of that lobster and the taste were unique; he never ate it before in his life such a lobster, although he had eaten even in France where he was also exporting to them live lobster from Limnos Island in Greece.

The dinner ended with sake that allowed them to have a dizzy head, and it was wise to go to the hotel for a good sleep, and next night, he would take Alex to the geishas, another dream of Alex's but also for him a repeated dream.

The hotel had beautiful kimonos, and one could buy such before leaving the hotel and buy kimono for him and Alex but also to give as a gift to Angel and Melissa, imagining them to remove that kimono and nothing else below but their gorgeous bodies.

The next day, they were both prepared to visit the geisha's house. He got the best place from the hotel concierge, and there, they were in full anxiety.

The taxi driver stopped in front of that place, but they, in full anxiety, instead of going left where the geishas' place was, went to the right, and to their surprise, they entered a very peaceful home. The door was opened; they entered and found themselves in front of a whole family watching TV, all smiling at them. The man of the family, with his typical Japanese smile, knew why they were there, as probably many tourist men did the same mistake; he showed 'opposite'.

In that place, a man feels a real man a masculine. Geishas are there to please the man and all his desires. They are carefully selected and trained and have maybe the best soft skin and bodies in the world and are so welcoming, friendly and not any fake smile, but a unique pure smile.

The sex they offer is incomparable, soft, tender and with charming motions in the bathtub or out of it. Miraculous sexy manoeuvres that could capture the imagination of any man and give the ultimate pleasure. They know how to keep customers hot and knowing that older men like they were, it is not possible to go for a second shot very fast, so they keep the first one so skilfully, as long as possible.

Both Alex and him, after kissing the geishas and thanking them for what they offered to them, got out in the street for the taxi, having the feeling that they were even emperors; this is what these ladies want you to feel after you get dressed to go to your hotel, to feel that you are the champion, the master, and indeed, they achieve this by their own splendid way.

The next day, they were already in Shanghai, and they were supposed to visit the four different apartments that the two girls found, believing to be the more appropriate to satisfy their demands and preferences.

They found those selected apartments not according to the standards they needed ,so he gave the job to the real estate company that were looking for the first tavern place. The girls wanted to find an inexpensive apartment, believing that it would be economical for them, but as they would stay with them, they needed something more comfortable, cosy and preferably with a gym in the same building and pleasant view, such were the instructions they gave to the real estate bureau.

He was anxiously counting the days to hear from Karla about the gender of the baby, hoping it to be a boy, as he always wanted to have a second son. He told to Alex about this story, and he was shocked that he went to Denmark to meet an old love affair and what he finally did was fuck her daughter.

Good news was coming from the Bras de Ferre Nuuk tournament, as two of the Bras de Ferre committee members would visit Nuuk to meet Tuppi and Saka and, of course, Tupe, the Giant Viking, so also to see installations and accommodation facilities he hoped they would approve. So, a fake promise might become reality.

Two weeks passed, and he got a phone call from Karla, announcing that he is the father of a son. This, of course, made him happy, and he promised to her that he would be there when she approaches the last week or so for the birth of the baby. He was in deep thoughts as now he was in front of responsibilities that could radically change his life.

He has to deal with unexpected situations, how to present this to his wife, son and daughters and also how to face both mother and daughter in Denmark. The situation was complicated and needed clever handling, and it was not a must that his wife and especially his son and daughters need to know of the existence of a brother.

He had to be more cautious, and when he would live with Angel in same apartment, not such a new incident would happen, although the mixture of a Chinese girl with a Mediterranean man could bring an extraordinarily beautiful result.

He knows this from a seaman friend who married a Japanese girl and the son became the number one movie star in Japan. But he better remove from his mind any such thinking.

He had to plan a new visit to Denmark in maybe six–seven months and this time stay with Karla and Mathilde without Emma knowing this, as she would 'execute' him. He then would see how Nicolas was doing with the hotel of his friend Arne.

The two real estate agents, who got the inquiry for both tavern place and apartment, came with suggestions, and tomorrow, they were all going to see the suggested tavern suggestions where he would go with Alex and Sophia and for the apartments, where he would go with Alex and his Angel and Alex's Melissa.

They first had to visit the six selected areas where the first Spartan tavern was to be established in the suburbs of Shanghai with dense inhabitation and mainly middle-class citizens. All were fine, and it was difficult to choose the best.

Final one of the six was chosen, and probably, that was the best one to meet the standards that were required. Next were the suggestions from the architects and decoration offices to see on paper how that first tavern would look, and this, they expect by tomorrow from three different bureaus.

They then, together with Angel and Melissa, went to see also the suggested rent furnished apartments. They were all so nice, and the decision was rather difficult.

The have to select the building where they could have two apartments, and there was only one that also had a gym on the last floor, overlooking the whole of Shanghai. So, that was it; 26th floor him and Angel; on 14th floor, Alex and Melissa's apartment.

They asked both girls to immediately evacuate the apartments where they since then were living in and move to the two new apartments. That would take at least one week to settle all matters with the previous apartments' owners.

He and Alex moved the next day, and they felt there were great in these luxury apartments, and this was what they both wanted to make a pleasant living for the two girls. These two apartments were before given to those rent platforms, like bouking.com, and had all the must luxury fittings both in bedrooms, living rooms and in bathrooms.

They went right away to the last floor to subscribe as members of the spa that was the exclusive club for maybe only the apartments' residents, and this was much appreciated as they were there to meet all residents and maybe make new friendships.

Not to forget to mention that the massage ladies there were amazingly beautiful with divine body shapes. These were not only Chinese but also were two Romanian girls, one of them with an unusual seductive look that made him feel vulnerable to her persistent glances. Well, he better forget about it as he would have an angel in his apartment, so no need for new experiences as that girl could be a ruthless menace to their romance.

Lucky for them, there was only five minutes away by foot a tennis club with perfect installations recommended by their building concierge. That concierge seemed to be a clever guy 'smelling', so to say, what the residents were in need. He gave him a good tip so that he keeps him on his side, just in case.

Now all was in a progressive stage, and what was now expected was the bill of lading of the shipped from Greece in a big 40 feet container all necessary for the installation of the first Spartan tavern, which would take at least one month.

The week passed peacefully until Angel and Melissa were to move in, and this week, there was not any sexual contact as coincidentally both had the same week their period. The next day, he had to go to the office, and from the comfort of his desk computer and his office, he had to follow some important and big inquiries that needed his knowledge and expertise.

The real estate agency also recommended to them a good constructor/decorator, who, according to their approval by all three partners' plan, would bring up the first Spartan tavern.

So, the second step was now in process to make the contract with the owner of the place, and the decorator would create the tavern's decoration.

The container from Greece was due to arrive in three weeks, so in the meantime, the decorator would be already in a good stage. He also asked the advertising agency to work for them with a first simple leaflet, announcing that in two months, the Spartan first in China Greek tavern would be near them, so that they start spreading the news about it from mouth to mouth. This always helps adding anxiety to what is expected to happen in their neighbourhood.

So, the tavern project was on a very good track. The apartments that they rented were also ready, and Alex and himself moved in and expected the girls to join so they enjoy the superb, warm ambience and the excellent view of both apartments.

So, it happened the girls paid the previous owners of their apartments they were living before and moved with all their dresses and ornaments and beauty accessories each one to the apartments of their 'boys', him and Alex, in different flats but finally at the same floor.

That night, it was the night to celebrate the moving in. They specially ordered Japanese sushi and four bottles of white wine and two bottles of champagne from the nearby wine shop cellar, according to the recommendation of the building's very smart concierge, who would be very helpful for all their 'requirements' and also hide any secret encounters.

So, the party was to be held in his and Angel's apartment, and the other two came at about 7 o'clock. Both well dressed, as if they were going to a top art gallery opening. One could see on their faces happiness, but he also dared to say sexual satisfaction, having calmness on their faces a sign that especially a woman is sexually fully covered. Alex probably did a great 'job'.

The sushi delivery arrived, and the party started. The girls arranged that all was served in the dishes, and they started the culinary enjoyment. Wine was in all glasses; they purchased special glasses for the white and red wine as those in the apartment were only for water and some small for snaps. The mood was at its peak.

Alex was staring at him in such a glance of satisfaction, having on his side a God's marvel that was gazing at him as if he were the military genius, the Great Alexander.

That world's biggest ever conqueror's name woke up in him an idea or rather a dream that he would unwrap in the next to come days.

All was perfect. The champagne's time came next with small chocolates, and that was the ideal to finish a dinner that few, egotistically saying, could enjoy.

The girls seemed to be hot. Alex's glance met his gaze, and what shall they do to make a swap orgy or better each couple move into its own apartment? The latter was chosen as those girls were to be their dominance and not share.

Angel was dizzy, and he gave her that time her kimono gift. She went to the bedroom to put that on and came to an optasia, in fact, not metaphorically but in reality. That kimono gave such an extra champ to her body that he could not do anything other than stare with his mouth wide open, like a stupid boy seeing a naked woman, the provocatively half-naked wife of the neighbour.

She licked and sucked his ear, telling him, he knew what, "You will not give that experience only to those 'ugly'," as her jealousy called the German girls, "but you will give to me and in your best performance, am I clear?"

He felt a brain fade hearing that now she commands him. He said that this requires bed and additives. He told her, "Go to the side table of the bed and bring me what is there."

Indeed, she went there and brought the small Vaseline jar (the concierge helped for this also he knew just with description what he needed).

Without asking him, she dropped the kimono, and there she was naked and not only that but figuring out what the Vaseline was for, she turned and bent, and the impeccable asshole was there in front of his face. He kissed that anus was so sweet, a real 'angelic anus'. He dislikes to call that of her asshole; he would call it her second tight 'mystery portal'.

He was licking that profoundly; he asked her to bring her hand and caress her little, because little it was, pushy. After licking that spot, he applied Vaseline, and he tried to insert the small finger. but that did not find the way in, either she did not allow this yet or was so tight that even the small finger was impossible to go in.

She showed that she was tired from standing up, so he asked her to lay on the sofa and open her legs and push her ass higher up so that he has better facilitation.

Second attempt was more successful. The small finger slowly but steadily was going in; what a satisfaction. She squeezed it to entrap it inside, but then she loosened it; he grabbed the moment and pulled out the small finger and right away to keep the fantastic entry loosened and wide before closing back to the previous state.

He inserted the pointer finger and went slowly inside with a none whatsoever problem; right away a second finger with little more difficulty went both inside, and then he added movements in and out back and forth; the more he did the easier that worked.

Now is the time; he picked her up like a pigeon feather and brought her to the bed. She, fabulously, on the way to the bed she had the first climax, never before had he while carrying a girl to bed her to have a climax. He put her softly on the bed, turned her on her back and at the edge of the bed so that he could see that both could enjoy the soft penetration.

He pushed her legs as back as possible towards her face and tits so that the arse would be slightly uplifted and have the divine second tiny 'cave' there to accept and embrace his penis. Indeed, after he rubbed also his penis with Vaseline, he had the head of the penis to touch the lubricated entrance, and with not any extra effort, it dipped in; he asked her to look at it, and she did with an admirable look; she could not believe that the whole was in.

He asked her to squeeze so that she would fill it inside her, and at the same time, he took her hand to meet her clit and caress it.

All went so beautifully; she and him looking at that specific spot and the in and out; many times he took the whole penis out and saw that the 'mystery' hole remain opened like an inviting nest, that greatness she could not see as it was too low for her eyes, and then back in; she started to moan, very seldom for Chinese girl as they try traditionally to hide it. She was ready to come, with a first time from her to hear, loud scream; he with his gesture somehow ordered her to release herself and all she had; no one would hear her, and she did.

He felt immense pride for this so he now has all the right and his turn to go for a gorgeous orgasm and without pulling out that usually kills the orgasm's fulfilment. He emptied whatever was there to empty in her; she nodded bending her head twice, to show that she felt it; he lingered inside her for a while until the penis shrank.

Both fell on bed exhausted, but at the same time with massive relief, and sleep was not that difficult to come.

The next day, he called Alex if Melissa prepared for him breakfast. He said, "No, it is me to do this because after long sex performance, she is still sleeping." He laughed and felt happy that he enjoys kind of family life with Melissa.

So, Angel after breakfast would also go back to bed. He asked him to leave Melissa some money if they want to go for shopping.

He told him that in 40 minutes they two have to go to the office.

The technical team to decorate the selected spot for the tavern would start the decoration immediately. The advertising and designer company would suggest the logo and the labels and sign for the approval.

All were on track for the first Spartan tavern in China, and the enthusiasm was difficult to hide.

In the meantime, he felt that he needed more help for the Spartan tavern, so he asked a friend's nephew, a guy very similar in size and strength like the Nuuk giant, but that was a Greek giant to come to China to pay him well and follow all the Spartan projects.

Indeed, he was more than happy, and he came right away; his name was Giannis. So, Giannis was here at first; he would stay at the hotel and then his partner or the real estate agent that they cooperate would find him a small furnished apartment.

The good thing was that he spoke English so there would be no problem, then he was a man with many skills and capabilities. He knows well the machinery and equipment that would come from Greece as he met, before coming, the other guy, the purchasing guy; his name was Christos. Apparently, he was such a huge man that it was always good to have such a man in the tavern in case trouble appeared.

He introduced Giannis to his two partners, Sophia and Alex, and they were impressed by his knowledge and skills, and they both felt that he covers a big gap between partners and the Chinese staff that was to be employed. Sophia brought him to an express Chinese learning school so that he learns the language as fast as possible.

So, they have the man to run the first Greek tavern, the absolute ideal man for the job.

They have a 15 days' space until both the Spartan tavern decoration and the arrival of the container to come, so they had to look elsewhere and get busy those days and not just remain there playing tennis, intensive gymnastic to sculpt the bodies and make love to their girls; the adventure flows in his veins.

Here comes a life's dream and seems now to be the right time to accomplish. He always wanted to visit the Chinese Terracotta Army in Xian, not that far away from Mongolia. The reason was Alexander the Great, the indisputable and undeniable Greek legendary general worldwide, biggest ever conqueror in the world with not a single controversy about him, who was never defeated in any battle and under his name were named more than 70 cities and one after his horse, Bucephalus.

So, his dream was to visit that city, as it is said that there is a theory that the Greeks of Alexander the Great helped China to build the Terracotta Army, so after Afghanistan and India, he entered China, but to no deep extent.

He asked Alex if he wanted to follow up and see another China, the northern part of China. He was astonished by the idea; he was immediately ready to follow him to that new adventure; after all, Greenland was more or less a similar opportunity for an 'escapade'.

He gave all instructions to Giannis, and there they were at the airport for the Xianyang International Airport flight that took little less than three hours.

Before leaving, he asked Sophia to call if there was any relative or friend or whatever connection so that they get a well-paid tour guide with sufficient English to be with them all the time that they would stay there, which was not yet defined.

Indeed, the guy was at the airport with a funny paper note with the name of ALEX and not his. Nice guy, maybe 30 years old, named Likin. First, they asked him to bring them to a good hotel and no need to be any of the international hotel chains but Chinese, as they wanted to live in the Chinese ambience but without spa as they do not want this massage story to be repeated again as they had to abstain from any sexual encounter by all means and get a break, and so he did.

The hotel was a great, big, luxurious hotel, the same as in the Shanghai Chinese hotels, but to their surprise, there was always a massage parlour, so the temptation was always after them.

They asked Likin to leave them today to relax; they shall eat in the hotel and come tomorrow to bring them to the Terracotta Army. So, it happened they went each one to his room and at the room first thing to do was to make many phone calls.

He first called his wife, son and daughters, telling them that he follows the steps of Alexander the Great; they were happy as they knew that this was always a big wish, and now it was to become real.

The next to call was Karla to see how the pregnancy was going, and she was glad to hear that he was not just indifferent to what she was up to. She said all goes according to the doctor's plan.

Then he called Sophia; the staff was always with the enthusiasm, still bright. Giannis told him that he worked four hours daily to learn Chinese, and he promised in two months to be able to communicate; he was also following the decoration and also checking the advertising agency for the logo, the labels, the signs and the first to go leaflet. What a wise and pragmatic decision was to bring Giannis over from Greece.

He also called Angel and asked her to get for Giannis a nice girl so he would not lose his time to look around to find a girl as he was a young man and he needed a girl by all means; she promised to do this, and she also told him in severe way, reminding him of Emma's warnings, not to call any girl for massage. Oh God, he had again a jealousy to face.

He then called Nicolas to hear how he was going with the hotel management, and he got such an enthusiastic attitude that gave him the feeling of justification to choose that young man for the right job.

He also called Tuppi to see if there were any contacts form the Quebec Bras de Ferre Association; he said yes and that there would be soon news when they would send two persons there to check all on the spot.

There was nothing best than having all under control with not any unpleasant and unforeseen situations.

So, he went to the shower for a relaxed waterfall and put on the bathrobe, then someone knocked on the door, and there was a girl asking in Chinese, but knowing only the word 'massage'. He understood what she asked.

Beautiful, but he found the guts reserves to say no. God knows how that was difficult. She nodded OK and made a sign showing that she would come again tomorrow. What a smart girl; she knew that he would not deny for long. Alex called and said that this also happened to his door, and they laughed a lot.

They agreed to meet at the lobby in one hour to have dinner, and they read that there in the hotel was a mandarin restaurant, so there they were to eat the night's dinner.

Before entering the 'Mandarin' restaurant, they passed by the concierge, asking him which was the best restaurant in the hotel. There were three. He said they had to try Dashu Wujie Restaurant. This was the most famous in town vegetarian restaurant.

That was great; he never ate in China exclusively vegetarian, and that was a must for his culinary expertise enlargement.

So, there they were; they had to wait at the bar for 30 minutes so that a table would be available for them. That restaurant being crowded certainly means that they have something unique to serve.

A table was available, and there they were guided to sit. They called the maître and gave him the order to bring all; they wanted to taste all or almost all if there were too many. He understood, so he moved them to a big table, and not a table for two, where they have a big space in the centre to put all the dishes and plates. The dishes started to come. They were experiencing a culinary festival on their table.

The maître had difficulty explaining what each dish was and that was not necessary, what they needed was to please and indulge their uraniscus. It was unbelievable most were routs, when eating there was such flesh that you could easily believe that this is chicken or pork. The variety was immense broad beans, soybeans, braised eggplant, frayed lettuce, fried mushrooms, lotus root, oyster sauce and Pak hoi, fried tofu with peanuts, fried bean curd sticks etc., etc., etc. The big table was not enough to take all.

They were experiencing a totally unusual but veritable vegan dinner that anyone in his life must have the same chance to taste as an ordinary degustateur. Alex was amazed to have such a variety that in no case one could find in Europe, he knows this as for 10 years of his life he was vegan but he abandoned this as the flavour of meat was missing and the joy of the good red wine could not match those vegan meals.

The maître was still carrying dishes until they told him that was more than enough. He surprisingly answered, "But then you did not even reach half of the variety." They stared at each other with astonishment, is it at all possible what else could there be. They declared to him that they are more than full and that the next day they start from the second half.

The only complaint was that the beer was not cool enough so they asked him to bring a beer cooler with many ice cubes to put there to chill the beers. They enjoyed that dinner more than ever before but the female presence was missing that would add something more. At the bar they could see that there was at each corner of that bar one girl and both stared at them as if they were the catch of the day or better of the night.

They looked at each other and agreed not to drag themselves again in the same 'massage' approach with the consequences. During that meal he revealed to Alex the next adventure that he hid from him from the very beginning. He unburdened himself from another goal of his life and that was to visit at the very north the city where was said in many historical books that until there Great Alexander was or maybe some generals of his army maybe fugitives or deserters being tired of the many years of fighting in numerous battles under the leadership of Alexander the Great. They installed themselves there and got married and brought with them and spread the Greek culture diffusion.

It is said that there is a small village where people still speak a little Greek and they idolise or better worship the Greeks and their descendants of Alexander the Great. That was the positive aspect of conquering cities and civilisations. He told Alex he wanted to visit that village as an explorer.

After telling him all this small story he kept looking to Alex to discover in his eyes and brains if he would follow him to that outstanding venture.

He smiled, telling him, "You son of the bitch where else will you drag me to Mongolia or what else do you have in that chaotic mind of yours? No, I will not allow you to make alien discoveries and I also want to feel as an archaeologist." So, after two days in Xian, they take the fast train to Niya County, also from Mandarin as Minfeng County and within the Xinjiang Uyghur Autonomous Region, what an enigmatic trip that will be. They chose a nice hotel and signed the necessary reception papers and off to the lift for their rooms, there they found themselves squeezed like sardines in the tin box, between three girls. The one who spoke little of English took the energy to tell them, "As soon as you stay at the last floor where the VIP rooms are, then you could afford three girls to your bed to fly with you to heaven."

"Oh God, it was my mistake not to ask for a hotel of an international chain that do not permit all these girls to annoy the customers."

He asked them to leave them alone as they are not in any mood for any girls and so they let them in peace and away from any sexual desire. The sleep was fast and easy, but at 12 o'clock here again they knocked on the door and he looking from the small eye hole saw a girl whispering, "I am here for you." He called the concierge telling that this is not proper for the hotel to send girls at midnight. He apologised pretending that he does not know this, probably he sends them up to get his commission.

The next morning, after a good breakfast, Likin was there to take them to the Terracotta Army. They explained to him what happened with all those girls. He said this happens as the feminine population is 65%, so the jobs for them are very limited and they found a solution by selling their body at half the prices to what you get in Beijing or Shanghai. He even told them that if you pay extra, they can send a virgin girl.

Well, they better forget this for the moment and let them go to see the Terracotta Army or the emperor Qinshiguang's Mausoleum museum. The official guide admitted that China's artwork was a copy of ancient Greece's artwork and sculpture. When he told him that he was Greek he looked at him with and admirable look telling him that very few Greeks visit that army despite the fact that their culture is present there.

He was telling them about the tyrant Emperor Qin killed everyone that helped to build the underground army. Millions of people were enslaved over the 38 years it took to build his self-indulgent monument and many thousands were killed to keep anyone from revealing its location. It was then buried and hidden from any view of anyone who wanted to destroy this fabulous army.

He was feeling real pride about all this as a Greek and turned to Alex saying, "Look what they did, what my progenitors did and what did you do? Export the Viking brutality to England and not only."

He bent his face admitting that this is true, but he came back saying yes, those times, but now? They are exporting high technology to your ancient country. So, he then tried to balance the ancient with the modern history.

It was for both of them a magnificent exploit of ancient China's culture influenced by the Greek one.

They asked what else they could see as far as they are there, he said the Xian Museum with the 16,000 square metres with exhibits and artifacts, huge gardens and the historic temple.

Indeed, it was a unique and long walking sight of a museum that similar might not exist. They asked Likin to come for breakfast tomorrow and they would then decide to stay one more day or take a train to Minfeng County. Tired as they were, returned to the hotel for a nap, before going up to the rooms they passed by the concierge saying that they wish not to be disturbed and not to knock at their door because they are very tired.

It worked and no one disturbed although arriving at our floor they saw two girls hidden at the end of the corridor with sad faces. They agreed to sleep two hours and then go down but not any vegan dinner but kind of European with nice steak and good red wine.

They had a peaceful sleep and in two hours they were down at the lobby to decide where to go and what restaurant to choose. They are there starving as they have nothing for lunch.

They asked the concierge for a good western restaurant; he said there is a good restaurant in this hotel for Europeans but the best is not far away and there you could enjoy the best dinner in town. That was the Hampton by Hilton hotel, a real and maybe the only western restaurant.

Before booking he went to the 'western' restaurant of the hotel to see the ambience and the menu, it was not bad and the maître of yesterday in that vegan restaurant had shift this night in this restaurant. So, they felt in good hands as he was very helpful last night at the vegetarian restaurant.

They explained to him that they wanted to eat a nice steak with good French red wine but the steak must be medium-rare so they asked the maître, "Is the cook able to do this? Or they better go to that restaurant near Hilton?"

The maître answered, "Do not worry. I will deal with this." They then took the decision to stay there at this restaurant of their hotel and enjoyed a nice dinner with a French wine. To the nearby table he heard Greek talking, he tried to hear the Greek were Cypriot Greeks they have a certain accent to their Greek.

He approached them asking them why they came, they told him that they import from Minfeng chemicals. He has to say here that the Cypriots merchants are very smart and you could find them in all parts of the world in the very last corner of this planet doing business.

They joined them at their table and they had a nice evening. They drank quite a lot and they then told them that this hotel has maybe the best girls of the town and they usually come in the room in pairs not one but two for trios and is cheap and they know how to make you feel as if you are the emperor of a dynasty.

He looked at Alex with a questioning smile to see what he was thinking about. He did not want to give his consent or not in front of these two Cypriots but when they left, he said let's do it. The two Cypriots also gave names of the four best so what they had to do was to ask the concierge, his name was Chang and about 40 to 45 years old, to send two of the four to his room and the other two to Alex's room.

They were each one to his room expecting the gorgeous girls according to the Cypriots description, and this happened in only 10 minutes. Those girls were not at all looking like those three that were in the lift and not to those that were hidden at the corridor's edges. They had an absolutely different look to all the Chinese girls they knew. They had something else that cannot be described in words.

Their eyes were not the typical Asian epicanthic fold eyes as they are called but more rounded and closer to western eyes than to Asian but still had that special something of the Asian characteristic eyes look, in other words mixed features.

Impressive also were their breasts, very seldom to see such rich and well-shaped breasts, as usually all Chinese girls have small tits.

They looked not as girls that are for paid sex, they looked more as if they are girls 1.70 of height, taking part to a defile (model parade) of a famous designer who chooses his models to have a different exotic and original or better unsophisticated look. He felt too little to confront their superb appearance. He felt that if he made the gesture to pay them, they would be offended and give him a slap on his cheek.

Wherefrom those girls came and why they did this job when very easily could be on the front pages of Marie Claire or better of the Vogue magazine, how come that not any model's scouter discovered those beauties.

The girls were standing still looking at him as if he were a disabled man, usually hungry men for sex rush on them to get them unaddressed to admire their bodies but he stayed there completely stunned.

He asked them not to get undressed but sit comfortably to the sofas and got from the mini fridge a small champagne and offered to them. The girls were in a dilemma: is he gay or kind of kinky? But they appreciated the gesture of the champagne and seemed to feel in that VIP room in a different situation as they usually face and that was evident on their faces looking cooler and with not any tense in the calmness of their face, while shy smiles enlightened their awesome faces.

He then went to the bedroom phone and called Alex, he told him that he is in front of the same vision and he feels awkward like a boy for the first time going for sex to a brothel. He asked him to get the two girls and come to his room.

He opened the door and there were two equally splendid girls all almost the same height of little plus or minus 1.75, which means tall girls and almost the same age and curves of their body as if they all came from the same creator's mould.

New champagne was opened for the two new girls to feel equally comfortable as the two first ones that they were there, were already drinking champagne, these first two nodded to them as if they wanted to tell them that this is something new, unfamiliar for them that might turn to be marvellous from point of view pleasant with plenty of desireful atmosphere.

First to make them feel happy they gave each one 100 dollars, three times more than what they usually get, that turned them a little more bashful but at the same time more approachable.

To their surprise they also spoke sufficient English so that they could communicate, later they found out that this good English was due to their uncle who was many years in Vancouver and asked them to learn English so that one day he would invite them to Canada.

They ordered two more bottles to come, and not those mini from the fridge but Moet Chardon, and asked if there was also Iranian caviar but Beluga would also be fine and bring potato chips, mini toast canapes with smoked salmon and creamy cheese.

The goal was to create a very nice atmosphere and the girls to feel as if they were at their home or better to a future luxury home that they deserve to live in.

All four girls seemed to be dazed with all this behaviour that was unknown to them. Usually, their customers drag to bed to get a fuck ignoring that these girls also have desires and could also have the right to demand soft and gentle behaviour.

The champagnes and the accompaniments came; the girls were amazed at what was in front of them. The one timidly asked, "Is this caviar that the queens eat?"

He answered, "Yes, and you are not queens but princesses." This said the one that spoke better English turned to the others telling them in Chinese that they considered them as princesses and a sweet smile illuminated their flashing faces.

They enjoyed the caviar and the small canapes not with any bulimia but with an exceptional magic kind of charm. The mood in the room was obviously at its highest level, the girls threw away and unloaded the first phobic shyness and they displayed their intact pureness.

They had in front of them two old but handsome men, the one blonde with blue eyes and the other robust with silver haired and brown eyes but both looked to have the characteristics of gentlemen in style and expression.

Before asking to know more about them, he called the concierge telling him that he would get a good tip to allow them to stay here with them for many hours and he gave his satisfied consent.

They asked them about their family and more. They all were relatives, the two sisters and the other cousins, daughters of five brothers. There was in the family history roots from ethnicity crossing from both mother's side and father's side either from the north, but more, according to sayings and stories, to the western influence of conquerors.

One of their wiser relatives with accumulated knowledge of history was deeply searching their root and this due to the uncommon for Chinese rather larger and rounded eyes.

This said, they indeed searched in their faces to discover what was hidden behind those magnificent eyes, was baffling but certainly whatever it was, was a brilliant crossing outcome.

They also asked as far as they are so extraordinarily beautiful 'why you do the job of the paid sex?'. They were kind of reluctant to reveal what pushed them to do this. But this came out easily after the second glass of champagne.

The five brothers, their fathers, were lazy and rough to their mothers when she was asking for money to buy the necessaries to live but that necessaries were never there as they were jobless, so indirectly through a far relative who was hotel concierge pushed them to this job that had in many cases had to face cruel instincts and behaviour and disagreeable treatment, this explains why they looked at them as if they come from other planet.

He spoke in Danish to Alex saying what if they promote them to high level Paris designers for fashion shows these girls would conquer Paris and Milano and for sure also Tokyo. Alex could not grasp the notion and looked at him with his head bent to the side like the dogs do when you ask them to do something that they do not understand.

He then discovered what he meant and he said, "So what now you want me to become after a restaurant owner also becomes a model's manager?"

He said, "Yes, why not seize the opportunity that is there in front of you?"

The girls were trying with the beautiful questionable eyes to discover what they were up to. So, he took the initiative to tell them the plan and if they could get the consent of their parents to travel abroad, they would pay them well to get their OK.

They were hearing this with suspicion and scepticism and the one said that two other girls in the same family but in second family relatedness, had the same kind of proposal from two Serbian guys and what happened to them. They ended up as prostitutes in the streets of New York controlled by the Serbian Mafia and procurers.

It was a shock for them to hear this and they understood their reluctance. But right away they admit that they do not look like that type of men and feel overconfident that what they promise to them is true, honest and trustful.

So, now he and Alex are in front of a new unexpected situation, there was a new incentive, a new profession exploration, managers of models at the highest level.

They asked the girls if in the family are also other same beautiful girls like them, they said yes there are another five from two uncles, brothers of their father.

The atmosphere was very joyful and could not be any better. The girls felt equal versus equal.

The girls curiously became hot and it was rather them to seek for sex. Was it an expression of gratitude or the caviar and champagne played a role, or, and why not, they liked them and were seeking to offer high quality sex.

With the look of a true manager and not any fake one, he asked them for a demonstration of their bodies through a kind of parade. The suite was huge with two separate bedrooms and a big living room.

All helped to remove some tables and chairs so there is enough space, and then without asking them they started to get undressed in such a sexy way as if they were in a deluxe strip club with a pure sexy strip tease and not any professional to gain dollars in their culottes.

Shirts, skirts, bras, and panties all down what they saw were God's creations but probably that day God was in excellent mood to make such a perfect mould.

Areus asked them to imagine that they are at a Giorgio Armani Fashion Show (Défilé).

Surprisingly they heard that name. The music started and the Go signal was given.

The princesses, because that is what they were, started rocking their bodies and walked as if they were not at all touching the floor with excellence and finesse that even a professional model would envy. The 'audience', him and Alex, found that runway show spellbinding, keeping silent and stunned with fascination until the end of the performance and the girls in an extreme euphoria sat down to the floor dripping their sweat.

They told them this is more than enough and they could sit and enjoy the rest of the champagne and the caviar that fits excellent to their naked bodies.

Them being completely nude they charmingly approached them having the faces to turn from heavenly calmness to sex demanding look, probably the promises of a new brilliant career and, as previously mentioned, champagne and caviar made this easily to happen. They split after they made an agreement between them, followed by joyful laughter, and so two went with Alex and the other two with him and his bedroom.

The girls led them to the bedrooms and what happened there cannot find words to describe. It would take five pages to thoroughly express the details, the positions, the motions, and the one after the other moaning having repeated orgasms of both girls, it seemed they were very seldom to come to orgasm with customers.

Laughter and happiness were flying from one bedroom to the other, until, exhausted and having the room heated to the maximum, all exhausted fell asleep completely nude.

In the middle of the night, he woke up but the one girl was with her leg on top of him and the other girl on his left her whole arm was embracing him and one of her breast's nipple was piercing his chest, her knee was against his thighs and parted his legs, he made not a single movement not to wake them up and also not to disturb this scene that El Greco the Greek painter Dominikos Theotokopoulos, for first time leave Christ paintings to paint these Goddesses, he only could depict to a canvas this captivating portrait.

In the morning, rich breakfasts they ordered in the suite, the girls left the charm on the side and fell on the food like starving wolves. He pulled Alex into the bedroom and suggested that they extend the stay here for two–three days to see how this new 'plan' can turn to flesh and bones.

He reminded him, as he indeed forgot it completely, that Angel and Melissa were in Shanghai waiting for them and how could they present this to them? The only solution was in complete secrecy, get another apartment that they would stay there until they transfer them to Paris or Milano if this business would proceed with positive results.

He called that real estate agent and asked him to get a big furnished apartment not far from the one that we were already staying in but in total confidentiality.

He also asked him if he knows a lawyer who is good at making professional and totally bounding jobs contracts. He confirmed that he knows the best in all of Shanghai. This clearly said that he wanted to bind four fashion models with them as managers and not after they make their first appearance in Paris or Milano would be stolen by cunning talent hunters.

They asked the four girls to go home and discuss with their parents and see what they say, although as they said they are adult girls over 18 (in fact 19) and they could make their own decision.

They left and added to them another 100 dollars which they surprisingly denied to accept feeling that what they did that night was not a job but a pleasure, adding that they had so many climaxes that they forgot when and if they had so many ever before.

Well, the skilful tongues, he actually made special seminars to Alex to know how to do this, played an important role plus the numerous positions and the achieved altruistic duration bring always marvellous results.

Alex suddenly found himself not any more in a boring life but on the contrary to a full professional and diverse activities. They agreed that they stay two more days to see the outcome of their family 'council' and then go to Niya and discover that village where, as also Chang verified, Greeks are worshipped.

In the meantime, he asked Alex to give him 500 dollars, as he had only a credit card and no cash, to give to the concierge so they 'buy him out' and this worked excellently. In the afternoon, the four graces came with a wide smile which exposed the family's consent. To his wonder the parents asked for no money and let their girls free to go for a new and promising future.

The girls confessed later that they left them all the money they gathered the last three months so the OK was given and this due to their mothers' pressure on the lazy and useless fathers.

So, now they stay with them and either let them stay there in that nice suite or take them with them to Niya. This said he asked if they knew how to go to Niya, they were very astonished to have them go there and seemed to be ready for this as they heard in some storytelling of an uncle that their family had an unexplainable root from there.

They searched and found that there is a train to Niya, so they had to ask them to either stay in this suite while they were there or they could come with them. They definitely expressed their would to come with them, as if they were also looking for something in that 'village'.

First of all, they had to go to the best shop in town to buy for them a new impressive attires, to look like European ladies. They knew that this transformation would cost a lot but this is an investment.

They went, according to the concierge and also according their own suggestion, to the best shop and asked the girls to choose but not the final as this would be done in Shanghai in much more modern shops, just buy new dresses the very necessary.

The girls with new dresses were looking impressively beautiful, they could not even walk the distance to the hotel as they would look like girls just fallen from heaven. So, they took taxis to the hotel.

All was settled there was no need to stay two more days and so the plan was to take the train tomorrow. The girls, although they had the option to stay in that huge suite and spend relaxed days, they chose to come with them.

In the meantime, the real estate office sent photos of the best and big apartment he could find near their apartments of Angel and Melissa.

They showed it to the girls and they were amazed at what apartment they would stay in Shanghai. After having all settled in, they have to sit down and give to them names that would more fit to supermodels than the typical Chinese names they had. He for the better speaking English chose the name of Eleanor and her sister Louise.

Alex's two girls, Charlotte and Desiree, the last name must be one that would create mystery but also heritage so the appropriate name was Terracotta.

So, they have:

Eleanora Terracotta. Louise Terracotta.

Charlottela Terracotta. Désirée Terracotta.

Beautiful and easy names but also fragile and historical, reminding both Greece and China.

He was the Godfather the one to give the names and they all were more than happy with the new names, aiming one day to be known worldwide.

They all agreed not any sex endeavours but deep and sinless sleep as tomorrow the train was leaving early.

They packed, paid and confirmed that they would be back for at least one night but it was not yet fixed what that date would be. Linkin came to pick them up with his car and his friend's car, then seeing these four girls they almost fell down from dizziness.

He also arranged two limos to pick them up at the arrival, as limos are needed to take all their luggage but also provide to those princesses a physiological upgrading to feel as supermodels from now on and throw off the until then, simple Chinese girls' attitude. They paid him more than well for his services and agreed to call him one day before they were to arrive back.

Off they went, all six wherever they walked wherever in that train stepped in, all had to turn around to look at this group of two elder men, one blond and the other dark-skinned and four supernaturally divine visions.

After not that long they arrived there. Indeed, at the arrival there were two guys with labels holding the name of Alex. Two limos were almost not enough to take them and all their luggage but still much more comfortable even if they had four taxis. The girls started to win the air of superiority because this is what their intended purpose is, to look different, not arrogant but with the flair of Divas.

They asked the driver, who would also be their guide and his name was George, to bring them to the best hotel in that town and indeed so he did.

All six entered the lobby and there also the same elegance of four ethereal existences walking with the air of Channel Fashion Show models. They asked for a presidential suite and indeed there was the only one at the very top floor.

That suite was indeed a huge and luxury but could not be compared with presidential suites of the hotels in Shanghai, Beijing or Hong Kong. They wanted to walk around a little at the city but with these girls you cannot run around as it provokes the public feelings, also their national ego that these Chinese beauties preferred foreigners as companions.

So, they asked the girls to stay in the relaxation of the suite and order whatever they want from the room service and they would walk around to have a first acquaintance with the environment.

It was somehow a mysterious blinking at them from all that they were passing by, they also noticed that the one was whispering to the ear of the other pointing at them, well that was scary he does not know why, but they decided to return to the hotel. Imagining what would have happened if they had next to them on that small towns' streets, those four graces.

They managed anyway to see that the people around them were all Chinese but inexplicably different Chinese. They in general were short and 'pretty ugly' that word fits them as description.

Returned to the hotel approached the concierge telling him what they are here for. Looking for that village that still some Greek is spoken and there is evidence that they are descendants of Alexander the Great.

He shook his head and boasted saying, "Yes, I know, I also come from that village and left when I was a boy to find better living conditions. If you go there, they will make a feast as it is said as an 'oracle' that one day, the progenitor of Alexander the Great with the progenitor of Heracles will come, and what I see in front of me is you."

Alex indeed had the traits of Great Alexander and Areus those of Heracles but, of course, not that muscular but after all the characteristics give a match. He said he would take the day off, but if he is needed to be there, he would be immediately back as he wanted to accompany them there and this would be his honour and privilege. His name is Chang, another Chang concierge.

So, it is fixed for the two of them and with the limo of their driver George to go to that village. He said no limo could approach. There must be a 4 × 4 jeep, a wrangler, a heavy vehicle as the road to go there is rough if not dangerous.

So, who then would take them there, he said let me make some phone calls and I will call you at your suite.

Areus asked him is it appropriate to bring the four girls with them, he answered abruptly, "No, in no case, they will dislike this as it is not mentioned in that legend that these two will arrive there with women." Adding, "They will envy a lot, their aesthetic, their beauty and also the seldom height of these four girls, so definitely no." Areus asked Chang if he noticed that these four girls have not 100% Asian eyes and rather a mixture of Asian and European ancestry.

He said, "Of course, I did, and this reveals that they might also have origin from our places." As he said as where they go, they have the same kind of eyes but do not have the heights of those girls. This is not just seldom but never any girl there reached their height.

He seemed to have deep knowledge of Greek History and mentioned maybe those girls' roots might be the famous tall Generals of Great Alexander, Neoptolemus the son of Achilles who was the tallest General of Alexander's the Great.

Areus told him not to tell them this, because then they would also want to come with them and as he says they must not come.

He also asked him how could you be so sure that this village worships Alexander the Great when it is known that he did not enter China so deep but maybe very limited.

He said the history and legend says that he entered a little in China but those Chinese that they conquered brought girls from all China to please them and quite many of them married these girls and had children and they moved to our places. He was more than clear that these four girls have roots from the tall generals of Alexander and not from any nomads.

They were both stunned. He felt his heart beating fast as that was what he wanted to discover there.

They stayed there like Greek statues, Chang almost cried that he would be the one to bring those two to his village.

Alex felt bad as they would consider him as the descendant of Great Alexander while he is a Dane. "Yes, but remember you have Greek blood in your veins as your great-grandfather was Greek, and as you told me, you look identical to him, so where is the problem? Even your name refers to Great Alexander. What indeed ideal and glorious combination Viking and Greek. Both Greeks and Vikings were conquerors, so this is a great blend."

They fixed tomorrow to leave early; Chang would rent a big 4 × 4 jeep and they leave at six in the morning. They went up, the girls were there in best of temper and spirit, and they enjoyed room service and rushed to kiss them.

They told them that tomorrow they would stay there and they would go to that village that is extremely dangerous through mountains, so there is no way for them to accompany them. This was bad news for them as they wanted by all means to go there as they suspected that there is some kind of inheritance from the Greek conquerors and this explains their height as women and also the eyes difference to all other Chinese girls.

The girls probably have the right to come and identify their roots, but Areus had to hide this from them so that they would not insist to come with them as according to Chang they must not be there and destroy the festivities that the locals would certainly celebrate seeing the two tall men to arrive there who both meet the prevalence and power of the myth and folktale. All these made both of them feel awkwardly about what they would or would not encounter there.

In any case, this visit is a must, as this is what they travelled there for.

The four graces begged them to accompany them, they had to tell them as an excuse that not only the road is rough and unsafe but they could find only one jeep and that takes four as Chang would also be with them to guide them there.

They were very sad for this in fact, also because it was fair for them being so close and maybe solve the baffling puzzle of their roots.

They slept deep and without any temptation for sex involvement and early in the morning they kissed them and they went down to meet Chang. He was dressed as another Indiana Jones; he confessed that his family is there, and he left since he was six years old and never had the chance to go to his mother village and see his parents, his brother and sister.

He is curious to see how that village's development is, all those years he left there was in a primitive status.

The trip was indeed rough and kind of rocky so one could realise that it would be a very isolated village.

At the long distance they saw the village was not a small one but there were not any kind of high buildings and from a distance already one could obtain the image of what is there to see.

They reached the borders of the village and the first houses then at first sight kind of silence with no people to run around and kids to play. They proceeded more inside and there the first people were to be seen. In general, short people not well dressed, houses low with a kind of an abandoned appearance.

They were approaching the centre of the village, some of the pedestrians were looking at this jeep with curiosity as if since long not any such vehicle entered the village, but they also were watching who the passengers were and one of them opened his eyes widely and his hand to cover his mouth and the other pointing to the inside of the jeep and loudly yelled, "They came—they came—they are here—they are here!"

This gave kind of an alert signal to the whole community to spread around the long-expected message that was written even on the walls 'Will Return' as Chang translated to them. This slogan on the wall, of course, was not addressed to the return of Chang to his village but to a since many generations expected in the history books, the precious visitors.

All of a sudden, thousands were on the road converging to the main square and that peaceful village became a crowded and lively boisterous with people with a nervousness to locate what happened that brought them all there in a panic. The jeep could not move anymore under compulsion and all three they were obliged to step down from the car.

The villagers were in a wild enthusiasm and ran to touch Alex and Areus, the more restrained ones tried to make a circle around them to protect them from the craziness.

The mayor of the city with the whole city hall committee arrived and the crowd made space for them to go close to the visitors.

The mayor, an old man having the face and view of a sophisticated man, came close to the two foreigners that the myth and folktale says that they are descendants of Alexander the Great and Heracles the unbeatable historical legends after so many conquests, and one day would come together to this village. The mayor showed coins of Hermaios from archaeological digs and excavations that proved the existence of Greco-Barthian civilisation.

He also showed tapestries of men with large green eyes proving that Niya have been inhabited by dropouts from Alexander the Great's army and probably also generals. Both mayor and the committee president had those semi-large eyes that the four girls also had and not Asian dominant eyes form but more rounded closer to European eyes that proves elements of many centuries in descent from Alexander the Great's small troops who entered a small part of China with only one goal to bring to them the Greek civilisation and workmanship in sculpture and as result was the famous Terracotta Army. The mayor affirmed that Buddhism was influenced by the Greeks and found plenty of adherents in Niya.

The stunned mayor looked at them both, first the blond one and then the darker skinned, he spiritually knelt down and in an extremely loud voice for such an old man and tears in his eyes he shouted, in kind of Chinese but not exact Chinese, "Welcome we are expecting you for many centuries. Please accept the key of the small village of Niya. You are our distinguished visitors. The memorable tales are woken up."

That old man revealed his own prophetic abilities. All around him also knelt down and shouted, "Welcome and again welcome!"

They stood there with prudishness, were the only two to be standing up looking all these many hundreds in a deep bow, but they noticed that there were only men not any single female.

He whispered to Chang, "Where are the women?"

He said, "In such ceremonies, women must stay home; this is why I asked you not to bring the four girls." He added the women would appear in their local and traditional dresses, but not all; only the virgin girls would do the dancing as respect to the legendary oracle of the Two Greats' arrival.

All happened so fast and totally unexpected that both were in deep dilemma what to do what they have to say or say nothing and keep a serious and with elevated pride attitude, as this is what the situation demands.

The mayor stood up and made the lead to the so-called 'city hall' and they all followed making a long queue as there was to be one only as a row, the one behind the other, so that queue would make more than two kilometres. What an odd tradition the only ones that were side by side were the two VIP visitors.

The city hall and under strict hierarchy could take only 20 all the rest made that queue like a long snake. The mayor held a speech in that Chinese kind of language half of his speech, as they were told, was in the Uyghur Altaic language and half of the Chinese Mandarin language and referring many times of the undisputedly historic century of Great Alexander and Heracles and the extension of the Hellenic empire that reached them and praised them as if they were ancient Greek Gods.

Amid wild celebrations a long and boring speech was addressed to them, a monologue, and they all had to stand up and not sit on the benches, so this became exhausting after that long and very uncomfortable trip.

The speech after all ended, yet the ceremonial process was not over and a procedure was heralded. Then started the real exhausting phase of the idiosyncratic ceremony as they had to go out and pass in front of all and one by one so they worship them, they had to prostrate themselves, bending their faces down as if they were not allowed to meet the visitors' eyes.

They had to walk all that long distance to have this traditional worship with that kind of religious, humble, bending down their faces to touch the soil.

Doing these they looked at the houses, all windows were closed so that women cannot see the Glorious Visitors.

It took two hours and they were ready to collapse. Chang told the one who was following always to the end of that snake's queue, that they must rest and where this could be.

Not to forget to mention that all these hundreds of men were all having the faces to look at the earth until they left that square and stood up and looked up at the sky as if they were thanking God? Buddha? That he at last made them come.

The leader who accompanied them took them to the so-called emperor's palace. That was nice and spacious, only the two of them were allowed to stay there. Chang took with him the driver to his old home which he had not visited for maybe 30 years.

The problem in that palace was that they had not any translator and not a single one to speak any language. The surprise was that there they saw at last women kind of chamber maids but that is not the correct word for them. They were not allowed to look at their eyes, this reminded him in Saudi Arabia where he was prohibited to look the Saudi princess to her eyes.

In all the difficulty to make them understand what they want, they brought them to the bedrooms. Each one had a huge bedroom with a huge toilet and a kind of small pool as bathtub. Same but smaller as that the Romans offered as hospitality to seduce Genghis Khan with beautiful Roman women.

They left their luggage and were immediately taken by two girls. A lady supervisor in charge maybe 40 years old or even less, she commanded them, this was the correct word, to remove their clothes, right there in front of her and her two younger girls, her assistants, all of them with eyes down, but having the eyes down they could easily see their penises.

It is funny they are not allowed to see the eyes but are allowed to see the penises. He prayed God not to have that cock bastard to erect and with self-control he managed to have him half erected exposed to the glances of the two girls. Alex did not have that problem as it takes long for him to erect and needs the assistance of the blue pills.

The girls under the supervision of the 'elder' one put in that 'Roman steam kind of bathtub', olive oil, no soap and invited them to submerge in that bathtub that could take maybe six–seven people inside. It was exactly what was needed after standing up for many hours. They stayed in, always the girls surrounded the bathtub and were waiting to see when they enjoyed it and had enough to get out.

Indeed, after almost one hour in there they got out and the girls took each one over and a separate bed was waiting for each one to lay on. Their bodies were slathered in oil and they applied a kind of curved implement to scrape the oil from all the parts of the body. That this time, it was impossible for him to hold a hard-on. The girl was happy that she could pick it from the head and scrape all the way down from all sides but without any smile or any facial reaction at the sight of the hard penis.

Only the in-charge lady turned to the other side as probably that bigger size compared to the ones of their local men turned her on.

They scraped them from head to toe, even turning them around they scraped also the buttocks and with that curved scraper going deep in to reach to the anus and scraped even there and remove all oil from the body until the bodies were shining so then they covered them with towels to absorb any moisture.

They left them there for 15 minutes and then the in-charge woman showed them with her finger to go to the bedroom where all necessities were there, such as a kind of kimono but longer, slippers and new big underwear like shorts or boxers and they were at last 'allowed' to sleep.

Before sleeping he was thinking what other delights were expecting them but fell asleep in seconds. Two hours later they were woken up by that supervisor 'dame' making signs that dinner was served. They dressed them up and they guided them through numerous corridors like a labyrinth, and there, they were in a huge hall with a rounded big table that could easily accommodate 30 persons.

Already, the whole city hall council was there, and luckily also Chang so that at least they have someone to translate. They sit, and Chang whispers to him that they are to experience big manifestations among them; the virgin girls dancing. He added these traditional customs from the years of Mau Che Tung and for these girls is a big honour and privilege.

Both absolutely declined this, but Chang warned them that this will be a big disrespect, and no one knows where this can end; it is considered as cultural inheritance and no way to be ignored. There are almost six generations that not such a big event happened, and these girls are considered as blessed.

He noticed that Chang wanted to hide something, his face, attitude and his saying about the virgin girls was kind of questionable.

The lady in charge (dame) came again, bringing them new dresses, Chinese kind of wedding long dresses. They were wondering what for those ceremonial wedding looking attire. That looked, as one can read in old books, like old Chinese dynasty dresses.

When Chang was there, they asked him what these dresses were for. Chang did not answer straight and immediately, but he, with a kind of breaking voice, said that this was how they honour the distinguished visitors.

He asked, "When was the last time they had such 'distinguished' visitors?" He said nobody could really tell, but centuries, for sure.

He also said that he may have to leave tonight and return tomorrow as an important family matter calls him. But he would be present at tonight's sacred ceremony. He asked him, "Sacred, why sacred?" There was no answer to be given.

So, they both dressed in long gowns that trailed along the ground and inside some funny underpants, and they were led by the lady, not Chang, who for a while vanished, to the ceremonial event that would take place in a huge, similar to the 1860 French or British, ballrooms but not so glamourous.

The entire city hall council was there, and maybe 100 people were crowded all around and all dressed with the same dresses or maybe 'costumes', so Chang also came with that special ceremonial, or one could say, 'Fancy' costume.

The leader held a speech in that mixture of languages, but this time less Mandarin and more Uyghur kind of dialect.

They were bored during that long speech, and the old mayor was always pointing at the two visitors. They had to ask Chang, who seemed reluctant to give details of the speech, all the time he whispered into his ear, make no sound, do not talk when the leader speaks. The multitude was staring at them as if they came from Mars. The speech at last ended, but they wanted to applaud, but Chang held them, saying no.

Indeed, no one applauded as it was usually done after a long speech, but right away, a soft music started, and maybe 60 girls arrived, all young, from 17 to maximum 18 years old and started a charming dance. Chang whispered into his ear, "These are all virgins and are all at your disposal."

"Disposal? What disposal? Speak clearly."

He answered, "I will tell you later."

Both Alex, and he looked kind of terrified for what was going on and were kind of afraid asking for the plans they had for them. The dance was indeed nice, full of beauty and charm; the girls all the time were looking at them and smiled so cutely. They started to understand that they were there for a duty. He turned to Chang asking if they could leave tonight after the ceremony; he answered just with one word: 'impossible'.

The music stopped, and the girls made a parade, passing by them with a smile of adoration and pride in their faces as they were the chosen ones.

Girls left, and all stood up, looking at them as if they were the saviours or the liberators of that village, and all left except the lady supervisor, who was approximately 35 years old and Chang.

Chang had a clouded and perplexed face; he wanted to tell them something, but he did not know how. He, at last, took the courage to tell them that they were more or less 'blessed prisoners' as these 10 out of the 60 girls would come by your bedroom, and 10 from Alex bedroom, each time two from each bedroom, and you have to have sex with all of them for 15 days, as they want you to leave your 'holly' as they called this in their perception of 'genes', your historical genetics as they want those idolised heroes to remain there by leaving your descendants and worship them forever.

This said, they were completely freaked out and used fierce words asking, "You mean that we have to fuck all these girls and repeatedly?"

"Yes, and the 10 girls for each one of you are 'the' blessed ones and was always the dream of any virgin when time will come to be the chosen ones."

They answered, "Is there was no way to take us away from this bloody village?"

He could not find the right word, but he said that they cannot, as they could see, and he showed at the entrance, there were guards that were not there before. He also added that he was commanded to leave so that there was no car for them to escape, and that he would return in 15 days.

They were in despair because their age does not permit them to have multiple sex encounters while several intercourses was in demand. Alex, as if he were aware of what was to happen, he had his pill box full with the blue pill and sleeping pills. Both had to enhance their performances to the maximum to succeed in that obligatory task.

Chang probably could read their thinking. He said that they will feed you all day with horse milk, Mongolian beef meat as well as certain herbs and traditional 'medical' roots that would turn you into stallions, or better, into bulls.

He emphasised, saying, "Understand that these people and whole village was waiting for many generations and centuries for you to come so do not disappoint them. So, do what you are asked for; other people would have this as a dream and you want to deny it?"

He highlighted that, "Many virgin girls of many generations were waiting for you to arrive, and now they worship this holy for these girls' blessing."

He said have courage and left in a hurry. "I will fetch you in 15 days." They begged him not to tell the four girls at the hotel about this but find an excuse why they would stay the 15 days.

Give them all comforts, so they spend a nice time in their suite and in no case ask them to make any paid sex encounters with any one; this said, they gave him 500 dollars.

Two men as guards took them to their bedrooms. That supervisor lady, she had a strict but at the same time melancholic or rather depressed face, playing the role of the superior, 'a Gauleiter', and also a similar one stayed in Alex's bedroom to watch that the matrimonial sex process would be done the best way so those nice young girls would become afterwards pregnant if not all, at least some of them so their genes would be multiplied in the small community.

He wanted to get closer relations and gain the favour of that dominant lady so that she would be softer with him but also less strict to the girls. With difficulty, he made her understand what he wanted, and finally, she said that her name was Sarnai, and in a manner, she understood by the hand language that she would care about him, so as to say, "Leave it to me. I will make things easier for you."

Well, there was no other option than to do their duty for which they were supposed to be there for. He looked down at the guy below (penis), asking him, "Well, you are asked one more time to make an exceptional job and be in any way tireless." If the poor penis had a voice would certainly say, "I never let you down, but this time you put me in a difficult situation, but I will give my best. I know that I have large shoes to fill."

The two first girls came; all of them dressed in peculiar dresses that allowed their tiny bodies to be seen. Sarnai gave the order to remove the dresses, and so they did as if they were soldiers but not on at a compulsory duty but on an open hearted and volunteered duty as they were 'the' selected and privileged to take part of this 'sexual ceremony'. Fertile intercourse was demanded from them, aiming for children and are not there for their own pleasure but why not combine both?

Both girls came to the bed and undressed him; the same process was probably also for Alex in the other bedroom. All the time, the girls turned to Sarnai, asking what was next to do.

She gave the commands and started kissing him, both to a different body part, including the in the meantime hard dick. Sarnai looked somehow happy that there was a hard penis that needed no herbs to get erected. Sarnai gave a new order, the first one to mount on top of him and the tiny but cute girl tried with her small hand to guide the penis in her tiny vagina.

He stopped that as he knew that this would create pain to these tiny girl's untouched and untrained vagina. So, as far as there was not an escape from this, at least make it the proper and delicate way to make the girls feel nice and with not the least of pain, so do it 'his way' that he knows well.

He licked the small pussy of the tiny but extremely cute girl until he felt that there was slight moist on the beautiful mini wet pussy. Sarnai was curiously looking as if she showed something very unusual.

He asked her to turn on her side. He lifted her leg up and took her hand so as to caress her tiny clitoris, and he started to insert his hard penis, but how to do this? There was no way as that was almost sealed.

Sarnai was facing this whole procedure peculiarly as this was not in the 'menu'; he ignored her and removed the penis and started smoothly to caress the pussy and inserting his small finger. He, then with surprise, saw Sarnai, better called her 'Warden', to nod a probable 'Yes, you are great, and you do so well.'

The little finger started to slip inside as that tiny pussy was wet-slick enough, his finger even crooked inside her, the girl was enthusiastic that her small vagina started to respond with muscles squeezing.

He reached a stroke where all her sweat and the pussy smell was gathered, he asked her to lick his finger with her own pussy juices, she did it and liked her pussy smell and taste. The small pointer finger was removed and the bigger middle finger took its turn, she was almost ready.

Sarnai showed great satisfaction that she was almost ready to cheer and even applaud but controlled herself getting back to her serious face.

Moment came for the real action, the penis went inside very slowly, slipped with big difficulty as that tiny vagina was so narrow, but kept going deeper until he felt the virginity's last fortress, small thrust and that was it the girl with her eye looked at the lady at the corner and she nodded to her with a triumphal smile that yes this was done.

That sweet girl turned around to show to him her gratitude, and he kept that usual back and forth routine movements and this time there was no need to hold as the goal was to leave all his load inside her, but still he held back until he heard the small young girl moan verifying that she came with a tiny climax and he then let his 'babies' rest well inside her. Sarnai, in their language, asked her to lay on her back so as if the sperm were to slide deeper in her.

The other one was watching all the process very closely and asked the first how was it, she was so happy that she could not hide it not only for the pleasure she had not only because maybe she will get pregnant and carry a heroic baby, but also that she had not any single pain as all the other girls in their community were telling about the unbearable pain they felt when they lost the virginity.

He kissed her softly and passionately to show to her that what he was doing was not an obligation but he enjoyed that a lot.

Sarnai showed to him an expression of admiration that he did what he did so nicely and professionally she wanted to tell him something but he could not understand until a while she stood up and kissed the girl, he then realised that the first to come girl was her daughter. He somehow with the hand language he asked her and she confirmed that she indeed was her daughter and approached him and gave him a warm hug and kissed him on the cheek as if he were the husband of her daughter and the father of her grandson or granddaughter.

That strict and severe 'warden' as he called her, suddenly became a very sympathetic woman. He had to sleep and she with pleasure gave her consent showing to him with the fingers that meant to be that in 12 hours she will wake him up for the next girl who stayed in his bedroom and slept with him and get her beautiful naked body to keep him warm.

He had not the strength to go to Alex's bedroom to ask him how things went and slept deeply like a baby but satisfied that he corresponded to his duty ideally and also provided pleasure to that little girl and also to her mother. The plan was that she will have a new intercourse in the second round to seal the pregnancy.

The 12 hours passed fast and the supervisor lady came to wake him up with a smile in a way thanking him for offering such a sweet satisfaction to her daughter. There was a table with only two chairs with plenty of food that reminded him of the big Arabic tables.

There was horse milk (to explain what that milk she was brought him from an opening where at the square was the statue of Alexander the Great on his horse the famous Bucephalus). That milk included proteins and many vitamins, then beef and goat meat but also camel meat.

As a beverage, a green cocktail similar to the Japanese Matcha tea with curcumin is probably also nettle with many doping herbs.

On the table he had as company the second girl who he had to deflower after the meal. She was so joyful and always smiling and stared at him as if he were a superman. She watched the process of the virginity loss of the first girl and she was anxious and very eager to live the same with more than big desire and willingness.

All what he had as meal plus the gorgeous body of that tiny girl helped to obtain an outstanding erection and the repeat sex ran very well, what shocked him was that this time the lady who was always there she had in a clever way her hand inside her dresses and was caressing herself. Probably, she had such a suffering eagerness that she lost the serious status and control, while he hoped that she will also not ask for a fuck.

The second girl stayed again there for a while on her back for 30 minutes him turned her on her belly for a minute kissing her buttocks going deep to her tiny anus, this tickled her and turned to him with a virgin, but at the same time strange smile and a question mark. *What he wants? That even more narrow hole also?* He turned her back, and after 30 minutes, she left, and he went back to sleep after all he had no other to do as he was a 'sex prisoner'.

This reminded him in that small Greek country town there was a male donkey known as the stallion donkey of a big area and all farmers were bringing their female donkeys for breeding and he, one by one, was climbing on top of them doing his well-known job. Well, this example is not far away from what was happening here.

Another seven hours passed with a new plentiful dinner or lunch, he even lost the time knowing what was outside night or day. He wanted to go to Alex's bedroom but the guard that was between the two bedrooms did not allow this. He was worried that maybe that poor guy who often uses Viagra, might have had a health accident.

Two new girls always had the same procedure, they always send two girls fist to acquire the much-wanted erection and that the one learns from the other by close and careful watching how this is done and how she had to behave and allow her body to be smoothly and gently treated. To one of them after the main course, tried to insert his penis to her anus, as that was a marvellous anus, but that was not in the menu. Sarnai worked even more intensively on her masturbation seeing that, but he could not manage to do that without any Vaseline support.

The 12-hour break changed to 13 hours so he had more time to revitalise and refresh his sex desire. After all there was no other option, no other activity or entertainment for him to choose.

So, days passed all the girls in order to be compatible to the 'fucking schedule' must pass two times (two rounds) from his bed all with the same sexual pursuit, while the supervisor's daughter wanted a third and last encounter and this time she became more aggressive.

She wanted the sex not anymore to get pregnant but to get more than one orgasm as she knew that was her last time and her mother did not seem to have any objection to that after all she was always enjoying having quite some masturbations.

Her daughter made it clear she also wanted to lose also het backside virginity, but how without Vaseline, she will suffer. Mother wanted her daughter to feel this also and took under her apron and gave him a small jar with a green paste.

He looked at her and made him understand to smear his cock, and he in a way obeyed, but that was quite similar to the known Vicks that one uses for his chest relief in case he caught a cold, and in a way burned slightly the head of the cock and had a smell of lavender. Sarnai nodded to him now 'Go'.

To his surprise, that paste was miraculous; the penis slid in that tight arsehole in one single second without having the little girl to feel any pain. He thought of this green formula; he needed this by all means.

After the ceremony ended, the girls would get 'locked' in a house under guard so in no case try any sex until they get a baby so the father is 100% guaranteed either him or Alex.

He recalls that the time the task was completed and the job was done, Sarnai wildly tossed her dresses to the floor, remained completely naked and obviously sexually excited, showing her nice body; after all, she was just 35 years old. She begged him under complete secrecy; she also wanted to live the same sex as her daughter from both canals.

He showed instant docility, what could he do? Nothing but give her that pleasure peculiarly asking him to start from her derriere; she accommodated his penis with pleasure despite a small pain, as the small jar was not anymore in her possession hiding this in her home.

Right after, she enjoyed from the anus; she asked him to move to her anxiously waiting and already dripping wet pussy and him having the previous routine to ejaculate inside with not any objection; he did that to her also while she made not any movement to avoid that; on the contrary, she let go with comfort.

She embraced him very tightly, kissed him and with no waste of time ran away not to be seen; she had a happy and satisfied face of a woman who had before not any at all enjoyable sex in her life.

At this point, it is necessary to point out that to all these girls the break of their hymen was not same to all of them, many hymens, or one could describe as a rim of tissue at the outer entrance of the vagina, does not show any at all 'resistance'; and the penis feels not any membranous obstacle and not necessarily bleed during that intercourse, but the girl still loses her virginity.

Chang returned to fetch them up and return them to freedom. The goodbye was difficult, all the community came back again, and all gathered under the statue of Alexander the Great in the centre of the square.

It was the first time after 15 days to see Alex was fat, maybe he gained more than five kilos; he asked him, and he seemed to be content and covered with sex for the next whole month; in that moment, it was necessary to remind him that the other four girls were waiting and probably means more sex.

Whole community was there to pay ultimate tribute and say goodbye; they gave them as present two bronze helmets believing that these were from Alexander the Great's military flanks or maybe spoils from battles.

Chang with his jeep drove off, having all behind them cheering in happiness except the 20 mistresses, who were locked in a separate room for almost nine months.

First thing to do was to ask Chang about the four girls; he said all clear; he even bought four kinds of vibrators so that they lose any wish for outside sex. They laughed and thanked him for doing this.

He also told them that the festivities duration was for 15 days but nothing to mention about any kind of 'celebrating encounters' with the virgins.

They reached the hotel and ran to their rooms so happy that they would meet their tall girls as all those virgins were very cute but short between 1.50 and maximum 1.55 but extremely cute and sweet.

The warm embraces lasted long; they were so happy, but to the obvious observation, the girls were also hot, so God knows how they could deny being for 15 days and supposing to be without any sex activity so the girls could obviously think that they for sure have a big desire for good sex.

A weary excuse due to the long drive through uneven roads worked, and so they were allowed to have a short nap, which finally turned out to be rather a long one.

They woke up quite late and only had time for dinner. They decided to go down to have a goodbye dinner at the hotel where they met those wonderful girls.

They booked the western-type of restaurant where they could enjoy French wine as in those 15 days, they were fed up with the green teas and the unidentified hot beverages.

The mood on the table was excellent. The girls kept asking when the plan was to go to Milano and Paris. The plan was first Shanghai where there were many models' schools so that they get a first professional contact with the profession that they would strictly follow from now on and leave behind them and for good the previous life.

They never stopped asking what they did there all these 15 days; it was difficult to fill up all those 15 days with ceremonies and festivities, but somehow, they managed to convince them that they were pretty far away from any sexual incidents.

But what they told them and they were happy showing not any surprise, was that what they saw there and the girls and women that were present at those round tables, justifies their belief that they might have in their veins a Great Alexander's blood. Reason is that all the girls of that small community had likewise non-Chinese eyes, no Asian monolid eyes; the only difference was that they were not 1.75 but 1.55 at the tallest.

So, the presentation that they would make for them at those famous designer's houses was that you are descendants of Alexander the Great with a mixture of the highest ranked generals of the old Chinese dynasty that were tall like Gherkins Khan only as height example.

So, they would impress all seeing those, seldom to be seen in defile girls bearing the glorious legacy of Great Alexander.

The girls were full of joy, flying in the air, so to say, with all these plans; they told them tomorrow they would fly to Shanghai.

The dinner ended with champagne, and thank God, they also had brie soft white French cheese and that was a dinner for the girls long to remember as the last one to that city and hotel with their bad family and rooms visiting experiences, which must totally be removed from their memories and never ever reveal that to anyone.

Of course, now their Golgotha how to manage both in Shanghai, Angel and Mellissa plus the four Terracotta girls without the one girls' group to know about the other.

In the suite, a good sex was almost obligatory, but as they had an early fight, they persuaded them for a fast and ordinary encounter just to satisfy their 15 days long needs and sleep fast and relaxed.

In the morning, he gave his phone number to Chang so as to inform him about the possible pregnancies of the 20 girls and see how fertile they proved to be. A good breakfast and off they went to the airport.

At the Shanghai airport, no one was asked to pick them up as the four girls were to be there in total secrecy, 'incognito', to avoid complications.

They drove directly to their apartment that they rented for them. It was big with two bedrooms and four beds, quite well-furnished and in a central part so that all was within walking distance.

It was difficult to explain to them that they had to leave as they were long away, and they had too much to do and many people to meet that were taking care of the many businesses they had in Shanghai.

They asked them to get well installed and open the yellow pages and look as close as possible to their apartment any model school. They left them money and kissed goodbye for a short period. They asked for their phone number, but they told them that they would change the number as they want a new one for Shanghai. But they would call them on their apartment phone.

They went straight to meet Angel and Melissa and hear the news after they asked them to go back to physiotherapists' school and also somehow inspect the decoration of the first Spartan restaurant.

They first went to Angel's apartment, and luckily, Melissa was also there, the joy; the hugs and the kisses were numerous.

The girls looked so beautiful with a relaxed face after living comfortably and away from that spa 'dirty' job. He was sure that the one was pleasing the sexual desire of the other; after all, Angel knew that lesbian lust from previous experience.

They prepared dinner in the apartment, so they were all happy and in a nice atmosphere. He asked Angel if Giannis had a girl so that he could feel the hug of a girl and she confirmed that not only just a girl, but they were both in an awesome love.

Alex and Melissa moved to their apartment.

Angel dragged him to the bed and took off all her dresses; her gorgeous body was revealed in all the charms; well, he avoided to try the comparisons between her and the Terracotta girls as it makes no sense each girl has her own body and grace. The intercourse was unavoidable. He tried to put in all remaining effort so that she would not notice that something was wrong and in a way he managed.

The sleep was more than required, and that sleep was so welcome and especially having the warmth of such an angelic body contact. The next day was a very busy day, starting at the office to see that all went well. Sophia assured him that all went not just well but perfectly well, then went to the restaurant that was under construction where Giannis was to be there on the spot supervising the works.

Giannis was the man for the job, his girl was also there to translate the communication between him and the workers. He introduced her; she was another angelic Chinese beauty. Giannis seemed to be so happy with her presence next to him that his job turned out to be a real pleasure.

He informed Areus that the container was due to arrive next week and all goods have to be transported to the Spartan tavern that had already the sign on and many passed by asking what will there to be.

They all and Giannis went to the advertising agency to see the designs for the menu and the leaflet that would soon be distributed to announce the inauguration of the first in China Spartan restaurant.

The deep freezers and fridges would be on the spot in four–five days, so then comes the time to ask the Greek fellow in Greece to send by air the gyros and all first foods, such as tomatoes, and feta cheese and more.

He gave all contacts to Giannis to handle all these as he was more than clever and capable to do all by himself without any guidance.

It is worthwhile to mention that he made incredible progress with his Chinese, and soon he will need no translator. He suggested to him with all difficulties to still try to communicate with his girl only in Chinese and only so, he will make huge steps for the language.

They left the restaurant as all was in complete control of Giannis—what a clever choice that was. They went to the office again to have a shareholders' meeting as among others they had to decide when to fly to Hong Kong for the registration of the new company for the Spartan company.

From the office, he made several phone calls, first his own family to tell them where he was and that he was in good health, then call Karla to see how the pregnancy was going. He also called Nuuk to see if everything was progressing.

All seemed to be in good order so he felt that he did the best of a well-organised job.

He also called a good friend from old times, a Greek/Italian architect whose companion had an excellent relation with the previous prime minister of Italy.

He explained that he worked as manager, and he had four heavenly sent Chinese girls all 1.75 of height with semi-European eyes and gorgeous bodies and needs an Italian agent who would introduce them to the famous Italian haute couture designers to step into the fashion shows world.

He also added that these girls inherited their beauty from the Great Alexander short passing by China, after he conquered and seized India and Afghanistan and this certainly adds an extra value and glam, so to say, successors of the royal race.

He was very impressed and asked him to send as many photos and videos as possible.

The shareholders met at the office, and fast decisions were taken. They agreed two days later to fly to Hong Kong for the company registration.

He also called Nicolas to see how he was running the hotel of his friend Arne, and he heard an enthusiastic voice that showed that he was doing this extremely well and very seriously.

The unsolved headache was the four Terracotta girls and the parallel situation with Angel and Melissa both needing their presence.

They had the next day a meeting with a lawyer to have to sign a contract between himself and Alex and the four girls for exclusive managers' rights for the next 10 years.

An excuse was invented to Angel and Melissa that they fly tonight with Sophia to Hong Kong for the company registration and they might be away for three nights and would pass by to pick up the adequate suits. That was not very well accepted, but they explained business is business and all the luxury living and the soon to come their own spa requires capital so they had to run to bring money in.

They indeed passed by, kissed them to 'catch the flight', took a taxi, and they went to the other four girls. They brought good news that Milano is waiting for them and that tomorrow they have to do many things.

First, go the lawyer to sign the contract, then second, go to one of the best shops in Shanghai to buy impressive dresses, and third, they have meetings with a professional photographer to take photos and videos that are needed.

They added after that, there was no need to take any modelling lessons in Shanghai but that could be done in Milano, the second heart of modelling after Paris.

So, the faster they finish, all the better. They tried to avoid any sex as the next day was a very busy day. They signed the work done by the lawyer bounding contracts, and then to the shop where they bought such dresses that turned them into real princesses or better divas.

He had the wise thought that the first thing to do when they were in the apartment was to search French and Italian channels, and if they were lucky, they could see model shows, and so they did, and they got a first image of their to-come profession.

The photographer, who was suggested by their advertising agent and was indeed a fantastic photographer, he was 100% gay, but that was not so important, his name was Andre. Important was the awesome job he does, a startling photographer especially of women in swimsuits.

They stayed there five hours taking photos with all the new dresses and also dresses he had in his photo studio for such occasions and also videos. He confidentially commented to them, that such models do not exist in whole of Shanghai and that they could stay here and be very successful.

They told him that Milano was waiting as they aim high; he somehow agreed that they deserve much more than Shanghai.

Areus asked him if they could stay there another hour and get all the photos and videos; he accepted that, but it would cost some extra money, and so they agreed. The photos he delivered in both, actual paper photos but also in USB stick and a separate USB stick for the videos.

They stayed there and watched it all. It was an amazing job. He took such beautiful photos also with bikinis that he had there for the photography, and especially he took closer photos of their faces with their extraordinary eyes; as he said, having seen many models, such a combination of height and eyes were very seldom in China and are probably crossings between Chinese and European.

Having what they needed he sent already from there, from the photographer the photos and videos to his connection in Italy.

As it was already quite late, they invited Andre for dinner. He chose the restaurant, a famous Japanese restaurant, saying that there were often many celebrities, models, agents and producers and quite many of them from Japan. The girls chose to wear the best new bought dresses, and they went to the restaurant that was two blocks away.

When entering, they heard a kind of WOW as if Brad Pit and Angelina Jolie showed up. The entrance of the four girls was so impressive that some even wanted to stand up. They, he and Alex, were so proud and happy that they discovered this group of four awesome girls not ever seen together four and all looking exactly the same, as if they were all four sisters.

The maître wanted, as special VIP guests, to guide them to a private room, but Andre denied; he told him, "They want in the main restaurant so to have all to admire these four girls as an image must be built around them."

This said, a Japanese guy approached, wanting to talk to the girls, but abruptly he was stopped by Andre, telling him that what you do is not appropriate in front of their managers.

He immediately addressed Alex and himself and gave his card saying, "Call us please," and went back to his table where all were staring at them persistently and talking between themselves in a low but likewise 'conspirator' intriguing modus.

They showed his card to Andre, and he told them that this was a famous bureau for talent scouts. The photographer addressed them saying, "You see why I wanted to bring you here? It was a first gallop to see the impressions and as you see, these are more than encouraging."

They had a nice dinner; the girls were looking at him as a 'bon viveur' to learn more about how a lady has to behave in a luxury restaurant as such and much more glamorous restaurants they would visit in Milan and Paris and maybe later also in New York.

Andre asked them if he had the right to put the photos to the local famous Chinese magazine for ladies. They told him not yet; they tell him when and if, although that would be great but something told inside him that better not yet as it might be better to show photos as a 'premiere' to European world known magazines. Later, that proved to be a very wise way of thinking.

Andre ordered a limousine to take all to the girls' apartment. They invited him for a drink last night's drink, and he was happy to accept.

The girls seemed not to be happy with that as they were hot and wanted sex now more than ever.

Anyway, they were there in the apartment. The girls right after entering the apartment rushed to take all their clothes and made a complete naked show, after all Andre was a gay, and he was many times invited to orgies as that was what it was to be turned about.

The heat in that living room was like a hammam heat, obliging them to get also nude while Andre was impressed by the hard cock and many dirty things passed through his mind.

His interest suddenly changed. In a manner he wanted to rush and jump upon with a blowjob but then he stood up and said, "I better go as I am afraid that I might surpass the girls' impressive bodies and win the competition with my incomparable ass." They all laughed, and he left.

Well, what then happened was difficult to be described, the girls did not just want to offer their bodies but also their souls to them being so grateful for what a change they brought to their life.

They cleverly called Angel and Melissa with some excuses that they will not be there as they had to travel to Ningbo, a nearby industrial city, to see the next day a big factory that will be the one to manufacture the machinery for the next to come Spartan restaurant.

The next day, they stayed there with the girls almost all day as many phone calls were needed and that was not via a mobile phone.

He also wanted to seek all mails in his laptop to double check that all goes fine with the office and the German and Australian customers and see that new orders are coming. Although the trip to Hong Kong to register the company was two

days later, they told the girls that this will be with a later flight and asked them to stay home and not go out as in the meantime and according to Andre's suggestion. They called two ladies personal trainers in the apartment to give them the appropriate body training and massages to keep their bodies in perfect condition.

This will also keep them busy so no need to go out and have unexpected surprises, as those Japanese agents might somehow try to 'kidnap' them from their hands. They also asked Andre to send another gay guy to teach them, in that big living room of the apartment, charming walking like professional models, so they have a full program, he made clear, 'Gay' trainer.

Before leaving to go to Angel and Melissa the phone rang and there was the Greek/Italian Architect, his name is Aristos, in a delirious voice saying, "What the hell? You keep these beauties there? I showed it to the two major agents who organise and recruit models for all the designers, and they were crazily impressed, they want to sign contracts right away before Paris or Americans would discover them."

Areus made up a big lie and told him, "I am sorry, my good friend, but that photographer, after seeing the unbelievable, according to his experienced eyes, beauties, invited to his atelier, without telling me, three major Japanese agents and a private fashion show was organised in front of them."

They, in stunning situation, appreciated what the value of these girls was, and today first thing in the morning, knowing that they will go to Milano, offered 1 million dollars to the four girls for a one-year exclusive contract that will include 25 defiles and two first page's photos to the two major Japanese ladies magazines plus luxurious free lodging presenting them as the daughters of Great Alexander.

Aristos felt bad as he did all so fast and now, he does not know what excuse to find. He told him he has two days to get those agents either to make a counter offer or come here in Shanghai, before the girls, after signing, they have to travel to Tokyo.

He possibly made a mistake but risk is always a guidance to his whole life. They moved, telling them that they will go to Hong Kong and that all is organised for them with Andre in order them to improve their physical status and also lessons in house for 'défilé' runway showcase.

Kissed goodbye and they went back to Angel and Melissa, they were supposed to be back from Ningbo. To their good luck, the girls had their period, so no sex was asked but Angel knew the story ;the French girls have pussy but also asspussy' he still with different excuses, he managed to avoid that.

The next day, they went to Hong Kong for the company with the already done company registered by a local lawyer and they also went to HSBC to open the company's bank account.

So, the Spartan chain of taverns had the legal composition and structure. While in Hong Kong they also opened two private bank accounts for Alex and himself and also a separate common bank account for both.

Back to Shanghai, next night and to Angel's hug, and this time, he could not avoid the so-called 'French hole'.

He called Chang and begged him to delete any info about the past of the four girls and asked for his bank account to transfer some money. He was more than happy that he also participated in the success and transformation of those girls and swore to seal his mouth.

The next day, they had to go to the four Terracotta girls and see the progress and the progress was astonishing, their bodies were looking even more smooth, well-trained and their walking that they demonstrated to them was four angels flying not touching the thick floor carpet, it was the apotheosis of glamour and charm.

The two personal trainers' girls were there and they also put the girls on a professional diet, so to lost one maximum two kilos as no more was needed. He noticed that they both had extreme muscles for girls, the abs were kind of 'six pack' but also noticed that they had rough face characteristics referring to active lesbians.

He hopes they did not fuck their girls having them all nude on that massage bed. But as second thoughts that might not be bad so that they do not desire other young men.

When the trainers left, he asked them if those girls had sex with them; the two gilts blushed, and they nodded yes, adding that it was so nice. He told them that they must not get the bad name of lesbians that will ruin their career, and from now on, whatever they do must preserve and secure the good image that they are creating for them.

They said, "We know, but those two girls during massaging started caressing our vagina and what could we do else than enjoy it with two consecutive climaxes; it was difficult to deny as this was done in such a way that we had to surrender to their skilful hands and fingers but also to their talented tongues, and then we had to twist and turn around and kiss their vaginas; they had orgasms as they were also very hot."

He explained to them that these girls lick every day many vaginas, and obviously, they have the professional know-how and expertise of their tongues to bring satisfaction to the girls and mainly women that they are supposed just to avail for innocent massage, but there exists no woman in the world not to enjoy a pussy licking and even more from a woman than a man.

He was thinking that such a thing might happen and especially when they are not there; he asked the clever concierge to find for him dildos of all sizes, small and big.

So, telling them about that lesbian love, he presented them the dildos as well as vibrators. They knew that these offer good orgasm as such but less good quality were purchased for them by Chang when they were absent for 15 days.

Seeing the new ad softer and also more advanced big dildo, they were very happy.

Two were exclusively for the asshole. One of them took the courage to ask how this could go inside me. He told her, "Tonight, I will show you that what you could take in and even bigger." She was stunned.

Anyway, you must not do again that lesbian encounter with any other women and get used to it, but if you still miss it, you could do this between you the one sister with the one girl and the other sister with the other girl so they have the desired climaxes, and no one knows that you do such lesbian love, and you cannot be exposed to gossips that will harm your fame.

In the meantime, he sent many mails to all Paris and New York agents with all photos and videos with the intriguing title, 'The ancestral four of Alexander the Great with the name of Terracotta sisters'. Terracotta was known from the Crete Knossos Palace that was made of Terracotta and was connected with the legend of Labyrinth and Minotaur so that workmanship was taught by the generals and soldiers of Alexander the Great, reaching Chinese territories. They passed to the Chinese workers the know-how to build the famous Terracotta Army.

These fantastic girls were the descendants of this legend.

All this story alongside the photos and videos created a mystery that any agent will offer as such a legend to the famous fashion designers.

The fabricated story turned into reality when the renowned Japanese agent expressed to Andre their interest in meeting with the managers. Areus informed Andre that the Japanese representatives sought to uncover the official offers and instructed him to convey that Milan was offering a substantial one-million-dollar deal for a year-long exclusive contract. This package included 25 models fashion shows, featured on two major ladies' magazines' front pages, and luxurious accommodations at five-star hotels, presenting them as the 'daughters' of Great Alexander.

Andre was amazed how fast they work and are able to launch intensive promotion to the whole project, as this, in fact, became a high-class project.

So, now they have quite some interests on table, and the competition was becoming harder because in the fashion show business, all of a sudden appeared four girls with seldom height for Chinese girls but with half European eyes and a legendary story to accompany them.

All now they had to do was wait for the phone to ring.

Back to Spartan business, Giannis was doing an excellent job; the restaurant was almost ready, and next week, the machinery, supplies and wines would come. He already called Christos, the contact guy in Greece, to fly next week with fridge containers, the gyros meat and all the necessaries enough for the first 10 days.

The announcing leaflet was perfect and was to be distributed in 1 million pieces to all the wider community. Angel and Melissa were following express lessons of physiotherapists and masseuses so that they get their diploma and be able to have the licence to open their own spa.

The next day, he went to the office, expecting possible phone calls from Milano, Japan, Paris and why not also New York.

In fact, the Japanese agents accepted the offer, adding 200,000 so 1.2 million adding two TV presentations. He answered that he will consider their offer and will contact them again.

He fixed a gaze at Alex with the sign of two fingers, 'victory'. Alex could not believe that they indeed hit the golden vein.

Aristos from Milano also contacted, saying that the major model's agent would come with a counter offer early next week as he has to talk with all leading international fashion designers having the photos and videos of the magnificent Terracotta 4.

One of them wanted to see completely nude photos; Areus absolutely declined this and angrily said, "If this designer wants to masturbate, he can watch Pornhub on Google," in a way showing that he accepts no jokes in business.

They did not want to reveal to the four girls any of those offers so that they keep them well-grounded and not fill them up with high expectations.

He dialled Chang once more, urgently inquiring about any girls in his city, matching the criteria and requested immediate photo submissions. Areus relayed information from the initial four girls, mentioning five additional ones of comparable quality, all siblings' daughters. He emphasised the substantial payment if these girls proved to be equally stunning.

"Chang, swiftly visit the families of the five brothers and two sisters. Look for four or five daughters with identical roots, exceptional beauty, and matching height and eyes. We need these additional girls urgently; time is of the essence."

He also asked him to be in contact with the village authorities, where they went and stayed the 15 days to hear if there were any pregnancies out of the 20 girls they were forced to deflower.

Chang confirmed that if the pregnancies were certain, it would lead to extended festivities lasting at least 20 days. He mentioned a potential invitation for Areus and Alex.

Areus did not show any interest on those 20-day festivities, emphasising the importance of securing four more girls to cater to both Japanese and potentially European agents, highlighting the probable harm to their reputation as fashion model managers if they failed to do so.

While in the office, Sophia, his partner, told him that a guy from Milano was asking for him. He grabbed the receiver, but it was not Aristos but an Italian-speaking guy.

Fluent in Italian, he effortlessly communicated, introducing himself as Enrico Bertalomo, a Milan-based agent for fashion models. After viewing photos and videos, he revealed that his Parisian partner expressed strong interest in the unique team of four exceptional girls. Acknowledging the Japanese offer, Enrico's partner was ready to make a counteroffer, sparking a heated negotiation between the two agents.

The reason was that Enrico wanted to give his phone number but, Areus, pretending to be very busy, asked the French guy to call him. The Italian fellow said, no way, this French agent was the biggest in fame in the world, and he never calls, so better let it go.

Areus cleverly answered, "I understand but whoever is interested has to call me. If not then, I agree with you, drop it." Enrico insisted that the French number one agent in fashion designers models never ask or begs so change the mind and do not lose such a big chance.

The answer was, "Well, Amico, then let us forget about I go with the updated offer of the Japanese; thanks for calling; nice to talk to you; goodbye." He shut down the phone. It was very risky what he did to drop such a big challenge, but as he always says 'risk runs in my veins'. Alex disagreed, and they had a small clash, but he was sure that in one hour the French arrogant agent will call.

And this indeed happened in 1½ hours.

On the other line was a French talking guy, pretending that he did not know who he was, so he had to introduce himself as the French partner of Enrico.

"Oh yes, I see, how are you?" was his answer. The French guy probably was expecting a humble voice, but that was not at all so. Areus knew well that he had the advantage of having four diamonds in his hands, so he wanted to gain the upper hand in the conversation.

The French guy came right to the point. "I offer 1.5 million for 1 year for 30 defile, plus front page to the two major Paris magazines, two TV interviews, all expenses for travelling to Milan, New York, as well as Berlin, staying in a suite for four at the most luxurious hotels of each city and, of course, luxury apartment in Paris."

There was a few seconds' gap; he did not want to show enthusiasm. Areus very coolly answered that he will give his answer in two days.

The French was surprised, but he had to accept and wait for two days. The communication was over with the usual thanks and goodbye from both parties. Alex remains stunned. "What a bastard you are! How did you dare, as an unknown manager, to play the role of an arrogant to the biggest maybe in Europe and America fashion models bureau?"

"You see, at the end, I won, so next time, trust my judgment. What is important is to have four new girls so they satisfy both customers."

He called Chang again; he assured that he will meet the family and relatives of the four girls, and he mentioned that there was a good chance that such beauties were there, but he will know tomorrow.

The night they would spend with Angel and Melissa and await to have the call from Chang, so if need be, they have to fly there to see with their eyes the new girls' discovery. Angel was a little sick with flu, and they had to sleep in different beds.

The next day was important. First, they have to give the OK to the Japanese, but this depends exclusively on the new four girls. If not, then they have to go with the much better French offer and the French agent who was much flashier and, undoubtedly, of higher class.

First thing in the morning, they did what they had to do, from the very beginning before asking Chang, and that was to ask the four girls if they know other girls of the same class that they are with the same dominant characteristics, height and eyes.

And so, they did, and the girls assured them that there was a whole family all first-degree relatives, daughters of five brothers that all girls with unbelievable resemblance were almost like twins; the three cousins were younger, of age of 17; these three are sisters and are even taller and always the same eyes as this was their inheritance, but there was another first-degree relative; she was 20 years old.

They asked them how they could contact them; they said they could call them, and so they did. These girls knowing the good future of the first four were also more than happy to join the team.

They asked them to get in contact with Chang so that he also could meet the girls. All must be done fast; they called Chang and gave him the address and the girls' names and asked him to go there right away; he confirmed that it will take 20 minutes to reach them, so they anxiously awaited his comments.

He called, and he could not hide his enthusiasm; he could not find words to describe what he saw. The three sisters were even more beautiful than the first four, and their eyes were almost 50% western, for the fourth one was equally beautiful to the three sisters. He already talked to their family, and they gave the consent for the good of their daughters, as there in that town there was no future at all other than prostitution.

He requested Chang to promptly arrange for their departure, and Chang efficiently secured them seats on the first available flight. Upon arriving at the airport, they were accompanied by one of the four girls already in Shanghai, ensuring immediate recognition and a smooth introduction.

They remained astounded seeing the girls, one could identify from the distance as they were so tall. The more they were approaching, the more one could see that they were of unusual beautiful standards and very rare to meet not only in China but worldwide. This was obvious as all passengers at the airport looked at them as an extra remarkable group of girls. Some of them even lost their luggage seeing those divine visions.

The four new girls kissed their cousin, and they were all in a huge limo, heading to the best hotel to impress the girls but also feel that this was a new page in their life.

When entering the huge suite, the girls opened their eyes and remained amazed or, better say, shocked at what they had in front of their eyes.

There are two major elements that helped the situation a lot. There was an uncle who moved many years ago to Canada and was supposed to bring them over to Vancouver so asked all the boys and girls of all five brothers to start learning English and also obtain passports.

So, this was great as they were ready to fly any time and also communicate in English.

He called Andre, begging him to pick up in his Mercedes the four girls, bring to that well known exclusive shop for ladies dresses to dress them the way he knows and then right away to his studio for photos in dazzling dresses and bikinis. Andre came, and Alex gave him his golden Visa credit card so he uses his card for the shopping.

At the same time, Andre also organised express lessons for professional defile in his atelier.

So, now they have not four but eight diamonds in their hands to please both French and Japanese agents.

Late at night, they expected the photos and videos and also the comments from Andre about their walking style and charm.

All eight girls, as well as Andre, were at the big hotel suite, watching the photos and videos and those were so professionally done that it looked as if these girls were walking on a fashion parade of Yves Saint Laurent.

Alex and he were both feeling great and amazed but also a little frightened that having them known in those big modelling circles they might lose them as in that field there are many hunters and 'predators', working a little under Mafia rules.

What was important was to first bring the first four girls to Japan after they make the bounding contracts with the Japanese agents and at the same time open six bank accounts in Japan for the four girls and also for Alex and himself. They had now to give names to the new four girls, brand-new and not any Terracotta names.

The four Terracotta girls returned to their apartment, while he and Alex went to Angel and Melissa. The next morning, he called both the Japanese and French agents. He confirmed that there was a deal. The Japanese wanted that they sign the exclusive rights contract as already agreed in Japan. Areus definitely denied insisting that in Shanghai there is an internationally very well-known lawyers' office. Clarifying that they won't travel to Japan unless the contract was signed and the money was deposited to their Hong Kong bank account.

The contract will explicitly stipulate that the Japanese agents hold exclusive rights for the four girls solely in Asia and Australia for a duration of one year. It would be clarified that these rights do not extend to Europe or America, and there are no provisions for the usage of their images in any TV or media advertisements unless a new deal is agreed. Furthermore, any potential future deals would be limited to international perfume brands, creams, renowned ladies' bags, famous watches, and distinguished jewellery from renowned jewellers.

So, the Japanese agreed to all conditions, and tomorrow was the big day. With that French guy, they agreed to talk again in two days so that they could prepare the details of the contract. One month had already passed from the day that they had the task to impregnate the 20 virgins, and there was agony about what the result would be.

If delay of period appeared this was sign of pregnancy, and so there, they will leave their descendants for further breeding of a new Sino-European girls' and boys' mixture.

The Japanese called the next day, and all was agreed, so at 1 o'clock they were to meet at the lawyers' office with the four girls, the Japanese agents Alex and him. The lawyer had the contract ready, which he had already sent to the Japanese a day before, who read it and approved with slight changes. Champagnes were ordered, and there they all were in joy and contentment.

All were there, the two Japanese that were there were binding their company, signed, and at the same moment, via e-banking, the 1.2 million dollars was transferred. The money was at the bank, they could see online, so the champagnes were opened and drank in a nice atmosphere in full mood. They kissed all four girls, wishing to them best of luck to their new and widely promising career.

As agreed, each girl will get 150,000 USD in their account so that they will open bank accounts in Tokyo next week when they will also be there.

The girls were stunned for their first $150,000, which was big money for them, plus all expenses including a luxury apartment in Tokyo for one year were covered by the Japanese agents. But this is just the first step for them as many and much bigger would follow.

Alex won just like this 300,000 USD from the first four girls, and more he would get from the other four girls whom they would follow to Paris next week to sign the contract. He stared at him with a smile and a sign of satisfaction as this was the first money he made from business done by him and not money that he inherited from his father, showing his gratitude by giving a big hug to his partner Areus.

The Japanese agents made all necessaries for the luxury apartment with four beds and in the very centre of Tokyo, and they would all fly for Tokyo in four or five days.

The lawyer was also to prepare the contract for the French big agent; Marcel was his name, and that as it was more complicated, it would take two days. Not to forget, that the French fellow after all became friends, at least on the phone; he was calling twice a day as he wanted to make hectic preparations and presentations for the four 'brilliants' (diamonds) as he liked to call them.

The surname that was given to them was Alexander and the first names were still to be adopted.

The party continued at the suite of the Alexander girls, and that was a really rich party with champagne and caviar and all the rest. Andre was also there, who had indeed contributed a lot to the whole project. In his ear, he whispered that also boys were to be soon here who were brothers to these eight girls, and this time, his eyes were wide open as he, as a gay, was happy to hear such good news.

Imagining that if these girls were goddesses, the boys would also be heavenly sent existences. Chang was already aware of this, and he would visit the families again this time, looking for the boys who were also to follow the model career. All eight girls confirmed that there were many boys of always the same family of the five brothers; they were tall, around 1.90 and incredibly handsome.

So, Andre knew well that there was more to be done and quite soon. Meanwhile, Giannis was to clear the container, and all was soon to be ready for the grand opening of the first Spartan tavern.

He asked Christos from Greece to send immediately with the first plane the cook and his assistant who knows the gyros and the Souvlaki well and start teaching the Chinese assistants right away. The cooks arrived in three days as Christos did many interviews and found the best ones for this job. They paid them well so that they decided to come to China, and the opening day was to be fixed in 10 days, but the final date would be determined next week so that they all were sure that they would be able to serve many customers.

The leaflet was ready to be printed, but the date was still open and when that was fixed, they would print and the leaflet would be distributed to 1 million nearby inhabitants. This was a small sample, but they did not want that the very first day hundreds arrive so that they would not be able to serve and this could turn into a boomerang.

Giannis now had two Greek cooks, and with everyone's collective effort, the tavern was taking shape and becoming a reality. Andre, not being a specialist, was asked to capture photos, willingly contributing with a positive attitude. He developed a fondness for one of the cooks, a remarkably masculine guy; dreams and fantasies passed through Andre's mind.

Volunteering to stay at Andre's apartment until a suitable residence was found, his dream came true. Meanwhile, the assistant stayed with Giannis, who had an extra bedroom. The nature of the connection between the rugged cook and Andre remained unknown, but it was more than evident. With everything running smoothly and with the sufficient funds, the Spartan tavern was poised for success, aiming to establish a brand name and set the stage for future franchise expansion.

Nicolas called from Copenhagen, telling him that he managed, following the instructions he gave him, to increase already his clientele. Areus emphasised to him that the success of this endeavour would reflect positively to the hotel community circles, having that achievement as his background and CV as reference.

Arne also called saying how grateful he was after having so many positive comments from all his friends in the neighbourhood seeing how this brilliant young man upgraded the hotel and mainly the restaurant, obtaining fame even in central Copenhagen.

The bad news is that one of his daughters wanted to come to China and see the good things he does there and also help as she had the charisma of being sweet and good for public relations. But how could this be done when he lives with Angel and deals with great model girls. That would shock her, so he was looking for excuses to avoid this by all means.

So, he had to invent stories that would convince her not to come, and the best was that in China to run a restaurant you need protection from the local Mafia and this was very threatening if you do not accept and pay them. Her mother, his wife, prevented her and asked her to delay this for later when all was settled. It seemed that this worked.

The day came when they had to travel to Tokyo; here was again an excuse to be invented by Angel and Melissa, and that was that they were invited to Tokyo to start a Spartan tavern, as the concept seemed to meet the Japanese taste as a new trend to their culinary habits.

He hoped that they would swallow this excuse, and so they flew to Japan. To their surprise, there were many journalists and TV channels to greet the four Great Alexander's daughters, the four Terracotta girls, as this was the honorary given title to them by the Japanese agents. The girls got scared by the unexpected big manifestations.

So, they had to run through airport corridors to avoid all these media. They expressed their complaint to the agents, but they also had no idea that such a big event would take place; their assistants did this to gain publicity, and, more or less, they succeeded in doing this. That was also good for the girls as their fame advanced them.

The hotel suite that they booked was indeed great; it was a presidential suite that could accommodate all six. The Japanese agents told them that they must move next day to other rooms as it was not nice to get the rumours to run around that the four diamonds, Great Alexander's daughters, were sleeping with two old guys, even if they were their managers; this would harm their virgin kind of popularity. And frankly, they were right.

So, they explained to the girls that from now on they were on their own as they anyway have to return to Shanghai. They were not at all happy with that as suddenly they felt like orphans, but their most promising future requires and demands this for the sake of their refined fame.

The next day, they had to go to the bank to open six bank accounts so that they would transfer their money and also for Alex and him two bank accounts in Japan, just in case.

All was settled; they made it clear to the agents that according to the clauses of the contract they signed they must handle these girls with the ultimate gentleness and care and are not allowed to oblige them for duties and presentations other than what they signed for. The agents also agreed, adding that for them this was also a must that the name of these four girls remain unharmed and untouched as this was what they promote for their fame 'the impeccable God's wonder, the daughters of Alexander the Great'.

The next day, they went to open the bank accounts, and then the goodbye was not at all an easy goodbye. These girls did not consider them as lovers but as saviours from the miserable lives they had before. The hugs were such that they felt their hearts break, but it had to be done.

They left them there in a luxury hotel with money that would add to their life comfort, and they were also in good hands as the agents seemed to be decent guys, and according to what they found out on the spot, they were very serious and professionals; after all, paying all this big amount of money, they could only be big and strictly professionals.

Angel and Melissa needed another month to get their diplomas, so they had to look for the best place to open for them a luxurious spa. They gave this to the real estate agent.

In the meantime, the four Alexander girls moved from the hotel to the apartment that the Terracotta four girls left until they move to Paris.

The Spartan tavern now is fully equipped and Giannis, but mainly the cooks, started the training to two more local cooks and, they employed two more waitresses for serving the customers and three drivers for the three new motorcycles specially constructed for the orders that are to be delivered at homes.

It will take one whole week to have the system to work impeccably so they did many rehearsals by asking the staff of their office to bring friends and relatives for free meals and also ask some of their friends that stay in the neighbourhood to order according to the catalogue also for free.

Angel and Melissa were also there at the door welcoming and, in a way, entertaining the guests.

The partners did not care what money they spent because all must be perfect to work flawlessly and have customers to leave happy and spread from mouth to mouth that this is a good and new kind of tavern that all must visit or order for home delivery. In the first rehearsal days there were mistakes and malfunctions but the last three days all went perfectly well.

One million leaflets and catalogues were distributed door to door to all the nearby areas. The inauguration day was for next Saturday, so eight days are enough to optimise the services. Giannis was announced as the director who in the meantime learned quite good Chinese and all was working like a well-tuned musical instrument.

The next day, they were to fly to Paris and all arrangements are done, they have sent the contract to the French agent who made some minor changes, the lawyer made the minor amendments according to these minor corrections and they were flying with the four princesses created by the hands of God and that mould that he created these girls was afterwards destroyed.

Have to confess that the first night that they came and stayed at the suite Alex and he asked the girls, in order to appreciate the attractiveness of the bodies, for a private défilé with no clothes completely nude as they were born. It is absolutely unnecessary to say that what they saw was a shocking spectacle of unblemished bodies and the eyes were entirely due to their certain progeny.

Bodies that few men had ever had the honour to see in such a close distance. Where to start from the faces, the necks, the breasts, the waist, the buttocks, the endless legs, wherefrom to start and where to end? All were ten out of ten.

The girls wanted to show gratitude and offer the pleasure of their bodies to them but it was an abuse from them to take advantage and make sex to them.

They only asked to allow them to touch and caress their bodies but how to control the desire was impossible. They wanted to stand up and run and go away but they held them back, so an orgy was to take place in that suite as they observed that his penis was hard, they unbuttoned his trousers and held in hand caressing it with spontaneous lust.

Alex had such a shock that despite the many efforts his penis could not stand up and betrayed him, so all four had to enjoy the only hard penis in that room.

The girls felt their pussy wet already for quite a time, one after the other sweetly slipped the hard penis in their narrow vulva, two minutes for each one and again another two minutes as second round for each one and the third round always two minutes, as if they had a minute's counter.

The tongues were in coordination and very busy until the first came in such a pleasant manner that added extra power for him to perform better and have all the other three to come but this time in a quite terrifying explosive way.

All four with a delightful face they wanted to have him also to come and one by one started with divine blowjob not as obligation but was obvious only for their own pleasure until all four took their turn and the ejaculation was inevitable and they were so happy to watch him come with a 'roar' sound an enormous relief.

He stayed in dizziness for seconds watching up thinking is it true or is it a dream, he asked the girls to pinch his cheek and smack his buttocks to verify that all in reality happened.

Alex from the corner shouted, "Well you bastard, I envy you, you enjoyed it and me with no Viagra I kept only watching and this bloody penis of mine did not help me even to masturbate as what I saw was a scorching porno scene."

The next day was the day to fly to the big money in Paris and fly to the big career horizons for the girls that would allow their wings to open widely.

Before leaving for the airport, a call came this time from Nuuk in Greenland, Tuppi was in ecstasy, he triumphantly announced to him in excess dose of euphoria that end of the month is definitely the contest of the Bras de Ferre to take place in the city and 200 people are expected and 10 contestants from 10 different countries. "All want to express their gratitude to you, and you must come."

He told him that he will do his best but he was tremendously busy and in that time period. He was very happy that that fake promise for that tournament finally proved to become true. Alex and he with the four girls at the airport created a chaos everyone wanted to see and some touch these girls as if they were in a spiritual ceremony. They could not believe that such beauties at all could exist. They were protected by the Air France VIP lounge where all stood up to get a better view of these girls.

In the first-class compartment also were jealous glances not only from the passengers but also from the hostesses that they saw that they are very inferior to those beauties. The pilot himself heard about and came out to welcome them on board. Areus was worried after what he saw he might lose control of his cockpit.

Before leaving, he called the French agent, Marcel, who in the meantime became very friendly; he was to be in person at the airport to welcome them with a huge limousine, like those that one sees in Now York and California.

He asked Marcel that he prefers that he books on his charge, of course, as that was clearly mentioned in the contract, to stay the first days and week in the Four Seasons Hotel (previously was called George V where he stayed also and even worked 50 years ago).

Marcel, despite the descriptions from the Italian guy, as a strict and arrogant type of man, he was very friendly and became even friendlier when he came face to face with these four girls. The man stayed there speechless staring at them for a few seconds looking as if he were in a shocking exceptional admiration situation.

Marcel could not believe that such souls were now on his team. In the limousine, he told him in French so that the girls would not understand that he plans after what he saw to make a new much improved offer that would include the rights for all commercial advertisements in all media. He showed that he was not to accept such a clause, although inside him he was ready to do but needed not to show any enthusiasm as this is a game of bargain and negotiations, a game that he after all these years he knows well to play.

Alex, in Danish, he was mad, saying, "Are you off your head? You want to deny such a new offer?"

He answered in Danish, "Shut up and let me do my job unless you do not like much more money in your bank account." Alex showed 'obedience' and remained cool.

At the lobby of the hotel again those expressions of admiration not only from the director who himself came to welcome them but to all that were in that huge lobby. Marcel had the style of a proud man being the one that those models belong to.

The suite was the presidential one, the girls entering opened their mouths showing that this luxury cannot be true, he gently pushed them softly touching their ass to ask them to enter and not stay there at the door.

Marcel in the suite's living room called his Italian friend and co-partner speaking in Italian, believing that he was the only one in that suite to speak Italian that was a mistake done by him, so he could listen to what Marcel was saying to his partner in Milano and accordingly he would build his negotiation strategy. Indeed, Marcel talking to Giorgio (the Italian agent) confessed that he could never expect such beauties and, always in Italians, that they both will make a fortune out of these four girls especially in New York and California and even more if he could make a deal to include to the contract commercial advertisements.

Well, that is it, now he knows where he stands and how to handle and negotiate with Marcel's new offer to come.

Marcel left them to rest and he will come to fetch them for a super dinner as he called it.

There were three bedrooms in that suite so they all ran to beds as the trip was too long and tiring. Alex, this time acting like a sneaky fox, went down to the concierge to ask where a pharmacy was so he could buy Viagra.

They slept for five hours, the beds were not enough so two of them had to sleep in same bed, of course, not with Alex but with one of the three sisters. Only that soft warm touch of that body was the best sleeping pill.

They all woke up simultaneously and asked the girls to go to the boudoir and take care of their face, lips and especially eyes as that was their irresistible asset.

The girls had to get dressed with the best dresses that Andre selected for them, as the dinner was to be in the best restaurant in Paris the most famous one in Paris and worldwide, Le Fouquet's where all celebrities and all first-class couturiers (fashion designers) is a must to be very often there for their own show off.

This said and apropos Andre was on the phone, asking how things go and also, that was his main interest, what about the boys models the brothers of the girls. He was so eager not only to take photos of them but also bring them to his bed. He promised to deal with this also but first finish the job and in the best way in Paris.

He anyways called Chang asking about this and the answer was that there are five incredibly handsome men, brothers and first-degree relatives of the eight girls, at the age of 19 and 21 all very tall and incredibly good-looking.

OK was the answer, hold them and deal when back in Shanghai.

Chang added "if you wants to know how many of the 20 girls have period delay" of course, that was also a big question mark. He answered

"Hold something stable as you will be shocked to hear the number".

"OK, go ahead. I hold the golden metal bar of the matrimonial bed in my hand." Both him and Alex were in full ears. He said a number, 15.

"Fifteen what?"

"Fifteen probably are pregnant; their period delays."

Silence on both ends that was not easy to swallow, not easy to realise.

After one minute of silence. "OK, keep us informed." They were in such an anxiety to hear if that period delay was coincidence or if these 15 girls were indeed pregnant.

Not to forget that each of the 20 passed twice the sex process. Anyway, let's leave this behind as they were there for another big reason.

The girls finished their makeup, but he was not happy. He called the concierge and asked if the hotel hairdresser is now available, and he got the OK. So, he took the girls to the hairdresser to take care of their coiffure, their makeup and also take care of their nails (manicure). He called Marcel to come one hour later and he explained to him why.

While waiting for the girls to return from the hairdresser he called Japan to hear the four girls. They were more than happy and satisfied with the gentle behaviour of their Japanese agents, they handled them as real Divas. It was then a necessary warning to them not to get involved in any affairs with any Japanese or other men as this and at this stage, will harm their reputation.

They promised that this will not happen and following the given advice they satisfy each other's sexual desire between them. They are more than happy; they were advised also from their agent to better stay in the room until the time comes, and not visit the hotel bar as there are always risky and unforeseen situations that must be avoided by all means.

Their fame has already spread throughout Tokyo and there are many handsome men, sharks, professional seducers especially for inexperienced girls as they are.

The result after they came back from the coiffeur was splendid even the coiffeur himself came up to inform them that he never had the privilege to take care of such ethereal existences.

The girls' image under the French coiffeur's supervision was, couldn't find the correct word or better the actual phrase in any dictionary to describe to describe. The Greek word *optasia* maybe expresses the grade of their beauty.

They dressed well and then the concierge called that the limousine was waiting.

Marcel was already at the restaurant so the driver drove them there, him also looking from his mirror, to see what princesses were in that limo.

They arrived at the famous restaurant, the door opened, the maître welcomed them and took them to the table that Marcel booked. From that door to that table had to walk across maybe 10 tables. What and how many eyes fell upon them were countless; it was the 'apotheosis' of beauty.

Marcel stood up to make a show off, he wanted to show that he is the proprietor of these 'cabochon' diamonds.

There were fashion designers there trying to attract the eye of Marcel to make him understand that they want the priority.

Marcel was in the highest mood, he ordered whatever was the most expensive. The wine came with dust and spiders (that old story was now again there), the most expensive champagne, caviar was to be eaten with a soup spoon.

Such was the abundance and the high spirit at that table was more than obvious. One could watch that ladies that were at other tables made hard efforts to have the men at their table not stare so silly at Marcel's table.

The dinner was over and the limo took them to the hotel while Marcel stayed behind with the style of the emperor of the night. He probably wanted to get unofficial contracts with fashion designers or managers of fashion designers that were there that night.

Back to the suite the temper, the humour, the spirit reached, metaphorically, the top of 'Mount Everest'.

He asked Alex, in Danish, "Are you ready?"

He answered, "Yes, I took one blue pill one hour ago, and I already feel rebellion in my trousers."

"Well, it is time that you take the load off me as all four I cannot handle." The girls were kissing each other; champagne was ordered to keep the mood in its peak. Romantic music was carefully selected to bring an additional amorous atmosphere in combination with the candles with switched off lights.

The elder one (Nicolette that was her artistic given first name), gave a sign to the three sisters to perform a sensual strip tease in front of their 'Knights', because as such they considered them.

The striptease and at the end the nude bodies could wake up dead man from his tomb, such was the degree of the temptation. The finale was the four graces to turn around, bend and allow the full sign of the four gorgeous asses as if they were made from the creator from the one and the only same matrix.

Their anus were absolute immaculate gems. The tits were to be seen between the two legs and a small shimmer of the nipples joined a painter's masterpiece. Who could be that painter to convey what he sees on his canvas? No other than a painter with the skills of the unique Sandro Botticelli.

The striptease dance concluded a charming and unrepeatable first performing theatrical part, but the 'theatre curtains' did not fall and the second part unrolled. This time it was the two and only men to make a striptease for them but with their participation unbuttoning button by button, zipper down until all was thrown on the floor. The well-received surprise and with laughter came from the four girls seeing the hard penis of Alex.

There was a small 'quarrel', a bickering which of the two will go with Alex and which of the other two with him until the agreement was settled rather to his favour.

The two beds in the two bedrooms were ready to complain as they knew that heavy anomalies were to take place on them. If they had a voice they would shout, "Will you please behave?"

The poor beds they had absolute right, they felt like Hew Heffner and their bunnies but in a much more advantageous situation for the only two present men to be the enjoyers of an orgy.

The night was full of surprises he needed to reveal all his experiences of all those years. In the luxury bedrooms, excessive lust was dangled in the air, fingers, tongues, Vaseline and hard cocks were the actual protagonists to the sex carousel, the happy end emphasised and metaphorically 'sealed' the perpetual relieves and total climaxes' fulfilment.

Deep sleep was requested and that was the conclusion of the turbulent night, so an idle sleep is more than needed.

Next early morning, if 10 o'clock could be considered as 'early', they had a very rich breakfast in the suite and more than 25 croissants they consumed as that was and will be the specialty of the ex-George V Hotel pâtissier.

Around 12, Marcel was in the lobby, he reserved one small meeting room in the hotel so that they could talk about the contract and the extensions he wanted to add.

The submitted offer was unexpectedly high adding all the French, but not American, commercial advertisements in all Medias with the four girls for one year and a half year for the 'astronomic' amount of 2 million. Well, they had to hide any enthusiasm to be able to negotiate.

He suggested to Marcel 2.5 million including American commercial advertisements for only perfumes, branded creams, ladies branded bags, famous watches and jewellery for 1.5 years.

Marcel remains sceptical; the amount was huge but the incentive was also tempting. He asked for a one hour break to perceive the proposed deal.

He came back and offered his hand to shake and the deal was done but he added for the commercial advertisements must also add products such as: soaps, toothpastes, and chocolates. They gave their consent but making clear that if they see advertisement's with other prodders the contract will be cancelled with no money refund. He knew that he was in front of a gold mine and it was not in his interest to degrade it.

The lawyer was at his office waiting for the changes and after 30 minutes the changes were done. They made it clear that the same moment that they sign, the same moment they'll see the funds deposited to their Hong Kong bank. Marcel through his laptop transferred the funds and the funds were to be seen to the bank so the contract was signed.

Everybody was glad champagne was there to drink and the atmosphere was celebratory. They approached Marcel telling him that they will have to fly back to Shanghai tomorrow and asked him tomorrow to bring the girls to a major bank and each one to open a private account so that they could transfer their money.

All was settled, the girls are in the right hands of a very serious and professional agent who will do all to have the girls to have big success so that he will also have his investment well paid.

The next morning the goodbye was an emotional pain. To part from those girls that they consider them as guardians, protectors but also at the same time as lovers, is not so easy. They all had to make their heart stone not to break and leave as fast as possible as both parties had tears in their eyes.

The next day, they were in Shanghai and this time stay for good with Angel and Melissa needing not any more to invent stories and excuses.

In two days was the inauguration of the Spartan restaurant and they must all be there to assist for a most successful opening.

Giannis was conducting the staff impeccably and it all worked like a well-functioning team. Giannis had Christos standby to see how the first two days will run, so that he will load new supplies and fly by air.

At the same time, he took the initiative and in cooperation with Sophia to ask the office staff to locate pork stock-farmers and bring them on the spot so they could see if they could produce the gyros and the souvlaki meat for them in China.

So, they had nothing to do, all was done by Giannis and his assistants and he felt justified for bringing Giannis and making him leader of the project.

The day came, Angel and Melissa had the task to welcome the customers and the customers start coming and coming and coming, the telephone started ringing for orders for home deliveries and kept ringing. There was a long queue, this is no good as they will after all get tired and leave, but what could they do? No one was anticipating any such a success and any such crowd.

He made a fast decision, those at the end of the queue, they for sure will not be served, they got a catalogue with Giannis' signature and they could get a free meal delivered to their home. There were 60 such free meals but they left with a big 'thank you' and that was done for the first time in China to offer free meals just for not being able to serve them.

All staff reached their limits but as the comments were more than excellent this somehow reduced the tiredness. Giannis rushed to his laptop to order fast new supplies to come from Greece by air. They did not care what it will cost, the important thing was to have satisfied customers and the profits will come, it is not now the time to check if there were profits or not.

After all the customers left and the tavern was well cleaned they gave to all staff an extra bonus appreciating the fact that they worked with good mood and devotion to their duty.

The next day, they expected four suppliers from different stock-farms that will see what they import from Greece and see if they could do this locally and at what cost they must create for the future of the Spartan taverns a Chinese supply chain.

He asked Giannis to order one small 20 feet container filled up with gyros meat and as far as this comes deep-frozen must be shipped in fridge vessel.

So, they will have one container on the way by sea and fly smaller quantities until that container arrives in one month. In the meantime, they work for local production of all except the feta cheese that they will need to have in that same ship but in normal fridge and not in the deep-frozen section as the feta cheese comes in barrels with water to keep always fresh.

Their partner Sophia was extremely happy that this Spartan project seems to be a very promising one and she also went home for a good sleep.

Alex was tired but also satisfied that all projects that he follows are all going so well and far away from any expectations.

Angel and Melissa standing all the time were tired so they went home to have a good night sleep without any other 'occupation'.

The next day the three partners met at the office to recap what happened yesterday to the opening day. The satisfaction was obvious to all of them, even to Sophia who was from the very beginning the one to have doubts about the success of such a tavern in China.

They also called Giannis to come to the meeting so they get his actual report and hear what he believes that has to be improved. He was positive in all aspects that not any changes were needed, he only asked if they could hire his girlfriend to be the head of the waitresses as he wanted to have his mind clear and dedicated to the job, they all approved with not a single objection.

Angel and Melissa are not needed anymore as they also had to put all efforts and strength to get their diploma.

So, the tavern project is entirely in the good hands of Giannis and then literally was not needed there at all.

Chang called again reminding us that he has the five handsome young men between 18 and 20, standby to come to Shanghai.

They asked him to wait two–three days as they had to do market research to see what the demand for men models is. Undoubtedly the appropriate person for this was Andre.

Andre's opinion was that in Japan such boys who have the mixed features of Chinese and Western have less opportunities as Japanese were never too friendly with the Chinese, while they tend to forget if it is to concern girls or women. So, for the boys Europe is the right market, they have to contact their good friend Marcel and see if there is interest.

He called Chang again, asking him if there is any professional photographer to take nice photos of the boys and see how they will deal and also locate the possible interest.

He called Marcel asking how things would go with his four girls and if he opened for them the bank accounts and in that case, he needed the Iban, so he would transfer their money. He also asked him if he is interested in handsome boys' models of 1.85 height brothers and first-degree relatives to his four girls, same origin, and same eyes. He said yes but the market for male fashion shows models is limited but there is still a market.

Marcel added that for the four girls, he cleverly created a mystery fame around them, and the major managers of the big designers' houses started to ask persistently about these Sino-European girls. He has a strategy to hide them from the eyes of these sharks. He let the fame go around, create anxiety and expectations and then reveal them widely. "Well, Marcel, you are a real and best 'fucking' agent." He laughed and confirmed that in three hours, he will send by email the Iban numbers of the bank accounts of the four girls and copies of their passports.

After all these busy weeks he had to call Karla to see how the pregnancy goes as this is a serious obligation and he must in no case neglect and show to Karla that he does not show his serious interest.

The pregnancy goes well and he will also soon know how the cute Chinese virgins' pregnancies go as that is also a vital issue of direct concern.

Three months passed since those sexual encounters with the 20 virgins, so Chang must know by now the actual situation.

Chang concluded that nine finally are pregnant, so their fertility was excellent and descendance was planted in that community, but there is also bad news.

Chang asked him if he also fucked Sanrai the supervisor lady. He had to confess that he did not fuck her but she fucked him after she was present to all the virgins' sexual intercourses and she probably was tormented with sex desire, to such an extent that she could not resist to the temptation having all that relentless fucking parade in front of her eyes. She also confessed that she wanted to live the same experience like her daughter, so how to deny?

He said but that caused a huge problem as she is also pregnant and was kicked out of her home by her husband who anyway was an abrasive and harsh person treating her badly, she was always trying to endure the hardship of that tyrant husband.

The city hall council expelled her from the community to a kind of exile, as there was a superstition that those two 'blessed' foreigners must not have any sex encounter with a non-virgin woman as they wanted descendants from pure virgin girls and not from a woman of her age, having already obligatory sex several times by her brutal husband, and what will come out will be uncertain and probably not 100% original.

Chang said that he drove there and picked her up and she will live with him as he is single and apparently, he likes her a lot and he will adopt that baby as if it will be his own.

Areus unable to say anything hearing this unexpected fact, he thanked him a lot for his brave and emotional behaviour and he will not forget this.

Chang answered that he will be proud to have a son or daughter that will have the fundamental superb Sino-European characteristics.

Given this he felt an obligation to do something for Chang to create for him and Sanrai a very comfortable living. That could be done by making him partner to a new company that will promote on the worldwide fashion show business those handsome boys.

Alex fully agreed and praised Chang for what he did and they have to reciprocate to him all his cooperation and his kindness he showed to Sanrai.

The Spartan tavern has a great impact on an extensive area and new repeated orders for supplies follow the one after the other. Local suppliers came showing samples done and are very close to have the 100% food supplies done in China that will save a lot of money and shipping costs. The two major suppliers that will be selected will have to sign binding contracts with very strict clauses that they will exclusively supply to the Spartan taverns.

They expect to have the official tests reports that are according to the FDA and LFGB food grade standards and then only they make the contracts.

At the same time the real estate agent was instructed to search for a good spot for the second Spartan as this seems to be imperative if a chain of such taverns is to be the next step towards the franchising and a new 'modus operandi'.

Chang sent photos of the boys which they conveyed to Andre for his experienced judgement. Chang showed haste as it was promised to him that he will be a partner for this new company.

While them, Alex and him, found so much free time and having Angel and Melissa at the lessons they went up to the building's spa for a relaxing massage.

They were welcomed by the two Romanian masseuses and straight to the two single private rooms for the massage. The Romanian woman, of maybe 30 years of age, commanded, this is the word, commanded not asked, to take all clothes off and lay on his belly to that bed with a hole for the head. He felt a kind of thick sticky oil fall on his back that reminded a Nuru massage. She started with a kind of Shiatsu with pressure on all single spots of his back including his buttocks.

That manual physiotherapy pressure emphasised the tired body and thighs. The therapist masseuse one more time characteristically 'commanded' to stay there and not move while there was a pause and she returned.

He felt the bed to 'protest' from extra weight and that 'protest' was justified as she was with her whole body on top of his back. He felt her breasts starting a 'body massage'.

The breasts were soft, natural not any silicone and the nipples were hard, while her tits were on his back, her hand was caressing his testicles and asked him to lift up a little to bring the penis to be seen between the two legs somehow tilted and she caressed that with her unusual way always to outline that she is the boss, the commander and he had to obey.

Her hand was further excavated until one finger reached his anus and with an oily body that finger was easy to go in. He thought what the hell is she, lesbian, she will what fuck him or what?

But the whole was so expertly done that did not annoy at all on the contrary the combination of penis plus testicles plus anus in addition to the breasts massage, manage to bring a euphoria and the inevitable hardest possible penis being in that position started to feel uncomfortable as if the penis 'will break'.

He adjusted the lower part of his body as the erection hardened too much so he had to turn little on one side.

She knew well and with a fierce one more time or better savage way she turned him around and with not a second loss she started an extravagant masturbation same time looking with a rigorous look straight to his eyes, she wanted to feel the minute that she had to abandon the masturbation and proceed to the next phase.

Having her now in front of him, he could see her body and enjoy the exposure of such an extraordinarily well-shaped body with a six-pack abdomen, but her eyes were always so severe and not a slight shadow of a smile.

All suddenly in a magic way without even holding the hard penis she mounted on top aiming straight a penis intimately merging to her flexible pussy and softly she pressed herself to feel and enjoy the warmth of her vagina. Her eyes threw a gaze to him but this time there was at last a soft and a desireful smile to be revealed.

Breaths and heartbeats were on the peak the sexual flow state was approaching. She was a 'sex maestro'; she knew when the time was there for her to come in accurate and consensual status, coordinating his and her orgasm to be more intense.

That moment came to his surprise, it seemed that she lost the discipline and control and allowed to herself to explode with a loud screaming that for sure was heard also outside of that room. She did not care and never stopped until she felt inside her the flow of the ejaculated sperm.

That strong, hard and severe face revealed that in specific moments of erotic explosion a woman's face could be transformed to an angelic one even if that woman before the encounter had the air of a shrewish woman. She bends and kisses him passionately whispering into his ear, "I could not imagine a man of your age to bring me in such a gorgeous climax, climax that I very seldom enjoy with many of my customers. Your persistent duration did this." This said, he felt proud and overconfident of his performance but at the same time of his tactical capabilities.

Well, that whole was a porn highly upgraded episode, because that was a sexual episode of extreme charm that many cannot even live to their wildest fantasies.

He asked for her name, and she said, "Luana."

Oh God he had so nice memories from another Romanian name Luana who was a student in the University of Bucharest to become an architect and she only was coming in summer to Athens to make some selected sex encounters from already known customers for the last two years and this she did only for her shopping.

Luana was crazy with the good sex they enjoyed together and was happy when he was booking her for two hours. Usually, girls refuse to proceed to any blowjob without a condom but she did this without, and exceptionally for him.

He asked that Romanian new Luana if she is well paid, she answered, no not at all as the owner is a very miserable Chinese guy who pays peanuts and he does not invest some money to upgrade the spa which is located in the best possible neighbourhood.

He asked her if she wanted to work for him and she answered, of course, without a single doubt you look exceptionally gentle and gallant.

OK then what you have to do is go to that owner, who knows that you have no capital and cannot pay much and, and he cannot figure out that there is a backup buyer, suggest to him that you, the two Romanian girls, want to buy the spa, so that she will see what this guy is demanding. She agreed and seemed so happy that something at last maybe will change in that neglected and obviously declining spa and gym with only few members.

That would be an excellent opportunity to find the spa ready adding the appropriate gym and fitness equipment, hammam and sauna and a big pool; there was sufficient space for this, adding aerobic lessons and more facilities that will attract the high-class clientele.

Angel and Melissa were almost about to give the final examinations to get the desirable diploma that will facilitate things and obtain the licence for the spa and run it the right way.

In that case, they keep the two Romanian girls in certain private 'pink' room in case erotic massage is requested but without advertising such a service so to prevent damaging the reputation of the spa.

Additionally hire two male personal trainers and his idea, as explained to Alex, who by the way was the main investor, was to bring two Geishas from Japan which will offer something really new, special and exclusive.

So, Angel the manager, Melissa doing the professional massage but not erotic, two male trainers for the gym plus the two Romanians will do all kinds of massages and then the exceptional treatment of those Geishas.

A ladies' massage department will be added and one skilful for all ladies demanding male masseur and physical therapist and tanning. Preferably European masseur will complete an ultra-modern and complete spa-massage, fitness and gym, maybe the best in that extended residential area.

That project might become reality and professionally restore Angel and Melissa to a business that has a promising future but also turn the job to a well-paid one for the two Romanian girls.

After that fabulous 'massage plus extras' a good sleep must be in program and that was very easy just the lift will take them to their apartments and sleep in peace having still on their dicks the sweet smell of the Romanian vaginas.

Their girls returned from their lessons and found their two guys in deep sleep and they respected that with silence and no noises and disturbance.

Chang promptly forwarded the photos of the boys directly to Andre, with a copy of the boys' photo to them. Exact to Chang's description, they possessed the allure of movie stars, enhanced by the distinctive feature of having both Chinese and European heritage, adding a unique and special quality to their appearance.

Andre answered right away that he needs at least one of the boys to see closely and also make a first walking performance because being handsome does not ensure also nice masculine fashion show walkway ability.

Chang agreed to send first the one boy and they sent him the tickets to come and stay at a nearby hotel and according to the judgment of Andre they decided about the rest of the boys. Andre was sent to welcome him at the airport and bring him to them and then to the nearby hotel.

They arrived at the apartment where Alex also came and what they see, this young man could be the new James Bond. He had something of the French star Alain Delon. About 1.85 tall, Sino-European and has a very attractive innocent smile.

Andre was shocked he asked if he could provide host lodging at his apartment. They definitely denied this, as they knew why he wanted him in his apartment and it is not nice for a pure and timid boy to be introduced to the anomalies of Andre. A repeat story with that masculine cook passed by Andre's 'crooked' mind.

They accompanied him to his hotel and next day they arranged to get him and they all go to the atelier of Andre for photos and some simple rehearsals.

Andre already prepared the whole setting so both photos and video will look impressive. The boy was charismatic, he had a proud walk and that added to him extra confidence and superiority value. Andre insisted on taking photos with a tiny kind of thong—a men's brief, so as to allow the emerging of his penis and testicles to be seen, probably that he wanted for his private collection.

The son of the bitch, he wanted to see and estimate his hidden under that tiny string type of swim pant the rich and in abundance virtues. Indeed, almost naked that boy looked like Apollo or Adonis, the two ancient Greek Gods of beauty and desire.

His body was not any of those six-pack heavy trained men's bodies, obtained by heavy weights, bars and gym apparatus in addition to kind of drugs to inflate their muscles, but was a body anatomically perfectly shaped and naturally trained, as he explained after hard working at the father's farm.

This training in nature reminded him of Stallone when he was trained before fighting the Russian boxer, in Siberia, not in a gym but carrying on his shoulders heavy tree logs and cutting down with a simple axe big tree trunks.

Andre seemed ready to almost pounce on him, they held him back as for a moment the innocent boy got a scared look. They asked him to rapidly get dressed as they leave and asked Andre in two hours to bring printed photos and videos to the apartment. Hoping that Angel and Melissa will not yet be there, because seeing that young man they also would have been excited and this might be an unpredictable threat.

Andre came with extra sexy dresses showing his desire to attract the attention of the boy. The photos were great, so also the video and particularly the one where the boy was almost naked so Andre was justified to ask him to get naked and put on a small string type of swim pants.

He called Marcel's office to see if he was there, indeed he was and he explained to him about the five boys and if he is willing to see photos and video.

The answer was, "After the unbelievable success I have with the Alexander girls, of course, I am." And the photos and video were mailed to him right away.

Only ten minutes passed, and he was on the phone, and the question was, "How much? I want them all?"

He cleverly answered that he first awaits the answer of the Japanese and then he will be able to set up the price. The answer was angry, "Fuck the Japanese. I want the boys each for 200,000 for a one-year contract, including commercial advertisements in the media."

He intentionally showed no enthusiasm and answered sorry, I have to wait. He promised to wait for their offer and he gave his word and he won't break his word, so to show that he is a responsible person. Marcel was upset, he said, "Whatever they offer to you, I bid with 15% more." OK then, they know in two days and goodbye for now. Marcel added that he appreciates that he keeps his word, this means professionalism.

He called Chang to know that the four boys are of the same standard as the one who first came, and he assured them that they are indeed the same as if they were quadruplets. That is good and they shall know in three days, Chang was the one to be more interested as he will be partner in the new company for the boys' management.

The time was passing and the Spartan tavern was booming as a new trendy concept, and soon there will be a second one and a third and who knows how many more. It is clear that the profits will be seen after the second tavern starts the operation as then only, with the economies of scale, due to the fact that all raw materials are made in China and the internal function reaches its peak.

Luana, the Romanian masseuse called him asking to meet him not in the spa that she works at but to a nearby cafeteria type of shop.

Indeed, he went there to meet her, she told him that she asked the owner if he sells his spa and he with rather a relief answered yes showing that for him and his age this spa is a burden.

The price that he asked was ridiculous not for the space as this is not owned by him but for all the equipment and his clientele, which indeed was a long list but most left as they could not find there is a big number of equipment and exercise units to have a complete program.

Here is a big chance as the spa's place was unique at the peak, last floor, of a big building with hundreds of apartments and surrounded by maybe 50 equally big apartment blocks. Overlooking the city, the space was immense, allowing expansion and more fittings to be added, even making a quite big hammam type of pool.

They agreed that they give her the money but before that she will sign a contract that she acts as intermediate and the spa belongs to Alex and himself and she will be hired as an employee with a double salary to what she had now.

This was must to be done this way simply because if he sees that there are foreign investors he then might even double his requirements. He even asked her to beg him and bargain saying that she and the other Romanian masseuses do not have so much money and this just to show that indeed they are the buyers and their money is not enough to pay what he requires.

So, it was done, the lawyer prepared the simple contract and she went back to the old owner to play a begging game pretending that she and Alina, the other Romanian girl cannot gather the money he is asking and in order to proceed a discount is necessary of the initially offered selling price.

It worked, as he was so tired of running the place, he did not have any children to take over and he was about to lose it anyway as he owed three consecutive rents.

Luana came back announcing that the price is even better. They signed the contract with her and at the same time they gave her another contract that the owner must sign and the two Romanian girls Luana and Alina. The money was given and the contracts were signed. The owner gave the keys and left rather happily that he at last got rid of that business that he was not able to run.

A second game must also be played, this time the two girls with the actual owner of the property of the spa. He luckily was a customer in that spa and Alina was giving him quite often super erotic massages and he was kind of in love with her.

So, again, Alina this time and Luana approached the owner saying that they will take over the spa and showed him the contract. He was also happy as the previous owner owed him three monthly rents and he was sure that he would never be able to pay that debt.

Alina played it smart, asking for a good rent and they both one time per month and for free they will offer to him a trio massage with all the erotic tricks that he asked before but were not given and as he was a horny type, he heard that with big satisfaction and the rent was even lowered.

They agreed that they would come back tomorrow with the contract to sign. The lawyer made again two contracts one that binds the girl to transfer to them the renting agreement and another contract for them to sign with the owner and there were in small letters written that the girls are allowed to transfer this to third person or company the signed contract.

The girls signed took the money adding two monthly rents as deposit and that owner only with the phantasy of having both girls to offer to him a magic trio erotic massage signed without even reading the contract.

So, now Alex and he made a new company as an objective to run fitness centrer all over China. They did not want yet to announce to Angel and Melissa about this as they first wanted to turn this to a luxury super modern fitness centre and then add them both as partners to the company.

And the name of it will be 'Angel's Fitness-Spa and Gym'. What they need here is another Giannis, so the person who immediately came to their mind was Andre.

The meeting was fixed at the nearby cafeteria and they announced that he will become a partner at the most modern Spa in Shanghai. He was enthusiastic to hear this being sure with all his connections this Spa will become Number one in Shanghai.

Money is available for him to hire the best interior decorator and order all the fitness equipment, sauna and steam bath, new showers and toilets as well as locker room to change the whole and upgrade the Spa to first class.

It took four weeks and indeed that was a spa that one does not see even in America or Europe, the pool was quite big and all was ready to have the spa to get new members.

The next day, they invited Angel and Melissa to follow them for a massage to the last floor spa, not knowing yet that they are partners and that it was fundamental.

When the lift reached the last floor Andre was there and the two Romanian girls to applaud the two girls, a red ribbon was there and two scissors were given to them to cut the ribbon. They stood there stunned, not knowing what was happening.

They kissed them, telling them this is your dream that now became true.

They jumped up to the air, cut the ribbon and stepped inside, seeing and not believing that the almost abandoned Spa is now a super deluxe fitness centre.

New staff was employed all done with best of care, by Andre, personal trainers also that boy who was sent from Chang helped until they see where he and the rest of the young men will end up in Paris or Japan.

Not to forget that Luana promised that she will never reveal to Angel that they had a sexual massage a few weeks ago, that will be kept as their sealed secret.

The next day, first to the lawyer to make the new company formation including Angel, Melissa and Andre and then to the advertising agency to prepare the first leaflet that will be sent to maybe 1 million nearby apartments and all under the supervision of the experienced eyes of Andre. Another wise decision to add him as partner to the company.

The opening day was fixed in 12 days so that all staff will be accustomed to the new fitness equipment but also the actual role of each one.

Angel and Melissa are the bosses of the Angel's Fitness-Spa and Gym, so they will give to each one of the staff their duties and the frames that they will be limited in. It was agreed that there will be an isolated room for offering special massage but that to only very few and selected members and that must remain in full confidential cover so that the reputation of the fitness centre will not be harmed.

Of course, things will show how this could operate and offer such a service to VIP's but under total secrecy. Luana and Alina will still provide their good massage and if an erotic one is requested then Angel and Melissa have to handle this cleverly and confidentially.

They asked our friend agent in Japan who has the first four girls under his guidance to see if there is any possibility to send 1 or two Geishas to Shanghai to join and enlarge the horizons of the Angel's Fitness-Spa and Gym.

The question is, will it also be a new chain of spas and be spread to all neighbourhoods of Shanghai and not only? The first months will show if something big could come out of it. Because his motto always is 'Think Big'.

The delivery of the baby from Karla is approaching and he as the father must be there. Alex agreed to come as he also wanted to see some of his relatives.

All projects are under close supervision; the only thing that is pending is the future of that handsome young man who Chang sent over. At the beginning, until they see about his fashion show future, he will offer his services at the fitness centre, as the Chinese ladies but basically the foreign women who stay in Shanghai, are crazy to have this Apollo looking young man to treat their body and they are afraid that it will be the ladies to look and ask after erotic massage from this handsome stallion.

The day came to take the plane for Copenhagen and there they were. Called Karla and that very day she was admitted to the maternity ward, so a taxi brought them both there. It was a very touching moment to meet Mathilde waiting outside the maternity ward. It was a moment of embarrassment, was it her to slap his face? Or hug him. She also did not know what comes first. The hug was chosen, a very warm hug and tears on her eyes were falling on both her cheeks.

She did not want to let him loose from her hug until she said something in his ears in Danish that was well known from him and that was 'I love you'. They sat there in complete silence not a word, he just introduced Alex to her as his best friend.

Nurse came out saying that it is on the way and that there are not any complications. He was in a very unusual and awkward situation, what happened was only written in the Greek Mythology. Bringing to pregnancy the daughter of his beloved girl, not an often complication to happen and is absolutely nonfictional.

But that was now in second priority, important is that his son and Karla will be in perfect health.

Doctor came out looking at him and he recognised right away that he must be the father and asked him as well as the mother to come in. Karla did not know that he was there and when she saw him next to her mother, she had a shock but having the baby in her arms that was immediately forgotten. The baby boy was identical to him, dark-skinned but had the blue eyes of Karla.

He was looking at the baby without knowing what to do, kiss Karla or take the baby in his arms. Karla made this easier and held the baby and asked him to take the baby boy in his arms. That fragile small creature undoubtedly was his son but that mother on that bed was not his wife while the mother of the mother was once his beloved woman. Only the Greek dramatist Euripides could imagine and write such a 'scenario'.

He had to kiss the mother and she warmly welcomed this kiss, then her mother showing a big pure smile also kissed her showing that she is happy and there is not anything to disturb the playfulness of happiness in that room.

The baby boy was so silent not a single cry but looking deep into his eyes, as he was the first after his mother to stare at, as if he wanted to tell him, well now you have a second son. Doctors asked them to leave the mother to have rest and so also the baby.

Mathilde was asking him about his life, she wanted to know all about him.

So, he told her about his family and his adventures. It was obvious in her eyes, a darkness probably she could bring in her mind that if she was not to leave those old days for that badminton tour, being angry to get to know that he was cheating on her, she could be his wife and mother of their children. But fate and destiny turned things upside down. He told her that he will stay in Copenhagen one or two weeks until Karla and baby are home.

She had an unexpected question, if he wanted to give the name to the boy. Of course, he wanted that as nothing else in the world, but he allowed an astonishment to be seen, saying let Karla return home and they all then discuss about.

They left the hospital; Alex invited him to stay at his home as he has a huge apartment and he stays alone. He accepted but his mind was not there was in a blur trying to realise what he has done and what he has to do from now on. Cannot allow that boy to have his old father far away and never be there on his birthdays, but at the same time he has a wife, a son and two daughters in Greece. That was a complicated puzzle that had no easy solution.

He never talked to Alex about this story, hearing that he looked at him as if he were a monster, he explained to him that he was not the bad guy but Karla seduced him.

He answered, "OK, what is done is done, but do not dare to look after Emma or Lorna or that 22-year-old girl who you sneakily took her virginity."

He, with difficulty, assured him that he will not do this. There were two things that had to be done, one to visit and see the tennis club to see how they are doing and second go to that hotel and see how Nicolas turned this around.

They enjoyed a nice Danish dinner after a long time, asking him not to go to that family restaurant so as to avoid any encounter with Lorna because then all will learn about it.

The next day, they went to the tennis club and they all were so happy to see them again. The tennis courts were all full of players and the owners improved the installations adding a sauna and a small but well-equipped gym. They showed their gratitude and also brought him to see that one of the tennis courts bear his name.

There he also met those mature ladies that he was their instructor for a small period of time and they also were so happy to see him again and gave him a small demonstration of their tennis game progress plus tight hugs allowing their nipples to pierce his chest.

The owners insisted for lunch and they took them to that family restaurant with their car. He could not tell them in time 'no please not there' as he had no persuasive excuse why not and so there they were. He was praying that not any Lorna or maybe other nurses will come as there were quite a few that had repeated intercourses with him the last year.

Thank God, the restaurant was almost empty so there was not any possible face to face meeting with those nurses, nevertheless they were almost just next door and any 'unwanted' meeting could occur.

The tennis owners and friends were telling stories about the legendary victory at that tournament and all Danish old guys were upset, how they allowed a Greek who came from nowhere to beat them.

The joy on that table was great, jokes as this is his specialty, brought laughter, wine brought mood. He was narrating all the businesses he did in his life, all the ups and downs, all the adventures, all the love stories and what he is still doing and what he will keep doing, as the thirst for new things is still there.

They were all amazed. "Well, what the hell are you? A four-in-one man? A James Cook together with an Odyssey? A Midas, who whatever he touches turns to gold? A Casanova?"

Alex intervened at this specific moment, saying, "Well, what you describe about him is still not enough to portray him."

Then, bells rang, he saw who entered the restaurant door together with a young man of approximately the same age. That was the 22-year-old who took her virginity, he even forgot her name. He tried to bend his face so she could not recognise him but in vain, she not only recognised him but also rushed to come to his table hugged and kissed him tactfully and discreetly, at the same time introducing her brother.

He could detect in her eyes memories to pass as a parade to what exquisite happened in that VIP apartment. Frankly, it also passed through his mind that she was also not to announce to him that he is father as he remembered that they were not that cautious, but not any such announcement happened.

She gave him her phone number so that they could have dinner together. She wanted that so much that she made this show clearly with an almost begging face. Before leaving, he went to her table and whispered into her ear, "Please do not say anything to Emma." She replied that she left to Sweden deciding to bring her marriage back again.

That was a real relief for him as he could not forget the ferocity of her demanding sex, which, of course, he did not dislike at all; on the contrary, he was looking for that as an interval from the usual and many soft and gentle sex intercourses; from time to time a 'barbarian' sex wakes hidden wishes.

The next day, they took Alex's car, and they went to see the hotel that his relative, Nicolas, was running. The changes he did, the reforms he did, the new ideas he brought, turned a sleeping and sinking hotel to a hotel and, even more, the restaurant to a famous one. They arrived there at about lunchtime, and the restaurant was not only full but there were five families were making the queue, waiting for others to leave so they could take their table.

He embraced Nicolas, who was not expecting him; it was a surprise visit. He apologised for not having an available table, but they told him later as he also wanted to see the reception to see how many bookings there were. The hotel was 95% full, and these 5% were those 'pink' rooms with the porno TV, but even those they booked for three hours later and had a full house.

He had kept the maître, whom he managed to turn into a very happy man with a hearty smile—a totally new man. Probably, the full restaurant brought good money to his pocket and gave him a boost and metamorphosed him into a maître d' hotel who deserves the credits of the good service and the good tips. Apparently, he was surrounded by two beautiful young waitresses who also had a pleasing appearance.

Nicolas changed all the kitchen staff and followed his advice to have new boys and girl cooks from the hotel school, and they did a great job as he was telling him. Every day, with teamwork, they were improving the quality and the variety of the dishes that customers were so much tempted to come again and again, and some even almost every day.

He kept the chambermaid and added one more equally beautiful and all came from a good source: the hotel school. Step by step, but with no tactless increases, he was changing the prices so as to turn the whole into a profitable enterprise.

He called Arne already from there, telling him what he has in front of his eyes; Arne had no words to thank him, and he announced that he would suggest to Nicolas to become partner and get a good stake of shares, and if they decide, then sell it for good money so Nicolas will also have a good capital for his whatever future initiatives and plans.

They left Nicolas, and he was so happy that this ended so perfectly well and that he gave the opportunity to Nicolas to show his capabilities but at the same time open for him new horizons.

At that certain point, an idea woke up his mind to open a restaurant in Cannes, where among many fresh delicacies, live lobsters would fly from Greece, also the best in the world Greek boutargue will be served, plus among others, the Greek smoked cheese 'Metsovone' that won many awards and the Greenland smoked reindeer.

Nicolas was to be the major partner, and it might become a next-to-come project after Arne returns, and they had to decide what they would do: keep or sell the hotel. So, let this Cannes restaurant be parked in the project's warehouse.

Tuppi called, saying that the Bras de Ferre tournament was to take place in 15 days.

He told Tuppi that he might be there for the tournament but maybe not as he has many ongoing businesses to follow.

The next day, he had to go to Karla's home as she would be returning from the hospital with the baby. There was to face a heavily loaded sentiment and emotions as a father due to an 'illegal' or, better, abnormal relation that created responsibilities. For the sake of accountability, he was willing to take over not only for Karla but also for the boy.

He was heartily welcomed by both Mathilde and Karla; the boy was a very quiet baby but with the brilliant eyes of his mother. The more he was looking at him, the more he became softer and vulnerable to emotion. Karla took the initiative to talk, as they all were silent; she admitted that the mistake was all hers, and he was in no case to be blamed as it was not him to seduce her but the opposite. The only thing she asked from him was to come from time to time to see his son so the son also knows that there is a father and he is not an orphan.

This was promised not as an obligation but as a wish because he would like to see the boy grow and spend some time with him until the day comes that he will know the whole truth.

Karla also asked him what name he wished to give to him as this was a right that belonged to him. His theory was always that the good name follows always a boy and later a man to his whole life, so the name must have a certain gravity and such a name is Alexander, whole name and not cut to Alex. Alexander refers also to Greece and is euphonic, and this will make him proud to carry such a glorious name. They both seemed to like it a lot, and this was agreed.

He told them that he has enough money to support them, but they denied as they were very rich, after selling the factory.

Time came for him to leave; he kissed both and took the boy into his arms and kissed him with small tears, while the boy was looking at him with wide eyes, as if he were trying to explore his father's eyes. That boy will be the ideal combination of north and south with blue eyes and black hair with darker skin; he will be chased by many Danish girls in his teen years.

This time, he gave the correct telephone number so they could call him whenever they want and promised to be back soon.

He was always in telephone communication with his own family, telling them where he was, so that they feel not worried.

There are now two opinions: either he goes to Nuuk for the Bras de Ferre tournament or he returns to Shanghai for the inauguration day of the spa, which will be a quite big event in the town. He chose the latter as that was so important for Angel, Melissa but also for Andre.

Before returning, he could not resist the temptation to call Pia, the 22-year-old girl who because of him she was not anymore virgin. He called and got a very sweet response, inviting him to come to her home where she lives with another girlfriend, three to four years elder.

He took a taxi, without telling anything to Alex, and there he was in Pia's home, where he was well received by her but also by her girlfriend. That girlfriend seemed to him to have a rough face, indicating that probably she is gay, and she fucks Pia in her lesbian way; he was in front of an intricate situation.

Karin, that was her name, had an aggressiveness in her words, knowing that this old guy stole the virginity of her obedient girl lover and wanting to show in that room that she is the only one to fuck Pia, while Pia was imprisoned under her tight and persistent siege.

It seemed to him that since the last time that he had that intercourse with Pia, she found protection and sexual satisfaction with that masculine-looking dynamism of a dominant lesbian.

He was somehow feeling that he was in a hostile living room, Pia looking at him with a scaring glance, and before talking, she had to look at Karin as if she were asking for permission; she was totally subdued.

There were drinks served, music was on, and Karin threw rugging angular looks to both him and Pia. Karin stood up, starting dancing in a peculiar way without any feminism but with an extremely well-trained body that one could see even behind her tight shirt, her six-pack abdomen.

Pia joined her in that dance and always with a submissive way, so he had in front of him a 100% lesbian dance. Karin was angrily staring at him as if she wanted to tell him, 'Do not hope for any intercourse with Pia. I am the boss here, and she belongs to my appropriation. I am the dominant here, and Pia is submissive to my total wills and desires; is this clear?'

But Pia became wildly horny, and she got rid of Karin's embrace and rushed to him fast, unbuttoning his trousers and the already hard penis was exploring her mouth, and at the same time, she tossed down all her dresses to remain completely naked. Karin did not lose a single minute and knelt down starting to lick Pia's vagina showing not a least interest for his sexual organ already in the mouth of her submissive sex servant.

Pia turned around and started passionately kissing Karin, and at the same time, skilfully, she managed to get her also nude. That body of Karin was the same as this kick boxer ladies, hard muscles all over and a bush of hair around her vagina, so as to differ from Pia. Karin wanted to display the similarity of the men's looking bush of hair around their dick.

Having Pia turned around, it was so easy to get his penis in her vagina, a safe sanctuary, her having the joy to be fucked by both of them, as Karin stopped the kisses and demonstrated her pussy to be licked by Pia.

The whole thing was a scene that he never experienced in his long sexual life. What he now wanted and wanted badly was to find a way to get behind Karin, but that was not so easy, she threw blinks of wild denial. But with a juggler's acrobatic jump, and at warp speed, there he was behind her muscular bum.

She with her finger touched his penis and squeezed it as if she wanted to punish but also showed signs unthinkable for her, retreat, submission and always having her vagina licked by Pia.

She grabbed the phallus and directed with seamless access to her anus, an anus that was already wide open. How this happened, he could not find the reason, but who cares, and his penis was in her anus and went in full steam inside. Anus that was similar to that also flawless anus of that French queer boy.

Karin wanted to hide from Pia that she was fucked from her behind by pushing Pia's head down to have no possibility to see what was going on behind her back. Karin did not want to lose the dominant female-style, having the 'humiliation' of a shaft in her anus.

But that could not be hidden anymore as Pia figured out that her female fucker was also get fucked by a man, and that man was the same who took her virginity, and she frowned.

There were a few minutes of quarrel between them, but Karin was so much enjoying the penis in her asshole that she utterly forgot her dominance and turned around opening her legs and again with her hand, as a least of a sign of self-control, took the penis and inserted in her bushy hairy pussy. Pia left the room and burst into tears for two reasons; one that her female lesbian fucker was now in defensive fucking position and also that her lesbian lover stole her sex mentor.

Nobody cared in that room for the bitter abandonment of Pia in that other room and continued a wild and, in all senses, a hard-core fucking, him dedicating his power to satisfy the wild sexual requirements of Karin.

Her vagina was so much in need of a hard penis that she with her vagina's muscles drawn taut, were even able to smash his fifth member, and especially the top sensitive head part could easily be traumatised.

That sex was incomparable to any other; he was fucking a woman whose role was always to be on top and in charge and get submission from all her girls that joined her lesbian sex performance.

With her hand, she was randomly changing holes until she came with such a scream that outside one could believe that there is a crime inside that home.

He also came as it was impossible for him to hold anymore and him evenly loudly. From the bedroom, they could hear the tragic cries of Pia, especially when she heard their both 'thunderous' screaming of relief.

During that whole sex rough orgy, he noticed that the drawer near the sofa was opened, and what was in there to be seen? Maybe 10 dildos, two of them huge, even whips for sadomasochism. At the corner of that room, he saw a baseball bat. Was it to defend themselves in case of a burglar? He could not imagine that they could use the hand part of that bat as another sex implement.

Those huge dildos explain why her anus was so wide; she for sure applied a lot of those dildos in her anus. He also noticed during the intercourse to her vagina, in her voluptuous asshole a hard device or a small dildo but with the edge to have kind of a diamond shaped crystal that was well almost permanently inserted in her anus so she had double penetration from both entrances.

Him feeling shame for what he did and 'guilty', he quickly got dressed, gave a spank to Karin's buttock, who was still there, still enjoying her climax, and left the home without saying even goodbye to Pia, who was the victim and collateral damage of Karin's fierce and strongest desire for sex this time her to get fucked and not her to fuck.

He left that apartment with guilty conscience, and he never told about this to Alex as he would believe that he is not a man of honour, having almost next door a woman just to bring his son in life and he was fucking, and what? A lesbian.

Before leaving for Shanghai, he again visited Karla and the boy, kissed them all, especially and repeatedly his son and wished the best for all of them, and off they went for the airport.

During that flight, he still felt warmth of the asshole of Karin in his 'cock' and her vagina muscles to squeeze like pliers. That was a unique experience added to his collection.

At the Shanghai airport was Andre with a limo; he looked excited and full of satisfaction; the dirty mind could locate the reason as if not be other than he managed to have lustful moments with that Apollo young man.

He was happy to tell them that for the next day's opening, many celebrities were expected, among them many of the Shanghai city hall council, and everything was well prepared and ready to have a social event that will be vastly known in that prominent Shanghai residential community.

Angel and Melissa did a great job; they played the role of the boss excellently and a gentle disciplined professionalism by all the staff was imposed.

The fitness centre looked equal to the best of Europe and America, and the new technologically superior equipment added assets gave a completely new image to what it was until then, a worse-equipped spa.

Tomorrow was the inauguration; they asked the city hall vice president to cut the ribbon, and they all, with a glass of champagne in hand, were walking around, adoring the perfection of the fitness centre. Many wanted to subscribe as members, but they were not yet prepared for this. The two lifts were unstoppably, bringing people up and down; the success was far away from any prognosis.

After all the guests had left, all staff and the contributors of the event, were invited to the best restaurant in the area, in a private big room, and the new brilliant and significant activity was celebrated.

Could this be another expansible project? A possible rising venture parallel to the Spartan chain of taverns. This stimulus does not come from nowhere, but during that inauguration party, there were two businessmen who expressed interest in an Angel's Fitness Centre in their Shanghai suburb.

So, let the first Angel's Fitness Centre start the operation under the new management, and according to the generally expected guaranteed success, later decisions for expansion will be taken.

He asked to send invitation for next day to all the tenants of the building so that they will see with their eyes the reforms that were done and feel proud that in their building there was maybe, if not the best, one of the best fitness centres in Shanghai.

The tenants were impressed with the special prices they offered to them to become members, and so day by day, the list of the members became bigger and bigger to such an extent that new staff had to be employed.

The Geisha idea was finally abandoned as no more additional tempting services were needed; the centre was full with members and cannot attend and satisfy more members. This started to become a problem as they had to deny new members, so they must find a solution or it will turn into a boomerang.

There was no alternative solution, but still there was an empty big apartment in the same building just on the floor below. There, they could move and relocate some of the heavy weight bars and equipment for the real big men, who rather are a discordance between the young and mature ladies having those guys with huge muscles and sweating bodies to demonstrate their masculine superiority.

So, all these guys will be moved one stage down so the big floor of the centre will allow free space to expand and get more members as peculiarly 74% of the members were girls and ladies.

This, of course, did not prohibit the men to go from floor to floor and get massage and also to make their bodies to be shown as those big men like to be adored and have female eyes to fall upon them, but likewise also, girls and ladies are not at all feeling bad to admire well-formed men bodies and their rich sex organs easily to be seen under the tight pants, assigning massive and exhausting 'masturbate homework'.

So, this big problem was solved not ideally, but there was no other solution so the members that were denied, they were called to come and register.

The Angel's Fitness Centre was soon to open the wings and fly to other suburbs and cities, but this was still to be decided wisely and in the comfort of time. What is next to do is make the first new one to a suburb at the opposite side of Shanghai and then after proceed to the next step, exhibit it at the franchise fair in Beijing where Spartan will also have big booth or, better, a complete tavern installed in the big exhibition area.

There was already from the real estate agent suggested a huge space near the communication hub of Shanghai, which was the ultimate position.

The good fame that both Spartan and Angel's Fitness Centre started to obtain the aimed monetised concept.

Spartan's second tavern was also doing greatly, and as the one was not that far away from the other, when orders came for home deliveries and the one was full of orders, passed the orders to the other one to execute so all customers were well pleased. The Spartan partners were meeting tomorrow to decide the next steps.

His suggestion would be to give a small stake of shares to Giannis as this man is the heart of the Spartan tavern, same as Angel is for the Angel's Fitness Centre. He always adopted the bonus to reward a good manager by making him partner, Giannis deserved benefits for his contribution to the success.

His mind could not move away from Chang and Sanrai, as she like Karla was expecting a baby that will be adopted by Chang while he is the father. This time, if it is a boy, he will suggest to Chang to name him Heracles to have him to live and carry that honourable name that will add extra value to his life.

If that will be a girl, then Athena, the goddess of war, or Artemis, the goddess of hunt is a best name for a girl who will one day be the special one. Roxana was also a good name as was one of the two official wives of Alexander the Great. Within five months, though, the gender will soon be known.

The big, but still unanswered, question is that out of the nine virgin girls who are pregnant, how many are his and how many are of Alex's? That answer has to wait three more months.

In the meantime, Andre, the in-charge person to locate the best place for the second Angel's Fitness Centre spotted the real best one at the best area where prominent residents live as this was the exact clientele for Angel's Fitness Centre and right away started the purchase of the equipment and the decoration of it through a well-known interior designer in China. The main aim is to make a fitness centre equivalent to the Miami standards.

The grand opening day will be in approximately 30 days, and he plans to bring from Japan two of Terracotta supermodels from the agent friend and also bring two more boys from Chang so as to have an impressive reception.

On this day, Marcel will be invited to see the boys as fashion show models and also the Japan agent for the same reason as he is tremendously happy with the contracts he signed for these four girls with many Japanese, Australian and not only fashion designers. So, they plan to have a big event with TV and media's coverage.

Having all projects on an ongoing route, he decided to go back home and see his family, and Alex also expressed his interest as he had never before visited Athens.

His family was more than happy to see him after quite some time and hear all the news and businesses. Alex was also glad to meet his wife, his son and daughters, and they spent nice time in good restaurants.

Being always a restless business spirit, he suggested to Alex to go and visit the lagoon where the boutargue was produced. The Greek Boutargue, the amber delicacy with the distinct and fine aroma, is among the gourmet flavours and among the first choices of demanding gastronomy.

After going further north and seeing the trout fish farming belonging to the salmonid family. Rainbow trout is preferred, and this is the quality that is a Greek exclusiveness.

Both boutargue and smoked trout could join the live lobster of Limnos Island and the Greenland smoked reindeer and could make a perfect gastronomic exquisite selection for best restaurants in Europe and America.

Indeed, a big Range Rover was rented to drive there. The trip was nice; Alex was adoring the landscape, and also, they stopped for lunch at nice taverns with typical Greek food, and they both were delighted.

In both places, they met hospitable people. He, as the host, had to show to Alex a lot of Greece, such as the Acropolis and the Acropolis Museum, one of the most modern in the world and, of course, the Greek islands so he gets the idea of the superiority of the Greek islands. Alex was amazed; he admired all of Greece, including the food and the unique climate.

But they had to return to China for the opening day of the second profoundly elaborated fitness centre where many VIPs will be present. Marcel will be there from Paris to meet the new boys' models. Chang arranged three more boys to fly to Shanghai, and Andre was to pick them up from the airport and arrange for accommodation in a best hotel.

With the approval of his family, they flew back to Shanghai where Andre picked them up. They went straight to the new fitness centre, where all were there: Angel, Melissa and the four boys. The boys were of such charm and physical status that they were ready to win international beauty contests.

The Angel's Fitness Centre was of an extreme luxury, the equipment in that spa and gym was rare to see in any other fitness centre. The opening day was in three days, and all was ready to receive the elite of the Shanghai Community.

Angel and Melissa were so tired that they even had no wish to enjoy any sex; the few free hours they had to rest and sleep. So, they were also not to cause any disturbance. In the meantime, the Japanese agent arrived also one day before with the four girls to be also present at the inauguration day. He also wanted to see the boys and also meet Marcel so they might find channels of cooperation as two major models' agents.

So, there will be at the reception four absolute graceful girls, who now more or less look like ladies (femme's fatales) and four men who are scarce to meet anywhere, including Hollywood. So, at the entrance will make an arch, the four girls left and the four boys on the right to form a Triumphal Arch of Beauty, a flair, a charming style.

Marcel also arrived, and they booked for him a suite at the same hotel of the Japanese agent with his girls, where also the four boys were staying in a big suite.

The big day arrived, all was ready at the entrance; Andre next to Angel and Melissa were to welcome the invited prominent VIPs.

First, the city hall leader had to cut the ribbon together with Andre, and that was done in a celebratory ambience.

One by one, they were coming; they remained stunned at what they saw; the interior decorator had transformed this fitness centre in a Paradisiac Environment with a lot of green and even trees that made the whole to look so ethereal and exotic that those that they make their body trading there, they will feel that they are on a surreal habitat.

Marcel and the Japanese agent arrived coincidently at the same time. Areus, Alex and Andre made the introductions. It was funny when entering the Beauty Arch, they both stopped. The Japanese agent, Akira was his name, adoring the boys while Marcel became dizzy having to turn his head left and right, admiring the boys on one side and envying the four girls of Akira on the other side. They created a 'traffic jam' at the entrance; many more wanted to enter but those two stayed there, speechless. Andre had to gently push them to proceed to the main fitness hall.

It was extraordinarily crowded, the champagne and the canapes, specially selected by Andre waiters and waitresses were among the crowd.

The atmosphere was cheerful; people were asking how they could register members and what the conditions were; they were all addressed at a desk where there were all the leaflets of the fitness centre and on the last page were the details on how to become members. There were 1000 such leaflets; at the end of the day, they were all gone; many took more than one so they can give it to friends.

All were gone so Areus and Alex invited the two 'rivals' and challengers of the four boys for a dinner at the most exquisite restaurant of the town.

It was a very interesting meeting as Marcel and Akira were passing the one to the other ideas on how to exploit the most of the four girls that they have in their team.

Needless to say, they also were throwing the one to the other probing glances to search the grade of the interest for the four boys so as to supply the most competitive offer.

At that dinner, he proposed to them to share the boys two in Japan and two in Paris, so this will be determined the next day.

Marcel, the next day, made an unbeatable offer for 1 million euros for two years for the four boys, so Akira could not compete and resigned.

Back to the fitness centre and just one day after that glorious opening day, the membership's registrations were on fire and beyond any expectations.

The time passed, and Chang called with the news. Sanrai brought a healthy boy in life, while the other nine girls there were seven (one girl gave birth to twins) in black skin and were five boys two girls and brown eyes so his children, and four (again one girl with twins) blonde three boys and one girl with blue eyes—Alex's babies.

So, then the genes are five Heracles and three Great Alexander's, plus the three girls, two dark-skinned and one white-skinned, were uncharacteristically beautiful. Those girls would be the pride of that village and hopefully God will be generous and give them excessive beauty.

He, in a most cheerful manner, described that all 10 had outstanding and exceptional eyes combination. In hospitals, where the births took place, they were all stunned to see what a great Asian and European mixture saw the European descended characteristics to be more dominant.

Chang conveyed to them the invitation from the city hall to be there at the festivities that will last five days with fireworks and many other celebrations.

Areus and Alex were sceptical. What if they ask them to stay again as 'prisoners and hostages' for a new 15 days devirginizations so that their epic tale will be glorified with more descendants? Who could give any guarantee that not again those bizarre situations happen? From the other aspect, if they will not go, it will leave an enormous disappointment. The dilemma is big but needs to examine all hypotheses and consequences, either go or not go.

One is for sure that he will certainly visit Chang to see the boy and what face traits are visible out of the Chinese and Greek genes' juncture.

Marcel increased his offer slightly, and the boys belonged to him for two years at 1.2 million euros, plus unlimited advertisements on all medias. So, all were happy with the best possible deal.

Marcel, same as she did for the four girls, will also open bank accounts for the four boys for their money to be transferred.

The next month, the big franchise fair would take place in Beijing, and they booked a big space for both Spartan tavern and Angel's Fitness Centre.

There are 30 days without any obligations, and there must be an activity to cover that gap. The one option was to go to the festive events at the village, where the nine virgin girls brought birth to their descendants. And they were to be honoured as the 'conquistadors' to bring a new era to their historical village. The other option, which was brought up by Alex, was that he wanted to visit Tibet and in fact him also.

Chang called, saying that if you will not be there, it will be an offensive act for the whole village as they are the ones to give names to the 11 progenies.

The two were to sit and discuss what to do; it was for them also of primary interest to see what seed was sown, which according to all the witnesses the result was absolutely amazing.

So, they quite gutsily ignored any phobic syndrome, and they travelled to meet Chang, who was to accompany them to the village as he had done the first time. They met him at his home, where Sanrai welcomed them and gave both an innocent kiss to the cheek. Right after, she brought the baby.

He looked at this boy, and he was able to distinguish right away that what he sees is a blessed joining of Sanrai and himself.

Chang as the father, and Sanrai were looking at this boy with such affection and joy as if that boy were one day to become the most handsome man in all the Chinese region. That boy had the same eyes like the boy of Karla but with slightly less folded eyes like the typical Chinese eyes that added an element to adore.

Chang and Sanrai made a perfect match, the one was staring at the other as if they were 19-year-olds who had met for the first time to a love at first glance.

Areus was tremendously happy that Chang showed such a greatness of soul to take both mother and son to his home, creating his own family.

The next day, all three, plus a driver in that same jeep was on the rough road, heading to that village. From a long distance, they could see flags; all that village was decorated with flags of all kinds of colours, but all in the centre had both Heracles killing the lion with his own hands and Great Alexander on Bucephalus with his spear and helmet.

This time, they welcomed them from far away and not like the first time, entering the village where there was no one to be seen as if it were a sleeping or, better, a dead village. They all had on each hand one flag of Heracles and one of Alexander the Great.

They made signs to them to stop the car and walk to the square and greet one by one left and right all the people there were there. It took more than two kilometres, having left and right people to worship them, until they reached the square with big flags that added to the festival atmosphere but at the same time public curiosity.

The same old council leader, this time he bowed to them, although the first time they arrived, he was standing like a true proud leader.

He gave orders to bring them to the council's main large hall, where again, he held a speech, always pointing at them at the same time and bowing maybe more than 30 times. Chang nodded to them also to bow; this is the reason that he bowed 30 times as he saw that they did not follow his bowing. Seeing them bow, he made obvious signs of satisfaction.

The speech was stopped all of a sudden, and they all left the room, but this time all mysteriously bowing as low as they could, their faces almost touching the ground and emptied one by one the hall. They were there standing alone until a lady appeared and asked Chang to translate to them that they have ready their bath and beds to rest as the actual feast will take place tomorrow.

That new lady, another Sanrai, looked not serious as Sanrai looked in the beginning, but she was hospitable with a smile.

Chang approached, whispering in his ear that she is the mother of that girl who brought birth to the two twin boys. This made sense; she was staring at the 'husband' of her daughter and the father of her two boys.

There were girls waiting to take the usual last time bath and lead them to bed for a more-than-ever-needed rest after walking more than two kilometres on a rough road to greet them all.

The girls, carefully selected to be the one more beautiful than the other, undressed them fully nude, stood there looking at their male sexual organs and smiling with curiosity seeing the penises the one down the other high up. The joy of the legend, which was not at all fictional, became true and was right there in front of their curious eyes.

Him showing girls flashing at him, he could not manage to calm his 'junior' down, and he became fast, hard and erected in all its length. The girls, but curiously also that lady supervisor, were showing signs of celebration for obtaining to get his penis erected without even touching, while Alex's penis was sleeping already, needing the necessary pharmaceutical support.

They showed them to get in the big bathtub but separated them to two different bathtubs, the one not to be seen by the other.

Chang was not there anymore to translate, so they showed one finger making him understand that he could stay in that bathtub for one hour, but they did not go. They stayed there, four girls on one side of the bathtub and two from the other.

This time, they were not at all shy like last time when they had instructions not to look at their eyes, but this time everything was natural and joyful.

He was bathing them became hot as that room reminded a hammam; they looked at each other, and in seconds after the approval of the supervisor, they were naked and also in that huge Roman-type of bathtub also bathing and swimming charmingly, playing innocently and rubbing his back and his chest; there wasn't any sexual intention, just a play. He felt in that huge bathtub like Mark Antony with four Chinese 'Cleopatras' When he was swimming on his back, 'is penis was oscillating and emerging like a submarine, which made the girls hold their mouth to avoid loud laughter, but they did not touch, maybe unintentionally, they did, but there was not any intercourse in their minds.

It was amazing how the whole ceremony changed completely from the very serious and strict to the very loose and relaxed with no rules. Those probably were not virgins but well experienced in sex but had not any at all instruction to go for sex encounters.

One of them took the liberty by herself to take an innocent grab of his cock, but that was all, she let that go. He looked at the lady. She was also laughing, making signs to enjoy the bath and get ready to sleep. He nodded affirmatively, but the 'junior' was on fire and needed satisfaction. He was wondering what would happen if suddenly the community leader steps in and sees those four girls swimming nude in that bathtub.

That one hour that was prolonged having four nude sweet girls bathing together and touching each other on all possible body parts, him improvising ways by innocently tickling the girls between their legs and them while swimming clumsily and softly kicking his organ with their small feet, was so enjoyable that he wished not to finish by freezing the time.

The girls got dressed but still stayed there on the side of the bathtub until he decided to step out, and they gave him a gown and led him to the bed. They left, but the lady, 'his mother-in-law', came and kindly asked him to remove the gown, and so he was naked; she as an experienced woman she knew that a man who had so many naked girls around him touching him and rubbing their breasts on him and unintentionally he gets his 'cock' hard and does not ejaculate, he suffers with full balls.

With kindness and not any desire asked him if he wanted that she releases him from that inconvenient full of sperms balls and exercise a masturbation, and so he nodded affirmatively, and he extremely loudly ejaculated in her hand, apologising from his 'mother-in-law' for this.

Deep rest was more than must as that long walking distance, plus the handjob of his 'mother-in-law', influenced his strength and consequently his stamina. They both slept for quite a long time until dinner was served. This time, horse milk or bull and camel meat to enforce their libido was not on the menu, just an ordinary veal meal.

Chang was there also, and he informed them about the schedule. After the dinner, there were not any festivities but to relax until time came for the night sleep. Tomorrow was the important day of the names to be given to the babies, a kind of baptism but according to Chinese traditions.

So, they both had to sit and think about the names that were to be given to their babies.

For the men, the names are Alexander, Heracles, Achilles, Apollo, Odyssey, Leonidas, Hector and Adonis, while for the girls Athena, Artemis and Penelope.

The next morning, his 'mother-in-law' woke hm up and so was also done for Alex. It is funny to mention here that the 'son-in-law' is almost 30 years older than the 'mother-in-law'.

They again were dressed in a traditional ceremonial long gown down to the toes.

There were cheerful voices to be heard while approaching that big celebratory hall.

All were there, city hall council, the ex-virgin mothers and the 11 babies in a soft wicker basket filled with soft straws, quite odd as a baby cradle.

The time came, and he handed over to the old leader the names for the boys and the girls and left it up to them who takes what name. The Chinese kind of 'baptism' had nothing to remind Christian baptism; it was simple, and while the leader gave the name to each baby, they all bowed down as deeply as possible hearing the name that impressed them all, while the mothers had to kiss the hand of the leader, but at the same time kiss his hand and Alex's hand.

The ceremony was in excessive love and cheerfulness, what amazed them was that not any of the 11 babies cried, just were turned in such a way that all 11 were vis a vis to both of them, Areus and Alex, and those brilliant eyes were looking at them trying to discover who of the two is his or her father.

It took three hours while the leader called Chang and both went to the corner of the big hall so that no one could hear what they were talking about.

Chang heard what the leader was telling him but not in a commanding manner but rather in a pleading way. Chang's face looked surprised and sceptical about what he told him but with a head motion seemed to give a positive answer.

They both approached the 11 wonderful babies and gave to all kisses on their cheeks but also to all nine mothers; that was a touching moment as these were both their informal wives and the babies their unofficial descendants.

All were gone; they only stayed while Chang approached. He could not find words to what the leader begged him for. After some minutes of pause, he confided to them what the leader's wish was.

One of 20 virgin girls was his niece, but she was not impregnated, so what he asked them was that he wanted both to have again sex to her, hoping that this time she will give birth. Areus asked him, "What? You ask us to make a trio with that girl."

He said yes exactly this. "And what if we refuse?" He answered with a meaningful 'you better not', and he left in a hurry.

They looked at each other, understanding that they had no other option and went straight to their 'dormitories'.

This time, there was a new lady there; they assumed it was the mother of this girl and the sister of the leader. She asked them to remove the gowns in an extra-large bed; this time not the same as it was last time.

So, there they were waiting for the girl to come, and there she was; she kissed her mother, the mother did the same, and approached the bed getting rid of all her clothes. She was an extraordinarily cute girl, but one could see that this time she did not have the attitude of a virgin, but the air of a girl who had a one-time sex experience before.

Alex recognised her as one of the girls that passed by his bed. Totally naked, also in bed in the middle between them. Without any shyness, she grasped both penises and started a soft masturbation. Areus's phallus was as always already hard while Alex's was not. She let Areus's penis in peace and with a blowjob tried to bring Alex's organ up but in vain.

So, she abandoned him and turned to Areus to the side showing him that she is wet already and he could penetrate her cute pussy, so it was done. But what curiously happened was that the mother got undressed; she was not more than 35 and well-formed.

She went to Alex and grabbed his organ and started masturbation, having his penis in her breasts. She did that so excellently that after some time his phallus started to rise and with a nod asked him before the penis goes back to soft that he has now to slip it in her daughter's pussy.

So, the girl left Areus and turned her ass to Alex and asked him to go ahead on that doggy position, and so he did, while the young mother with horny tits was on his back, adding extra arousal having the nipples of one woman on his back while he was inside the vagina of the girl. That combination brought the result and maybe for the first time with no Viagra, and he ejaculated inside her.

She turned right away to Areus, but this time, she wanted to enjoy this having already planted Alex's seed in her vagina. He did not like that, but he was obliged to do so, and he offered her plenty a sex demonstrations, asking Alex to finger her asshole so she feels double penetration. That made her feeling superb, with two climaxes, the one with just two minutes' difference from the other.

Her mother was extremely happy seeing her daughter enjoying such a pleasure with both her holes busy and with a head motion asked him to ejaculate in her, and so he did, him also feeling one of the best orgasms.

Mother kissed both, also the cute girl having in her face that characteristic angelic look, kissed both and left, and so did they also.

They dressed them with their own dresses, and Chang showed up.

The welcoming from the city hall, the name giving, the 'baptism' and finally the trio were all done, and after everybody gave them an honorary goodbye, they left. What they now had to look forward was if that girl would this time bring birth and then become relatives to the leader.

Chang wanted to please them and offer them a dinner in his home where Sanrai cooked Chinese specialties, and they were all in a good mood. Areus told him that he will send him the contract and sign as he is partner to the boys' models business and also asked him his bank account to send him the first revenues. He was extremely happy that he at last got a good amount of money in his bank.

Back to Shanghai, next week, is the big franchise fair in Beijing, where both Spartan and Angel's Fitness Centre have big booths. Giannis and Andre have to make an impressive presentation of both contemporary concepts so that both will expand rapidly in all Chinese regions as beyond any expectation a successful infrastructure was there already.

Tuppi informed that the Bras de Ferre tournament was very successful, and their hero reached the final, but he lost to a Polish giant. That was a success anyway, and Nuuk owes a lot to him for succeeding to have that tournament in their city.

The Angel Fitness Centre had a problem as the one Romanian girl, Alina, revealed the secret that Luana, the other Romanian girl, had sex with Areus.

That brought a quarrel between them, and he had to intervene as a fireman and extinguish the fire and calm both girls that this was just a weak moment of him, and Luana was not responsible as he was the one to demand sex, and she was obliged to follow, and that time she did not know that Angel and him were a 'couple'. Apologies were given, and all went back to normal.

Angel that very night in their bed was a volcano having as fantasy him to fuck Luana.

She was asking him all the time what she did to him, how she did this or the other to him, is it this way or that way, so she was extremely horny having in her mind, the scene of him fucking Luana, and she enjoyed that instead of the contrary. She was aggressive asking him, "Do you want to fuck me and her together and make an orgy?"

"If you want, I could ask her to be here tomorrow night and make a group sex as I am also missing the lesbian encounter." What could he say? If she wanted this so much, why deny it? After all it will be a sex party between those three.

Obviously, that will mean the start of a flexible relationship between boss Angel and employee Luana, which might lead to loss of discipline. Anyway, let him enjoy this and then see the professional part of this story.

Angel indeed invited Luana next night and made great preparations that this will indeed be an orgy. Not only food delicacies, wine and champagne but also vibrators and dildos of all sizes she purchased. He could not imagine that Angel was hiding such a sexual deviant, and openly, she declared that she misses the lesbian sex.

Luana arrived with tight blue jeans that allowed her gorgeous arse to be seen in all its perfect shape. She almost did not enter the door, and Angel rushed to her and kissed her on the mouth, so she also returned this kiss, and they stayed there for one whole minute kissing passionately each other. He always seeing two women kiss each other turns him on.

When watching porn videos, scenes where two women kiss each other, he gets extremely horny, and that happened, watching them kiss each other but with passion and lust.

They finally were on the sofa after Luana got rid of her coat and revealed her European big and well-shaped breasts; Angel was looking with enormous arousal and lust.

They enjoyed the dinner with much fun and joy. The vibe was explosive; they drank wine and champagne that fuelled passion, and the air was smelling wet and demanding vaginas.

Angel rushed to Luana, kissing her and at the same time was undressing her, first the shirt and the bras, and she then sucked her big nipples. Luana was horny, but it seemed to him that she rather wanted a dick. To his surprise, Angel was the dominant girl and not Luana, who was rather accepting all Angel's sexual desires.

He was expecting the contrary, the big woman, the Romanian, to be the one to 'play' the masculine role and not Angel, who was almost half of her size. They were both naked with their voluptuous bodies to form a horny portrait of sexuality, and as the floor was covered by thick carpet, they were on that, performing an unbelievable lesbian sex.

Such a lesbian sex that is his favourite to watch in porn videos; he never saw any similar reaching the borders of raunchy sexual shocking behaviour.

Angel, with her hand, searched and found on the corner of the sofa under the pillow, a big dildo and demanded Luana to wide open her legs, and she did it with such a pleasure and not as an obligatory task because her boss was asking for this, but she craved for it.

He was stunned to watch that huge dildo how could slowly slip in her pussy while Angel grabbed a smaller one and with her hand, she skidded that to her own anus and let that stay there half in half out. The huge dildo was effortlessly going inside, and Luana was, at that moment, not on the earth but on the clouds, enjoying this with moans and screams of relief that escaped from her mouth.

It did not take too long, and she came squeezing the dildo in her pussy, feeling grateful for what pleasure she experienced from that silicone plastic kind of big male sexual organ.

The roles changed, Angel down, leg wide open while the small dildo was always stuck in her anus. Luana with that tongue, which he knew from own experience when he lived one month ago in that same spa, was licking Angel's pussy and, at the same time, was moving in and out her asshole that small dildo.

Angel was sweating; girls' sweat is his fetish smelling like nectar and always makes him extravagant horny; she then asked Luana to get the big dildo and opened her legs even wider; he could in no case believe that this huge dildo could enter her tiny vagina, but it gradually slid in. He was wondering if the dildo was two times thicker than his own penis, and he felt a minority complex.

But it is true that all ladies admit that size does not play any role for a woman's orgasm to reach their highest point or a stormy relief. Luana felt that she abandoned her own anus, and she made a sign to him to approach and get his cock in her anus while she was with the huge dildo 'fucking' Angel.

The invitation was warmly welcomed; she took saliva from her mouth and rubbed the tip of his cock so to be more slippery at the same time also inserted that wet finger in her arsehole, so he was inside her without any difficulty probably Luana's not any maiden anus was well-trained and exercised with dildos and for sure needed not any saliva; she was the epitome of the compulsively sexual woman.

Angel surrendered to the rhythms of the huge dildo's insertions, and she had repeated but loud orgasms that she never had with him having sex. Was it as she claimed, 'I missed lesbian love', or the huge dildo did a better job than his dick?

No matter what, he was enjoying at Luana's anus, a great fuck and seemed she was also to explode loudly same as Angel as she was with her other hand touching her clit for a perfect masturbation.

The roles changed; Angel wanted also her anus to be filled with a real phallus and not that small dildo with the fake diamond on the backside so to hold the dildo, not get vanished inside her pretty asshole.

So, his sex organ so far was jumping from asshole to pussy, feeling the damp and warmth of a wide-opened vagina. Angel having the ongoing satisfaction of his penis in her derriere, it was her turn to please Luana with a pussy licking.

All this orgy filled in already one hour and counting, but what else were those horny girls to invent to amuse their impassioned lust? If there were feminine Viagra, one could say that they had Viagra because only so could justify that extreme libido.

The fucking was well on track, changing from the one to the other 'doors' to one and the other girl. Luana suddenly acrobatically jumped over him and came behind while he was inside Angel's vagina and inserted a finger to his anus and although he did not like it at first, but then accepted that allowing Luana to play the masculine role and please both her in such moment of madness and him having a tiny finger in his anus while at the same time, he maintained the achievement having his shaft in the warmth of Angel's vagina.

The orgy party ended; having all the satisfaction engraved in their faces, all were exhausted; Luana could not even walk to her apartment that was not that long away, but she rushed to the bed of himself and Angel, which is a big bed, but for three is a bit narrow, so they had to squeeze themselves all naked, and no one cared what body part his male genital will touch or whose breast touch whose face or whose knee is inside the other's arse because deep sleep dominated.

His concern was if Angel gets an addiction of lesbian sex and obtain a dependence on that sex variation or abnormality that might destroy their sexual harmony.

They all woke up at almost the same time and rushed for a rich breakfast and to each other's job, then to the spa and himself to have a meeting with Giannis and Andre for the upcoming franchise fair in Beijing, which was of utmost importance.

The decorators are working to present the two concepts impressively, so to attract franchisees who will apply for the one or the other, but why not for both concepts and one day a big brand name with the revenues that will enable the one or the other to become a public company in Hong Kong or the Shanghai stock exchange.

In the meantime, he got many photos from the four girls in Paris, the Alexander girls and the four of Japan, the Terracotta girls, but also the boys, sending impressive photos of fashion show défilés but also front and first page covers in major magazines.

One of the boys attracted the interest of an American producer, and he might make a career in the movie business, and that will be good for both Areus and Alex as they are his agents. They also have great demand for products from TV advertisements such as whiskeys, aromas and all kinds of cosmetics. Their future is brilliant and very promising, and that justifies his judgment.

The day came for the Franchising Fair in Beijing, and they asked the Japanese agent of the Terracotta girls to send the four girls to be at the reception of both booths, Spartan and Angel's, and so he did.

The two booths were side by side and looked impressive, best job done from both Giannis and Andre. At the Angel's booth were two of the Terracotta girls with Angel and Melissa and also one boy who was sent from Chang of the same family of the other boys who were already in Paris. These were indeed the best and most beautiful booths of the fair.

The Spartan had the two Terracotta girls as receptionists, distributing leaflets as well as Giannis' girlfriend who was also very pretty.

The doors of the fair opened after the Beijing mayor cut the red ribbon, and many businessmen rushed to visit all 100 booths.

In the beginning, it was not as they predicted, and there was a disappointing atmosphere, so the first day passed, but not any big number of visitors passed by as it was anticipated and made them all very sceptical. The idea came through Areus' mind to make the Spartan work as they had all the infrastructures, and so not just show a tavern but also show a working tavern and also offer to taste the food to all visitors.

So, immediately and overnight, food supplies were ordered to arrive first in the morning parallel for Angel's; they corrected the mistake to save money and not allow all the working staff to be there, so all staff, including the two Romanian girls. Areus also asked Luana to offer free tickets and hotel accommodation in the best hotel in Beijing to five to six good customers, three men and three ladies with well-trained bodies to come and make there in the fair their daily exercise so that one could see a fitness centre in operation. Limo was ordered to bring them all overnight to Beijing.

The next day, all was as planned; the two concepts were in full operation; the Spartan was distributing to all visitors to taste the gyros and the souvlaki and sit on the 20 Greek-styled tables to enjoy also the salad; and the Angel's Fitness was amazingly well done, seeing big movement girls to massage men or ladies and their guests men or ladies making their daily exercise using all machines and equipment so to make a fantastic image that gained not only the admiration of all businessmen visitors but also staff from other booths to come and enjoy the Greek specialties, and also if they wished to have a nice massage, having two special rooms dressing spots so they could get rid of some heavy coats and enjoy a massage and utilise the most advanced fitness equipment.

The second day started brilliantly. The best ambassadors of both concepts were the staff of the other booths, who from mouth to mouth were sending visitors that passed by the booth to taste the Spartan food and also watch the great installation of the Angel's Fitness Centre and get a relaxing massage.

It was Areus' idea to allow to spread around to all booths that after the fair was over for the day, they were all welcome to have a relaxing massage and rest their feet on the special instrument for this reason and also have a free dinner, and that invitation was also for all the fair's employees and guards so making them also advertisers of the Spartan and Angel's.

The second day was a good day. There were 30 businessmen from different cities of China to show serious interest to become franchises; 60% for Spartan and 40% for Angel's Fitness Centre. Four contracts were signed, three for Spartan and one for Angel's.

That second day's closing of the fair, a huge party took place in front of both the booths.

Many were tasting the gyros and Souvlaki; equally, many were enjoying the five minutes for each one massage and use of all equipment. That was a really successful movement as all those will be tomorrow the last day of their 'ambassadors'.

Areus told them to be prepared for the third day because after the very positive rumours of something different as concept in that fair, ran not only in that fair but also all over Beijing.

The next day, both booths were crowded with many business decision-makers and businessmen. The one was pushing the other to be first to register and sign a pre-contract, and that was indeed beyond any expectations.

Maybe 200 showed very serious interest, and another 200 that they would study both leaflets and they would either call or come to Shanghai to discuss.

The fair's last day was over, and they sat down to see and get a tally how many they, in fact, signed contracts and what as pre-contracts and how many were those that would come to talk in Shanghai.

It was amazing; there were four from Shenzhen, Ningbo and Beijing, who signed for both concepts, and there were also 10 for Spartan and four for Angel's, and more than 200 would come or ask for the contracts to be sent to sign. That was a tremendous success.

Giannis, as well as Andre and Angel, must be prepared and organised with secretaries for numerous inquiries to come.

After the fair, they all went to the hotel and were asked to take a bath and come down to the main restaurant of the hotel, where they would celebrate the 'victory'.

They indeed were exhausted but still had the guts to come down to have dinner and live in the best mood of the 'triumph'.

Areus held a small speech, and they all ran like wolves to have dinner as although they were in a tavern in the fair, their own tavern, they still had not the time to eat anything.

The next day, they all flew to Shanghai, and the Terracotta girls left for Tokyo, while the Chang's specially sent boy would stay in Shanghai as he indeed was extremely useful.

After reaching their apartment, sex was the last thing to think, while sleep was must.

The next day, he was meeting at the office to discuss the Spartan Fair results. The immense extent of the success was totally unpredictable. Giannis was also present, who by now spoke almost fluent Chinese.

He was instructed to employ two secretaries to be able to respond to all inquiries, and as there was no space at the tavern, they could have here, in these offices, two desks to feel more comfortable.

Same meeting was also held at Angel's and also needed to have one secretary with the only task to follow the franchisees and newcomers' inquiries.

All was running as was carefully planned, but there were still some issues that would soon be put under priority categorisation.

First, he called his family to assure them that his health was perfect and there were not any whatsoever worries.

Karla was next to call, and she was very sweet on the phone, saying that this boy would become the Don Juan of Copenhagen with blue eyes and black hair and darker skin. He confessed to her that he had dreams for him to become a tennis champion and asked Karla to give him, from that age, any toys related to tennis so that he will love that sport from that early childhood. She totally agreed; he even asked her whenever there were TV tennis matches to let him watch.

It would also be nice when he reached the age of four that she move to the nice city of Nice in France. There was the best tennis academy, where both the Greek Tsitsipas and the Danish Rune became the best players in the world. If they are close enough for him to visit, he also has many good connections in both Monte Carlo and Cote d'Azur cities.

It was amazing that he was the father of so many newborn sons and daughters, and he could make plans for them all, at least of the two Alexanders of Karla and Sanrai, though at this age, parenthood, even if not legalised, was not an easy task to handle.

Having always in mind that he might need a few years to retire and slow down a little, he started interviews to provide a high managerial position to all three activities. So, the office would get one well-experienced manager, preferably a German who knows the German business mentality, but he would never present himself as German as German companies were very suspicious for competition purposes.

Also, the Spartan chain as now were already six, and four more franchise candidates were on the way and also a manager next to Andre and Angel as there were three Angel's Fitness Centre and expecting more to come.

The interviews had excellent results, and he chose for all three projects three very experienced managers that through their knowledge to run a business would also gain the indispensable respect from all staff and assistants as well as the co-owners.

So, he prepared the ground to slowly step back and give authorities and initiatives to the managers and co-owners Sophia, Giannis, and Andre with Angel.

After one month, all seemed to match each other, and there were not any internal turbulences; on the contrary, they achieved the optimal collaboration.

He felt justified for his decisions, and so he had more time to exercise his body; after all, Angel's spa has all facilities for that, plus the nearby tennis where both him and Alex could compete.

All was running exceptionally, well, but there was bad news from Wuhan that there was a virus that had hit the whole city, and that might spread to all of China.

The virus was called Corona or COVID, and indeed, it spread fast all over China, and businesses were collapsing. Spartan could still work very well with orders to be delivered at home, but Angel's Fitness had to close for an unknown period. The office could still work as the employees could do the job from their own home as there were repeated lockdowns. The borders were closed, so one couldn't leave the country.

Situation was deteriorating as Corona hit also Europe and Germany, and also the businesses there were in trouble. The one year after the other was passing with lockdowns and suffering of millions of people and definitely also businesses.

His wife and two married daughters, the one with a doctor, the other with a ship-owner, and the son a good lawyer were in a bad physiological situation with him being far away not able to psychologically support them.

Four years passed, and the situation started to get slightly better, but not at all as it was before the virus. He often talked with wife and his daughters and son as well as with Karla to know how Alexander was doing.

He was now 74, and he made a radical decision; he left China, maybe for good; after all it was well managed and in perfect hands; he only held as business the agency of the eight girls and the four boys, who needed nothing else to renew the contracts.

The borders were opened so he could fly home. But not alone, Alex would also follow him as he was his only good friend to whom he owes a lot for revitalising his whole life.

He asked Karla to come to France and so also asked Chang with Sanrai to move to France. Both of them were more than happy and excited. Karla and Chang-Sanrai with their four-year-old Alexanders to be close to the famous campus tennis training Clinique, where maybe later would take over their tennis progress to aim one day to become champions.

Karla enthusiastically agreed to go to Nice and change to a new life in such a nice city, while Mathilde wished that she stayed home as her health was not at its best.

Chang and Sanrai definitely wanted to, but they did not have the financial background. He assured them that he would support them adding the necessary money to the profits he earned from Chang's commission from the boys' contracts, as he was co-owner of that boy's agency company.

The days were approaching for the heart-breaking goodbyes. Angel was in a deep philological fall down, but he told her that he would always communicate with her, but it was time for her to find a young man to get married. She had a lot of money, so she could have a comfortable life. Same situation was also with Melissa and Alex, who emotionally was more touched by this separation.

Giannis was able to marry his girlfriend as they had a perfect match; he was also in a perfect financial adequacy to live a relaxed and nice life.

The day of the departure came at the airport. There were all to say goodbye. Sophia, whom he assured that he would always attend the mails, and when a big enquiry comes, he would handle from any distance; he would be for one more year, but then she would take over all of it.

The overwhelmed melancholia was more than evident to both Angel and Melissa, and both busted in tears. He whispered into Angel's ear, "Try to forget me and get a good and chivalrous husband that you deserve."

Giannis was there and thanked him for all he did for him to get a good job and find also a good woman next to him. It was not an easy goodbye, but it was done, and Alex and he were flying to Greece, leaving behind the two beloved girls Angel and Melissa but also three well-organised and profitable businesses.

At the Athens airport was his son to pick them up. They had a whole family dinner with his wife, the daughters and their husbands and children. He announced to his whole family that he would go to France for two reasons, one to improve his tennis in a special academy and second to fulfil his old wish to study wine gastronomy and sit again at the age of 74 on the students' benches.

So he and Alex left for Nice.

First thing to do was to go to a real estate agent to ask for four apartments. One for him, one for Alex, one for Karla with two bedrooms and one for Chang and Sanrai, also with two bedrooms.

While the two real estate agents were working on this, they went to the tennis campus to register as members, so they start, having no businesses in mind, to train hard and keep their bodies fit as in that campus was also a most advanced gym.

One week passed, and they went to visit the options that were available, and the decision was difficult as all were nice apartments with excellent views of the sea.

He sent mails with the apartments' photos and called both Karla and Chang/Sanrai to get ready to move with the two Alexanders.

All, Karla, Chang and Sanrai, were delighted to see the photos of the apartments; their life would change drastically as Karla would leave the dark Copenhagen for a distinctly different city, the sunny Nice, and Chang with Sanrai would leave their boring Chinese city for the incomparable and picturesque Cote d'Azur.

The time came, and Karla arrived with Alexander; there were hugs and kisses, and with a car that he bought in Nice, a Volvo, he drove them to their house.

During that short car trip to the apartment, Karla was holding his hand as if she were in love with him; after all, he was the father of her son; he could not take his eyes from his son, Alexander, who was already at the age of four, an extremely nice boy with the characteristics of a Scandinavian and a Mediterranean, the ideal mixture that would turn the French girls crazy.

When they arrived at the apartment, Karla stood there astounded and enchanted, watching the full view of the sea.

Small Alexander rushed to play in the big garden while Karla and he entered the house, having Karla open her eyes to what was unbelievable to be seeing.

In fact, he lied to them by sending them photos of an apartment while finally he changed and rented a big house with a big garden. She kissed him and thanked him for caring so much for them; she right away took photos with her mobile phone to send to Mathilde.

That night was a special night; all three were having dinner prepared by their lady house cook, who would also take care of Alexander, and her name was Aicha from Morocco. Aicha did an excellent tournedos ala Rossini, and they all enjoyed it; Karla and himself drank a good Bordeaux red wine while Alexander had his cola.

During that dinner, he heard for the first time from this boy and was very touched; Alexander called him Dad. The night advanced, and Aicha took Alexander to his bedroom to sleep.

Aicha left for her nearby home, where she lived with her daughter, to come again early to prepare breakfast and take Alexander out to see the surroundings. It was time for them to go to sleep; they had a separate bedroom as he did not know if Karla wanted to continue what they left four years ago. He wished her goodnight and went to his bed calmly and peacefully. It did not take long until he heard Karla coming in his bed, kissing him and her hand trying to see if after four years an old man of 74, he still has restlessness under his underpants.

To her surprise, she felt as if not any day had passed since the last four years; the same hard penis was there at her availability. A good sex was on the way, her feeling great and in a passionate excitement so also him, but no tricks that time, maybe in another day as they both were tired and a bit dizzy from the wine.

After both had a remarkable climax; they laid down side by side, so he had to tell her the story of Chang and Sanrai that they were to arrive tomorrow and the boy, who was also called Alexander. For a few moments, she was shocked, but after a while, that was not anymore a problem.

He also asked her these four years if and how many sex intercourses she had. She recounted that her old time Tunisian boy who was not a boy anymore came back to Denmark looking for her with proposal of marriage, but he wanted that as he was for many years jobless, and when she saw him at the age of 44, she was not fond of him anymore; he had turned ugly with rough characteristics, and she found an excuse saying that she was married to a Greek and has a boy with him, so to let him go.

She, at the same time, thanked her mother for not allowing her to marry him when they were young. How time in some cases is so unfair to turn a so cute boy to a very ugly man.

For sex, she was using her beloved old times vibrator, and that satisfied and calmed her desires. Only one night, she was asked by a girlfriend of her age to go dancing, and there, she met a guy and had rather boring sex in his apartment, and that was all.

The next day, he was at the airport to pick up Chang and Sanrai and also little Alexander.

Alexander was an extremely good-looking boy and seemed, for his age, also quite tall.

It was obvious that he does not know that Areus was, in fact, his father, but, in a way, sooner or later he would find this out.

Areus drove them to their apartment, and they were amazed at what a luxury apartment they would stay in.

Areus let them relax after a long flight and returned to Karla and Alexander Junior; to avoid complications with the other Alexander, it was decided to call him Alexandros.

The next day, they were to meet the family of Chang with both Areus and Alex. They were all in the best mood and had a nice breakfast on the huge balcony of Chang's sea-facing apartment. With time, Alex seemed to become somehow depressed.

The reason was that he was rich but did not have any heir, even though he already had a son and daughters left behind in China. His wish was always to have a daughter with him and near him. Areus sat down with Chang and talked about how they could organise an operation, a kidnapping from China of one of his daughters with or without her mother.

They did this in full secrecy so that Alex would not get hopes and if the operation fails and he gets even more depressed.

Chang has a friend named Liu, an old-type kind of merchant on the move; he with a big truck, full of any kind of houseware and tableware as well as bedroom fittings and towels, visited that isolated village where the 20 virgins were given as trophy to Areus and Alex, with the only obligation to leave behind 'historical' descendants.

Through her sister, Sanrai contacted, under complete secrecy, the young Chinese girl who gave birth to the daughter of Alex. Sanrai's sister, named Chung, showed photos where Sanrai lived in Nice, so to tempt that girl, her name was Hua, to move with Penelope, her daughter, to France always under total secrecy.

Hua was impressed but, at the same time, was very afraid of what would happen if this escapade failed. Chung was also in serious danger as intermediate to this kidnapping would be in serious trouble.

Chung also explained to Hua that her daughter would be the heir of a very rich man and she would be a very rich girl.

Those girls who were the descendants of Areus and Alex were in strict surveillance not being afraid that they would be kidnapped but that these descendants would remain pure and intact and had for each of those boys and girls a special supervisor parent who were state employees. The mothers must every week visit at their offices and hospital for medical examinations and a general monitoring.

The good thing with that mother and daughter was that she had no parents; they both died and they lived alone, so no one would be accused for allowing the disappearance.

The girl, after pressure and under total night cover of Chung and Hua's contacts, took the decision seeing in what life she would live both her and her daughter.

Areus secured a good amount of money to find a way and channels to send good money to all, Liu, the driver, and Chung, Sanrai's sister, so that they risk but at least they get big money.

But that was not possible so that money was sent to Andre, asking him to make that trip and meet Chung to deliver to him the money, and Andre had not any objections, as because of Areus, he was now a rich man.

Areus also asked Andre to stay there as long as needed and get the girl and the daughter to Shanghai.

The whole operation was now well-planned, hoping not any problem would destroy that effort that would bring happiness to both Hua and the daughter (Penelope) as well as to Alex, who still had no idea of this secret operation.

Chung got the money, and he was very happy as that was a big money amount, and also, he got the good money also to be delivered to Sanrai's sister for her valuable help.

The crucial day approached; Liu took his truck to go to the village according to his usual plan. At the same time, Hua pretended that she was sick and asked not to give any presence this week to that office and hospital, so that there would be a good time to be moved by Andre to Shanghai.

Liu arrived with all the merchandise to that 'mystery' village, and all rushed to see the newly arrived merchandise and what they needed to buy. Liu made all negotiations slowly so that the night would fall.

So, he asked for permission to stay there and sleep in his truck, as by night, the road was dangerous without any lights. The permission was granted. The house lights, one after the other, started to be turned off, and the village was 'sleeping'.

Now was the time; at 2 o'clock, Hua and Penelope, walking on the tiptoes, reached the truck, and Liu had arranged that the truck was turned towards downslope, so the only thing he had to do was to release the breaks, and the truck started going downwards with no lights and not any engine sound at all until that was quite far away, and then he turned on the engine and lights and quickly leave, and all in that truck had the smile of success and happiness. They arrived; Andre was there ready and, with not any minute to lose, rented a car and, as fast as possible, drove to the nearest airport and reached to Shanghai, taking with him also Liu as this man had not anymore any future there as on-the-move merchant. He had plenty of money to live a comfortable life, and Andre would give him a job at one of the fitness centres.

After a long time, they were in Shanghai, and they all ran to make all necessary passport and visa formalities and managed Hua and Penelope to be on the plane for Paris and hence to Nice.

The next day, they arrived at Nice airport, where Areus was there, together with a Sanrai, to pick them up and carry them to the unaware Alex.

They reached his luxury apartment with three bedrooms and knocked on the door, and there was Alex. Areus hide Hua and Penelope in the corner of the house, and Alex asked him, "Why do you wake me up so early?"

He said, "I have a present for you."

"What present?"

He answered, "A present that you could not even imagine in your best dreams."

And he nodded to Hua and Penelope to come to the door. Alex right away recognised the girl; he was ready to burst into tears; he embraced both Hua and especially Penelope and gave also two kisses to the cheeks of Areus, saying, "My good friend, what else you would do for me? You made my life new and nice and now also happy—thank you."

So, nice, all were happy; all were there, and soon they took all three, Alexandros, Alexander and Penelope to the famous nearby Tennis Academia so that from the age of four they started holding a tennis racket.

Two teachers were also employed to teach them all English and French to both mothers and kids.

He asked both Alex and Chang to take close interest in their tennis lessons, and he would move for six months to Bordeaux to attend a wine gastronomy and Degustateur high school.

So, here, he was at the age of 74, five sitting on benches with young boys and beautiful, fresh attractive but seemed also thirsty for sex experiences, French and not only French, girls aiming a good job as wine degustateur (sommelier) in big luxury hotels and restaurants.

He was there in that school, the pole of attraction not only for his guts to be there as student but also for his deep knowledge due to his hotel management career.

Next to him, he had a 19-year-old French girl called Charlotte, and to his left was another one equally beautiful called Antoinette. Only those names and their gorgeous figure became tinder for erection.

All of them saw that he arrived at school with a luxury latest model of Volvo and was always well dressed as a real gentleman making known in a sneaky way that he lived in the most exquisite loft apartment of the highest building in town, intriguing their interest and tickling their treasure between their legs.

One of the professors, of about 45 years, in that school, was making a demonstration on how to evaluate the wine and how the wine pleases the uraniscus. He always, in good humour, was posing questions with deeper meaning, such as, "My dear, Mrs Lafante is the feminine uraniscus and mouth appropriate to taste a wine leaving a space of hint."

The professor blushed, showing in a shy way that she caught the deeper meaning. The boys laughed, also the girls. Charlotte, next to him, pushed him with her elbow, telling him, "You bad boy." The teacher called him privately after the school time, asking him not to make jokes that have 'sexual' hints.

He protested that his comment was completely innocent, unless a sexually deprived girl or woman wanted to discover a different meaning. At that point, she showed signs of intimacy and in such feelings looked at him as a woman being in a state of lack of quality sex, allowing him to build vivid hopes with her in due time.

The lessons were very interesting; he narrated to them the preference of Mireille Mathieu to the Alsace white wine Riesling to accompany the lobster and also the incident with the old and expensive wine from the cellar that he wiped off dust and spiders, but that incident led to a mysterious situation with the beautiful companion of that German Von…All the girls and teachers were stunned to hear that story.

At his bench, both Charlotte and Antoinette wanted to know what was behind that 'mysterious situation'.

He simply answered, "Use your imagination."

Before coming, he decided to shave his head, and every day, he came to the school with a different suits and fancy ties, with real leather belts and shoes that showed an aristocratic look, and with a bald head, he hid maybe 20 years of his age, plus the intrigued fame that bald men have high libido. Bald, well-shaved head and having no forehead wrinkles, no one could guess what the age is.

During the lessons, he was always throwing hints, such as good old red wine with nice yellow cheese is good for a honeymoon dinner and is like a woman of 45 with all her sexual acts and experiences she carries that can wake up even a dead man. The teacher flashed as that was addressing to her; the girls looked around them to see the boys, who were rather indifferent for his meanings.

At his bench, another girl was on his back; she caressed his bald head saying, "You will turn us all crazy." And everyone there laughed.

His answer was again, "Exploit your fantasy in your bed, and open your bed table drawer, and you will find a convenient solution there until next."

All three turned red. Charlotte even tapped his lap not far away from his penis. The start was on track, but he faced the insufferable jealousy of the teacher seeing the three girls circling him, protesting that they are not focusing on her teaching.

The next day was 17 of June, and his birthday, so he invited all 16 students (6 boys and 10 girls) and the teacher to his apartment for his birthday.

What a night! Ten girls came, and the teacher and two only boys, the one was gay, the rest boys were sabotaging that party as they were not happy with what they saw in the classroom.

He welcomed them with a Japanese kimono; he looked like Hugh Hefner.

They were astounded to see the luxury of his apartment and the amazing view, and on purpose, he left the door of his bedroom so they could see what was huge and soft, allowing fantasies to circulate the living room.

Wine, champagne, Beluga caviar and best Royal Swedish fish red brick, smoked reindeer and smoked salmon canapes, and Greek boutargue was served by two waiters that he hired to run around, and the glasses were emptied *plusieurs fois* (several times). There was also a DJ in that big living room to turn the night into a crazy night.

The lady teacher drank quite a lot, and her serious outlook turned to excitement. One of the girls who drank three glasses started in the centre of the room a sensual striptease; no one dared to stop her; they were all in such ecstasy that they were enjoying, some even touching their pussies without any shame.

Charlotte and Antoinette came close to him and wanted to see what was hidden under that kimono; he whispered to them, "Later."

The gay boy joined the strip tease girl, and he offered an even more sensual dancing, pretending that there was a dancing pole in such a skill that one could believe that indeed there is a dancing pole.

The strip tease girl was drunk, so they carried her to the bedroom. Charlotte and Antoinette showed dissatisfaction as they intended to be on that bed after the party was over, but they were not the only ones. The teacher was so horny that she completely lost control and grabbed the penis of the only non-queer boy who was there and made clear that someone must fuck her either man, boy or girl.

The party turned to an orgy, girls doing whatever lesbian acts, girls rushed to fuck the only one male waiter, while the black waitress was after Areus; she reminded that old incident in Denmark where he declined that black beauty, but this black waitress maybe was hornier and with a fantastic shaped body and admirable tits.

She grabbed his cock under the kimono telling in French, "*Je veux que tu me baises ici et maintenant* (fuck me here and now)." Well, this time, he would, in no case, deny it. He pulled her by hand to the bedroom, where the naked drunk girl was sleeping, but there was wide space left in that bed, and he, with his always in good mood shaft, fucked her while the bedroom door was opened, and three girls were watching the whole act and were masturbating. He during the fucking of the black pussy and having to his side the sleeping girl's naked ass, inserted his middle finger in her anus; she from deep sleeping woke up and lifted up and wigged her arse cheeks so that the fingering would be more enjoyable.

The three girls ran to that bed and a lesbian heavenly trio was ongoing. There were no vibrators or dildos in the apartment, so they took three unripened bananas to substitute the dildo in indescribable orgiastic situations.

In the living room, the waiter was fucking all the rest girls, even the teacher, who seemed to be the one with the loudest moaning, reaching a high-pitched climax; she was certainly lacking for long time, from her geologist husband, a good sex outbreak.

Two girls slept there, one on his bed and the other on the sofa, all naked as the heat in that room was to the maximum.

The next day was Saturday so there was no school, and they all relaxed after the outburst of the probably wildest orgy party in that city area. He felt responsible to what happened, and having also the teacher to be somehow humiliated with her crazy fuck, he decided to pack and leave without any goodbye so that he leaves that classroom back to normality.

He drove back to Nice after 1½ month. He learned quite a lot about wine, and now he had to concentrate on the future tennis champions. He made the mistake to give his phone number when enrolling to that school. Charlotte called him, telling him that the whole classroom fell after his absence into deep depression as his humour was not there anymore. All the girls in that classroom showed sadness because they missed to enjoy the enigmatic genius old man's capabilities designed to fulfil the uppermost desires.

She also scolded him that he preferred to make love to the black waitress and not to them as they wanted to suck all his experiences and his sex tricks that he activated all to that black waitress, and they thrilled witnessed under unbearable lust, wet panties and an already moist so only the bananas could heal their horniest ever lust.

He was soon to become 75 years old; he had all on good track, his own family, his mistress desireful Karla and their son Alexander, Chang and Sanrai and his son Alexandros, Alex his best friend happy also with companion, bound with civil contract, a young Chinese girl and his daughter Penelope. The three future tennis champions.

Him having done all and not just almost all, having in his quiver adventures and experiences that maybe few could obtain in a life's time. Now, he allowed himself to settle down for the next peaceful decade and why not longer, practising with his daily hard gymnastic and playing tennis and in singles, not the relaxed doubles.

Living in Nice and close to Monte Carlo, he decided one afternoon to take Karla and Alex and visit Monte Carlo and relive the nice nights he enjoyed with his wife many years ago when he was cooperating with the casino management.

Karla dressed impressively also he with a fly as the Salon Prive of the casino required, and took their car for the casino.

He presented to the Salon Prive entrance guards his credentials, and they were allowed to enter where only VIPs were allowed to gamble and also dine.

The atmosphere was always glamourous, and he, as well as Karla and Alex, enjoyed the luxurious ambience. He was a fanatic non-gambler; he only wandered around the roulette tables and the baccarat, while Karla enjoyed some gambling so did Alex, and they went to the impressive restaurant for dinner.

They ordered Scottish smoked salmon as starter, and they continued with Lobster Thermidor, accompanying the lobster with a nice Riesling white dry wine that fits well the lobster.

Nearby and very close to their table was another couple speaking Arabic. He was quite old, maybe 90 years old, while she was maybe 55. The two tables were in full mood, and one of the Arabic couple invited them to have dessert and cognac at their table.

So, they moved to their table, both spoke fluent English; they told them that they were staying at the next-door hotel, the famous Hotel de Paris, and so Areus also narrated them that he was here many years ago for almost every weekend, staying at Hotel de Paris as young man with his wife, newly married, where they enjoyed those unforgettable weekends.

They drank some aperitif sweet wine, and the conversation moved also to the business activities: what one's business is and what is the other's.

Areus told him about only a few of his business ventures because to tell them all he needed a whole night. So, he told him that they have a chain of restaurants in China and he is also a fashion model manager.

The other guy told them that he was Libyan and was one of the closest persons to be near Muamar Gaddafi, when the latter was still the head of the state. He deals with petrol, having the right sources and under-the-table support of the Tripoli temporary government, so he finds ways to export petrol to many countries, especially in South African countries.

Areus and Alex were very impressed by his business as it was known that traders of petrol make big money.

He asked for a meeting with them to tell them more details about this oil business. Indeed, the next day, they were at the suite of the Libyan guy in the Hotel de Paris. He described it as an easy business, but he was now quite old enough to be very active. He felt that he could be comfortable with them to make a partnership.

Areus told him that before he engages himself and Alex to any partnership, he needs to meet those Libyan guys who with their connections they are able to get the state oil at a very good price and sell on their behalf at very higher prices with extraordinary profit.

That guy, his name was Aziz, had no objection, but this means they have to travel to Tripoli to meet them, and saying this, he called Libya there in front of them and talked to another guy in Arabic and later in English. He passed the receiver to Areus, and they talked directly. He sounded as a very confident fellow who has close connections at the highest level in the Libyan government.

They agreed that Areus, when and if he decides to step into that partnership, would contact him.

A lunch followed at the Salle Empire of Hotel de Paris with Aziz, him feeling comfortable as he probably found the appropriate partners so he could retire and enjoy his money with his beautiful escort.

The general picture was that they were in front of a new venture, and new ventures always were welcomed to the blood veins of Areus. Areus, despite his age, felt strong to proceed to that business, while Alex, as always, the conservative one, was reluctant. They had many meetings with Aziz so as to gain trust and confidence in what new business they would or would not be going to step in.

They held meetings, and it was decided to take that trip to Tripoli to meet those guys. Karla was absolutely negative to this trip, knowing that the situation in Libya was in a turmoil and obviously very dangerous. The decision to take was difficult, and he had to consider that indeed the situation in Libya was far away from secured. His motto was always think big and there was no success without risk. He talked many times with Abdullah, that was the name of the Libyan connection, who assured him of his security as he would have the Tripoli police guard 24 hours.

The challenge to get into the oil trading business was a big incentive.

So, the decision was taken that he would go to Tripoli without Alex, who was scared to follow, plus he wanted to enjoy life with his Chinese wife and daughter.

Areus landed at Tripoli, and Abdullah, with a squad of four policemen, welcomed him under total secrecy, something that put him in deep thought. What was such secrecy for? He is a businessman and not any politician on a mission.

They took him in a military vehicle followed by another, one more interrogation point. Why military vehicles and not a limo or a nice car? He started to feel uncomfortable.

Abdullah was not in his car but supposed to be in the one behind, leaving him with three local policemen or at least seemed to be policemen. What made him feel even more annoying was that he noticed that the three 'policemen' were not speaking Arabic but Turkish and were staring at him not in a friendly manner.

Suddenly, the car behind disappeared in a cloud of dust; it seemed that it was forced to stop, and the car's abrupt breaks created the dust, and Abdullah's car was not anymore to be seen.

He turned around and pushed the man next to him, asking him to stop and see what happened, but he shouted to him angrily in Turkish, probably asked him to shut up, even gave him a painful strike on his shoulder, and they not even stopped but, on the contrary, accelerated in extreme speed as if they wanted to avoid something or were being chased.

He started to realise that there was trouble ahead, and he was in a totally hostile car. The two in the front were laughing, turning around looking at him as if he were a ridiculous person, and their eyes reflected hate on him.

He protested in English, but they seemed not to comprehend anything in that language and even did not care to listen to him but kept laughing with pleasure and satisfaction that they had him on their hands, which was clear from their body language. The bastard next to him, an ugly, unshaved, brutal-faced man, made a sign again to shut up with no strike this time but showing him the handcuffs that he had on his belt.

Everything was clear to his mind that he was probably abducted from maybe a military foreign legion group pro-or anti governmental commandment. The fact was that he was in a severe and frightening situation without knowing why.

Was it that his local guy was arrested by pro or anti governmental forces, or was it because he was Greek, and the Turkish's hate against the Greeks is known for many centuries?

Suddenly, the road was with no lights in full darkness, and the car also turned off the lights. They stayed there in deep silence for unknown reasons and for almost half an hour. In that deep and terrifying silence, one of them lit up a cigarette, and that was it, right away a huge car the size of a tank collided with them, breaking the car into pieces and threw them all out of the car.

The last thing he remembered was that he landed with his face on a big stone, smashing his teeth and a metal part of the broken car crushed both his hands cutting all or many of his fingers, and he fainted.

After quite a while, he somehow opened his eyes, half opened as the one eye was blurry, and he could slightly see around but in a totally painful body, and his mouth was almost closed or half opened, but he could not feel his tongue as if there was no tongue; his teeth were certainly gone.

He found himself in front of two men in beards with rough faces and gave him a kick to make him wake up or kind of wake up. That kick worsened his pain on his face. They were talking to him; luckily, he could at least hear, but it was impossible to talk, and looking down to his hands, they were unrecognisable, tied up and covered by short of a dirty bandage. They were talking to him in a strange language, probably Russian. He could not understand a word, only he could identify one word 'Turk'.

He figured out that they wanted to ask him if he was Turkish. He moved his head in denial trying to tell them, "No, I am not Turkish." But they laughed, showing clearly that they do not believe him.

It was obvious that when that crash happened and as it was in full darkness, maybe some of the nearby local inhabitants stole all he had on him, money, papers, passport, a watch, even shoes, all and left him there half-dead and 90% naked.

The probable Russians left him there in a dark, damp, filthy basement. He tried to turn his face with difficulty left and right to see where he was. Certainly not in a hotel or in a hospital but in a dirty basement and next to him was another guy, who was in an even worse situation, and it seemed to him that he was the driver of that car that had abducted him from the airport, and he was Turkish.

There were chains on the wall and ropes hanging from the roof; it seemed to be a torture room.

His eyes closed, feeling so tired with a killer headache and pain on his whole body but more on his face. He thought that he better not get himself in front of a mirror, anyway not such a comfort existed there, as he would probably look like a monster.

His mind was in Greece with his wife, the two daughters and son, thinking if they could know where and how their father is, they would be in a shocking situation. Karla was right and so was Alex, who had warned him not to take this trip, but he ignored them, and now he was paying for his insistence to make such a risky business in a country where instability and foreign legions dominate.

He made a try to enunciate and say a word, but it was impossible, so he realised that he lost the ability to speak, which means he was voiceless.

His tongue was also injured, and in his mouth, the tongue was an orphan being alone and not touching any teeth, so making the speaking impossible. His hands being covered and could not feel if at all fingers were there, so what if he also loses the ability to write, how could he reveal his identity and tell them who he was?

He wanted to sleep, but he was thirsty, and no one came into that damp basement. But even if they come, how could he make them understand what he wanted?

That neighbour was unrecognisable, probably the driver of that military vehicle that was smashed by that huge other vehicle, if not that was to be a heavy tank.

He turned his body towards him, and he showed what a horrible situation he was in, but he could speak as he tried to address to him some words, but in Turkish that was impossible for him to understand. But one word was clear, and that was the word 'Francia'.

He thought that as far as Areus came from France, he probably is French. He thought that, well, he couldn't speak so how to tell him that he is Greek so he decided to nod affirmatively that he indeed is from 'Francia', so more or less those probably Russians know that he is neither a Turk nor an Arab.

His eyes closed, and he fell in deep sleep, a sleep of pain and tears; tears falling in the dust of his cheeks, as he knew that he would never be the one he was before. The man who had families and wealth, and he was now in that filthy hole.

Someone kicked him to wake up, so he did. He noticed that those guys were indeed Russians as they had the emblem patch on their uniform of the famous Russian Wagner Legion, and there was with them a Turkish-speaking fellow, also in a state of despair. They were angry at him as they did not know with whom they dealt and what secrets he carried as if he were a spy. The Turk kind of translator spoke to him in Turkish but made a sign that he did not understand, so they moved to the Turk next to him.

He answered to the interpreter that he is Turk, and then they asked him if he knew him; he answered to them probably no, but he told them that he is from Francia. That was a good sign, and they immediately changed their attitude towards him.

They two Russians spoke to each other, and in a few minutes came with water and a food that even dogs might consider as trash, but he had to eat. Again, how to eat? He could not bite, and what they brought him a kind of bread; he made them a sign that he couldn't bite, so the one guy left and brought a soup. What was in that soup was not easy to discover, but whatever it was, he must swallow it.

To the neighbour, they did not give anything, and he looked at him with a look full of hatred, showing that he got water and soup because of him telling them that he was from Francia and not from Turkey. Areus had all the will to share what they brought him, but neither him nor that Turk could move as they were in a horrible physical situation but also tied up on that metal 'bed' with not any mattress. He made a sign to apologise, but that was of not any help for him.

The time was passing, probably because it was already night, so his painful and exhausted body forced him to sleep, but the neighbour was shouting, asking probably for water, but no one seemed to hear him shouting.

He was feeling bad; he was the one to save him from thirst and hunger, but he could not offer any help to him. He was exhausted; the tiredness, the deep disappointment, the uncertainty made them both burst into tears; the tears led to sleep just to forget where he was and fantasise where he was supposed to be.

The supposed morning came, a morning in deep darkness, and the bad smell of that hole was unbearable.

People were heard to come down, and they turned on the light. They were holding a 'kelebia', a long Arab cloak they threw to him, making a sign to wear it on, but how? His hands were in bandage. They unwrapped the bandage, and there he saw in what situation his hands were, two–three fingers were missing from each hand, and the rest were smashed, seeing that he fainted.

After a while, he was kicked to wake up, and he found himself in that long Arabic kelebia. They brought him up to the ground floor. He noticed that in one of the rooms was maybe an officer in charge of that small soldiers or kind of soldiers' squad.

They pushed him to the entrance, and with a kick, they showed him to walk, but walk with no shoes under that burning sun and the burning desert sand. He walked few hundred metres; there was nothing there, just desert and dust and that half-ruined building. His feet started to burn. He rushed back to that building, begging them to keep him there.

They took him to the chief. That chief looked more civilised and gentle. He looked at him and then looked to his soldiers in a very angry manner, telling in their language something like, as Areus probably figured out, that he told them in angry way, "He is French; we have enough enemies like the Turks and Khalifa Haftar; you want also the French to be against us?"

He allowed Areus to sit in front of his 'office', which was full of Kalashnikov arms. He gave him one to hold, but with almost no fingers, he managed to hold it, but he did not know how to hold it, and the officer laughed so loud. But that laughter was the laughter of a kind man.

He gave him a nickname, Louis, after the French comedian Louis de Funes. He showed it to him, calling him Louis de Funes, and he again laughed so as to retain the Louis as name.

He ordered one of his guys to bring tea for both. The chief, his name was Boris, noticed with admiration the way that Louis was holding the teacup with only two of the three fingers, and he figured out that he has good manners so he must be of a good family and maybe of high society in the French community.

All of a sudden, a bomb was heard to be quite close. They were all in a panic, probably other forces or other legions were after them; he gave orders, and they all gathered all the arms they had and took him with them in a military vehicle like those we see in movies that US forces used in Afghanistan.

He noticed they had many metal cans full of oil so they could reach far away, and so they entered deep into the desert, going probably south. Left and right, behind, in the front, nothing other than desert and clouds of dust that driver could hardly see in front of him more than two metres.

They were driving for more than five hours when at last they saw in front long distant trees, maybe a small oasis. Five fully armed black Africans stopped them; it seemed they knew Boris, and they lowered down their guns. A very tall African, he later knew that his name was Abdul, was called, and he embraced Boris in a friendly manner.

The centre of the oasis was full of carpets, and in those carpets were few fully covered in black dressed women. Abdul gave strict orders to bring food and tea. Boris approached Abdul, showing Areus and whispering a few words into his ear. Abdul looked at him in a respectful way and ordered to bring liquid food as one could see that there were no teeth in his mouth. They all sat down on a different carpet circle, eating and drinking tea.

Areus noticed in a corner under the cool shadow of a palm tree there was a full crate of Tuborg beers. He showed them the beers; they all laughed, and again, Abdul ordered to bring beer to him. At last, beer, in that heat he could not understand how they could drink tea even if it was chilled and not beer.

He drank or rather swallowed two beers almost with no break, holding the bottle with the three fingers of each hand. They all burst into laughter, even the women who looked at him as if he were dropped in the desert from the sky from another planet where they drink beer and not tea; it was very curious to that black race or whatever it was. He tried to recall in his mind the African map.

To be so tall, they must be either Sudanese, or Nigerians, but maybe also Algerian, but mostly, they looked like Sudanese. He would prefer them to be in Chad as there they speak French, and he could at least understand what they say. He knew Sudanese people as he was in Sudan many years ago for a project.

He tried to bring in his mind the Libyan situation and conflict between the eastern National Army of Tripoli and Haftar in Benghazi. So, if these are Sudanese, they are backing together with Qatar and Turkey the Tripoli government while Khalifa Haftar's counterrevolution was backed by Egypt and Russian Wagner. So, probably that small squad of Boris were Wagner deserters and chased by the Wagner legion to kill them for deserting.

The discussions between Boris and Abdul seemed to turn around arms. Boris ordered one of his guys to bring all the arms they had in that vehicle, and those were many, well hidden under the car, under the seats and in the back under the oil tanks. So, with the arms, they bought hospitality in that small oasis.

The stay there was for Areus as if he sleeps in a suite in a Four Seasons hotel in comparison to that damp hole he slept three nights before.

The hospitality was impeccable, and all there was peaceful until one morning they saw a cloud of dust approaching their camp. It was a wind storm, a Saharan wind storm. They all ran to cover whatever was to be covered and protect themselves.

They have the know-how as they have such wind storms very often, but for Areus, this was a new experience. The wind storm smashed down even palm trees. The storm passed but left damages to the camp, but for those strong men, it was easily reparable.

Areus was still unable to speak, unable to write and explain to them that he was Greek and a very wealthy man.

All were busy to bring the camp in good condition. Boris seemed to be worried because he was looking at the sky all the time, and he was right there. They saw a drone making circles around the camp. They tried to shoot it down but with no success. Now he knows that Wagner and Haftar located the four deserters, and they would, for sure, chase them with all the possible means.

They have to leave even more south inside Sudan, but even there, they were not safe as there were Sudanese tribes that were not at all friendly with any Russians, either they are pro or anti Tripoli temporary government. They loaded as many supplies as possible, but no car could travel through the desert, so they were on camels, but not any of them was familiar with these animals and knew how to ride them.

They were taught by the locals how, and they started a probable very dangerous and exhausting trip. The Sahara Desert is not at all hospitable, the heat and the often wind storms makes the trip very difficult and especially for the inexperienced in such situations and on camels.

That drone discovered them, and they were afraid that the Wagner legion might send a helicopter to kill them all being completely unprotected. But in front of them, there was nothing but desert, so they had to accelerate their riding to find a shelter or anything that could hide them from an offence from the sky.

All of a sudden, at a very long distance, there was something big to be seen, but it was not clear what it exactly was. The more they approached, the more they saw that it was probably a big tent or something similar.

They reached close, and that was a huge tent that reminded the tents of Muammar Kaddafi but was abandoned, seemed as something happened, and they left the tent with all that was inside, carpets and more fittings and left in extreme hurry. Who was staying in such a luxurious tent?

What could have happened? Next to the tent was a well; they checked and there was water, which solved one of the most major problems.

The decision was what to do, stay there but soon the food supplies would be finished. If they continue, they are again wide open from any attack from a helicopter, but the same was also with the tent; that tent did not offer any protection.

They decided to make a stop and relax in that tent and then they would decide what to do. They had water and food supplies for at least one week, but that was not enough as they did not know how far they were from any borders of any country and if that country would be friendly, as they had not any compass to guide them to where they were heading to.

They stayed there for two days, and their physical status strengthened, so off they went towards the unknown.

The unknown became clearer as they saw in distance, buildings. Where were they? They found out at last that they were in Sudan.

Sudan was close to the Russians, supporting Haftar; they were Russians but they were bad Russians as they were deserted and were wanted dead or alive.

Tall, black Sudanese guards asked them to deliver their arms and follow them. They had to follow as they were more than 50, and they seemed to belong to a kind of ferocious tribe. Are they rebels as there was always, and for years, a civil war in Sudan between south and north.

They asked for any credentials, but they did not have, or they pretended not to have before they get to know to which side these 50 soldiers belong.

Those black Africans were staring at Areus as if he were an anthropoid—so ugly and scary he looked without teeth and no fingers; he was probably looking like a second Quasimodo, or the latter was another Clark Cable compared to Areus.

One of the Russians spoke Arabic, so he explained that they left Libya and they got lost in the desert. They could not be believed because of the distance that seemed impossible for them to survive in the desert for so many kilometres under the burning sun with no supplies.

They looked at one another to decide what to do with them. The Russian who could speak Arabic explained to them that they found a very luxurious and well-preserved tent empty and abandoned and they rested there for three days, having also a well with water, and they managed to survive.

They seemed worried about who could be in that tent and what would cause them to abandon and leave in a hurry like being chased. Such a tent must belong to a tribal chief, but they never leave such a tent behind as they always, when they move, uninstall the tent and take with them, so it was a puzzle who could that be and if that was one of their tribes; they must find the way to support and bring help to him wherever he went with his accompanying group.

One of the guys pointed at Areus, asking who he was as he does not look Russian. The interpreter told them that he is French. That was not good as French were not that welcomed to Africa while Greeks were welcomed.

They approached him with a hostile attitude. An idea passed through his mind; he took a spear from one of the guards, and he drew with great difficulty in the sand the map of southern Europe, so he showed Spain, then France, then Italy and then Greece.

He slinked that spear on Greece. One of them who seemed kind of better-looking shouted Unan. He nodded with tears that yes, he comes from there. They all changed completely the way they stared at him with a friendly smile. That same guy who seemed more educated, he cried Acropolis, having the air of the wise man the African Einstein. He nodded yes, with tears, but also with effort he made a kind of smile.

They were curious how this happened to him. Boris asked the Russian interpreter to tell them that his car was attacked, and he almost lost his life but with hard injuries that turned him to look so horribly ugly.

He took the spear again and made the map of Africa and showed Khartoum; he always wrote with extreme difficulty the year 1985 and, next to that, the word Nimeiry. They all were happy as they were fans of Nimeiry as president of that decade of 1980.

That story, a true story, completely changed the attitude of all of them. He took the spear again and engraved in the sand the map of Khartoum and the Sudan hotel with the zoo and the Nile and the nearby city of Omdurman, so they were 100% sure that his story was true.

In fact, all five, the four Russians and Areus, were in a way their 'prisoners'. They gave as task to the Russians, who were professional soldiers with deep knowledge of arms and ammunition, to train the African 'soldiers' for the secrets of actual war, as in war, they were, and in the fiercest of all wars—the 'civil war'.

They had a not that comfortable accommodation, especially the Russians who were younger, between 40 and 55, needed women; they needed sex, that was there in no way to get as they were isolated far away from the whatever possible civilisation of that country.

Many times, many of those soldiers in full armour were leaving the camp, probably to kill and frighten whoever were there and were considered as enemies and returned after two–three days but not all returned and many were injured.

The months were passing, and the years were passing. The routine became boring. Areus had not any task, but he had to take care of his physical body status.

Every day, he was walking all around that 'military camp', and many times he even ran for quite some hours. But there was an obvious problem: he started forgetting things; was it a sign of Alzheimer's?

He started losing his memories, even who he was, who he is now. He lost count how many years they were there. That camp was built with stones, so he was counting the stones every day, and engraved the number in the dust but well-hidden, trying the next day to remember how many stones were last day. The first days, he remembered the exact number of stones, but later, after a few months, he made mistakes, and more mistakes unrolled. He ended this 'hobby' as more sadness was bringing.

One of the Russians died; nobody ever learnt how. His other companions believed that either he committed suicide living there more or less like animals or he tried to escape, but there were so many guards that it was impossible to escape.

They gathered trying to make their life a little fun by singing Russian songs; there was no alcohol, just a beer made locally, which was horrible and of course not chilled.

In fact, they knew that they would leave their bones there, with no possibility of an escape or any other option to make their life tolerable.

White hair on the heads of the Russians revealed the many years they were there in that filthy environment, which for the local soldiers was considered as luxury because their wives travelling quite long were bringing them food supplies and also stayed there for one or two nights so that they could have the necessary sex.

One night, and after many years, five black women came, but these were not wives; the chief offered to them these women for a night to at last empty their balls, but those women were just cans with a hole, still it was an obligatory solution to the Russians, but Areus denied that sexual humiliation. One of them approached him as the Russians took each one a 'woman' and went to their 'cave'. She was so ugly and fat but with a sweet smile. He thought better masturbate, but with what 'tool'? What cock? His cock was in eternal sleep. She showed with signs that she must do this with him or else they would punish her; he understood and took her inside and slept with her side by side. She was so sweet; she cried seeing him in that situation and caressed his face, and that was all until the morning; she kissed his head and left.

One night, there was an obvious turmoil in that muddy camp; they all were running left and right; they took their guns and grenades and made a wall for protection. They called the Russians to be on the front line. The Arabic-speaking Russian heard that there were rumours that two tribes, the most fierce, wild and dangerous tribes, arrived from the south of Sudan, and they were close to their camp.

He heard that; after being with them for so many years, he could understand their language, but he also managed to learn Arabic as he had that talent and gift to learn languages fast. He was amazed by how he could learn languages and understand what they say while his memory abandoned him for good. It was a mystery.

Indeed, one could hear those characteristic loud and wild voices like hyenas approaching. They were all scared, knowing that they were an undefeated ferocious tribe, and that guns and grenades would kill many, but they would come in big numbers so, it was impossible to exterminate them all.

So, as it happened the Russians were killed on the spot being in the front line; the chief was captured, and all the rest were killed with poisonous spears the same that they use to kill lions and elephants in their jungle in the south of Sudan in the city of Juba. Areus was well hidden in the dirtiest spot that one could hide himself, and that was the shit hole of the camp.

Shit hole that saved his life. It did not take long, and they discovered him.

They poured water on him to see what was under the shit, and that was a human-looking creature they had never seen before. Those fierce fighters who were not afraid of lions showed a kind of fear seeing the status of that man, who looked more like an anthropoid than human. One of them showed the sky as if he wanted to show that he fell from up there.

They dragged him but peculiarly with sort of respect to their chief. The south Sudanese chief asked his captured chief what is that. He said, "Unani."

They all stood up as if they heard that he was the golden heir of an unknown universe. He gave orders to take care of him the best way and smiled to him in a very friendly way. They looked at him as there was magic, a mystery hidden inside him. They kind of worshiped him as if he were a legend or maybe the spirit of their tribe. They immediately gave him clean clothes, and the chief made a sign that he wanted him always next to him as he brings luck to him as his lucky charm.

So, now a new adventure was ahead of him; he must take advantage of this situation, hoping that they have the support of the central Khartoum government so that he could find a way to get into the Greek Embassy.

They stayed there for two days to redraft their next move. That was a new attack to a similar camp to that one that they conquered, and after they exterminated that also, they started their triumphal march towards the capital, which was none other than Khartoum.

Getting into the first houses of the Khartoum suburbs, they all were glorifying them as liberators until they reached the government building where thousands were gathered to worship them.

They were the heroes; the authorities gave them a luxury stay in Sudan Hotel, and what a coincidence; they gave him a room in that same hotel where he was many decades before. In that same hotel also stayed the chief with 50 of his generals. In the two days, there was a full program of celebrations of their many victories.

All these many years he was in that filthy muddy camp, he tried after he stole from the chief's office a kind of primitive pencil to write something on a paper. He was trying, but most of the time unsuccessfully, to hold that pencil between the two fingers of his foot and write a message. After many attempts and failures, he managed to write in English a message, which said:

"I am Greek and a wealthy businessman; I was for 12 or more years abducted, and after a car crash, I am unrecognisable anymore, having injured my tongue and lost all my teeth so I couldn't speak and my hands and fingers are mashed.

"I was a hostage to different Libyan rebels, Russians of foreign legions and Sudanese tribes. Help me reach the Greek Embassy. I am about 94 years old and have lost 90% of my memory, and I don't even know my name." That same night, in his room, he managed again in the same way to add 'Room 178'.

He preserved that paper so well although it was very filthy, but one could still read it.

In the morning, accompanied by the chief and four of his generals, they went down for breakfast. The chief knew that Areus understood the Arabic language so he was always telling him that he would never let him go as he brings luck to him and that he would always take care of him as if he were his father.

All these years being unable to speak, he improved his hearing and smelling. This always happens; when one loses one of his senses the others get ameliorated.

Drinking his tea, he heard from a table quite far from their table, Greek speaking, he cautiously turned to locate from which table that Greek language came. Their table was the honorary table as they were the heroes.

He made a sign that he wanted to go to the toilet; at first, they did not understand what he wanted, but later with some gestures, he made them understand what he wanted, and they all laughed.

Luckily, the toilets were close to that table where the Greeks were. He stood up, and with his almost cripple walking next to their table, he purposely fell down, and one of the Greek guys stood up to help him, so he found the way to slip in his pocket the message.

He returned to his table, and again, he managed to turn around to see if they got his message, and it seemed they did. He was happy it might be the end of his nightmare.

At 3 o'clock, he heard someone knocking at his door, hoping that they would come; he was dressed and ready to go. He opened the door, and there they were, the two Greeks, plus another one, maybe from the Embassy. Indeed, very silently he told him that he is the embassy secretary and rushed to the car in front of the hotel.

They went down like shadows and reached down; the car's engine was on, and they left. He was on the backseat, crying in tears; he could not believe that this might be, after so many years, his liberation.

At the embassy, they tried to make him tell them who he was, but no way. The ambassador came and gave him a hug and gave orders, "Forget the interrogation, take the car, a private plane is waiting at the airport, rush as they will find out what happened and first thing they would do is to come here for him."

That one-hour drive was for him a century. They reached the airport. There was indeed a private plane; they rushed on it, and they flew away.

He was crying all the way; he could not imagine that he would be back to his county and his family. Was it real or a dream?

After four hours, they reached Athens airport.

A big black jeep picked them up and drove to a hotel for him to rest as he was a wreck.

He collapsed and fell asleep right away. He could not know what hotel that was, but he did not care; he was sleeping in a Greek hotel, on a mattress and clean sheets and pillow.

In the morning, they came. It was two policemen and a doctor, probably a psychologist to help him recover.

They were asking him who he was, what was his name, where his family stayed, but nothing; he didn't remember anything and he could also not speak or write. They brought him to the central police station. They made many tries to get something out of him, but it was completely unsuccessfully. He tried but in vain; nothing was in his memory.

The head of that police station asked them to drive him around Athens. Maybe he sees something that would remind him of something.

And that was done. They were circulating him looking from the window to locate something that would ring bells to his memory. They were six hours driving with no result. The policeman stopped at a gasoline station to fill up his oil tank.

He looked around and saw high trees on the one side that looked kind of familiar. The policeman came back and started driving. He pushed him, showing him the high trees. He smiled and said this was the central cemetery of Athens and drove away. He pushed him again, he said, "What?" And he made him understand that he wanted to visit that cemetery. He called his chief and asked him what to do, and he got the order to take him to the cemetery; maybe there he gets his memory back.

They stopped, and by foot, they entered the cemetery. He started walking faster and faster and was heading through the different tombs. He accelerated; he knew where he was going; he stopped, looked left and right and then on his right there was a big family tomb. He knelt down and embraced a marble tomb plate that had his name engraved. He showed the policemen making the sign that this was him.

The policemen made the sign of the cross; they could not believe it; they called the chief and told him that he found his own grave. He looked next to that, and there was the name engraved of his wife and his brother, and on that big standing marble plaque were the names of his father and mother also engraved. So, now they also have the surname, and they knew how to search for his family. It was easy. They brought him straight to his hotel as he was exhausted not only from tiredness but also from emotion.

The next day, he woke up late after a long sleep. Someone knocked on the door; He opened and found himself in front of his whole family, the two daughters and his son with six grandsons and granddaughters. Hugs and tears; they were all in a high emotional state; they never, ever had any hope that their father was alive, so they made for him a funeral that was attended by hundreds of friends and relatives.

What an unexpected total happy end. The policemen made some formal papers to be signed, and they left for the one daughter's home. What was now more than necessary and urgent was to bring back the speaking ability.

Surgery was required to bring the tongue in prior condition, and teeth had to be implanted. Prosthetics were needed for the hands to be able to work as fingers and possibly even be able to use the computer keyboard.

But the major of all was to have the appropriate pills and whatever other medicines that were appropriate to bring back as much memory as possible.

All these would take time, but after all, he would be able to have a human outlook and not have his grandsons and granddaughters to be afraid of him with the look of a monster.

The warmth of the family elevated his morale, but the nightmares made him suffer at night, bringing back the miserable life of those last 12 or maybe even 14 years as he completely lost the year count.

The weeks and months were passing fast, and the doctors were doing a great job, and slowly, but safely, he gained confidence, and the mirror started to show an almost ordinary man, who soon would also be able to go out and have dinner with his family.

He asked his family not to allow any of his old friends, although just two were still alive and God knows in what status, or relatives to come and see him as he was still ugly, and he did not want them to get shocked with that scary image.

One night, on TV and especially the athletics channels, he was watching a junior's tennis championship. The commentator was talking about a phenomenon where a boy tennis player at the age of 15 was almost ready to compete at the ATP tour with men of high-ranking.

His name was Alexander with a Danish surname. That boy had a rather Mediterranean look, and according to the details about him, he lived in Nice and worked hard at a famous tennis academy in Nice. That intrigued him, but he did not know what and why.

He tried to remove this from his mind and concentrate on his rehabilitation. But the image of that boy tennis player was always in front of him, causing anguish to him again and again.

Next week, the prosthetic fingers would be tested, and then he might be able to search on Google about that phenomenal tennis player.

It took one whole month, and Areus was again the old Areus and still fit at the age of 94 with brilliant teeth; he could speak as an ordinary man, his fingers were perfectly adapted and his memory had started to come slowly but steadily back; names were coming back; he remembered a guy called Alex and a lady called Sophia in China.

The first thing to do was to search on Google about that boy tennis player, and what he found about the boy shocked him. His mother was called Karla and his father was dead. Karla, that name rang bells in his mind. On Google, there was also his phone number.

So, he called, and there was a woman's voice. He asked her, "Are you Karla, the mother of the tennis player, Alexander?"

She answered, "Yes, I am."

"Do you know any man called Areus?"

"Of course, I know; he is the father of Alexander, but he died many years ago in Africa."

"Well, what if I tell you that I am Areus?"

She answered, "Would you please leave me alone, and this is not a joke; Areus died." And she hung up the phone.

He called again. "Is your mother's name Mathilde, and Areus came to meet her, but you revenged her for not allowing you to marry a Tunisian young man and you made love to Areus at the kitchen sink?"

A big silence on the other side. "If you are Areus, what is the name of your friend from Denmark who has a daughter from China?"

He answered, "Alex, and I think that there is another Alexander with two Chinese parents."

Karla could not believe it. She remained speechless for almost one whole minute, then shouted with happiness, "Areus! I cannot imagine that after 14 years, I will hear from you again; your son will be the happiest boy on earth as he knows that you are his father and it was your wish to become a tennis champion; he is indeed on that way, and he does this for you."

"Alex, your good friend and partner, is still in depression, blaming himself for not insisting you not to take that trip."

Areus told her that he was under medical attendance, and he believed that in one or two months he would be able to travel and come to Nice if the doctors give their consent. He gave his phone number so that Alex could call him and also his email address for them and also Alexander to get in touch and send many videos of his tennis matches. Karla also mentioned that Alexandros was the most handsome boy at both his school, with both Mediterranean and Chinese features; he does not play tennis, but he is a phenomenon in mathematics; they call him Einstein.

The daughter of Alex was the sweetest girl; she plays tennis and probably one day would be a champion. Areus asked about her mother, Mathilde. She told him that she passed away, and the last five years of her life she stayed in Nice, and she was so well living with the family, and, of course, she also missed him and was every day in church praying for him.

They said goodbye and she sent him kisses, so he also would like to return that kiss, but he still could not manage to do this yet due to his tongue and lips with the teeth that were not yet in harmony.

His memory started to return step by step, after taking the pills they gave him, and he could remember about his eternal love Anabella, Sophia, Angel, about Spartan and Angel's Fitness Centre, about Nikolas, Nuuk of Greenland and Tuppi; slowly, all was coming back as a memory parade.

One hour later, Alex was on the phone with his usual way of expressing himself. "You bastard, I almost had a heart attack suspecting that you were probably dead. Where the hell were you all these years? Did you get a new mistress, or what?"

"Well, no, this is not true, my good friend Alex; you can never imagine what situations I was involved in against my will. I was brutally mistreated and abused, losing my dignity, my face was deformed, and I lost all my teeth; my tongue was cut in the middle, so for 14 years, I could not speak at all; my fingers were mashed, and I lost the ability to write; you want me to continue?"

"No, you better not. I do not want you to recall all these tragic incidents; get better, and we all are waiting to see and hug you."

The next day, a new phone call and a boyish voice was heard. "Dad?" Again, "Dad, I am Alexander, your son from Nice." Areus was in deep emotion.

"My boy, I am sorry that I was away from you for 14 years. I saw you on TV and your mother sent to me videos of you playing tennis. I love you."

"So do I, Dad, and please come soon to Nice."

So it all happened. The end was a happy end. Tennis, he cannot play, but golf, maybe he can. This man traversed a life with plenty of fantasy, eternal love and tribulations, variety and adventures that many could only see fictionally in movies.

Life is an imagination, but get that explored, or else life would become very boring but also relentless.